the language
of Sisters

Books by Cathy Lamb

JULIA'S CHOCOLATES

THE LAST TIME I WAS ME

HENRY'S SISTERS

SUCH A PRETTY FACE

THE FIRST DAY OF THE REST OF MY LIFE

A DIFFERENT KIND OF NORMAL

IF YOU COULD SEE WHAT I SEE

WHAT I REMEMBER MOST

MY VERY BEST FRIEND

THE LANGUAGE OF SISTERS

Published by Kensington Publishing Corporation

the language of Sisters

CATHY LAMB

KENSINGTON BOOKS
www.kensingtonbooks.com

KENSINGTON BOOKS are published by

Kensington Publishing Corp.
119 West 40th Street
New York, NY 10018

All Kensington titles, imprints, and distributed lines are available at special quantity discounts for bulk purchases for sales promotion, premiums, fundraising, educational, or institutional use.

Special book excerpts or customized printings can also be created to fit specific needs. For details, write or phone the office of the Kensington Sales Manager: Kensington Publishing Corp., 119 West 40th Street, New York, NY 10018. Attn. Sales Department. Phone: 1-800-221-2647.

Kensington and the K logo Reg. U.S. Pat. & TM Off.

eISBN-13: 978-0-7582-9511-8
eISBN-10: 0-7582-9511-1
First Kensington Electronic Edition: September 2016

ISBN-13: 978-0-7582-9510-1
ISBN-10: 0-7582-9510-3
First Kensington Trade Paperback Printing: September 2016

10 9 8 7 6 5 4 3 2 1

Printed in the United States of America

For Jimmy Straight

1

I was talented at pickpocketing.

I knew how to slip my fingers in, soft and smooth, like moving silk. I was lightning quick, a sleight of hand, a twist of the wrist. I was adept at disappearing, at hiding, at waiting, until it was safe to run, to escape.

I was a whisper, drifting smoke, a breeze.

I was a little girl, in the frigid cold of Moscow, under the looming shadow of the Soviet Union, my coat too small, my shoes too tight, my stomach an empty shell.

I was desperate. We were desperate.

Survival stealing, my sisters and I called it.

Had we not stolen, we might not have survived.

But we did. We survived. My father barely, my mother only through endless grit and determination, but now we are here, in Oregon, a noisy family, who does not talk about what happened back in Russia, twenty-five years ago. It is best to forget, my parents have told us, many times.

"Forget it happened. It another life, no?" my father says. "This here, this our true life. We Americans now. Americans!"

We tried to forget, but in the inky-black silence of night, when Mother Russia intrudes upon our dreams, like a swishing scythe, a crooked claw emerging from the ruins of tragedy, when we remember family members buried under the frozen wasteland of the Soviet Union's far reaches, we are all haunted, some more than others.

You would never guess by looking at my family what some of us have done and what has been done to us. You would never sense our collective memory, what we share, what we hide.

We are the Kozlovskys.

We like to think we are good people.

Most of the time, we are. Quite good.

And yet, when cornered, when one of us is threatened, we come up swinging.

But, *pfft.*

All that. In the past. Best to forget what happened.

As my mother says, in her broken English, wagging her finger, "No use going to Moscow in your head. We are family. We are the Kozlovskys. That all we need to know. The rest, those secrets, let them lie down."

Yes, do.

Let all the secrets lie.

For as long as they'll stay down.

They were coming up fast. I could feel it.

2

"A Italian!" my mother, Svetlana, howled, slamming a cast-iron pan onto her stove. "What is this? My Elvira marrying a Italian? Why not a Russian? What wrong with Russian? I been cursed. Like black magic spell."

English is my mother's fourth language. Russian and Ukrainian come first. She is also conversationally fluent in French, which is the language she likes to swear in. Her English is never perfect, but it goes downhill quickly based on how upset she is.

"That sister of yours, Antonia"—she put her palms up to the ceiling—"Elvira is a . . . how you say it? I know now the word: rebel. She a rebel. I pray for her, but I knew when she born, your aunt Polina say to me, 'This one, she will cause your heart to cry!' And see?" She pointed at her chest. "Tears."

"Mama. Your heart is not crying. Ellie says she is in love with Gino."

"Love! Love!" she scoffed. She pushed a strand of her black hair back, the same color as mine, only mine fell down my back in waves and hers was to her shoulders in a bell shape. Our blue eyes were the same shade, too. I looked at her and I knew what I'd look like in twenty-two years. Definitely encouraging.

"I know about love. I have it with your papa. I know about this passion I have for him. He and I, we have the, what you call it?" She lowered her voice, for effect. "The biology in the bedroom."

"Chemistry. You and Papa have chemistry." I rolled my eyes

and braced myself, then ate one of her chocolate fudge cookies. They are beyond delicious.

"No! Not chemistry. That chemicals. I say we have the biology in the bedroom because biology is body. He cannot stay away from me, from this." She indicated her body from neck to crotch with one hand, head held high. My mother is statuesque. She curves. She still rocks it, I have to say.

"I cannot stay away from his manly hood, either." She grabbed a knife and held it in the air, as if making a solemn vow. "I say that in the truth."

I was going to need many chocolate fudge cookies that afternoon, that was my truth.

"But Antonia, *your sister*"—her voice pitched again, in accusation, as if I were in charge of Ellie—"she cannot have the biology for a Italian. She has it, it in her blood, for a Russian! A strong Russian man."

My mother started banging pans around, muttering in Ukrainian. I loved her kitchen. It was huge, bright, and opened up to the family room. There were granite counters, white cabinets, and a backsplash with square tiles in every bold color of the rainbow. My mother loves bright colors. Says it reminds her, "I am no longer living in a gray and black world, fear clogging my throat like a snake."

She had her favorite blue armoire, formerly owned by a bakery to showcase their pies, built into the design and used it as a pantry. A butcher block counter was attached to a long, old wood table that had previously been used in a train station. Blue pendant lights, three of them, fell above the train station table. The windows were huge, at my mother's request. She wanted to be able to look out and know immediately that she was in America, not Moscow. "Free," she said. "And safe from evil."

This kitchen was where all of her new recipes for my parents' restaurant, Svetlana's Kitchen, were tried out. This kitchen was thousands of miles away from the tiny, often nonfunctioning kitchen of my childhood in Moscow. The one where I once watched her wash blood off her trembling hands—not her blood—in our stained and crumbling sink.

"Elvira should marry Russian man. She will grow to love him, like a sunflower grow. Like a turnip grow."

"You were in love with Papa when you married him. No one asked you to grow to love your husband like a turnip."

"Ah yes, that. I in love with your papa when I see him at university. I told my father after the first kissy, you must plan wedding for Alexei and me right away, right now, because soon I lay naked with him."

Oh boy. Here we go. I poured myself a cup of coffee. My mother makes coffee strong enough for me to grow chest hairs.

"I make the love with him." She grabbed a spatula and pointed it at me. "I say that to my father."

I imagined my mother's sweet, late father, Anatoly Sabonis, hearing that from her. Poor man. I'm sure he momentarily stopped breathing. "I know, Mama, you told me."

"It was how I felt. Here." She put her spatula to her heart. "So in one month I am married to Alexei, but my father not let me be alone with him for one minute before wedding. And still, in the bedroom, your papa and I—"

"I know, Mama. You love Papa. Like Ellie loves Gino."

"No! Not like that." She smacked the spatula on the countertop. "Elvira fall in love with non Russian. A nonrusseman."

"A nonrusseman?"

"Yes. I make that word up myself. It clever."

"Is it one word?"

"Yes. One word. More efficient. More quickly."

"Are you done?"

"No, I not done. Never done. That Italian not Russian. Does not have our genes. Our pants, you know? The jeans. Not have our history in his blood."

"Mama, what's in our blood is a lot of Russian vodka."

"Yes, devil drink. Fixes and dixes so many Russians, but we are Russian American. American Russians. We marry other American Russians."

"Unless we fall in love with Italian Americans, then we marry them. Or we marry Hawaiians, like Valerie did."

"Kai is my new son." My mother adores my sister's husband.

"Not this Gino. No and no. He not enough. I see them together and I no see the love."

I didn't see it, either, from Ellie to Gino, but Gino loved Ellie. I decided to keep my mouth shut.

My mother whipped the spatula through the air like a lasso. "But she plans a wedding. Me oh my God bless, Mother Mary help me."

"I like Italian food."

"Italian food!" My mother gasped. "*Italian* food? At the wedding of my Elvira? No. *Russian* food. We have Russian food. If we not have Russian food, I not come."

"Ellie wants you to come."

She crossed her arms over her impressive bosom. "No. Not unless Russian food."

"It will be Russian and Italian food, I heard. A blend." I tried not to laugh.

"That not happening." Fists to air. She looked to the heavens for divine intervention. So dramatic. "It cannot be. I am good Russian mother. I be good to her and now! A Italian. My Elvira choices it. Where went I wrong?"

"Gino is not an it."

I watched my mother stomp around the kitchen as she yanked out more pans. Her pans, cast iron, from my father, are her favorite possession. She cried when he brought them home many years ago as a gift, when I was a teenager, as did my father. It wasn't about the pans. It was about loss, despair, and a promise kept.

My mother loves to cook, and when she's stressed she cooks until the stress is gone. The cooking and baking can last for days.

Her customers love it, as when my mother is stressed she makes specials for the restaurant. It is a quiet message that goes through the Russian American community. "Svetlana is upset? What is she upset about?" And then, quickly, "What is she making? Last time I had fish soup with salmon, halibut, and lemon. It warmed my bones. Do you know if she's making that again?"

The restaurant is packed, always, but when the Russian community hears about my mother's temper going off, we are more packed than usual, line out the door.

She banged those special pans, muttered, in English and Russia, swore in French, then it was back to English. She has a doctorate in Russian Literature and used to be a professor when we lived in Moscow before our lives collapsed.

"You children and your papa, though he tire me out in the bedroom, you are my whole life. We love the children. But constant it is!" She yelled and swung another pan onto the stove. "Always these problems. Elvira want to marry a Italian it. Your other sister around the bad criminals, all the time! And you"— she pointed at me, this time with a wooden spoon, wielded like a sword—"you write about the crime. That make criminals mad at you. Why like this? More worries. More anxious for me. I worry, all the time!"

Yes, I write about crime for the *Oregon Standard,* our state's largest newspaper. But to my credit, I hate it. I would probably quit soon. Another problem, which I was not going to share with my mother so she would not get "more anxious," is that the dock where my home is—a yellow tugboat—is about to be shut down. Yes, I live in a yellow tugboat on the Willamette River.

I was also climbing my way back up from a soul-slashing experience that had knocked me to my knees, then whipped me to my butt, then pushed me down face-first into the dirt and there I lay for a long time. I am now breathing, and I have told myself that I will not be facedown in the dirt again, but sometimes I say that when I am facedown.

"Lookie. See my hair. White streak. From the worry. It my worry hair."

My mother did have a white streak. It started at her widow's peak, to the left center of her head, the same place where Valerie, Ellie, and I had our widow's peaks. It's where the language of sisters and brothers comes in, she's told us, handed down through the Sabonis family line, to communicate, silently, with our siblings. It's not rationally or scientifically explicable, so I won't try, but sometimes I can hear my sisters talking to me in my head.

"It's vogue, Mama."

"No, not vogue. This old woman hair. Caused by my children. Nieces and nephews, too. All the peoples in the Kozlovsky family. I blame you, your sisters. And!" She slammed down a container of flour. "You know who, who worries me the most!"

I knew who. I worried, too.

She flung a pile of spice bottles down on the counter. "We are Kozlovskys, we are good people, but this not right. You talk to Elvira, Antonia, I tell you, you fix this." She shook her finger at me. "Fix it right up, like you do. Quick. You do a quickie. No nonrusseman."

When I left, she gave me cheese dumplings and a container of roast goose with apples and dill. My mother has to feed her children. A daughter leaving the house without a container of food would undoubtedly starve by noon tomorrow, her skeleton pecked at by crows.

"I love you, my Antonia." She hugged and kissed me.

"Love you, too, Mama."

"Now I make new recipe. I call it 'My Childrens Makes Me Worry.' "

I headed home to my tugboat.

Six months ago, I sold my home in the hills above Portland and moved to my yellow tugboat with red trim. I was in a dark pit I couldn't crawl out of because each time I looked around, a memory bashed me in the face.

I cried for days when I sold that home, but I knew it had to be done. The house was white with blue shutters with a willow tree in front. Now I live on a dock in a marina with other people who live on houseboats.

You have to walk by three houseboats to get to my three-story yellow tugboat with red rails and trim and a red door. Petey, a friend of my father's, used it for twenty-five years to haul timber, grain, sand, and gravel on barges up and down the river, but he retired and didn't want it.

I wanted to live on the water, away from the city, as natural as I could get without a long commute to work, so I bought it from Petey, who moved to a condo in Miami. I then had it gutted and remodeled before I moved in, with a full bedroom added to the second floor. I needed something to think about other than the memory bashing, and it helped to have a project.

I rented a slip on the dock and settled in.

The whole tugboat is about a thousand square feet. I painted the small entry white. Two square windows on either side let in the light. I've taken photos of my river "pets," which include two mallard ducks that always wander up on my deck named Mr. and Mrs. Quackenbusch; a blue heron named Dixie; a bald eagle, which disappears for days, that I call Anonymous; a golden eagle I named Maxie; two beavers named Big Teeth and Big Tooth; and river otter. There are a number of river otter, so I call all of them Sergeant Ott.

I matted the photos in blue with white frames.

I have a tiny hallway, then a bathroom off to the right. I have a shower over a claw-foot tub. Across the hallway is the kitchen with a huge window over a white apron sink. I had the cabinets painted light blue; the counters are a beige, swirling granite; and the backsplash is made of blue, gray, and beige glass.

The kitchen opens to my family room. I have white wainscoting on the lower half, light beige paint on the top half, and a blue couch in the shape of a V. The blue couch has a multitude of pillows, made from thick, shiny, fuzzy, painted, mirrored, arty, lacy, silky fabrics from all over the world, sewn by my sisters and me. I have a glass dining table in the corner near the French doors, which leads to the tugboat's lower deck. On either side of the French doors are more square windows.

Up a skinny spiral staircase, on the second floor, is a semicircle office with a desk; a closet with shelving on both sides to house my clothing collection/obsession that used to house the crew in bunks; and my bedroom, the comforter and walls white.

The bedroom has windows on both walls, and another set of French doors leads to a second deck.

A ladder in the office leads to the wheelhouse up top where Captain Petey used to steer the tugboat up and down the river. The wood captain's wheel and an old, gray clunky phone with a silver bell on top of it are still there, as is the dark wood paneling on the lower half. There is also an array, on a panel in front of the captain's wheel, of radios, levers, switches, gauges, and controls to drive the tugboat.

The top half, into the ceiling, is all windows so Petey could see in all directions. The roof windows make it excellent for stargazing.

I had a three-foot-wide bench built up in the wheelhouse, raised over four feet. I added a long red mattress and a pile of red and white pillows with fabric from India, Thailand, Norway, Pakistan, Mexico, China, and Hawaii.

I can sit on the bench in the wheelhouse and have an incredible view of downtown Portland if I look one way and the ruffles of the river and towering trees if I look the other way. Sometimes I go up there to cry.

Outside I have another "house," built on my side deck. It's not a real house. More like a shelter with a door. I don't go in there. It hurts me too much. When I moved in, I shoved in what needed to be there, then shut and locked the door.

Locked. It's locked.

I can't see unlocking it anytime soon.

An hour later I called my father from my deck, Mr. and Mrs. Quackenbusch in the water by my feet. "Mama's upset about Ellie."

"I know, I know," he said, his voice sad, moaning. My father is tall, balding, with a chest like a bull, a broken nose shifted a bit to the side from his boxing years in Moscow, and brown eyes that have seen way, way too much. In Moscow he was a physics professor at the university before he was arrested and entered prison/hell, his scars our reminder.

I could hear the restaurant sounds in the background—plates

clanging, waitresses chatting, a chef yelling, lively Russian music. "My poor Svetlana. She worry. I okay he a Italian, you know what I saying, Antonia? But I no think those two, not a up match. . . ."

I knew he meant "Not a matchup." My father's English gets worse as he gets upset, too. I listened as he told me what he thought of Gino, Elvira's fiancé. "He handsome. He funny. He love Elvira, I knows, I see it. But Elvira . . . she not, what you call it? She not over the sun for him."

"Over the moon."

"She not over sun or moon. I worry. I don't like that Gino's hair. Vain. Why a man care about his hair? Not me. I no care. He not enough for my Elvira. What his real job? Huh? You tell me, what his real job?"

"Entrepreneur."

"Entrepreneur." He slung that word out long and slow. "That mean he want to be leech off my Elvira's pillow business."

"I don't think so. He does own parts of a number of businesses." Gino did well. So did Ellie with her pillow-making business.

"What your mama making?"

"She had chicken, walnuts, coriander, flour, and white wine out. She said she's drinking wine for inspiration. I don't know what she's cooking. She's experimenting, throwing things in, chopping like a fiend. If she likes it, she says she'll make it at the restaurant tonight. She says it's called 'My Childrens Makes Me Worry.' "

My mother liked it. She brought her recipe down. First diners sampled it.

Word travelled fast. It was a ninety-minute wait into our restaurant that night.

Two nights later, he called.

"I'm having the flashbacks, Toni. And the nightmares."

"They're back again?" I slung my feet over my lower deck, then rubbed my forehead, right by my widow's peak. It was nine o'clock at night, stars blocked out by clouds. I felt a mixture of sorrow, horror, and overwhelming guilt, my usual feelings when he was upset.

"Yes."

"Where are you and which ones are you seeing?"

"I'm in India. The southern part. And I'm seeing the woman. Her blond hair. The one I think is my mother." His voice crackled, pain and memories blending together, an emotional tornado. "And that blue ceramic box is back with the carriage and the fancy lady with the parasol and the butterfly. The box keeps opening, and that red and purple butterfly is flying around. I'm trying to catch it, trying to talk to the butterfly, but it keeps flying toward the woods." He took a shuddering breath. "The woods are so scary, I know there's something in there, or someone. I think they're from my past, not just random things."

"Okay, breathe with me . . . one, two, three . . ."

He breathed with me, raspy and ragged. "I'm seeing the wooden ducks. I'm seeing them being thrown. Yelling. I'm scared of someone there. It's a dark shadow, and I don't know who it is. The blood is back, too, Toni. All over me. I can feel it. It's all over her, too. She's bleeding. I can see it in her blond hair. I'm trying to get to her, but I can't. I wake up and I can't breathe."

I lay down on my deck, holding the phone. I had been told never to tell him what I knew, what I saw, what I guessed at.

"Where is all this coming from?" he asked. "What does it mean?"

Never tell, Antonia, never, ever tell.

I was a secret keeper, and I could not hold the secret much longer. It had been twenty-five years and he needed to know. He deserved to know. But not tonight. "Breathe with me again, okay, here we go . . ."

Over the next few days I received a number of calls and texts from family and friends who had had my mother's special named "My Childrens Makes Me Worry." They wanted to know what we Kozlovsky kids did to make my mother worry. The older people who called from the Russian community also gently chastised

THE LANGUAGE OF SISTERS   13

me, in Russian, of course. "Don't make your mama worry, Antonia. You know better."

The regular dishes at my parents' restaurant all have family names. "Elvira's Tasty Treats," which is a selection of desserts; "Valeria's Dumplings," which are beef dumplings on a bed of lettuce; and "Antonia's Delight," which are cheese crepes.

But the specials . . . well, those are a crap shoot.

In the past, my mother has named specials "Alexei Not The Boss," after she had a fight with my father.

And "Teenagers Big Trouble," when we were younger.

And "I Wish Valeria Quit Her Job."

I had "Antonia Not A Criminal," simply because I write about crime.

Ellie endured "Elvira's Bad Choice" when she got engaged to Gino. It hurt Gino's feelings.

As my sister Valerie says, "I'm a state prosecutor. I try to maintain respect, a professional image, then Mama puts out a special called 'Valeria No Call Mama Enough,' and even the criminals are asking me why I don't call my mama more."

It goes on and on. Don't make my mother mad, or you'll hear about it on the Tonight's Specials board of Svetlana's Kitchen.

On Saturday night I heard a knock and opened the door of my tugboat. I knew who it was.

"Hi, Toni."

I smiled. "You're up late."

"So are you. I saw the light on. Want to come over?"

"Yes."

He put out a warm hand, and I took it. He smiled, kissed me on the cheek, hugged me close.

I locked my door, though I didn't need to, and we walked down the dock. He opened the door to his houseboat.

"Want dinner? I bought crab legs for us."

"No, thank you."

"Wine? I bought that white wine you like from River Valley Vineyards."

"No, thank you." I wanted one thing.

Relief.

It was incredible sex, as always. I am turned on by touching his hand.

He asked me to stay, he always does. I said no, thank you. He said that he wanted to wake up with me. I said no, sorry. He said, "I need this to change."

I said, "I already told you it's not going to change."

I rolled over on top of him and kissed his cheek. He linked his fingers with mine, then rolled over on top of me, our hands above my head. He wasn't happy. I ignored it. I disentangled our fingers, pushed at his shoulders, climbed out of bed, and got dressed. I ignored his unhappy face and walked out of his houseboat.

He followed me and made sure I returned to my tugboat safely. I don't know why he does this, I'm perfectly safe. I opened the door. I did not look back at him, but I knew he was hoping I would.

I didn't turn on the lights. I went to bed and stared at the ceiling, the river a lonely thing wrapped around my tugboat.

Then I did what I always do after these nights with him.

I cried.

It was Kozlovsky Sisters Night at Svetlana's Kitchen. Valerie, Ellie, and I were at the bar. It was crowded, as usual.

"Valerie," I asked. "Do you sometimes feel like you're the Lock 'Em Up Queen of Portland?"

"Yes, I do, Toni," Valerie said, tapping the side of her martini glass.

Valerie likes her job as a prosecuting attorney. She is almost two years younger than me. She's tall and thin, and has risen through the ranks at work like lightning. I told her it's because of her fire-and-brimstone nature, the bonfire beginning in our childhood. She agreed.

Valerie has short black hair, blunt cut, her widow's peak naturally pushing her hair away from her face, as mine does. Her eyes are blue, a little lighter than mine. She is married to Kai, who is a burly Hawaiian and a captain on the Portland police force, and they have two kids—Ailani, who is ten, and Koa, who is three. Ailani knows way more about crime than she should and finds it fascinating, and Koa likes to dress up like a monster. Both the kids have a widow's peak. Or, perhaps I should say that Koa has a cowlick.

"They commit the crime, they're arrested and locked up. If they're guilty as sin, I grill 'em, chill 'em, and bake 'em."

"That's an interesting way to describe your job," Ellie said.

"It's very chef-like—grilling, chilling, baking," I said.

"Only it's people," Valerie said. She took a long drink of that martini. "More complicated."

"You love it," Ellie said. Ellie is almost two years younger than Valerie. She has wavy black hair, to her shoulders, same thing with her widow's peak. Her eyes are blue green, like the sea. She curves, like our mother. She believes she's fat. I believe she has a perfect figure. Ellie owns the pillow-making business that my father thinks Gino wants to leach off of. It's called Ellie K's Pillows.

"I love it most of the time," Valerie said. "Call it childhood revenge." I knew, by the way she closed her eyes, that something from our childhood had come up and clawed at her.

As a crime and justice reporter for the *Oregon Standard*, I don't write about the crime, or the court proceedings, if Valerie has the case. That goes to Shamira Connell, my colleague at the *Oregon Standard*, as clearly there's a conflict of interest. Valerie did not change her name after she got married—"We're Kozlovskys forever"—so it wouldn't do to have the reporter's name the same as the prosecuting attorney's. However, I'm often familiar with her cases because I wrote about them at the time the crime occurred.

"Any info on the job you applied for?" Valerie asked me.

"None." It was probably hopeless. I had applied to be a reporter for a new magazine inside the newspaper called *Homes and Gardens of Oregon* and had heard nothing. The attraction was that I would not be writing about crime. The other attraction was that I might be able to avoid a nervous breakdown.

"How are you doing, Toni?" Ellie asked.

"I want out before I have an embarrassing nervous break-down." I wasn't kidding.

"Shoot, Toni, I'm sorry," Valerie said. "Quit. I told you. Start over. New career. Take time off."

"Quitting scares me. I've never quit anything in my life. I don't want to talk about this. It makes me want to go home, get in my bathtub, and eat an entire box of chocolates. Ellie, let's talk about your wedding."

"Got it covered." Ellie's voice was falsely cheerful.

I winked at Valerie, and she winked back.

"All flowers ordered, cake chosen?" Valerie asked Ellie, try-ing not to laugh.

"Got it covered." Ellie, our poor younger sister, paled.

"Menu set with Mom for the wedding reception?" I shut my mouth on my chuckle.

"Got it covered." Her hands shook as she dug in her volumi-nous purple purse and pulled out a paper bag. She blew into it.

Being engaged to Gino was giving Ellie panic attacks. She didn't want to take any sort of "tranquilizer fit for a horse," so she kept a paper bag in her purse at all times.

"One breath in," I said, slowly, almost singsongy.

"One breath out," Valerie said, also slowly, singsongy.

Bag went in, out, in, out, Ellie making wheezing sounds.

"It's a euphoric time of life for her, filled with excitement, wedding bouquets, champagne, and choosing hors d'oeuvres," Valerie said.

"She can't wait to walk down that aisle," I announced. "Vir-ginal white dress . . ."

"I can see the white veil now, flowing in the breeze."

Wheeeeeze.

Ellie choked out, "I don't want to talk about the wedding."

Valerie and I laughed and took another sip of our martinis while Ellie put the bag back over her face. I glanced at Tonight's Specials board over the bar and choked. One of them was "An-tonia You Fix That Problem." The special was cabbage and sau-sage soup and salad combination. I shook my head. Why does Mama have to do this type of thing?

Svetlana's Kitchen, which my parents started a little more than a year after we arrived, dead broke, in the United States, is fairly formal. The 1920s building is all brick, and the outside has a patio and trellis with a blooming wisteria vine. The front door is red, the windows clean and wide, with an elegant sign, painted in gold, that says SVETLANA'S KITCHEN. It's three stories tall, the restaurant on the first two stories.

When they could afford it, my mother insisted on circular tables, leather booths, white tablecloths, candlelight, crystal, a few chandeliers, and heavy silverware. There is exposed brick, a slick mahogany bar, subdued lighting, and a fountain in the corner. It has an old-fashioned, classy Russian bar feel, and all the food is authentically Russian with, as my mother says, "A twist of American tastiness."

Translated, that means that my parents are in business, and if she has to soften the recipes, or add different spices here and there, or invent a whole new recipe and pretend that it's Russian, she'll do it.

My parents' office and an employee breakroom are on the third floor. There are also two remodeled rooms—one for Ralph, an African American Iraqi war vet who has a dent in his head and a traumatic brain injury from an IED, and the other for Charlie, who is musically brilliant and mentally ill. They live there for free and are two of the gentlest men I have ever met.

Ralph is in charge of helping to clean the kitchen when he is able. He is easily confused, and now and then he'll stare off in the distance, but he makes sure that the kitchen shines. He salutes all the Kozlovskys. "There not a germy in that kitchen when Ralph done with it," my mother says. "Anya could come over and eat on floor, I tell you that."

As my cousin, Anya, is germophobic, this is high praise.

Charlie plays the piano for the restaurant unless he is in a state. He can be triggered by a half moon, bare trees, or barking dogs. Charlie likes Mozart and Tchaikovsky; they calm him down, so my father bought him an iPod and filled it with both composers.

Charlie writes his own piano concertos in addition to playing the classical masters. My parents bought a piano for the restaurant and he'll come down and play it, no sheet music, all memorized, for hours, then abruptly he'll go upstairs and that's that. My parents give Ralph and Charlie leftovers and some cash.

"What?" my father said. "They need help. Ralph and Charlie, they can't work no normal job. We can help, so we do. We give a blessing to them."

"God tell me to do it, so I do," my mother said. "That could have been us. Poor in Moscow. Poor in Germany. Poor in America, but we healthy. Minds clear, only a little messed up." She tapped her head. "But them? No. Cannot fix. So we take care of Ralph and Charlie, praise God."

That night my mother was talking to customers, table to table. We never get to order what we want when we come to our parents' restaurant. My mother orders for us based on what she wants us to eat. We'd had salads, and the dinner was coming.

Mama was wearing a blue velvet dress and matching shoes. My father was working hard in the back, the waiters and waitresses rushing to and fro, almost all of them stopping to chat with my sisters and me. Most of them have been with my parents for years, and five have been with them twenty years. My parents provide health insurance and retirement packages.

"We have to talk about something besides my . . . my . . . wedding or I'm going to lose it in this bar," Ellie said, then said to herself, in a whispery voice, "Be serene. Be quiet within your soul. Breathe in calmly, like a calm meadow." She turned to Valerie and spoke through her paper bag. "Tell us about the Tyler Barton serial murder case; it will help me to relax."

"I'm going to trial soon against a murderer. Multiple victims. I have a bad feeling about it."

"Why?" I asked. "You've done this before. What's wrong?"

"I don't know."

"Do you think you'll lose?" Ellie asked, the paper bag expanding as she blew into it.

"No. I'll win, but there's something . . ."

"Something?" I felt cold inside, an instant hit, sensing Valerie's fear. Fear, as in my hairs were standing on end all over my body and getting ready to run.

"I can't figure it out yet. But it feels different. He's a scary guy, his family is scary. They're unpredictable. Unhinged."

"Now I'm scared. We're a trio of problems. Valerie's prosecuting demons, Ellie can't breathe because she's engaged, and I am actively trying to avoid a nervous breakdown and it isn't working." My phone went off. I glanced at the quick alert I received by e-mail. My e-mail, and the police scanner, were always a source of current mayhem, murder, and chaos. "I have to go. Another shooting."

"Have a splendid time," Valerie drawled as she stood up and gave me a long, long hug and kissed my cheek. My father hurried over, his kind face wreathed in concern. "What wrong, what wrong?" His face, his dear face, so worried.

"What is this? Why is my Antonia leaving already?" my mother said. She cupped my face. "You no eat dinner yet, it up in two minutes, you need to eat dessert, too. I make ptichye moloko cake. You too thin. Not enough skins on the bones."

"I'm off to a crime scene."

"That crime scene," my mother said, shaking her head, which somehow seemed to shake her whole body. "I don't know why you must write about the criminals. We come here to America, get rid of crime. You can work here in the restaurant, I tell you, many times, your father tell you, many times. Come. Work with us. You be the boss of the desserts. You are happy girl with desserts when you younger, you bake like Mary, mother of Christ—"

"Yes, like mother of Christ," my father agreed.

"There's no mention of Mary, mother of Christ, baking in the Bible," I said.

My mother ignored that comment. "You go to school and become lady who write about shootings and murder and the bad mens." She threw her hands up. "What I do wrong make you do this? What? Curse on me."

"No childrens working the restaurant. Bad for us." My father shook his head. Even his slanted nose seemed sad.

"Bad for us," my mother echoed.

"I burn food," I reminded them.

"*Tsk,*" my mother said. "We fix that."

"*Tsk,*" my father said. "I teach you."

"I have to run." I hugged my parents and my sisters; waved at Ralph, who saluted me; and at Charlie, who was playing Mozart, who smiled back dizzily, not everything clicking on all cylinders in there.

I told myself this was my last murder.

I knew it wasn't.

The scene was busy, loud, ugly, as always. The police were there, more coming, lights flashing, sirens on, yellow crime tape surrounding the sight. Men and women in suits, detectives, one taking photos of the crime scene, passersby with their cell phones out, also taking photos. I parked, half up on a curb and started run/walking to the scene. I had a peek at the dead people, gang members, lying on the ground.

Looked like teenagers. No more than eighteen. Skinny. They got up and got dressed this morning, ate breakfast, and this is where their lives stopped. They were about three feet apart from each other. From where the guns dropped, it looked to me like they probably took their last breaths staring into each other's eyes, their hatred gone, their lives fading.

They had mothers. Fathers. Siblings. Friends. Those people would never recover.

Captain Martin Belbee gently moved me out of the way. Martin and I went to high school together. "Sorry, Toni, gotta back you up there. How ya doing? How's your sister, Ellie? The wife bought one of her pillows the other day. Red with a lion on it. The lion was blue and green. The wife said it made her feel like roaring. We're going to your parents' restaurant tomorrow. Hey, do you think your mother is going to make that special called 'Menopause Nightmare'? Lamb and beef. It was delicious when I had it before. The wife loved it. She's having hot flashes."

I backed up with Martin, answered on automatic, told him I'd check with my mother and let him know. I asked Martin questions about the crime, and he answered with what he could. I knew he'd call me later with more info. I mentally started writing my story that would go up on the *Oregon Standard* Web site immediately. I would add to it as more details came in. That was my job.

Yes, I write about crime.

It's not for sissies.

Neither is it for people like me. I wanted out.

My mother would make "Menopause Nightmare" for Martin and his wife. I e-mailed him. Martin e-mailed back, "I cannot wait. Thanks, Toni. Thank your mama for me. Is she still mad at Ellie for her bad choice? And why do you and your siblings make your mama worry? I saw that on the Tonight's Specials board the other night, too. You shouldn't do that to her. She's a good woman."

Hours later, at two in the morning, I climbed in my bathtub with a box of chocolates. I ate them while I soaked. Not the whole box. Half of one tray. I like to eat treats in the bath. Makes for a tasty time, and it sucks away my stress.

3

At seven in the morning, I heard Ellie in my head. She said, *Toni.*

I'd been awake for two hours already. Once I'm awake, I have to get up immediately, have coffee, and make the choice to stay up. I have to make the choice not to hide under the covers. I have to make the choice not to give up on life that day. I learned that the hard way. If it's not raining, I have coffee on my deck and watch the river, check on my river pets, search the sky for Anonymous, and read the newspaper. Sometimes I'm having coffee in a down jacket, hat, and gloves.

Toni.

I called her.

I knew it was about her wedding.

We arranged to meet at the end of the week at Ellie's for Pillow Talk.

Which means we sisters get together and sew pillows and talk and laugh.

Now and then there's a fight. A few things have been thrown: a spool of thread, fabric, a handful of buttons, pillows—for sure nonweaponry-type things.

No scissors, thankfully.

Sometimes I can hear my sisters, Ellie and Valerie, talking to me in my head. It's rare, and it only comes in emotionally intense times—when we're worried, scared, in danger, falling apart, or conversely when something perfect happens to us. All of a sudden, I hear them.

I do not know their day-to-day lives. I don't know the minutiae of their thoughts. I don't know when they're making love or fighting with someone.

Some might say that we only *think* we can hear each other because we're sisters, and best friends, and in tune with each other, that it's nothing remarkable. Some might say we're making it up, or it's some sort of natural reaction because we know what is going on in each other's lives. We know the truth.

"The brothers and sisters of the Sabonis family can hear each other. Gift from God," my mother says. "It comes from all the way back, from the time of the Romanovs, those spoiled fools, to Lenin, that mass murderer, may he be whipped by the devil each day; to Stalin, a much worse mass murderer, may his body be set on fire in hell; to Germany's invasion, those sadistic Nazi thugs; to the siege of Leningrad, to the Cold War, we have heard each other.

"We have called for each other, Antonia. We have begged for help. We have said good-bye as we lay dying, crying as we gave birth. We have shared secrets and joys. It is passed down to all of us. It's the language of brothers, the language of sisters."

My earliest memory of this special language was in Moscow, when I was six and Valerie, called Valeria then, was four. Ellie, Elvira then, was two, and she was asleep in her crib.

Valeria and I were in the kitchen of our tight, dingy apartment making our mother's Russian tea cakes with pecans and powdered sugar. Our mother had managed to trade eggs for powdered sugar with a neighbor.

Our kitchen was small, the walls sometimes damp and weeping, the oven didn't always work, and the refrigerator made a clanging sound like a ghost's chains, but my mother was clever with what little she had.

As I was sifting the flour, I suddenly couldn't breathe. I could feel myself shutting down, getting dark inside, floating. "I'm dying," I told my mother, my voice weak.

Valeria, her hands covered in rolled dough, stilled. Her head tilted back and she went pale. She gave a tiny gasp, a choked breath lodging in her throat.

"Mother of God, what is it?" our mother said, dropping a bowl, one of only two mixing bowls that we had. It shattered as she reached for Valeria, when she fell straight back, her face growing more sickly, splotchy white by the minute.

I felt a pull into that blackness. I knew it was death. I collapsed to the floor, then lay on it, curled in a ball. I wanted to help Valeria, but I couldn't. My mother shook Valeria's shoulders. "Valeria! Valeria!" she screamed, then crawled over to me, "Mary, mother of Jesus, help me. Antonia!" She slapped my face, not hard, as I closed my eyes.

I heard babbling in my head. Baby babbling, the same sounds that Elvira made, but they were scared, panicked. "Elvira," I whispered. She cried, a weak wail, sadness.

The black pulled in tight, sucking out my breath, my vision. I felt myself floating upward. My mother shook me, yelled my name as I felt myself spinning. I closed my eyes.

"Antonia!" My mother shook me, screamed again. My vision cleared, I breathed in again, ragged and hoarse, and the spinning stopped. As soon as it had come upon me, the wave of suffocation headed back out. Death's hand danced away, as forcefully as it had jammed its way in. I exhaled, the blackness gone, the pull gone. I heard Elvira's cry again in my head, a baby's sorrowful cry, a sigh, a last breath. . . .

Valeria stood, wobbled. "Elvira! It's Elvira. I hear her!"

"What?" my mother said, on all fours, trembling. "The baby is not crying."

I grabbed my mother's shoulder to pull myself up, then Valeria and I both ran, stumbling, tripping, to Elvira in her crib. She was blue, tears on her cheeks.

"My God and Mother Mary have mercy!" My mother picked Elvira up in her arms and whacked her on the back, then turned her over and began CPR. She breathed in, twice, not too hard, then pumped her tiny chest with her fingers. She sank to the floor and laid Elvira out.

Her hands shaking, my mother breathed and pumped, breathed and pumped.

Valeria and I kneeled, right by our mother, her tears streaming down her face to Elvira's, mixing with Elvira's tears, that blue tint seeming to glow, her body limp, her face sweet, a dying angel.

I heard nothing in my head. Nothing.

Valeria glanced at me, her face stricken. "She's quiet."

"Mother of Christ. Saint Peter. Saint Joseph. Help me," my mother begged. "Help me."

Limp. Blue. Still.

Breathe. Pump.

"Jesus help me. Breathe, Elvira, breathe!"

Dead angel.

Breathe. Pump.

"Damn it, God," my mother begged. "Are you deaf?"

Breathe. Pump.

Elvira's eyes flipped open and her cry, robust, outraged, a scream from heaven entered too early, burst into the room. My mother, now cradling Elvira, fell back into the wall, white as vanilla ice cream, trembling, holding her baby, rocking her back and forth as her screams pierced the room. Within a minute, my mother had calmed her, and I heard the babbling again, the sweet talk of Elvira *in my head*. I looked, stunned, at Valeria.

"She's talking in my head," she whispered.

"Me too."

My mother studied us, exhausted. She'd aged a hundred years doing CPR on her baby angel. "How did you know?"

"Elvira was dying, and she gave it to both of us so we would come and get her," I said.

"She talked to us and said 'Help, help,' " Valeria said. "Mama, you look bad."

"Yes, Mama," I said, young and blunt. "Very bad."

My mother, reeling from the shock of her life, kissed Elvira, then dragged in air. "You have it then."

"Have what?"

She closed her eyes, head back, then opened them, a new light inside. Pride, maybe? "The language of sisters, the language of brothers. I have it with Uncle Leonid. We can hear each other, inside our heads when something is wrong, or when something is especially beautiful. Now and then we can feel each other. It started when we were children. My father had the same language with his sister. My grandfather had it with his brother. My great-grandfather had the gift with three brothers. It comes down the line, like genes, like our widow's peaks. Father to son. Mother to daughter. Then the sisters and brothers, we hear each other.

"It's a gift. It's a curse. It is us. The Sabonises. Praise God and Jesus and, most especially, Mary, mother of God, who never got enough credit for her sacrifices and her courage." My mother reached out to brush my hair back from my widow's peak, then Valeria's, then baby Elvira, who had a visible widow's peak when she was born. She pointed to her own widow's peak. "This is where it comes in. Through the widow's peak. We all have one, my father, my grandfather, my great-grandfather."

We curled up next to her and she hugged us tight while Elvira cooed. She bent to kiss Valeria and me. "My two angels saved the youngest angel. Thank you, daughters."

"Do you think I'm a better angel than Antonia?" Valeria asked.

"No, I'm the better angel," I told her.

"You are not."

"Yes, I am."

"Am, too!"

"You are both angels," she said, then glared. "Most of the time."

That night, our curtains drawn against people who would spy on us, wish ill on us, especially as we were secret Christians, I peeked out at my parents from our closet-sized bedroom. My mother was still holding Elvira, and they both held straight shots of vodka. My father kissed my mother, tenderly, and she kissed him back, then they headed to bed.

I heard them that night, as I did often.

My parents didn't realize how thin the walls were.

It was like rock-a-bye baby music to me. I went to sleep to my mother's laughter, my father's whispered comments, then the bed's headboard hitting the wall.

Elvira slept in her crib that night, next to my parents, and Valeria and I slept together in our bed, curled up together, as usual.

"I'll always listen for you, Antonia," Valeria said, tapping her peak. "In my head."

"I'll listen for you, too, Valeria. I promise."

We put those widow's peaks together, held hands, and went to sleep, clutching the stuffed bears our grandmother Ekaterina had sewn us.

I took three phone calls on my way home from work the next afternoon. This is why I'm glad I have a headset in my car. My family is large, complicated, and they like to talk on the phone.

The first call was from my aunt Polina, who was in a tizzy about Ellie's wedding. Aunt Polina wanted to make sure that I knew that she was not—*not!*—going to sit by my aunt Holly, as Holly is a "... body busy. You know what I say, Antonia? Body busy!"

"A busybody?"

"No, body busy. She always want to know my business. That not right. And, I say to you, that body smell. Yes, Holly smell. She say it perfume, I say it like this: rat fart. You no put me by her at the wedding table. How you are, my sweet Antonia? I see your mother yesterday at Svetlana's Kitchen. You know what name of special was? No? I tell you: 'Antonia Quit Your Job.' "

I groaned.

"We worry about you, Antonia. I bringing you my borscht. You love the beets and cabbage and the pig's lard, eh?"

My cousin, JJ (Nadja when we were in the Soviet Union), Aunt Polina's and Uncle Yuri's daughter and one of my best friends, called to confirm dinner next Saturday night downtown. "Don't bail on me. You need to get out, Toni, and you know it. Boris, Anya, Tati, and Zoya are going. So is Valerie and Kai and Ellie and Gino. And Jax, of course."

JJ owns JJ's Salon. She has ten stylists in her modern, brick, cement-floor downtown salon. Her brown hair is parted down the middle and curled on the sides. She wears fashionable clothes, impeccable makeup. I had heard her speak bluntly to her customers on numerous occasions.

"No, I won't allow that haircut, Amie. Your face is shaped like a square. It'll make it fatter. Here's what we're going to do. . . ."

"No. We will not dye your hair that red color. It's a terrible choice, Maureen. You'll resemble a middle-aged clown. If people ask where you got your hair done, it'll be bad for business. I'm going to dye your hair a golden blond. . . ."

"What in heck happened to you, Addy? Did you stick your hair in a blender on high?"

Miraculously, people keep coming back. She is blunt with me if it has been a while since I've been in. "Toni, stand still. I'm going to cut your hair so you won't resemble a Russian sheepdog."

"This is my and Jax's first night out in a long time, Toni," JJ said. "I need action. I need adventure. I need to feel like a woman again, not a mother of two teenage girls, so I need you and everyone else to play a part in our date fantasy. Listen up. Jax and I are going to meet at the bar and we're going to pretend we don't know each other and don't have two teenagers together and aren't dealing with his sick dad and business stress. He's going to hit on me and pick me up. I'm going to introduce you."

"You're going to introduce me to Jax, even though you two have been married for eighteen years?"

"Yes. Except that his name isn't going to be Jax. His name is going to be something else. It'll be a surprise. And my name isn't going to be JJ, it's going to be Stephi. I'm telling everyone. We're going to flirt and then I'm going to a hotel with him for a one-night stand. My parents are taking care of the kids."

"I can't wait. Fun idea."

"I know, isn't it? Stephi is going to get laid, not JJ. *Stephi.*

Zoya and Tati are going to give me a black bustier and a gauzy tiny skirt, too. Hopefully Tati and Zoya will be dressed appropriately and not in their stripper clothes. It's not necessary to *always* advertise their business, is it? Anyhow, gotta run, another client walked in and she looks like a tornado hit her." She held the phone away and shouted, "Laurie, did you walk through a tornado? What the heck?" She turned back to the phone. "Be there or I will hunt you down. You won't pretend you're sick, or hide or say you have to work late again, right?"

"I'm coming." I was dreading it.

"We love you and miss you and we want the family to be together. All the Kozlovskys. That means you." She hung up.

"We want everyone to be together" was a common phrase in our family. But we are together. All. The. Time.

The third call was from my cousin Anya, an actress and a hypochondriac who said she was sure she had "Gangrene. In my toes. Not a lot, but I think it's growing. I think we can stop it before amputation. I hope." Her voice wavered.

Anya has thick, straight brown hair and golden cat eyes. She's gorgeous. You would never guess at the head case beneath the beauty. "I like stage acting better than TV because I can lose it in front of people if the role calls for it. I mean, totally-freak-out lose it, scare-the-audience lose it, let-my-brain-out-of-my-head-and-let-it-run-up-and-down-the-aisles lose it."

I assured her that I thought her toes were fine, and she took a gulp of air and said, how are you, and I said, I'm fine.

"You're not fine, Toni, I don't think. You're healthy fine. Physically. I worry about you. Worrying about you makes me more susceptible to colds. In fact, I'm not blaming you, but in the last two years I have gotten more colds. I know I was bordering on bird flu once, and another time I am sure I had symptoms for scarlet fever, and I do think my worry about you has caused them. Please stop making me worry. I hope you know if you want to talk, I'm always here."

"I know, Anya, I do."

I didn't want to go out with my cousins, though I loved them. I wanted to be alone.

By myself.

"See you next Saturday night, Toni. I'm so glad you're coming. We want everyone to be together. All the Kozlovskys. JJ is turning into Stephi, did you hear? She's going to have a one-night stand. And don't worry, I'm going to bring the antiseptic spray."

"Antiseptic spray? For what?"

Anya gasped. "So I can spray down the table at the restaurant before we sit down! Do you know the kinds of germs that lurk on restaurant tables?" She made a gagging sound, authentic, as she was gagging at the thought, and explained these germs to me in high-level bacterial detail. "Do you understand now?"

"Yes."

"Love you so much, Toni. See you soon."

My family is huge. Do not try to keep track of all of the members. It's impossible.

We have all immigrated to Portland from Moscow. We are in and out of each other's lives constantly. My father calls it "The Great American Kozlovsky Escape, Praise America."

My father's father, Konstantin Kozlovsky, was murdered in the Soviet Union. I can't say more about that now. His mother, Ekaterina Kozlovskaya, died about a year before that.

My father has three brothers. They are all tall, barrel chested, and grizzled. Black hair turning white. They would not win beauty awards. They all used to box, and none of them have straight noses. They all have scars, small and large, on their faces, and they wear the stoic expressions of Russian men, their jaws hard.

Beneath the rigid stoicness, soft, loving, and tender hearts reside. These are men who believe in, and love, our family.

My father's oldest brother, Uncle Vladan, came here first when I was very young. He had been to college but worked in a factory as he refused to be a card-carrying member of the Communist Party. He spoke out against the government. He wanted more money for factory workers and their families who were crammed into dormitories. He wanted a free press, freedom of speech, a fair justice system, and freedom to worship. He was, as all Kozlovskys were, a secret Christian.

The government didn't like that, to say the least. Uncle Vladan was imprisoned. He escaped into a winter storm. He froze on his escape but kept running, and later had to have two toes removed and a finger. He went to Poland, Czechoslovakia, then Germany, then came to the States. He was in poor shape during his journey and worked any day job he could get, even through pneumonia, starving, and an infection where his toes used to be. He met my aunt Holly, a hilarious and loud person, here.

When Aunt Holly met my uncle, she was a kindergarten teacher, and he was starting a landscape business, which meant he was mowing a lot of lawns.

Uncle Vladan met Aunt Holly when he was mowing her parents' lawn. His English was poor, her Russian was zero. They fell in love anyhow. He told Holly, "I give of my word to you, I make fine husband. I not always be a lawn mower."

Uncle Vladan kept his word. He owns a huge landscaping business now, for residential and corporate clients. He never mows lawns anymore. He cried when he bought his house ten years ago, brand new, with a sunset view. "I promised my Holly I buy her pretty home one day, and I did it. What you think, Holly?"

Holly hugged him. "I think I love you, and when you told me you would not be a lawn mower forever, I believed you." We all laughed.

Aunt Holly and Uncle Vladan have two children. The oldest is my cousin Anya, the actress and hypochondriac.

When Anya told Uncle Vladan in high school she wanted to be an actress, he gasped, hand to heart, and yelled, "What? Woe on my life. You on the stage? No. Not my daughter. You not loose woman. You go to college, you get married, have the babies, like nice Russian women do."

Their son, Boris, steals cars. He runs a chop shop. It's an embarrassment to the family. Boris has served time twice. He will again. Uncle Vladan currently likes to pretend to believe that Boris is a full-time mechanic, his wily ways behind him.

"Aha! My son. He fix anything. He know everything. Has own mechanic business now. Obedient son. Soon he marry Russian woman, have the babies, like nice Russian men do."

Boris is a funny guy. He steals fancy cars, "only from the rich and spoiled," but he also has season tickets to the Oregon Symphony and the Portland Opera. He's addicted to it. He goes to every single concert. He begs me to come with him all the time, and I do, sometimes. He literally brushed my hair and got me dressed when I could hardly get out of bed two years ago. "Come on, honey. Get up, Toni. It's Rachmaninoff's Concerto Number 2 in C Minor. I know that was your uncle Leonid's favorite. You can't miss it, you simply can't."

I have a real problem with him car stealing, and I have told him many times, often yelling. But I love him, he's my cousin, so what to do? Relatives can cause difficult moral conundrums.

My father's second brother, my uncle Yuri, is married to my aunt Polina. Uncle Yuri is an electrician, and Aunt Polina owns a florist shop. Aunt Polina and Uncle Yuri left Moscow about a year before us. Their daughter is JJ, the cousin who harangues people about their hair.

JJ and Jax have two teenage girls. Chelsea is seventeen, a rebel with dyed black hair, black eye shadow, black leather, and black nails. JJ says Chelsea needs a chastity belt and a leash to keep her from sneaking out at night. Hope is eighteen. She is a straight-A student and athlete and Pollyannaish, and very, very sweet. Hope has had the same boyfriend—Macky Talbot, a truly nice, intelligent kid—for two years.

My father's third brother, my uncle Sasho, who owns a trucking business. That's what he did in Moscow, before he escaped with his wife, Yelena, and my twin cousins, also about a year before us.

Uncle Sasho is divorced from his wife, Yelena. Yelena ran off with the plumber ten years ago. They don't know where she is, but now and then they get a postcard. Yelena leaving was, in some ways, wrenching for her kids, but she was also a faceplanting alcoholic and mean as a python, so there was relief mixed in with the cauldron of emotions.

Tatiana (Tati) and Zoya are the twins. They are in their early thirties, and they are wild. Tati and Zoya own their own business selling stripper clothes. The business is called Tati and Zoya's Light and Lacy Delights. They do the whole costume thing for the strippers—Scottish dancing lady, doctor, executive—down to the pasties and thongs.

They are next-door neighbors in condos overlooking the city, and they have a sewing/office space downtown. Business is booming. Zoya handles the business end, marketing, sales, and the Web site. Tati is the designer and deals with the fabrics. They are curvy and daring and, shall I say, refuse to be monogamous.

"I cannot limit myself to one man," Tati told me years ago. "How boring."

"I feel the same," Zoya said. "Three is a . . . tantalizing number."

"Yes, three," Tati nodded. "Tantalizing."

"You can rotate." Zoya made a swirling motion with her finger.

"Yes," Tati agreed, rotating her hands. "Rotate. Who wants to get bored or tied down?"

"Well . . ." Zoya mused.

Tati clapped her hands. "Fantastic-o idea! We should make licorice straps. What do you think, Zoya? You could eat your way out of being tied down."

I couldn't imagine handling three men.

Uncle Sasho also has a son. It was a surprise when Yelena got pregnant. We are not sure if Sasho is Pavel's father, as Yelena was running around a lot back then, but we don't ask, we don't talk about it, and we love Pavel as Sasho does.

Pavel is a junior in high school. He told me last year he wanted to be a dancer but swore me to secrecy.

"How long have you been dancing?"

"Three years."

"You want to be a dancer after high school?"

"Yes."

"What kind of dance?"

"Jazz. Modern. Tap. But what I love most is ballet. It's so

graceful, it's so hard. And to be dancing in roles that other men have danced in for a hundred years..." He teared up.

Several months ago he said, "Can you help me with my dad, Aunt Toni? I've been lying to him about where I'm going after school all these years. He thinks I'm studying chemistry."

Pavel is well groomed. Long and lanky. Huge smile. Enjoys clothes and fashion. Sensitive. Gentle. Hopeful, but sad eyes. He is keeping another secret from his father. "I will help you with your father."

He smiled, relieved, hugged me tight. "I love your heels, Aunt Toni! I think your color wheel leans heavily on blue."

(I am almost done with my family line, don't worry.)

My mother, Svetlana, maiden name, Sabonisa, had a dear mother, Lada, who died in the Soviet Union when I was young, with what they think was cancer, but are not sure, as the medical care was poor. Her father, Anatoly Sabonis, almost fifteen years older than Lada, died a year after his wife of a heart attack. It was undoubtedly because he missed Lada, but it was also because of what happened to Leonid, his son, my mother's brother. There is only so much one can take.

Our families get together all the time. Birthdays. Christmas. Anniversaries. On Fourth of July my family hosts a huge parade in our neighborhood for hundreds of people. There are homemade floats, decorated bikes and wagons, and a barbeque at the end. The American flag is prominently displayed.

Unless you are in the hospital you are expected to come to all family activities. However, if you are in the hospital, the dinner will be brought to you, because you cannot possibly eat hospital food, my goodness no. It will kill you. Russian food will build your strength up again, and here is a small shot of vodka.

We recently went to see Uncle Sasho when he was passing kidney stones.

We are a chaotic bunch. We phone, e-mail, and even have a separate, private Facebook page for Kozlovskys only. We fight, although I try to stay out of all of them. When I had a dinner at my tugboat a month ago, Zoya pushed Boris into the river because she is sick of him stealing cars, even if it is from the "rich piranhas."

Tati told our aunt Polina she needed a colonic cleansing so she wouldn't be so uptight. That made JJ mad—no one is allowed to speak ill of her mama—and she told Tati she was a lingerie-wearing slut. This did not offend Tati as much as one would think it would.

Valerie told Anya her hypochondriac tendencies were giving her an ulcer. This alarmed Anya, and she had to sit in a corner and look it up on the Internet to see if it was a possibility.

My mother told Uncle Vladan that his mind was as closed "as a clam. Shut like a snap." Uncle Vladan said, "That not true, Svetlana." Then he said, after a few minutes, "I think you right. That hurt my feelings." And he got all teary and my mother had to hug him. "I not be a snap clam anymore, Svetlana."

Things go on like that.

If the argument gets too heated my father steps in, solves it, and says, "This is my final word." The matter is then done. Until a new matter/fight comes up.

We're like any other American family.

We're a mess.

But we're the Kozlovskys, and this is how we live. It is not always peaceful. But we love each other and we will do anything for one other.

Especially if a car is stolen. We know to contact Boris. He'll get it back for us.

The next day I was sitting at my desk, working, having just gotten off the phone with an assistant police chief when my editor, William Lopez, who is ex-military from Vietnam, stomped up and said, "Why the hell does your mother want you to quit? I saw it at the restaurant last night on the Specials board. 'Antonia Quit Your Job.' What's wrong, Kozlovsky?"

"It's my mother, William. What can I say? She wants me to make desserts at the restaurant."

He grumbled. "I had the kebabs with plum and lemon sauce.

I couldn't have the special because the name of my favorite reporter was on it. You're not quitting, Kozlovsky," he said, jabbing a finger at me before stalking away. He shot back, "I need a draft on that story you're writing on the Ramburg embezzlement charge in one hour."

He left. Charged back on full speed. He pointed at me again. "And don't you even *think* about quitting."

I was quitting. Soon. It's always best to avoid nervous breakdowns when one can.

4

On Thursday I went shopping. I don't call it retail therapy. I call it Keeping The Monsters At Bay: Shopping Defensive Strategies. I found an emerald-green wrap dress with a low V neckline; three lacy bras made by Lace, Satin, and Baubles, my favorite lingerie company; and a red leather coat with a belt at the waist.

I love clothes.

I love knee-high boots and skirts with slits. I love lace and ruffles and clean lines. I love tight jeans and shiny silver dresses. I love red high heels and sandals with bling. I love silky scarves, dangling earrings, and bracelets that jangle.

My love of fashion is not based—much—in vanity or self-absorption. It goes back to Moscow. I shop to remind myself that I am not living in poverty anymore, that I am not doing things I wished I didn't have to do, that I am not poor, scared, hungry, and desperate. I am not a street urchin.

I shop for that warm coat that will take away the memories of that ceaseless snow in Moscow. For that thick cable-knit sweater to keep the freezing rain from Red Square out of my mind. For warm boots that chase away the thoughts of ice hanging from our apartment windows—on the inside.

My love of clothes is also related to being an immigrant, knowing no English, scared in a new country, a new state, a new school, and not fitting in at all.

When we arrived in Oregon, my sisters and I wore our long

black hair in braids wrapped around the tops of our head with a fluffy bow on top.

We were stared at, and the kids giggled behind our backs. Several of the kids pulled on our braids. No one in my class had long braids wrapped around their heads like the Kozlovsky girls. We wore uniforms in Moscow, and though my parents were happy that we were not wearing uniforms here, that didn't mean they would let us wear pants or anything casual to school.

We had to wear dresses. Flowers. High collars. Prim. A little lace. My mother sewed us our dresses. We looked like overgrown dolls with an overabundance of weird braids.

Not only did the kids make fun of our clothes, they made fun of us because we were Russian and didn't speak English. Not all the kids. Many of the kids were nice, and we're still friends with them, but when you are young and scared you remember the kids who made you feel like nothing, a freak, the most.

On a sunny afternoon, two weeks after starting school, at home in Uncle Vladan and Aunt Holly's basement, I chopped off about a foot from each of my braids, then brushed my hair out. It was thick and shiny. I loved it. When Valerie saw me, she insisted I do hers, too, as did Ellie.

When our parents arrived home that evening, from their jobs with Uncle Vladan's landscaping business, their mouths dropped open at the changes in their daughters. Then we threw them another shock. We told them, "At school our names are Toni, Valerie, and Ellie now, not Antonia, Valeria, and Elvira."

The kids had made fun of our names, too. They called me "An-TOE-nya," or "Toe." They called Valeria "Valeria Malaria," and they called Elvira "Virus."

My father swayed. My mother sank into a chair. Our parents spoke to us in Russian, though we would all soon be trying to always "speaky the English" to each other, as my father said.

"Who cut your hair?" my mother asked.

"I did."

Their eyes bugged out. "You cut it, Antonia?" my father said. I nodded, scared.

They stared at us. They stared at each other. They sighed. They reached for each other's hand.

"Girls," my mother started.

We all flinched. Tensed. We were ready for our punishment, but it could not be as bad as what the kids at school were dealing out.

"Daughters," my father said.

Our parents exchanged another look, then they both sat straighter and tilted their chins up.

My father cleared his throat. "Your hair is pretty."

"We Kozlovskys are proud of our hair," my mother said. "I am impressed with your hair-cutting skills, Antonia."

What? We were not in trouble for cutting our braids off?

"And we are not wearing dresses again," Valerie announced, though tentatively, not wanting to hurt our mother's feelings. She had stayed up, late at night, sewing those dresses. "No one wears flowered dresses here, Mama, I'm sorry."

My mother's face . . . Oh, that hurt. I saw my father pat my mother's hand. My sisters and I had to bite our lips not to cry out.

But then . . . my mother smiled. "Your uncle Vladan said that he is bringing us clothes for you all tonight. A collection from the church was taken. Perhaps there will be clothes in there that you like. As soon as we have a little money, we will take you to get new American clothes." She raised a finger. "Not expensive."

"Really?" I said, breathless.

"Yes."

"Yes. Okay-dokay," my father said, then laughed, and went back to Russian. "That's a new phrase I learned today. You can dress like American girls. This is my final word."

"We are proud Americans, from Russia, and you can dress how the girls do here," my mother said. "Thank you, Jesus, he brought us here safely. May all the people who hurt us in the Soviet Union find that their feet are infected, their tongues flattened, their hearing dying." She smiled so sweetly at us, then flung out her arms for a hug. "Praise Mary, mother of God."

"Praise Mary, mother of God," my sisters and I said, hugging her close. She was the best.

And that was it. My parents were smart enough, open-minded enough, not to force the old ways on us here in this country.

We found jeans in the pile of clothes that night. Tennis shoes. T-shirts. Sweatshirts. The next day we went to school in American clothes, our hair brushed straight down. We changed our names. When the kids made fun of us, we punched them.

I loved clothes from then on out. Fashion, for me, allowed me to blend in at school, blend into America.

Clothes helped me then, and now, to fake confidence. To fake that I'm strong and brave, when often I feel neither. To fake that I know what I'm doing at work when sometimes I don't. To fake that I am an insider when I don't feel that I am. I've lived here for over twenty five years, but old insecurities cling like crimes.

I always search for bargains and sales, I always pay cash, and if there's a coupon, it's in my hand. My parents are strict savers, and it was drilled into all of us that we should save money. One of the Kozlovsky favorite family mottos: "Save your money so you will not starve to death."

It's a helpful motto, and I do save.

Another helpful motto, this one from my mother? Always put on lipstick and earrings before you leave the house, unless the house is on fire.

Clothes are my armor.

There was only one time when my love of clothes fell apart and I didn't care anymore.

That was when everything tumbled into hell.

He called late the next night.

"How are you?"

"Fine."

"Where are you?"

"Mexico. I needed to move on from India."

He had been volunteering in an orphanage in India for months. "On the beach now?"

"Yes. I'm volunteering in a local school and talking to people."

"Sleeping?"

"No." He laughed, but it was sad, too close to the edge. "Currently I'm being followed by the vegetable garden again."

I would laugh, but it wasn't funny. He was haunted by a vegetable garden.

"I'm also being followed by someone scary. I wake up all the time to this black, lurking presence and screams. Not my screams, a woman's screams. I don't get it. Why is all this getting worse these last months? Why am I seeing all these things more lately?"

Maybe it's because you know you've been lied to all these years, you're twenty-eight, and you're searching for the truth and I am a disloyal sister. "Are the memories making any sense?"

"Not much, but I can feel my mind opening up. I'm getting snatches of memories here and there. I keep seeing a rocking horse that's rocking on its own, no one on him. It's creepy."

I shivered. A rocking horse that rocks alone. A blue ceramic box with a fancy lady on it, and a red and purple butterfly that flies toward scary woods.

No wonder he thought he was losing his mind.

"I think it's all from my childhood, but it's the blood that's the worst, Toni. I see it on my hands in my dreams. It's driving me straight out of my mind. Why do I have blood on my hands? How did it get there? Was it mine? Was it someone else's? Was it hers? Or is it all in my imagination?"

"It's not in your imagination." *I remembered the blood. Never tell, Antonia, never, ever tell.*

"They know more than they're telling me," he said.

"Yes, I think they do."

"I need them to talk to me."

"I know. They will."

"I miss you."

"I miss you, too."

When the moon was high in the sky, I walked over to his craftsman-styled houseboat. I brought a bottle of wine. "Tired, Nick?" I asked when he opened the door.

"Not for you. Come on in, baby."

Nick Sanchez's houseboat was modern and streamlined. Wood plank floors, darker wood kitchen cabinets, quartz counters, open shelving, and an island in the middle. It had one open room downstairs, and then his bedroom, a guest bedroom, and an office upstairs, which was lined with books. It was a manly-man houseboat.

Nick had made manicotti and a salad and heated up bread. He is a thoughtful person, kind, even though he often resembles a blond criminal, depending on where he's working at the moment.

We ate in bed, then we had sex, then I went home.

He sighed as I let myself into my tugboat.

"I heard that, Nick."

"I heard it, too. Come back if you change your mind."

"I won't change my mind."

"I'm always up for a night in your tugboat."

"I know."

"I'll keep you warm."

"I have heat."

"Not personal heat."

"Not tonight."

"A night soon?"

"Nick—"

He held up a hand. "I won't push. But I'll miss you. My bed is way too big without you in it."

"Your bed is way too big, period."

He laughed.

I shut the door to my tugboat. I do not spend the night at Nick's, and I don't allow him to spend the night at my place, either. The answer is no. What I am doing is already bad enough.

Nick said hello to me on the dock when I first moved in.

"Hello," I said, then froze. Nick was an intimidating giant. He has blond hair and light blue eyes, and those eyes stayed on me, full attention. The blonde and blue eyed part makes him sound pretty, but there wasn't a pretty bone on him. His hair was down to his shoulders, and he had a mustache and a goatee.

He was all man, rugged, tough, pretty serious. He had a faded scar on his left cheek and a faded scar on his right temple. He had nice teeth. I don't know why I noticed his teeth.

"I'm Nick Sanchez."

"Toni Kozlovsky." When he shook my hand, I felt that my hand was going to be permanently lost in the size of his.

"Moving in?"

"Yes." He had on a black T-shirt, jeans, and black boots. It appeared that he might have a criminal history of slamming heads together.

"Welcome. I hope you like it here."

"I think I will."

"I live right there." He nodded toward his houseboat.

"I love your home."

"Thank you. I love your tugboat. Creative way to live. If you have to, you can probably haul my home down the river."

"Probably. It's a retired tugboat, though, so to speak. It's tired. It doesn't want to work anymore."

"I feel the same way sometimes."

I laughed. "Me too."

"I like the yellow paint and the red trim."

"Thank you. It's . . . it's been remodeled on the inside. I'm not living in a real tugboat. Well, it's real. But not real in a . . . tugboatty type of way."

He smiled. I caught my breath. *Wow.* I remember thinking. *Wow.* Full lips. Not so scary when he smiled.

"I bet it's interesting to live in. A lot of river history there."

"Yes, it is." That would have been the moment to invite him in, but I couldn't. The words wouldn't come out of my mouth. What to say to a man like that? How could I invite another man into my home, anyhow? I couldn't do that.

"Are you from around here?" he asked.

"Yes. We live, well, I lived, I sold our house." Simple question, complicated answer. "It's about thirty minutes from here."

"Ah." Something flashed in his eyes, covered up quick. He caught my confusion. He wondered about the true answer behind it all.

"Yes. So now . . . here I am at the tugboat. I'm here." I decided to study the deck. I had lost confidence in the last long months. I had been humbled to the floor. I had been gutted. I was not myself. I didn't think I'd be myself again.

"I see you have a kayak. I love kayaking. There are a lot of animals and birds right here, but if you kayak that way"—he turned and pointed downriver—"it gets quieter near the curve and there are even more."

"I'll go that way." No, I wouldn't. I would not get in my kayak and do that. I glanced down again as his eyes were seeing too much of me and I was not up to handling someone tall and studly like Nick. "Thank you."

"Sure." He held out his hand again. "Nice to meet you, Toni."

"You too." His hand was warm. My hand was cold.

He walked off the dock as my parents headed down, holding boxes.

I watched him go.

I heard him say hello to my parents; they said hello back, smiled.

My mother put a box down on the dock and hugged me. My father wrapped his arms around both of us. My mother lightly tapped both of my cheeks with both hands, put her widow's peak to mine, and said, "Okay. Now we have things to do, things to get done. No?"

I wiped away tears and kept unpacking, my sisters coming down the dock with boxes, too.

That's what Kozlovskys do. We brush away the tears, and we get on with life. We always have things to do.

"How are you feeling about the wedding?" I asked Ellie.

"I feel perfectly pleasant and peaceful about it." Ellie, at her sewing machine, continued to sew white lace around the edges of the light blue fabric. When she was done, she was going to paint blue irises and lily pads on the pillow. "Be one with your life," she whispered to herself. "Embrace your fear, then let it go floating into the sky."

"You sound perfectly and pleasantly insane," Valerie said.

The three of us were at Ellie's house sewing pillows. Some women meet for lunch. Some women go away to Vegas and be naughty. My sisters and I sew pillows and talk, so we call it Pillow Talk.

When we were younger, we sewed pillows to make money in the midst of a long and blisteringly cold and starving winter in Moscow. Then we sewed for our lives; now we sew because that's what we do when we're together.

All the pillows the three of us make during Pillow Talk go to a children's hospital in town, so they have to be extra special. We all work on them at home after our Pillow Talk nights. When we get a bunch, we bag them up, haul them over, sometimes give them out to the kids ourselves, then we go back to Ellie's, have a couple of celebratory vodka straight shots, and make more pillows.

Ellie lives in a two-story blue home in a quiet area on the Willamette River. It's set back from the river about twenty feet. The home was old, so she had the whole thing gutted and had all the walls painted white. That was where the boredom ended.

Ellie loves fabrics. She has floor-to-ceiling window treatments in the most lush, intricate fabrics on every window, all different designs and bright colors that somehow blend. She has taken fabric from India, China, the Netherlands, South Africa, Australia, etc., and framed it for her walls and used it as furniture slipcovers. The world looks like it landed in her home.

Upstairs she knocked out a wall between the living room and kitchen, so it's one large room, with two bedrooms down the hall and a bathroom. Downstairs she knocked down four walls, so the daylight basement, with two sets of French doors, is completely open. This is where she runs Ellie K's Pillows.

She has four women who work for her. She sews and sells her pillows all over the country. Ellie has a Web site where all of her pillows are pictured. I sometimes get on the Web site to relax myself because the pillows are so creative, fun, funny, bodacious. She also has a page about her, her life, her home, her cats, the river, and her pillows in progress. She's made her business personal, a slice of her life on the river, in the woods. The business grows each year.

"That's it?" Valerie asked. "That's all you want to say, Ellie? I would think we'd get some bridal gushing, some enthusiasm, some wow—wow, I can't wait for the legal bang bang." Valerie bumped her fists together. Her pillow would have a country scene with white and black chickens that wore red velvet top hats. "Get what I mean?"

"I think we get it, Valerie," I said. "Since we do have brains." I was cutting out leaves from many different fabrics from around the world, then I would paste them onto a tree on a three-foot-long blue, rectangular-shaped pillow.

"The wedding planning is going well," Ellie said, standing up, breathing deep, her hand to her widow's peak, which is what she always does when she's nervous. "Except that Mama and Papa don't like Gino. Family war."

"Not a war," I said, choosing my words oh so carefully. "We have . . . concerns."

"Please. Let's not hide behind politeness," Valerie said. "We think you're making a mistake. Let me spell mistake for you. G.I.N.O."

"Please stop it, Valerie," Ellie said. She took another deep breath and chanted, "I don't need a paper bag. I *don't* need a paper bag. I am in control of my lungs, my air, my breathing, my life, and my calm demeanor. I am in control of myself."

"I'm glad I'm not warring with Mama," Valerie said. "I don't want to have to deal with her evil eye and curses and muttering. She does mutter a lot. I think she's muttering more the older she gets."

"And she's swearing more in French," I said, crossing my legs on the couch. The couch had a slipcover made from fabric from India. Red. Elephants. Gold trim. "Back to the wedding. Ellie, I want you to be excited."

"I . . . am," Ellie said, chanting once again. "Breathe, Ellie. Relax. Bring the peace of the world unto yourself. You're happy."

"You're not," I said.

"You're a stupendously poor liar," Valerie said. "I would rip you apart on the stand. Like a lion shredding flesh and swallowing it whole. I hope you never commit a murder. In fact, if I went back to being a defense attorney, I wouldn't even let you testify, because you'd incriminate yourself. Spill your guts, Ellie. Tell us the truth."

Ellie stopped working at the sewing machine, leaned way back in her chair, then came up right. "Gino is . . . he's . . . I've never met anyone like Gino. He walks into my house and everything lights up, and I light up, he's like electricity, and he's exciting and fun, and we're always doing exciting and fun things and it's entertaining and exciting and fun."

"I think my cat is entertaining, I'm not going to marry her," Valerie said.

"I think I've had all the excitement and fun I can take," I said. "Do you love him?"

Ellie hesitated. That infinitesimal hesitation. "Yes. I do. I wouldn't marry him if I didn't love him." She then whispered, "Don't get uptight, Ellie, breathe in slowly. Feel your soul. Arrange your aura. Reach for serenity."

"Ellie, keep sleeping with Gino," Valerie said. "Have your fun and excitement with a condom attached to his pistol at all times, but fun and excitement does not carry the day. Or the years ahead. I tell ya, I find sexy in faithful and loyal. Somebody who listens. Kai may not light up a room and suck the light right out of it from everyone else, but he shines a light for me. Last night, this is so funny, he brought a flashlight into the bedroom and we got under the covers and—"

"I don't think we need to know about flashlight sex right now," I said

"Fine," Valerie said. "But I want you to have this look of total lust and passion on your face whenever you say the word 'Gino,' and you don't have that, sister."

"Gino and I have a physical passion together. . . ." Ellie gave up. She grabbed a paper bag that she had stashed under the emerald green cushion of a chair and started breathing into it. "Capture your inner calm, Ellie. Decide that you are in control. Embrace your harmony. . . ."

I groaned.

Valerie groaned, too, then tapped the armrest of a chair. The chair had pictures of the Eiffel Tower on it.

Ellie doubled over with the bag, then stood up, pale. "Gino is nice to me. He pays attention to me. He always wants to be together."

"And what would be wrong with that?" I asked. "Did you want him to head for the mountains screaming when he saw your face?"

"It's a bit . . . suffocating. I turn around, he's there. It's leechy. I can't believe I used the word 'leech' to talk about my fiancé. But he started talking about us and how things will be after the wedding." She made a wheezing sound.

"Sit down, Ellie, you're making me nervous," I said. "Now I feel like breathing into a bag."

"There were things he talked about, like money. I've never told him how much I make. He's told me what he makes, and he makes more than I do, but he wanted to sit down and make a budget and talk about savings, retirement. He said that from now on we should both talk to each other before we make purchases, not the little ones, but medium-sized purchases and the expensive ones."

"That sounds like a plan to me," I said.

"I've handled my own money for a long time. And I don't want to sit down and talk about money. I don't want him, or anyone else, to tell me how to spend or save my money. I don't want to have to ask for his permission to go out and buy a new coat or new furniture or if I need something for my business or if I want to go on a trip."

"Kai and I do that, though, Ellie," Valerie said. "Not with everything. He buys clothes sometimes. I do, too. We both buy things for the kids and we don't get approval for that from the other person, but we both know the budget, we both know how much we can spend. And I would double vasectomy Kai if he went out and bought a motorcycle or a car without discussing it with me."

"I know in my head"—*gasp-gasp*—"it's reasonable for Gino to ask that we do that, but I don't like it. It feels controlling to me. It feels like I'm losing my financial independence. I don't want a man, any man, even my husband, telling me how to spend money.

"Gino and I were also talking about family." She put the bag down, her hands trembling. "And we were talking about, specifically, his mother, who is always complaining about something. Her back hurts. She has migraines. Her feet hurt. She's in her seventies, and Gino jumps to her beck and call.

"I'm glad he loves her, but she can't stand me. I know it's not personal. Gino told me she has never liked any of his girlfriends, but I don't like being around her. His father deadens himself with alcohol each night and checks out. Anyhow, Gino said that when his parents aren't healthy anymore, that he will want them to live with us."

"Torture. That is akin to torture," Valerie said.

"It would be like living with a battle-ax and a stoned aardvark," I said.

"I can't imagine living with his parents. I told him that, too. I told him that if they weren't healthy, they could go to assisted living, that we could be there every day, and he was angry. He said that family is family and he would never put his parents, or our parents, in assisted living."

She collapsed beside me on the couch, and I put my arm around her. All this bag blowing was making me nervous.

"If I have to live with a woman who hates me and a man who drinks steadily to dim the noise and nagging of his wife, I will lose my mind. It will fly out the window and disappear."

"Then tell him no, Ellie," I said. "I couldn't do it, either."

"I did. We had a fight about it. It was unpleasant." She put the paper bag over her face again. "I reminded him that I work, full time, at home. Who would take care of them? And he said that wherever we live we'll make sure there's a place for my business in the home, so I could take care of them and check on them during the day."

I threw up my hands. "So he wants you to give up your time, and your business, to help care for his mother, who hisses at you, and his father, a drunken man, when they're ill."

"Yes. I think I want to die thinking about it. It's making me feel like I can't breathe."

"Watching you not be able to breathe is making me feel like I can't breathe," Valerie said. "I feel light-headed."

"Ellie, you have to work this out," I said, fanning my face for more air. "They're older, and they may well need help soon."

"I know," she wailed. "I can't, and won't, do it. Gino knows how his mother treats me, and I'm angry that he would even suggest that I take care of her, that he would not understand, or refuse to understand, what her being in my home would do to me, to us."

"How did it end?" Valerie asked.

"It ended with Gino angry and saying that I'm selfish, that he would help my parents. Am I a terrible person?"

"No," Valerie and I both said.

"You're saying that you can't live with his parents because of their alarming dysfunction," I said.

"Because they'll drive your brain out of your skull, and it will fly out the window," Valerie said.

"I love Gino but not enough to take care of his mother." Ellie collapsed on the couch, exhausted from her anxiety attack. "Maybe I don't love him enough."

"Yep. Give me that," I said, and put the bag over my face and breathed. That helped.

"Hand it over, sista," Valerie said, swiping the bag and putting it over her face and breathing in. "I think I need a bag for this upcoming trial. The Bartons are psychotic."

We had a group hug on the couch. Ellie leaned against me and I leaned against Valerie, arms and legs entangled.

"Love you," we said to each other. "Love you more than Mama's Russian tea cakes."

I have three kayaks. Two singles and a tandem two-seater. I keep them in the little house/shelter on my deck. I loved kayaking. Being outside, in nature, was my peace. Being one with the river, sunk down into it, along with the river animals, watching the leaves flutter above me, the sun shine on the water, the wind blowing through my hair . . . well, there's nothing like it.

I won't kayak again.

Going to work downtown, in the *Oregon Standard*'s boxy, four-story, concrete and glass building in the middle of the city, was getting harder and harder. Each day I left my tugboat, said good-bye to Mr. and Mrs. Quackenbusch, and Dixie the blue heron if I could see her, who reminds me of him, and headed into a full day of crime.

From blue herons to drive-by shootings.

From Sergeant Otts to robberies.

I meet regularly with William to discuss my long-term projects, my short-term projects, and any story I am working on for that day. I often sit in mind-numbing meetings, then head straight out whenever someone commits a crime. The crime gets me out of the meeting, which is the only positive aspect.

When a reportable crime is committed, I interview the police, witnesses the perpetrator, and the victim if he or she is willing and still living. Interviewing dead people is difficult. I then attempt to carefully talk to family and friends to figure out what happened, the back story, the angles, the people involved, and the motives, especially if I sense a broader story or need to dig deeper to find something I'm suspicious about. When I know someone is lying to me, I go into pit bull mode and don't let up.

Sometimes people want to talk to me, sometimes they don't. A few times they've shown me how much they didn't want to talk by holding up a gun. That usually has me flying off the front porch as if I could sprout wings on the way down.

I also write about court proceedings.

For longer or more in-depth stories, I talk to prosecutors, including my sister (quietly), defense attorneys, judges if I can get at them, detectives, FBI agents, DEA agents, victims' and perpe-trators' families, friends, neighbors, schools, anyone involved in their personal lives and history, etc., to get the whole picture and quotes.

Some crimes appear to be one crime, but you do your research and you're looking at an entire criminal network. If not a criminal network, you're often looking at a total breakdown in one part of society.

There's nothing easy about my work.

I majored in journalism and English at the University of Oregon, then earned a master's in journalism at Columbia. I started working for the *Oregon Standard* when I was twenty-five years old.

At first I wrote obituaries. That bored me to death. What a way to put it. I started looking for human interest stories to throw at one of the senior editors, William.

I found a homeless teenager and wrote about him and his life, why he was on the streets, why he'd meddled in drugs, what his hopes and dreams were. "I know I can be someone. I just need help," he told me. The story got him help. Counseling. An apartment. A job. A scholarship for community college.

I found a woman who was transgender, man to woman, and wrote about her. She was a biologist. "When I was three years old I refused to wear swim trunks. I wore a bikini, like all the other little girls. I tried to pull off my penis when I was five."

I found a man who fought in Vietnam and worked as a peace activist. He told his war stories, wrapped around his belief that war was never an answer. "Once you've seen a man destroyed by shrapnel and you hold him in your arms as he dies, you know that war doesn't solve a damn thing. It makes all of us worse."

William loved the human interest angle of the stories. He grunted, edited; we worked on them together. I didn't have to write obituaries anymore.

I like truth. It stems from my childhood, particularly from my mother. Professors, doctors, musicians, journalists, writers, and artists, and my uncles and aunts, bringing my cousins with them, all crowded into our apartment in Moscow.

They ate my mother's chopped herring salad, or fried potatoes with what few eggs she could find that day, while she and my father talked about freedom of speech, religion, press, the right to protest, a fair judicial system. They were adamant that a free press was the pillar of a free society, and they were vociferous in their belief that they should be able to worship, as Christians, in the open, with no fear.

"No religious freedom, you smother the soul. No freedom to vote, you suffocate and endanger your population. No free press, no truth," my mother would say, as people nodded. "When the government controls the press, they smother reality."

I exposed the truth. I loved journalism. I loved writing. I loved the awards I now and then won for my longer, more in-depth pieces.

I do not love it anymore.

I work long, harsh hours, as one cannot predict when crime will occur. Criminals do not schedule their criminal activity with me. Full moons are bad nights. Heat waves are grueling. Gangs pissed off at each other as leadership shifts are a mess. Wives leaving controlling, narcissistic husbands might mean I'm up at two in the morning as they take off running . . . and so do their tormentors.

The crime and justice beat is all negative, all the time. It's senseless. Whenever someone says to me, a pious note to their voice, "I believe that everything happens for a reason," I see an incredibly naïve and shallow person who has no idea what's going on outside her front door.

A woman named Ricki Adelman is the editor for *Homes and Gardens of Oregon*. I have heard nothing about my application. I would love writing about homes. Why?

Because it all ends happy. Someone gets a remodeled kitchen with handles in the shapes of teacups on their cabinets. Someone else repaints an old dresser red and adds a Picasso-type design. A living room wall is decorated with reclaimed wood from a barn.

If I don't get the job, I'm leaving. I will have a nervous breakdown if I don't.

* * *

To keep my nervous breakdown at bay, I indulged in Keeping The Monsters At Bay: Shopping Defensive Strategies after work. I bought a pair of pink tennis shoes and red skinny jeans. That night I made peanut butter cookies and ate them in my bathtub. I put a glass of milk on the rim of the tub and accidentally dumped it in the water.

5

There are six houseboats off our dock in the marina. There are more houseboats all around us, off on different docks, and moored boats, but when I walk down the main dock, then hang a left onto my dock, which is down aways and off on its own, there are six floating homes.

A miserly, fish-faced man in his eighties, Herbert Shrock, used to own the marina, under the umbrella of his company Randall Properties, but he died and now his grandsons, Shane and Jerald Shrock, smarmy and ignorantly arrogant and too immature to know they're ignorantly arrogant, have caused us a huge problem.

I will probably lose my neighborhood.

Tweedle Dee Dum and Tweedle Dum Dee, as we neighbors refer to them, want to build a condominium complex on the land behind us and do not want the dock and houseboats in front. What they truly do not want is to make the sewer, electrical, gas, and dock repairs and updates that have to be made, that the city, and we as a neighborhood, were insisting upon.

Tweedle Dee Dum and Tweedle Dum Dee were also slumlords, left over from their grandfather. They owned apartment complexes slung up in poor neighborhoods all over the city that had problems with electricity, inadequate water pressure, mold, safety hazards, repairs that weren't made, and fire hazards. There were lawsuits pending.

I sighed and cursed Tweedle Dee Dum and Tweedle Dum Dee.

The first houseboat, which actually branches off our dock onto its own dock, belongs to Lindy Hughes, a high-priced hooker. She goes by the professional name of Desiree. Even she rolls her eyes at that. Her white houseboat somewhat resembles a two-story Queen Anne home, complete with white gingerbread, a wraparound porch, and a purple wisteria vine that drapes around the house. Her front door is blue. Lindy and I are friends. I wish she wouldn't do what she does, she knows I wish that, and we move along and have wine, cheese, and crackers and talk about our mutual passion: books.

Vanessa and Charles Oldham are next. They have a traditional, two story, large, light blue houseboat. Vanessa is white and a high school English teacher, Charles is black and a college professor. Charles likes to grow vegetables, so he has two raised beds on his back deck. I love the vegetables—radishes, tomatoes, corn, chives, carrots—that he gives me.

Next to the Oldhams is Jayla OHearn, a nurse in the ICU at the hospital, and her wife, Beth Diaz, who is an emergency room doctor. They're in their thirties. Both are very social. I've been to their houseboat, they've been to mine. Their houseboat is new and modern, with a huge semicircular window above the front door and lots of glass. It looks like a Frank Lloyd Wright house, only on the water.

Then it's me, in my yellow, three-story tugboat.

Next to me is Daisy Episcopo. Daisy's house is light purple, white trim, two story. She has planted an abundance of daisies, all colors, in flower boxes and pots that surround her home.

Daisy is eighty-five and has taken a short dive into dementia. She was always eccentric, as I understood from others, but I think she's turned a corner the last few months and wandered down a curvy road. All the neighbors, on all the docks, watch her pretty closely. Daisy is about five feet tall, has white curls, and always wears a daisy. She sings at the edge of the dock almost nightly. She owns taverns that don't have too many fights, two bowling alleys, a midpriced hotel, and a shooting range. They are all now run by her sons.

Unfortunately, her sons are wealthy criminals, with their own "businesses." They have been charged with embezzlement, fraud,

money laundering, now and then assault against other bad people, etc. Periodically, they're jailed, and they get slick lawyers to
bail them out. Prosecutors have not been able to make evidence
stick. Their crimes, to note, are never against women or children.

They wear black, they're tall, and they have pockmark scars
from acne and scars from other "problems" on their faces. My
mother saw them once and crossed herself. "Look like Russian
mafia. Only these two, not Russian. Sicily. Yes, I say Sicilian."

She was right. Daisy's grandfather came via Sicily. The oldest
son is named Skippy. Skippy is not his real name, it's what Daisy
calls him and it's what he invited me to call him. His real name
is Arthur Episcopo, otherwise known as—wait for it—"Slugger." The other son's name is George Episcopo, otherwise known
as—wait for it again—"Slash" because of the scars from a knife
fight on his face that resemble slashes. Daisy calls him Georgie.

Skippy and Georgie are devoted to Daisy, though I have
heard, and seen, her upbraid both of them on numerous occasions, their heads bowed in shame. She even grabbed Georgie's
ear once and hauled him down the dock. Georgie greeted me as
if nothing unusual was happening, "Hey, Toni, nice to see you.
Skippy and I were down at Svetlana's the other night. Had the
special—the poached cod with parsley. I thought I was in heaven, which I ain't never expected to achieve. How does your
momma make cod taste that damn delicious?" His head was
tilted down toward his little, haranguing mother. "She named it
'Antonia Not Come See Me Enough.' Is it true? Do you not visit
your momma enough? You gotta go see your momma."

His own mother pulled harder on his ear, and he winced.

Skippy and Georgie were eager to meet me when I moved in.
Both of them gave me all of their phone numbers, four each,
and their e-mail addresses, two each. "Please let us know how
our mother is. We give her a visit every day, but if she seems sick
to you, tired, anxious . . . or, uh, if she's doin' anything not normal,
call, will ya? She, uh, seems to be gettin' . . ." Georgie paused, unable to speak the words, his face flushed.

"We think there's an old age . . . problem." Skippy tapped his
head, then teared up.

Georgie patted him on the back, took off his dark glasses, and took a swipe at his eyes.

They both sniffled at the same time, then took out handkerchiefs and mopped up.

I noticed they were both carrying guns under their $3,000 suit jackets.

I assured them I would call. And, indeed, I have had to call them in the past.

"Skippy," I said, to a brisk, menacing 'hello' one morning. "This is Toni Kozlovsky."

"Who the hell's bells is Toni? How'd you get this number?"

Scary. I almost hung up. "Toni Kozlovsky. I . . . I . . . live next door to your mother, Daisy, in the tugboat."

"What? Tugboat? Yes! I know that. Toni! Toni! I'm sorry. Forgot my manners. Don't tell my mother. How are you? Oh no oh no. Is somethin' wrong with Momma? Is it Momma?"

Momma wasn't feeling well, I told Skippy. I saw her on the dock, sitting down, dizzy, singing like a flute but forgetting the words. I helped her inside her light purple houseboat, gave her some lemonade, put out a plate of fruit, told her I would call her sons.

"Those boys are naughty!" Daisy yelled at me while I was on the phone. "Naughty." Then she lay back on her couch and groaned. "I oughta smack them from here to the Dakotas on their behinds for what they done."

Within fifteen minutes, the naughty sons were both sprinting down the dock to their mother. Their guns were not hidden as their black designer suit jackets flew open, dark glasses on their worried, scarred faces.

Despite her objections they hired round-the-clock nurses to be with her for a week to help her get over . . . a cold. A doctor also confirmed some dementia.

"What do we do, Toni?" Skippy said, holding his head in my tugboat living room after that particular incident. "We can't put Momma in a nursin' home for the rest of her life. She loves her home here. She's been here more than thirty freakin' years, and this blippin' river, all her friends are here, including all her animal friends. She's got names for all the"—he swirled his hands around toward the sky—"birds and shit."

"If we take her home away, she'll kill us," Georgie said, wiping his eyes. "Don't think she won't. She will take aim and fire away."

"She does like her guns," I mused. "She walks up and down the dock with a rifle sometimes. To her credit, she does tell everyone who passes that she won't ever shoot animals."

"Heck, no. She wouldn't," Skippy assured me, aghast. "She's an animal lover. She thinks they understand what she says." He ran a hand over his bald head. "She says they understand her, too. Especially the whales." He moaned, stood up, and started pacing.

"The amount of money she makes us give away to her favorite animal shelters is . . ." Georgie shook his head.

"It's embarrassin' to say." Skippy coughed. "Because of our . . . uh . . . business. Can't be, like, softies. You know. Like we care about meowin' cats or dogs or . . ." He paused, exasperated. "Goats. She likes homeless goats. Who worries about homeless goats? But we gotta write a check to this animal place for homeless goats."

"And monkeys. Where are the damn monkeys again, Skippy?"

"Africa. That's where monkeys live. We sent 50K to monkeys in Africa last year. F-ing monkeys."

"But the gun thing," I said. "Maybe she shouldn't have guns?"

"Even if she pulled the trigger, nothin' would happen," Georgie said. "We've taken all the bullets out of the house."

That was a relief. A clever move. "She's fine right here for now. She's happy. She loves everyone. Plus, her voice. Did she train to be in the opera?" Daisy's voice was truly, utterly remarkable.

"No. She trained as a take no prisoners bar owner who regularly beat up men who twisted her day in the wrong direction," Georgie said.

"I would rather die than put Momma in a nursin' home," Skippy said. "Beat me up, tie me with rope in a sack, add forty pounds of rocks, and throw me in the river."

Whew! He sure knew what to do.

"She's a hell of a woman. *Hell of.*" Skippy was a true admirer of his mother. "But we worry about her feet gettin' cold. She's little. When we were younger, her feet would get cold. Like ice."

"Icy," Georgie said. "That's why we buy her warm boots and lots of socks. For her cold feet."

"We all have your numbers and e-mails," I said. "You come all the time to visit. If there's a problem, if things get worse, then you might have to make another decision. But she eats, she bakes for everyone all the time, she's clean, she's comfortable . . . let her stay for now."

I received a huge bouquet of flowers from Skippy (Slugger Episcopo) and a gift certificate for a fancy dinner from Georgie (Slash Episcopo).

So Daisy is in houseboat number five. She sings at the edge of the dock—show tunes, opera, rock, drinking songs—and her voice is one of the best I've heard.

But that sixth houseboat? The one next to Daisy's? The manly, craftsman type with a black door and a wood deck all around at the end? The one with a boat named *Sanchez One?*

That's Nick Sanchez's houseboat. Studly Nick.

Marty.

Nick.

Marty.

Marty.

What a mess.

Nick Sanchez works for the Drug Enforcement Agency. He speaks fluent Spanish, learned from his father, and Italian, learned from his mother.

Nick was adopted out of the Los Angeles child welfare system when he was a baby, hence the blond hair even though his father's family is from Mexico. His father traces his lineage to Southern California back hundreds of years, when that part of America was Mexico. His mother's family is from Italy, ironically, given my mother's fits about Gino. Her family immigrated in 1950.

Nick said to me one time, "My father is a tall, proud Mexican American who wears a cowboy hat and boots. My mother is clearly Italian, with a lot of black hair. She tries to feed anyone within ten feet of her. And I'm blond. We look like an advertisement for the United Nations."

His parents own the family's cattle ranch in California, so Nick grew up roping cattle, riding horses, branding, taking care of other animals, hauling hay, and driving tractors and other farm equipment.

Nick was undercover when I first met him, which explained why his blondish hair was to his shoulders and why he had a mustache and a goatee. At six five, he looked like a man who was the head of a drug ring, who'd been in his share of fights, and always won, someone you would be scared of. I was certainly scared of him.

Then that undercover case wrapped up and he had his hair cut shorter, but not short, and he shaved off the goatee and mustache. When he went back undercover on a new case he shaved the hair off his head entirely and grew a beard and stuck an earring through his left ear. He looked, once again, scary.

I would sometimes see him on the dock, pacing, on his phone. He would walk to the end of the dock, then back, head back out. He'd leave for days, or weeks, at a time.

Before we got together, when I knew he was home and out on his back deck, I'd sneak below the window line of my bedroom, grab my binoculars, and spy on him. Yes, I'd spy on him with my binoculars. I am utterly embarrassed to say that I did. Pathetic.

He never brought women home, which was divine, because I would have wanted to push them into the water. Which would be rude.

Nick's hair was longish now, no beard or goatee. Totally sex goddish.

I tried not to think about what he did undercover, who he had to talk to, what he had to do, how dangerous it was, the threat to his life and safety. I couldn't think about it.

But it was always there, and I asked myself often if I could possibly ever marry a man who had such a dangerous job, even if I ever wanted to marry again, which I did not and would not. But why get emotionally involved with someone who was courting danger and death all the time?

I tried extremely hard not to get emotionally involved with Nick.

There were other reasons I tried hard not to get emotionally involved, which included my ever present avalanche of guilt.

It was Kozlovsky Cousins Night Out.

Ellie and Valerie came and met me at my tugboat. Their eyes traveled up and down, head to foot, and they said, together, semi-aghast, as if I'd grown a second head, "You're wearing *that?*"

"What's wrong with it?" But I knew. I so knew. It was old blue jeans and a blue T-shirt. "I don't want to get dressed up."

Ellie said, "You're a clothes horse. You gallop in clothes. You love them."

"Only for work, not for going out." I didn't go out much anymore, except for required family events. And certainly not to bars.

"You cannot go in that," Valerie said, her black blunt cut swinging around her ears. She was wearing a shimmery purple, low-cut shirt and a short black skirt. "What? Are you planning on gardening afterward? Maybe painting a house? Do you want to mop floors when we return?"

"It's not that bad." It was.

"Yes, it is bad." Again, together.

"Up you go, Toni," Ellie said. She was in a blue wraparound dress and knee-high black boots.

Ellie pushed me, none too gently, toward my stairs, and we all trooped up together to my closet. I envisioned the crew members in bunks who used to sleep there. I bet no one ever bugged them about their clothes.

"I don't want to get dressed up." My tone was belligerent. I wanted to scold my own self for it.

"Why not, Toni?" Ellie said, standing next to me in the crew quarters/my closet. "You wear pretty clothes to work. You haven't wanted to go out and have fun for so long and then when we make you, when you can't wiggle out, you don't want to wear any of your pretty clothes."

"No reason," I lied. I knew they knew I was lying.

"There's a reason," they both said.

"It's that . . ." I swallowed. "I don't really want to go out."

"Toni, just this once," Valerie said.

"You know it's not just this once."

"You're right." Valerie smiled. "It'll be many times, hopefully."

"Everyone's going," Ellie said. "We want all the Kozlovskys to be together. We want you there."

I leaned against a wall and decided to tell them the truth. "I don't know if I'm ready to have fun. I don't know if I remember how. I don't know if I *should* have fun. I don't know if I deserve to have fun."

"You should have fun, you deserve fun," Valerie said, those eyes pleading.

"You'll remember how to have fun, Toni," Ellie said, her eyes filling up.

They wrapped their arms around me and gave me a squeeze.

"Hug tight!" Valerie said.

"I'm hugging tight!" Ellie said.

We talked a bit more, we cried a few tears, they unceremoniously yanked off my clothes, and I ended up in tight jeans; a red, flowing shirt; and high black heels. Ellie did my hair. She took it out of its messy ponytail, grabbed the dryer and a curling iron, and went to work. Valerie shoved a few chunky bracelets up my arm and dangly earrings.

"Now you're ready, hot stuff," Valerie said.

I studied myself in the mirror and wrestled with all my insecurities as they popped out and roared at me. There was me, all poofed and glammed up. The me I used to be. Before. "I don't think I can do this."

"You can, Toni," Valerie said. "Kick some butt. For you, not for anyone else. You."

"Try," Ellie said, gentle. "Try it for one night."

"And you are so gorgeous." Valerie crossed her arms. "Actually, get in your frumpy dumpy dull clothes. All the men will be after your tight tail."

That made me feel sick. I did not want any men after my tight tail. But . . . I tilted my head and stared at myself in my full-length mirror. I had missed my high black heels. I had missed my necklaces with all the charms. It's shallow. It's silly. But I had missed getting dressed up for a night out. "Okay. I will try." I took a shaky breath. "I can do this." I shook my hands to get the nerves out. "I think." I bent over, hands on knees, and my sisters bent over with me.

You can do it, Toni.

"I heard that, Ellie."

We'll be with you the whole time, Toni.

"I heard that, too, Valerie."

She grinned. "Let's go.

On our way down the dock, laughing, we saw Nick.

"There's the Jolly Green Giant Sex God," Valerie whispered. "Look at those hips. I'm a hip woman. I like a man who has hips I can grip. Like Kai's. I like a man whose hips are enough to make me feel like a woman and he . . . wow. He's a hip man."

"You said he's a DEA agent, right, Toni?" Ellie said. "I think I might want him to arrest me."

"If I wasn't married, I would leap on him like a cheetah in heat," Valerie said. "I see him and I want to salivate. Do I have any salivation on my chin?"

I didn't even search for salivation. "*Shhh!*"

"I don't think I can *shhh,*" Valerie said. "I want to moan and groan."

We walked a few more steps and Valerie called out, "Hi, Nick!" Under her breath, she said, "I think I could orgasm if I stared at him long enough, and I adore Kai."

"Hello, Nick!" Ellie said. Under her breath she said, "How have you been able to resist him, Toni?"

I didn't answer. Ellie turned to me, quick as a hot snake, and whispered, "Ohhhh. You didn't tell us . . ."

"Hello," Nick said. "Nice to see you again, Ellie, Valerie."

He stopped, smiled, shook hands. I didn't know what to do with him. Shake hands? Flash him my boobs? No. Not appropriate. I smiled and said, "Hey, Nick."

"Toni." He smiled at me, and I saw that familiar heat in those light blue eyes. "Going out?"

"Yes," I said. I remembered our last position in his bed. I am glad I am so flexible, but it made meeting those blue eyes difficult.

"You look beautiful."

Dang. I wanted to stay home now. I wanted to stay home at Nick's home and show off my flexibility.

"She does, doesn't she?" Valerie said, her voice a tad high pitched. "She didn't want to get all fluffed up, but we stripped her down and shoved her jeans on and a bra and—oh shoot. I didn't mean to say the bra part. I meant, we shoved her in jeans and a shirt."

I turned toward Valerie. *What in the world?*

"But a bra under the shirt," Valerie explained.

What the heck?

"Not over the shirt."

"What is wrong with you, Valerie?" I asked.

"Nothing. Not at all." She was starting to sweat. Mrs. Prosecutor was *flustered*. It was Nick. I wondered if she having her orgasm. "I was clarifying."

"There's no clarifying needed, Valerie," I said.

"No," Ellie said, "It's a given. The bra part. Red."

I turned to Ellie. I was beginning to feel like I was being whipsawed. "Have you lost your mind?"

"No. Still here." She tapped her head.

"Let's go," I said. "Bye, Nick."

"Bye, Toni. Have fun." He smiled. Now I really wanted to stay home with him. At least I wasn't Valerie or Ellie, gaping at Nick and talking about red bras.

I grabbed Ellie's elbow as Nick walked away and dragged her up the dock, my black heels tapping. I stopped. Turned back around.

"Are you coming?" I hissed.

"What?" Valerie asked, taking her gaze away from Nick.

"Are you coming?" I hissed, once again.

"My God, Toni. Not now!" Valerie snapped, then realized what I was talking about. "Ah. Yes. I'm coming . . . up the dock, to the stairs. Not the other coming. Right-o."

"Get your tongues back in your mouths," I told them as we climbed the stairs to the parking lot.

"I think I almost orgasmed," Valerie said.

"I almost forgot I was engaged," Ellie said. "Gall. Anxiety attack. *That word*. Engaged." She dug in her purse, brought out the brown bag, and blew into it.

"You should date him," Valerie said. "Why aren't you? Then you could tell us everything so we could live vicariously through you."

I climbed the stairs, hurried to my car. Ellie panted into the bag, wobbling across the parking lot. Valerie gasped.

"You are!" Valerie said, toddling after me on her high heels. "Oh my goodness and badness and craziness, Toni Kozlovsky, you are sleeping with the Jolly Green Giant Sex God. I am so happy for you and why didn't you tell us?"

"I didn't tell you because I didn't want to talk about it."

"Well, that notion is over," Valerie said. "I want to hear all about it."

Ellie pulled the bag away from her mouth and leaned against my car. "Well done, sister. You have bagged a stud. Get it? I'm breathing into a bag and you have bagged a stud."

"Please, I'll tell you, but don't tell Mama and Papa. They'll name a special after him at the restaurant. It'll probably be called 'Welcome To The Family, Nick.' Or they'll make an announcement in church, or start calling him their future son-in-law . . ."

"They'd do all that and more," Valerie said. "Mama would be talking to the minister at the church to reserve a date."

"She'd be at Aunt Polina's florist shop that afternoon picking out roses," I said.

"And she'd probably start ordering the invitations all by herself," Ellie said. "Oh no. Just thinking about invitations . . ." The bag deflated, inflated.

"Yes. All that. Can't get her hopes up," I said.

I felt guilty. It felt like a black blanket around me. Two reasons. One from the past and one because I was sleeping with Nick, and here I was, all dressed up with heels and hair and we were definitely "going out," and I hadn't invited Nick, although Valerie's husband and Ellie's fiance would be there.

But as Valerie drove toward downtown Portland and my sisters and I chatted and chortled and Ellie put down the paper bag, it felt right, too. The windows were open, we were laughing, I could see the stars, I would be with my crazy cousins soon, and finally, finally I felt like living. For one night.

"Give us all the salacious and juicy details," Valerie said.

"It's been over three months for Nick and me. . . ." I said.

They cackled and we high-fived each other and they told me I needed to talk to Zoya and Tati about new lingerie, then they pried for more details, few of which I gave, and we laughed some more.

The Kozlovskys went to a place called Dolly Ann's. It was famous in Portland. Dolly Ann was a man who dressed as a woman, and he sang down the house every night. Dolly Ann wore sparkling dresses on his six foot two frame, with a towering blond wig; a matching, golden, gem-stoned headdress; and glittery makeup. It was rumored that he was on stage in New York for years.

It was rumored that no one knew his real name.

It was rumored he was gay and had a husband.

It was rumored that he worked as a female model for years.

None of that was true. How do I know? I know because I'm a reporter and we know. The dull truth?

Dolly Ann's name was Johnny Ohlsson. Johnny had a wife named Margie. Margie was a high school biology teacher. They had five children. They've been married twenty years. They lived in the suburbs in a sprawling white house with a picket fence, no kidding, and a huge yard for the kids to run around on. Oftentimes truth is dull.

My cousins already had a table waiting for us. We had wine, clinked our glasses together, and shouted out, as we always do, "To family. To the Kozlovskys!"

"There he is!" Anya cried out, holding up her hand sanitizer spray, which she'd used on our table before we sat down. "Dolly Ann! Dolly Ann!"

The room was packed, the candlelight flickering off the chandeliers, burgundy curtains hung on every wall. Everyone went crazy for Dolly Ann. Dolly Ann was hilarious. He sang with a baritone voice, a husky timbre, and a beat that wouldn't quit.

Boris was to my left. He'd taken a night off from being a "mechanic." Tati and Zoya were to my right. They were both wearing negligees as shirts. They had arrived with dates we all knew we would never see again. The dates were charming and friendly and handsome, the usual.

"This is our new line," Tati told me. "Don't you love it? Feel that silkiness, feel it!" I touched the silk at her stomach. "Soft, isn't it? Like a camellia. That's why we call it The Camellia. Get it?"

"I get it. It's one of your best."

Zoya's lacy negligee was burgundy. "You gave me the idea for this, Toni, because you said you love this color. We call it The Toni K."

"It does me proud," I said.

Kai gave me a hug with one arm, his other arm around Valerie. He was funny and friendly as always, wearing a Hawaiian shirt. Kai is my sister's weakness. She is totally in love with him.

Gino came in, handsome and well dressed, gave everyone a hug, bought us all a round of drinks, and had his arm around Ellie the whole night. He was smitten with her. I did not see the same from her to him, her smile tight, her arms close to her body. At one point she bent under the table and blew in her bag. To his credit, Gino bent down under the table with her.

JJ arrived by herself in a silver-sequined shirt cut low and tight jeans. She met her "date"—her husband, Jax—and they pretended to pick each other up. JJ told him she was Stephi, a technology executive from out of town, here for only a night, and he told her he was Kyle, from Florida, a musician with the Florida Symphony.

We all played into the imaginary date, shook "Kyle's" hand, introduced ourselves, asked him about himself, where he lived, etc.

They danced closer and closer all night.

"He's cute," Tati said, joining in on the pretend date. "But he has a dadlike quality to him, which is not attractive to me."

"Stephi will sleep with him for one night and that'll be that," Zoya said.

"I hope Stephi's husband doesn't find out about this," Boris said.

"She definitely shouldn't marry him," Kai said. "Too nerdy."

We listened to Dolly Ann sing, joined in when he invited everyone to sing along, and we laughed at his jokes. When it was time for audience participation, my family nominated me and dragged me to the stage. I ended up sitting on Dolly Ann's lap, on top of her silken dress. I had had too much vodka.

Dolly Ann, sparkling and glittering, sang a song about an Irishman in love with a mermaid with black hair and blue eyes, ogling me, then asked me what talent I had. I showed him. I did a drunken handstand, "hand walking" across the stage, my red shirt down, my stomach bared. The Kozlovskys about died laughing.

The crowd went wild.

Dolly Ann, drag queen, father of five, faced me and curtsied.

I walked up my dock at six in the morning to the parking lot above the marina to go to work. There had been a murder under the Freedom Bridge, so I was rushing. Rushing to a murder. I do not like this part of my life at all.

"Shoot!"

My car was gone.

I have a sleek black MDX.

I opened my phone and dialed a number.

"Boris," I semishouted. "My car is gone. Again. This is the second time—"

Twenty minutes later Boris drove up with my car, followed by another man, bald and the size of a dump truck.

"Sorry about that, Toni." He gave me a quick hug and a kiss on the cheek.

"Your mother would kill you if she knew you were still doing this, Boris, if your father didn't kill you first."

"I know, I know."

"Why are you still in this business?"

"Lucrative."

"You're going to jail again. They'll catch you."

"I know. But my mechanic business is doing better and better. I've hired two real mechanics, they're a fortune, but soon I'll quit—"

"Yes, I'm sure. As soon as I quit breathing."

"I have tickets for *Madame Butterfly* for Friday night. I've been asking you and you keep putting me off. Please, Toni, can you come?"

I was going to stay no. Then I could be alone. Or with Nick.

"I'm going to take that slightest of slight hesitations as a yes, Toni. Meet you at The Grill first?"

I changed my mind. It was fun to be out last night, despite the double guilt. I danced and laughed for the first time in too long. "Sure. Yes. Thank you, Boris."

He stood up on his toes, thrilled. "I love *Madame Butterfly*. So emotional. The costumes, the cultural differences, the history, the music, the poetic words and heartbreak. The deepest betrayal."

"You know all about opera and yet you run a chop shop and steal cars."

"I don't steal them."

"Give me a break."

"I'm giving you a hug instead." He hugged me, then his voice became pleady. "Toni, do you have any of your mama's pryanikis in there?"

"I do." I gave him the baggie of honey spiced cookies, glazed in sugar. I would miss those cookies today.

"Thank you." He kissed my cheek and headed back to the bald man the size of the dump truck. The bald man got out of the car and walked toward me, not smiling. "Hi, Toni. Sorry about the car. New guy."

"Hi, Mac."

He gave me a hug then headed back to the car. He turned around. "Were those your mama's pryanikis?"

"Yes. Tell Boris I said to share."

The dump truck smiled.

On my way to and home from work, I drive by a one-story white house with a red door. Often the garage door is open. Inside, up on some type of wood platform, is an old tandem kayak. I see the husband working on it sometimes. The red paint is chipped. He has a wife. They are white, but their two young boys are black. Everyone always seems happy. I'm happy for them, being so happy, but it's a stab in my gut, and I look away quick.

6

Moscow, the Soviet Union

We lived in Moscow in an apartment complex owned, as all were, by the government. We were able to live there because my parents were professors at the university. It took years for my parents to get the apartment. Before that, we were in a dormitory room—*one room*—with one kitchen on the floor that was shared with ten other families.

Our apartment building was concrete, many stories tall, and one of many other concrete jungle apartment buildings. It was a middle-class lifestyle.

However, middle class in Moscow should not be associated with middle class in America.

We had a small bedroom for my parents, and a miniscule bedroom for my sisters and me, which fit a double-sized bed that took up most of the room. My father built a wood table, which took up much of the family room/kitchen. There was room for a couch and one chair.

The walls of the apartment were cracked and bulging here and there as if the apartment wanted to come down on us. My mother painted them yellow, "to add the sun," she told us. The wind, like an invading cold army, would swoosh through, rain would leak around the windows; and when it was snowing, ice froze on our windows on the inside, making us feel as if we were in a snow cave. We were not able to adjust the heat—that was done centrally.

When the hot water stopped flowing, it could be gone for days, weeks, or months, same with the heat.

In Moscow, the sky was often dark and moody, or overcast and snowing. Snow, snow, snow. Cold to the bone it was, the cold slithering through your body and into your marrow where it stayed all winter, an icicle pulsing through your blood.

We were near Red Square and St. Basil's Cathedral, which I loved because the tops looked like soft, swirled ice cream in blue and white, green and yellow, and red and green, the crosses perched on top.

My mother told me that Ivan the Terrible had had it built. "He was insane, brutal. May he be stuck in the circles of hell, suffering for every soul that he tortured." The name alone scared me, but the colors and swirls enthralled me.

I liked the State Historical Museum, too, all red with white on the top of its spires and points, as if were holding perpetual snow on the outside, while the inside held perpetual treasures. In my mind it was a red castle. The Kremlin, along the river, with its wall, twenty towers, cathedrals, and palaces, was overwhelming. My mother talked about how Moscow was filled with "Stalinist architecture," which I did not understand as a child.

The impressive architecture did nothing to alleviate the stark quality of life, however. The streets were crowded, fear hung heavy. We often didn't have enough food, and it was the same food all the time. Plus, there were long lines out of each store. I waited with my parents, my sisters, for hours in line, it seemed like every day, and sometimes we'd get to the head of the line and there would be no more bread, or dumplings, or chicken, or whatever we had been waiting for.

There were many things going on that I didn't understand. My parents' friends—other professors, artists, writers, musicians, doctors, scientists—were over all the time. They brought the food they had: chicken soup, potato cakes, Olivier salad, lamb dumplings, pickles, sauerkraut, braised cabbage, rye bread, sweet beets. My mother added a spice here, salt there, and somehow made it better. Everyone said so. They talked and laughed and argued around our wood table.

And they whispered. "Hush . . . quiet . . . let me tell you, tell no one . . . we need higher wages . . . voting . . . free elections . . . religious freedom . . . you must be careful, you must stop talking so much, Alexei . . . You, too, Svetlana . . . the time is not right for protesting . . . still dangerous . . . don't trust the government . . . you are being watched . . . they are listening . . . the newspapers, simply an extension of the government . . . propaganda on television, always they lie to us . . . it's not safe for us . . . no one knows what happened to Professor Popov . . . to the priest . . . to his brother . . ."

We were told, my sisters and I, not to talk about what we heard around that table. Our parents were, officially, members of the Communist Party. It was be a member or live a life of destitution with few job or educational opportunities. But we were secret Christians. In the Communist Party there was no God, no Jesus, no faith, no Christianity allowed.

Had anyone known, my parents would have lost their jobs at the university. We would have been moved out of our apartment. My parents would have been able to find only low-paying jobs in a factory, if that. They might have lost custody of us or been sent to an insane asylum.

Schools were state run and promoted and taught atheism. There were Russian Orthodox churches, more steeped in tradition, song, ritual, and liturgy, than God. In fact the KGB had infiltrated the Russian Orthodox church. They pretended to be priests and took confession. The Communist Party had demolished or closed thousands of mosques, temples, and churches over the years.

We held church services in our home, with my uncles and their families. My mother's parents, Lada and Anatoly, came, as did my father's parents, Konstantin and Ekaterina, all loving people. My grandparents had known each other for decades.

As kids, Valeria, Elvira, and I could smell fear around our family's wood table, as well as our mother's sugar-sprinkled pancakes. We could smell people's pervading sense of distrust and hatred toward the government, alongside her baked cinnamon apples.

It was a government steeped in corruption, cronyism, spying, paranoia, and violence. Suspicion and obsession with possible dissidents ran high. The television was used for propaganda, the press controlled. The KGB peered into everyone's lives, and chased down and jailed without justice.

The economy was stagnating, the government owned everything, the wages were pathetic, and a battle waged each day to buy enough food. Moscow, along with the rest of the Soviet Union, was suffocating and suffering. Life was too hard.

But I was a child. I had loving parents who protected me from all they could. My mother and grandmothers taught my sisters and me to cook and sew. We loved to sit with them and sew small pillows using scraps of silk, cotton, even burlap. We lined them with rickrack, lace, or ruffled edges, or we embroidered flowers. We were taught to make our stitches precise, tight, and to use different stitches for different designs.

Plus, I had my sisters who I could now and then hear in my head through my widow's peak, the Sabonis gift coming down the generation to me. We had friends. We played outside, bundled in coats.

We went to school in uniform, with strict teachers, and we were called Oktyabrenok—October children, in reference to the revolution in October 1917. We were to behave well and study hard and memorize the party lines and songs and when we were older, we could become Young Pioneers, and wear the red scarf of the Communist Party. We did what they told us to do.

We tried to ignore that tingling, black, confusing shadow that swirled around us, the hushed voices, the unexplained tears from our mother, and our father's tight face. We let it flow over our small shoulders.

Then it all changed.

* * *

On Sunday I went over to my parents' home for dinner. My mother was babysitting Ailani and Koa because Valerie had work to do for her upcoming trial and Kai had a late shift. She was outside playing with Koa, who was dressed as a white monster, while Ailani and I cut out sugar cookies on the train station table.

Ailani is in fifth grade. She has long black hair and likes to talk to her mother about crime and court proceedings. She said that school was sometimes "boring" and that she got in trouble when she made a speech recently.

"Oh, uh." I could hardly wait to hear the topic. "What kind of trouble?"

Ailani's forehead furrowed as she pressed the rolling pin down on the dough. "Not bad trouble. The teacher, Mrs. Phillips, said we all had to stand and talk for one minute. A lot of the kids were scared to be up in front of the class. Like they were afraid of getting bullied or something. I wasn't scared, because I knew what I was going to talk about."

"Which was?"

"Defensive wounds."

Oh, my Lord. "A fascinating topic for a fifth grader."

"Yes!" She grinned at me and picked up a flower cookie cutter. "You get it, Aunt Toni, I knew you would. You know what defensive wounds are, right?"

I sure did.

"I also told the whole class how to defend themselves against a kidnapper—poke out his eyes, bite his hand, smash his face up, stomp on his inner foot, scream your head off. I showed them how to put their weight on their left foot and bring their right foot up superhard into the man's nuts, and all the kids practiced kicking a kidnapper in the privates and poking out his eyes and then I had crime photos that I . . . uh . . . I . . . uh . . . borrowed from Mom . . ."

"Like for props?"

"Yes!" Way to go, Aunt Toni! Ailani smiled. Then she frowned.

"That's when I got into trouble. The teacher said the photos weren't appropriate. I hate that word: appropriate. But I said you don't want to end up dead like this, and the teacher said no more photos. Some of the kids said they were scared, and a boy started to cry."

Whew. Well, that's our Ailani. I picked up a cookie cutter. It was a four-leaf clover.

"Then I wanted to talk to the kids about how to get out of the trunk of a car if they got kidnapped, but the teacher said I had run out of time. She looked kinda tired." Ailani's face was confounded. She frowned, then she smiled. "But I think I'm getting an A because it's important to know about defensive wounds and how to escape from kidnappers, right?"

I hardly knew what to say.

My mother opened the door to the backyard, and Koa toddled in.

"Hey, Koa!" Ailani bent down and hugged Koa the monster, then said, "He tried to eat my lizard today."

"You tried to eat a lizard today, Koa?" I clamped my lips together and tried not to laugh.

He smiled at me, not a lot of teeth. "I eat lizard."

I brushed the hair back from his cowlick. "No, don't. They don't taste good."

"Taste good." He giggled.

"You need a lid that he can't lift off the lizard aquarium, Ailani."

"I know. Mom's getting it."

"If you don't, Mr. Grins here is going to eat him for lunch."

"Brass knuckles," she said, rolling out more cookie dough.

"What?"

"The lizard's name is Brass Knuckles. You know. The weapon."

"Yes, I know."

"And I named my new goldfish, too."

"I can hardly wait to hear their names."

"Nunchucks and You're Arrested."

"You have a lot going on in your head, don't you?"

"Yes, I do. Sometimes it's too much and I have to lay my head on my pillow to get my mind turned off."

"I can imagine."

"It gets bad sometimes, Aunt Toni," she whispered. "My brain is too fast."

Ailani went off with Koa the monster to read him a book on being a detective. I stuck the cookies in the oven and poured myself a cup of my mother's coffee. I resisted the urge to check my chest to see if the strength of the caffeine had made me sprout hairs.

My mother turned and shot me a stern glare, and I knew I was in trouble. For what, I didn't yet know. It could be several things.

"I think you not try hard enough, with this wedding of Elvira, Antonia. It is no." She made a chopping motion with her hands. "No wedding."

"Mama, I have tried. I've talked to Ellie. She's in her thirties, remember? She owns a business. She can do what she wants."

"Ack! No!" My mother shook a metal spatula at me. "She cannot. You not try hard enough, Antonia. Why my Elvira still marrying that Italian? Italian stallion, that joke I hear. I need no stallion for my Elvira, I need real man. I feel here"—she pounded her heart—"he not make my Elvira happy. You see my mouth? Right here?" She pointed to her mouth in case I had forgotten its location.

"I see your mouth, Mama."

"I taste this. That Italian leave bad taste right there." She switched to Russian and muttered a few words.

"What did you say, Mama?" I knew what she said, but I simply had to make her repeat it for entertainment purposes.

"I say to you, I can taste people. I know good taste, bad taste. You see? This Italian stallion, you say like that, he not right for my Elvira. I worry. You talk to Elvira again."

"She loves him—"

"Ack." The spatula flew back up into the air, and she swore

in French. "No, she not. She has to have bag on face. That mean she don't love. Why marry then, I ask that?"

"I don't know, Mama."

I gave her a hug. She held me tight, then took me by the shoulders, the spatula right by my ear. "You do something. Already the family want to plan that party for the bride. What it called again? Bridal bathtub party?"

"Bridal shower."

"That right. They call me, I say not yet, I no know who does it. Already, the family is fighting. Who gets to do which party? Bridal bathtub party. Bachelorett-y party with the naughty things. The dinner on the rehearsal night. The lunch breakfast after the wedding. You stop this right now, Antonia. You talk to that girl. I talk, she not listen to her mama.

"Ah, see here. Here come your Papa. I surprise I walk today. That man, your papa." She glowered at me as if I had put him up to it. "He tire me out in that bedroom last night. I try to sleep, can't sleep . . . he can't stay away from—" She indicated her body, boobs to butt.

"Mama, please."

She glanced in an entry mirror, patted her hair, swiped on red lipstick, and pushed her boobs up. "Alexei!" She opened the door, smiling. "My life. You are here." She hugged him tight, kissed his lips.

You would never guess my balding father with the barrel chest, who was devoted to his children, was a roaring love machine.

"Svetlana. So beautiful today. God gift me. And here she is. Our Antonia, our daughter." He hugged me like a bear would.

"I not see you for a week!" my father said, aghast, then started in on the questions. "So, start with the Sunday. What you do . . . okay, yes . . . now tell me, what on Monday? What happen . . . your job? . . . Now Tuesday . . ."

When we were done discussing my week in minute detail, I sniffled. I do not know how I got so lucky. Two parents, loving people.

"What wrong with our Antonia?" my father said to my mother, worry creasing the lines in his face.

"She needs tefteli," my mother declared. "Meatballs. My special sauce-y." All would be right with her meatballs, she knew it.

"Yes, you are *right,* Svetlana," my father said, so proud of his wife. "You always know what right for everyone. I tell you, Antonia, I am lucky man."

"I make tefteli, meatballs for the restaurant tomorrow night," she said. "I name them, Svetlana's Meaty Balls."

I coughed. *Svetlana's Meaty Balls.* Oh, the phone calls I would get.

I saw my father pat my mama on her butt. She swatted his hand away. "Not now, Alexei. We have a child here. Wait."

I rolled my eyes.

I will not discuss the calls I received two days later about "Svetlana's Meaty Balls." Apparently, though, they were delicious.

I wrote up my resignation letter. William would have a fit.

I had not heard from Ricki, the editor of *Homes and Gardens of Oregon.* Ricki is a rough-talking, head-knocking sixty-year-old woman with vivid red hair and chronically stylish high heels. We get along well, and I would have liked to have worked with her, but I assumed I had not been chosen for the job.

I wrote "Sincerely, Toni Kozlovsky" at the end of the e-mail.

I was burned out, fried, and exhausted. I would take a break. I would figure out what I wanted to do.

Maybe I would work in a different field altogether. Maybe I'd work with my parents for a while at Svetlana's Kitchen and learn how to not burn desserts.

Maybe I'd work with Ellie. She was constantly asking me to come to her company. Maybe I'd learn to paint. Maybe I'd be a ceramicist. Maybe I'd move to a farm and grow blueberries. Maybe I'd sell everything and move to a quiet cabin in the backwoods of Montana and have a nervous breakdown. Being a hermit had its appeal.

I would wait a couple of weeks, finish two long-term stories I was writing—one about a family with one kid in a gang and how they'd turned him around, and another about a woman who runs a women's shelter—and I'd wrap things up.

I was shaky. Crumbling on the inside. Fighting back depression. I was almost, but not quite, in free fall.

Again.

I was done here.

The kayak house beckoned me again, about one in the morning. I opened the door and pulled the tandem onto the deck. I climbed in.

I didn't cry.

I pretended to paddle. I'm sure I looked ridiculous. Paddling a kayak, on the deck of my tugboat. I really couldn't have cared less. That I was even able to sit in the kayak felt like the tiniest of accomplishments in a terrible way.

When I was done paddling, I cried. I had to. Sometimes I do this. I put myself in a situation that I know will make me cry. If I don't, the tears get all backed up and they come out at times when they're not supposed to come out. I can control things better this way.

When I went back inside I didn't put the kayak back in its house. Before I went to sleep, I peeked out at it.

Still there. Still alone.

I went to *Madame Butterfly* with Boris.

We both cried. He handed me his silk handkerchief. The costumes, the cultural differences, the history, the music, the poetic words, the heartbreak, the deep betrayal.

It was too much.

He called at eleven that night. He knows I can't sleep. He can't sleep, either. He asked how I was, what I was doing, what I was writing.

"How are you?" I pulled my comforter up to my chin.

"Fine."

"No. Tell me."

"I don't remember the orphanage at all, Toni."

I wanted to tell him what I knew, what I remembered, all those years ago, in another land, another time, but I had promised I wouldn't.

"I would think I would remember kids, a whole bunch of kids, cribs, food, something. I've read what those orphanages are like, though. Maybe I blocked it out."

You didn't, I think, but I don't say it.

"And the other day I saw potatoes and beets, together, side by side on a plate. I thought I was going to be sick. What is wrong with me? I try to put all this behind me during the day, but at night, when I'm sleeping, it all comes out in my head. Disjointed things, but I think they're tied together. I'm getting afraid to go to sleep."

"I love you, Toni," he said thirty minutes later.

"I love you, too."

I wondered if he would still love me when I told him what I knew, about the blood, and how I, the secret keeper, his adopted sister, had never told him.

Never tell, Antonia, never, ever tell.

"Those sons of trash, lice in hats, and weasels with buck teeth," Daisy Episcopo announced in Vanessa and Charles Oldham's houseboat. The living room, with a wall of windows overlooking the river, was comfortable, like an indoor pillow, with wide couches and plush chairs, fuzzy throws and soft blankets.

Vanessa's schoolwork as an AP English teacher was on one table, and Charles's history books were stacked in bookshelves that stretched up two stories, with a ladder attached to read the highest books. "I'm a book nerd and proud of it," he said.

Lindy, high-priced call girl, fellow book nerd, stared in awe at those books as Daisy spoke. Lindy loves going to the library and staring in awe at books. Charles, Vanessa, and Lindy were always exchanging books, then would discuss them over wine. I often went, too, if I wasn't working late or getting naked with Nick.

"Tweedle Dee Dum and Tweedle Dum Dee are my enemies. And I'm not moving my boat!" Daisy was wearing a fisherman's hat with a red daisy in it, a yellow dress, a hunting jacket, and black boots that I knew cost two hundred dollars, a gift from her sons so her feet wouldn't get cold.

"I'll get those trash-eating vultures." Daisy grabbed a fake daisy from a pocket in her dress and pretended to use it as a gun. "No one's kicking me into the river to talk to the whales before I'm ready."

There were many people in the Oldhams' home, people who lived on houseboats all over the marina. They were not happy. Some were baffled by Daisy.

"I'm confused about how Tweedle Dee Dum and Tweedle Dum Dee can shut down an entire dock, an entire marina," Jayla said. She was still in scrubs. Beth nodded beside her. Both looked exhausted. There had been a train wreck the night before, and they'd both been on shift. "I know they're slumlords and for some reason they're getting away with it in other parts of Portland, but how can they do this?"

"How can they make us move our homes?" Vanessa said. "It's not right. You couldn't force people to move from their houses if they lived in the suburbs."

"No," Charles said. "It's not right. We need to rally against Shane and Jerald Shrock and Randall Properties."

"I'll write a mass letter to the city and everyone else I know in government," Vanessa said.

"I'll talk to the mayor," Jayla said. "I know him because my father used to be his chief of staff. The problem is that this is private property, owned for decades by their grandfather, so Tweedle Dee Dum and Tweedle Dum Dee may have been grandfathered in under different rules and they can shut it down. . . ."

The ideas flew on how to save our water neighborhood. "I'll call the assistant to the governor. My brother dated her years ago. Uh. No, wait. I won't. Bad breakup, I think there was a stalking charge against her. . . . I'll call the mayor's wife. My mother and she drink martinis together. . . ."

I would contact a reporter I knew at the *Oregon Standard,* too. I wasn't happy. I was worried. I had a sweet deal here at the dock. I liked living here on this blue-gray ribbon of river, being in nature, watching the weather. I liked my river pets, most especially my blue heron, Dixie, who reminded me of him; Mr. and Mrs. Quackenbusch; Anonymous, who I hadn't seen for a while; Maxie, who soared by to say hello; and the Sergeant Otts. I liked my neighbors, especially my favorite neighbor, Nick.

"Those scruffy badger boys have a stick up their buttocks, big as a tree," Daisy said. "The tree wiggles, and they pee. I'm going to go see the president of the United States of America about this and give him a piece of my mouth."

"Don't bring that gun, Daisy," Lindy said. "The Secret Service won't like that at all."

"This here gun?" Daisy pulled a gun out from behind her back. Most of the people in the room hit the ground. The rest of us knew there were no bullets.

"Let me tell you something, streetwalker." Daisy did not mean this meanly—she and Lindy get along fine—but a number of people looked confused by the "streetwalker" accusation, as Lindy kept her business quiet. "I am not afraid of jail. I'm not afraid of those bull dykes in there, the dumb-ass criminals, the white trash, the space aliens, the gang banger wasters, the hos, the ghetto women."

I sighed. Filter for Daisy? Gone.

"This is our neighborhood," Daisy announced. "We got a black guy who can't dance, that's you, Charles, who should be able to dance because he's black. He's living with a white woman who is an older hippie and smokes a joint now and then when she gets her panties in a twist. They're an Oreo cookie. We got two lesbians, both pretty. Most lesbians look like dykes. These two don't. We got a hooker running a business out of her houseboat.

"We got a man who disappears sometimes and he's packin' a pistol in his pants and looks like he could kill someone, but he is a man I want to make a human sandwich with and I'm the toast and he's the banana, and we have Toni." She pointed at me. "News reporter. Tough. Something bad happened to her. Huge family all over the place. Svetlana's, my favorite restaurant. Russian mafia food. Her cousin steals cars and her sister locks criminals up. Sometimes she's sad and she cries in her kayak, and then we have me." She pointed at herself. "I'm crazy. Crazy Daisy. I think my mind might be flipping and flopping, hello whales, I don't know."

Those of us who lived by Daisy were not thrown by her rant, but the other people, from different areas of the marina and downriver, were. Silence descended.

"Hey," Daisy said to Jayla and Beth, leaning forward, the red daisy in her hat bouncing. "Now I'm sorry about that. I don't think you two lesbians are bull dykes."

"Thank you," Jayla said.

"We appreciate that," Beth said.

Daisy started crying. Beth put an arm around her, and so did Jayla.

"Now, now," Jayla said.

"It's okay, Daisy," Beth said.

"What's wrong?" someone whispered.

"I don't like when I hurt the lesbians," Daisy cried. "I don't mean to."

"Don't cry, Daisy," Beth said. "We're not hurt."

"I am stupid. Stupid!" Daisy said, hitting herself in the head, twice, until Beth gently caught her hand. "Did I hurt your feelings, Charles, when I said you can't dance?"

"No, Daisy. You're right, I can't dance."

"I could teach you to wiggle to the beat. And I'm sorry you're sad in the kayak, Toni."

"No problem," I said, trying to be reassuring. "It's the truth. I'm working on it."

"I know you're sleeping with the man with the pistol behind

his zipper. And I don't care that you're a hooker, Lindy girl. I don't. A girl's got to do what she's got to do, and you read books, too."

"It's a steady job, not many hours," Lindy said, "and I can buy my own health insurance."

"I'm a flying idiot," Daisy muttered.

"Let's continue," Jayla said, while Daisy blew into a Kleenex and I patted her knee.

"You don't need to worry," Lindy said. "The marina is not going to shut down."

"How do you know . . . why . . . that's not what we've heard . . . we all received the notice . . ."

Lindy brushed a hand through the air. "Forget it. I'll have it handled. All will be fine."

But Lindy wouldn't explain that comment, so the meeting dragged on. What could we do, could we turn the marina into a co-op? Could we become the owners? How much money would we need? Could the city take over? Could we do this or that?

Later, I stood with Lindy on the dock. "You don't think the marina will shut down?"

She grinned. "No. Don't worry. I have it all . . . handled."

"How?"

"Trust me. I do." She started off toward her Queen Anne houseboat. "I have a nine-er. Early for me, so have to go. Want to go out on my boat tomorrow evening? I have a four-er, that's it. Maybe five-thirty?"

"Yes. Thanks. I need some river time."

Hadn't had that in too long. . . . I avoided my kayak as I went inside my tugboat that night.

Daisy stood at the edge of the dock about eleven and sang "Maria" from *West Side Story,* "I Dreamed a Dream" from *Les Miserables,* and "I Could Have Danced All Night" from *My Fair Lady.* It was like sitting in a concert hall, but there was no stage, only a river; there were no costumes, only an older lady wearing daisies. There were no other actors, only a woman whose mind was crumbling, door by door, shutting down, but the voice was still there, pitch perfect, melodious, the notes sailing all over the marina, wrapping us up in the magic of a musical miracle.

Nick's arm tightened around me as I tried to get off of him on Saturday night. We had had sex that was so seductively brain cell busting that I had accidentally fallen asleep on top of him, my head on his chest, his blankets covering me.

"Let go, Nick."

"I would rather not, baby. Please stay. You're warm. I'm warm. Together we're warm."

"That's why you have blankets."

"Take pity on me. I had a bad week and need a long night hug."

"I'm sorry you had a bad week. I'm still leaving."

"I'll make you pancakes in the morning."

I paused. I love pancakes. "No. Thank you."

"One night, Toni. Stay."

"No, I can't."

"Can't and won't. Same thing."

"I know. Good night."

I pulled back, he pulled me down into one of his kisses, and I sank into it until I could get the strength to leave.

He got up and walked me to the door of my tugboat. I kissed his cheek. He was unhappy. I could feel the unhappiness and his anger.

I was unhappy, too.

I closed my door, the river around my home so lonely tonight.

The first few weeks after I moved to my tugboat, Nick would stop to chat when he saw me and I would try to utter something semi-intelligent, which often didn't work. I didn't have a lot to say, because all my words clogged in my throat when I saw him. By then it had been almost nineteen months and the fog was lifting, but only now and then.

He told me later that he thought I had taken an instant dislike to him. That wasn't true. I had taken an instant, lusty physical attraction to him, but at the same time he scared the heck out of me. I wasn't ready to be attracted to anyone. I felt guilty being attracted to Nick. I felt lost and sad and overwhelmed.

Nick was skilled, though, at conversation about the weather, the river, the animals, restaurants, politics, movies, work, etc. I liked him. I liked how he always asked about my day, not a flippant "how are you" and then when I said "fine" he moved on. No, he sincerely wanted to know how my day was.

As soon as he knew I was a crime and justice reporter, he read my articles and chatted with me about them. Because he was a DEA agent, we had a lot in common with our work. He told me once that he became a DEA agent because one of his cousins died from an overdose of cocaine. The cousin had been trying to get clean, but the drug dealer was relentless. "My family, truly, has never recovered from losing Casey."

He was in college when it happened and decided then that he would do what he could to help prevent any other family from going through what his had been through. Nick often had to leave in the middle of the night for work. Holidays. Sundays. Erratic hours. Long days and weeks and months. "Drug busts don't adhere to a nine-to-five schedule," he'd said.

He was wise, measured, calm, compassionate. He sympathized when I told him about the sad stories I was writing about and seemed genuinely upset for the families affected by crime.

He asked about my parents, who he had met that first day, and said he had been to Svetlana's Kitchen many times and he loved it. I instantly pictured him going on a date there, and I also instantly didn't like his vapid, shallow date.

As if that man could read my mind, he said, "I have a bunch of buddies from college in the area, so we meet there about once a month."

I learned that he liked to make his own pizza. I told him that I liked making white coconut cake. We talked about traveling, which he wished, as I wished, that we had done more. We talked about books. That was a clincher for me. A man who likes to read.

About a month after I moved in, despite my inability to hold a decent conversation, he asked if I wanted to go to dinner at

Pepper's Grill. Pepper's Grill is an expensive restaurant with a view over the river downtown. I said, no, thank you.

He smiled and said, Another time?

And I said, Maybe. Not now.

Those light blue eyes were gentle, but it felt as if he were looking right into me, exploring around.

I couldn't date. Couldn't go out with him or anyone else. I was struggling. One step from going over the edge of my own life.

Nick and I went back to general chitchat. In that first three months he was gone for a few days, even a couple of weeks, at a time. He always told me when he was going out of town. I started to miss him. I didn't want to miss him.

One time he came back with a bruise on the left side of his face. I said, "Were you in a fight?" and he said, "Yes."

"With who?" *I felt my stomach clench up.*

"Someone who didn't want to follow the law."

"Did you win?" *His injury made me feel sick.*

"Yes."

"And where is that person now?" *Why did someone hurt him?*

"Jail."

"Ah. That's an unpleasant place." *I'm in an unpleasant place. I don't want to see this, and I don't want to feel this.*

"It is."

"Glad you've made it back home to the dock," I said. *I was more than glad. I was relieved. I wanted to cry.*

He grinned. "Are you?"

"Yes. Of course." *I was going to cry. I needed to leave.*

"I have steaks. Want one?"

I hesitated that time. He was beat up and I was so attracted to him, but I couldn't. I shouldn't. It was wrong. "No, thanks."

"I won't burn yours."

"I'm sure you won't."

He smiled. "Okay, Toni. Some other time?"

"Maybe." I felt like a smashed ant. He was hurt, he wanted company. I wanted to eat steak with him. I wanted to go to Pepper's Grill with him. I wanted to go out on his boat, *Sanchez One,* with him. But if I went out with Nick I would drown in guilt and betrayal, and I was already drowning. I turned away, a vision of that bruise stuck in my miserable head.

"Night, Toni."

"Night, Nick."

My husband, Marty Romanowsky, was born in America, though both parents were from Leningrad, now St. Petersburg. His given name was Makar, but in kindergarten he apparently changed his name himself. Five years old, and he announces that he's Marty.

I met him at church one Sunday when I was twenty-four. Usually I could escape going to church—organized religion is not for me—but my mother had been pestering me for a long time and I gave in when she promised to make me her Russian pancakes with whip cream and her homemade strawberry jam afterward.

On the way there, my parents, once again, regaled me with information about Marty Romanowsky.

"Remember, he Russian," my mother said, with a full and rolling R. "He a doctor. He kind. Look like a . . . What that bird called I think of, Alexei?"

"Blue heron."

"Yes. The blue heron. Marty like that. Graceful. Long on the arms. Long on the legs. Listening. He a listening bird. Gentle. But, important now, what I next say: He Russian." She again emphasized the hard "R" with gusto. "I tell you that already?"

"Many times. He's a Russian blue heron," I drawled. "I've always wanted to date a bird."

Tall, brown curls, thin, lanky, glasses. Marty was an oncologist. Thirty-two. Never married. He had been out of state for med school, his internship, and residency. Now he was home. He had a smile that was friendly and inviting. His mother, Raina, loved him; his father, Zakhar, was so proud he could burst. His father was a doctor in the Soviet Union, but here they own hardware stores. Raina is the CEO.

Marty was an only child. Our parents were friends.

Which is exactly why I did not date him, nor was I particularly friendly that Sunday, but our parents were determined.

My parents would sneak Marty and his parents over, springing them on poor, unsuspecting me when I arrived for Sunday dinner. "That nice doctor boy, Marty, he coming too, with his mother and father," my mother would say to me as they walked up the driveway. "You be polite, Toni." She would threaten me with a wooden spoon. "I choose this man for you. Your papa wants him for you, too. Don't upset your papa."

My father agreed. "Antonia, this man, Marty, listen to him. Open your heart. I tell you, I know him, he is right for you. I love you, I am your papa, I want what's best, and Marty is best."

I would move to scuttle out the back door, but my mother would stand firmly in front of me, arms crossed over her bosom, and glower. I'd sigh and stay.

Marty was kind. He asked me questions about my work and my life. He seemed interested in me as a person, as a woman. He kept smiling at me, that Russian blue heron.

I avoided him because I was twenty-four, out on my own, working at an alternative newspaper, with a loft downtown, and I didn't need my parents dictating my life. I was also dating a fellow reporter who was free spirited, gorgeous, and not too bright.

Marty was already too settled, I thought. He was a doctor, with a home, and a pair of glasses. He liked reading and going to plays. He loved his parents. His hair was receding. Too dull. Too old. Too conservative.

I kept running around, bar hopping with my sisters, my crazy cousins, and my girlfriends. I kept traveling. I kept shopping. I dumped the not too bright reporter because he wanted to spend too much time with me, then started dating a man who worked in the governor's office. Zack was quick, ambitious, focused, and supersmart politically. I broke up with him at lunch one day and I didn't even know I was going to do it, but I did and felt better.

Zack stalked me for two months after that, and I had to get

the police involved. One time he stalked me to the door of my loft downtown when Marty was there. Marty had come by to say hello. He arrived with a huge bunch of red and yellow gladiolas

Zack took immediate offense to Marty and his gladiolas. Zack yelled, threatened, and swung a fist, right at Marty's face. I didn't know that Marty had a black belt. Zack crashed to the floor of my loft like a squished and shocked fish, sputtering.

Marty helped Zack up, peered into his eyes with a small flashlight attached to his key chain, had Zack tell him how many fingers he was holding up, checked him out like a doctor would, then told Zack, calmly, that if he bothered me again he was going to break his teeth away from his gums. I never saw Zack again.

It was then that I started to see Marty differently. I started seeing him as tougher than I thought. Stronger. Protective. Even . . . sexy.

He smiled and handed me the gladiolas.

I smiled back at him.

7

Three nights later my mother called at six. I had left the *Oregon Standard* after finishing a story on a man who had been locked up for twenty years for being a low- to mid-range drug dealer when he was nineteen years old. "I'm thirty-nine," he told me. "I earned two degrees in prison. It's been twenty years. Is that not long enough?" The rest of the story was about the excessive length of sentences given for nonviolent drug crimes, and how black men were statistically proven to go to jail for far longer than their white counterparts who had committed the same crime.

"I need you to come and waitress tonight, my Antonia. We are handed on the short."

I did love the way my mother used American phrases and turned them around.

"Party coming for fifty. Please. I call Elvira. Valeria can't come. She going to get that killer, you know."

The truth is that my parents don't ask my sisters and me to waitress often. They know we have other jobs, but sometimes they need us, so we go in. Valerie, a prosecuting attorney; me, a reporter; and my sister, who owns a pillow business. And there we were, trays high in the air, just like in high school and college.

Svetlana's Kitchen is not a quiet restaurant, and when people come to party, especially the Russian community, it's a party. Songs, toasts, vodka, my mother's dinners, which people come from near and far to eat. Ellie and I made a pile in tips. We visited with Ralph, who saluted us, and Charlie, who played Rachmaninoff in our honor.

The only bad thing was that the special that night, borscht beet soup, was named "Valeria Get The Killer."

"Valeria Get The Killer" was popular, especially among the Russian community. When my sister found out about the name of the soup, as someone called her and told her it was one of our mama's best specials *ever*, she had her rename "Valeria Get The Killer" immediately. My mother huffed and puffed, but she did it.

New name? "Valeria: Don't Tell Mama What To Do."

Valerie then received calls and e-mails admonishing her not to tell her mother what to do.

I fell into bed that night.

It's hard to have your family's private life up on the Specials board of a restaurant.

"How's the trial going, Valerie?" Pillow Talk had begun at Ellie's house, surrounded by stacks of her fabrics. We'd had tostadas and beer, then chocolate pecan pie.

I had finished the tree pillow with the leaves made from fabric from all over the world, and now I was sewing a pillow for a teenage boy. The blue-and-white-striped background was done, and I was piecing together a skateboard for the center.

"We're almost done picking the jury." Valerie was making a pillow for a little girl. All pink, two layers of white lace around the edge, and a huge rose in the center where she was going to embroider "Girl Power."

"How's Tyler Barton's family?" Ellie asked.

"Still sitting in the first two rows, and they hate me. Would like to see me flattened by one of the trailers they live in, or shot by one of their many guns, or trapped in one of the traps they use to catch their food. Like possums."

"That bad?" Ellie put her pillow down. She was making a pillow for a teenage girl. The pillow was made from a white cable knit sweater and would have six red buttons down two sides.

"Yes. It's a violent sickness that runs through the whole family. I'm putting their beloved son/brother/cousin in jail for a long time. They're missing teeth, they come in dirty, the men have long, straggly hair, and the women look like they've been through a meat grinder."

I felt that chill inside again. A chilly snake wrapping around my spine. Valerie was scared, I could tell. She never gets scared of criminals. She likes to smash them.

"I'm sure they won't do anything. . . ." Her voice trailed off, and she fiddled with her widow's peak, which is what she does when she's worried. "But the rat face hatred comes at me in waves."

"Family members of criminals have hated you before," Ellie said.

"Yes. Definitely. And I understand why. The weird thing is that sometimes the family members don't hate me. They were the criminal's first victims and they're actually there to make sure he goes to jail. But this case is . . ." She hesitated. "Different."

"How?" I asked.

"They're creepy, dangerous, uncontrolled people who have no morals or ethics. They think and act instinctively, with violence."

"Any outstanding warrants on any of them?" I asked.

"No, we checked. They have criminal records, but they've served their time. They have a right to be there. Tyler is one sick monster. The creep knocked off four women, at least. The defense attorney didn't want all four victims in one trial, but he lost. Anyhow"—she took a deep breath—"I don't want to talk about this anymore."

"You're an excellent prosecutor, Valerie," Ellie said.

"Maybe. But I'm not an excellent mother."

"What do you mean?" I asked.

"The kids aren't happy."

"Why?"

"I'm gone all the time. I work all the time. The other day Ailani told me that she wished I could be like the other moms who drive carpools and plan the class parties." She put her pillow down. "She did say that she likes our conversations."

"What do you talk to Ailani about?" Ellie giggled, then stopped herself and put on a serious expression, as if she didn't know.

Valerie squirmed.

"Yes, do tell, Valerie." I leaned toward her and had to stop myself from cackling. I knew what she talked to Ailani about.

"I am trying to educate my child." Valerie sat up straight. So pious! Sanctimonious!

Ellie and I could not contain our laughter.

"There's nothing wrong with teaching your daughter about depositions, grand juries, admitted evidence, and all the vocabulary of a courtroom." So righteous! Superior in her mommy skills!

"And?" Ellie giggled, then stopped *again* and tried to arrange her face into that serious expression.

"Hmmm, what else could there be?" I mused.

"Let's talk about something else," Valerie muttered.

"No. You talk to your ten-year-old daughter about how to run a murder trial, admit it," I said.

"You can't sneak out of this one," Ellie said. "Remember that paper in school that Ailani wrote last month? She detailed, at length, what would happen if someone murdered someone else and everything that detectives do to comb through the crime scene to find the identity of the killer."

Valerie rolled her eyes. "I had to go in and talk to the teacher about that one. . . ."

"I'm sure you did," I said. "She talked about blood splatters. She talked about DNA and various weapons and point blank range. I believe she mentioned a .45 and how bullets match a gun."

Valerie wriggled. "She's precocious. She asks me about my work and I tell her. I don't tell her the details—"

"She knows an awful lot about serial killers and compromised crime scenes," I said.

"She took one of the books I like to read and read it. When I found it, I took it." Valerie ran her hand over the rose pattern on her pillow. "Perhaps I might be accused of being a wee mite tiny too graphic with her."

"A tad," Ellie agreed, chortling. "You have a ten-year-old with more than a basic grasp of criminal activity, criminal analysis, prosecution, and punishment."

"Motherhood is a difficult balance." Grumpy now! "I have done my best." Holier than thou defensive!

Ellie and I cackled. Poor Valerie.

"Where's the wine, Ellie?" She groaned.

Work the next day was the usual. I listened to the police scanner. The news was grim and grimmer. The scanner never announces that we have had a bounty crop of tulips this year, the sun is still shining, the beach is particularly pleasant today. No, it's the blood and guts, rage and tragedy, of some people's real lives.

My other stories were almost done—the story about the family who had one kid in a gang and how they'd turned him around, and another story about a woman who runs a women's shelter. I'd interviewed a number of the women in it, first names only, so they couldn't be tracked by psycho ex-husbands and boyfriends.

I was in edits with William, who again pointed at me and told me I was quitting over his "dead kidneys." When they were done, photos taken, stories printed, I'd hand in my notice before I crumbled like a stale, old cookie. William would have to deal with his dead kidneys.

I listened to a police report, heard what had happened, grabbed my purse and my notebook, and headed out of the building.

I stopped my car at the curb, the white bungalow in southeast Portland surrounded by police, crowd control in place. Shoot. I wished I'd gotten here earlier. I grabbed my notebook and bag and scrambled out of the car. I scooted toward the house to be closer to the action, trying to avoid detection.

"Hey, Toni," an officer name Mikey said to me. Mikey is friends with Kai. They were partners for years. "Nice to see ya.

No, no, no. You know you can't do that. Don't go any nearer. Anything happens to you, and your mama would never let me come for dinner at Svetlana's again and Kai and Valerie would kill me."

"Toni, hi," an officer named Laura Hart said. "Saw your sister, Valerie, the other day at the courthouse. She's going after a sick son of a gun, isn't she? That guy, Barton, he's a psycho, and his family looks like they've come up from a swamp."

"I've been hearing that."

"Your sister, man, she gets men's balls in a sling," Mikey said, slapping his hands together. "I've seen her go after those criminals. It's like watching a human ball crusher."

"She likes to win," I said.

"I love it when I know she's prosecuting a case, because I know that guy's going to the slammer," Mikey said. "She gets all the lunatics, and those boys gotta get locked up. I got daughters and I can't have them walking the streets with my girls around."

When a bullet blasted through the front window, I hit the sidewalk, Mikey on top of me, Laura to the side.

"Well, dang it," Laura said, calm, so calm, as if she'd lost at a game of cards. "I didn't think this one was going to get ugly."

"Darn," Mikey said. "And I'm off shift in an hour. I'm supposed to be at my grandma's by three."

Mikey, Laura, and I scrambled to get behind the open door of a police cruiser, then Mikey and Laura moved behind a different car, closer up to the house, guns out. A second and third bullet rang out.

Beside me a captain named Harriet Chance rushed in, crouched down. "Hello, Toni."

"Hey, Harriet."

"Stay down low. I'm coming to Svetlana's with my new boyfriend tomorrow night. Is your mama . . . uh . . . stressed?"

"I know what you're asking, and no, she's not stressed. Not today."

She seemed a little disappointed.

"I do, know, however, that's she's making her beef stroganoff and homemade bread."

Her face lit up. "Really? I love her beef stroganoff. That's the recipe from her mother, right? She calls it 'My Mother's Tasty Beef.'"

Harriet stood, briefly, and aimed her gun at the house. *Boom!* Glass shattered, then silence. I covered my ears.

There were no more shots that night.

I saw Harriet and her new boyfriend at the restaurant the next night. She appeared to be savoring "My Mother's Tasty Beef" and the home baked bread. She stood up and gave me a hug.

"Nice shot," I told her.

"Thanks!"

When we arrived in Oregon, we were traumatized, exhausted, and broke. But three days later, after long nights of sleep and tears of relief, my parents went to work for Uncle Vladan at his landscape business. Two college professors, shoveling bark dust, planting trees and flowers. Yet they were grateful for the work.

My father took on a second job as a janitor at a hospital three nights a week. They immediately started going to community center classes to learn English and started "Speaky the English" at home, which became our family's motto: Speaky the English.

My mother's contribution to Uncle Vladan and Aunt Holly's home was to cook for the family with Aunt Holly. My parents could not get over the food in the supermarket, the amount, the range, the prices, and no lines. My mother had always cooked, the best she could, with limited amounts of everything, but in her heart, she was a chef. Now, finally, for the first time in her life, she could truly cook, and she lit up that kitchen like a culinary firework.

I had never tasted food like that before. Everyone loved my mother's meals and treats. Aunt Holly, an enterprising American woman, encouraged her to sell her Easter cake with vanilla, cinnamon, and raisins and her baked cheesecake at a farmer's market. They rented a stall, and my mother cooked all night. She and Holly brought the desserts in early in the morning, with help from my father and Uncle Vladan.

They set out samples and sold out by eleven o'clock the first day. They sold out by ten o'clock the next week as word got around. They started making more. And more. They sold desserts and they sold dumplings, potato cakes, and all kinds of soups. They took private orders. Soon my mother made more money baking than she did working for Uncle Vladan.

That was when the idea for the restaurant was born. My parents insisted on paying Uncle Vladan and Aunt Holly rent the first month we arrived, then they saved every penny they had to rent a space for a restaurant. After about a year of scrapping and saving, they found a place, put in used industrial-sized appliances that they bought for cheap from a restaurant that was going out of business, bought wood tables at Goodwill and garage sales, threw white tablecloths and candles down, and had a scene of St. Basil's Cathedral painted on the wall by a local art student.

They named it Svetlana's Kitchen and opened up.

They worked night and day, my father at the landscaping business during the day, then at the restaurant weekends and nights. My mother was at the restaurant full time. They were wiped out, but they were happier than I'd ever seen them. They loved the restaurant. My mother loved to cook. My father took care of the books, the hiring, the interior. The food was delicious, plentiful. The Russian vodka flowed from the bar. We were soon jammed.

At the end of the second year, my parents had saved enough for a down payment on a house in a neighborhood within a ten-minute walk of the restaurant. It was a rambling 1930s home, two stories, white, and needed a ton of work, but we loved it. We could not believe the amount of space. We could not believe that we each had our own bedroom. We still couldn't quite grasp that we could adjust our own heat, that the government didn't own our home, that the stove and the refrigerator always worked, and hot water would always flow when you turned the knob.

In the Soviet Union, we knew not to trust our neighbors unless we knew them well and were close friends. That's why curtains were always shut and why people whispered. But here, in America, we learned that neighbors were different. Uncle Vladan and Aunt Holly got along well with all of their neighbors, and they kept their curtains wide open. "We not hide anything," Uncle Vladan said.

My parents kept the curtains in front of our home open, too. "I no want people think I hiding a dead body," my mother said.

My parents were afraid we would not be accepted in our neighborhood because we were Russian. To not have friends around us, in this new American land where you could trust your neighbors, was unacceptable, so my mother made oreshki for all of our neighbors when we moved in and brought it to their homes herself, in a pink box with a pink ribbon.

The walnut-shaped cookies with a dulce de leche cream inside were all they needed.

They invited my mother in, my father, us.

We were welcomed. We played with their kids. We chatted with their parents. We knew our friends' grandparents.

And they all came to Svetlana's Kitchen.

My father eventually quit the landscaping business, my uncle Vladan cried because he would miss him, and my parents both worked full time at the restaurant. They started renting the second floor, too, and then they bought the whole building.

My mother kept cooking.

"Oh. My. I can't *believe* this."

I held the phone away from my ear as my cousin JJ yelled into it as soon as I said hello. I was practicing the art of Keeping The Monsters At Bay: Shopping Defensive Strategies, which meant I was at my favorite store. "What's wrong?"

"I'm calling about *Anya*."

"What about Anya?"

"*She* wants to give the bridal shower for Ellie." The tone was accusatory, as if Anya had robbed a bank, then firebombed a car, all while kidnapping an entire city, and she, JJ, crusader of righting wrongs, was reporting back on that heathen.

"Okay." I studied the beige pencil skirt in my hand with black cutouts down the side and a black, lacy sleeveless shirt.

"I want to, Toni." Stubborn tone. "I want to."

"You do? But you're so busy with the salon and the kids."

"So is Anya! She's rehearsing for that play right now. I would be better at giving the shower. I have heaps of stuff in the back room, shampoos and rinses and crap like that, that I can give the ladies as bridal shower gifts. Plus, I'm going to bring two of my girls and we're going to do everyone's hair. Wouldn't that twirl your skirt up? It would mine.

"Anyhow, tell Ellie I want to do it. And are you using the curling iron to make a few curls like I showed you? You're not. I know you're not. I don't want to see your hair like it was at the restaurant a few nights ago. It's bad advertising for me.

"Also, Chelsea keeps sneaking out at night. She keeps getting piercings, too. She is a rebellious, out of control, horny rabbit. Hope, on the other hand, is an angel. I have to go. My client is here. Devil Dee Dee coming in. The woman can talk for an hour about her manicure. If I started talking about how my leg had fallen off, within twenty seconds we'd somehow be talking about her again. Ugh. I'm doing the shower. I love you, Toni. Bye."

I bought the beige pencil skirt. New clothing armor.

I was called again in five minutes.

"Toni," Anya said, breathing hard. "I'm in rehearsal, have to be back up on stage in minutes here, and my eyelashes are falling off and my bladder is full."

"Why are you calling me? Shouldn't you be in Zen mode or practicing your lines or something?"

"Because I need to talk to you." Anya lowered her voice, still panting. I recognized the pant. It was the hypochondriac pant. "About a slight medical issue I'm having. I have an itch. Under my left arm. Do you ever get itches only under one arm, not the other?"

"Uh, not usually."

"Oh Lord. There's something wrong with me, then. I'll bet it's an organ. One of my organs is sick and causing me to itch. You release cortisone when your body is fighting something, and that causes the itch. The other day I had a bump on my leg. It itched, too. What is that bump, I asked myself? I looked it up on the Internet. I determined it could be a tumor, a bunched-up vein, a bone that was broken that I didn't know about, or the beginning of a benign growth that could grow up to six inches long."

"And what did it turn out to be?"

"I rushed to the doctor and he said it was a spider bite." Her volume rose. "Isn't that awful? I asked, 'What kind of spider bite?' And he didn't know. So I researched spider bites." She rambled on about spiders and what type of nasty spider it could be, and the possible cataclysmic health problems that could ensue, now and in future.

"Don't you have to go onstage soon?"

"What? Yes. One minute. So, tell Ellie I'm going to do her bridal shower. And watch out for spiders, Toni. I'm not kidding. I might have poisons in me right now, as I speak, that will cause me to become paralyzed, on stage. Shoot, someone's yelling my name. Don't forget, I'm doing the bridal shower. I'll make first aid kits for all the ladies for gifts and add a huge bottle of hand sanitizer."

Anya hung up. She is an outstanding actress, and the Kozlovsky families all go to her plays. We would be going to this one, opening night, even though my uncle Vladan clutches his heart, his daughter an *actress*, and mutters, "Woe on my life. A actress. What? No husband? No babies? Why this happen to me? Woe on my life."

The next day, Zoya and Tati called me. They were both on speakerphone.

"How are ya, Toni?"

"Tati and I want to do Ellie's bridal shower, Toni," Zoya said. "It'll be a par-tay! We're going to have a theme. Ready for it? Hang on to your bustier. The Stripper Shower. Like the sound of that? Tati thought of it, I can't take credit. She thinks of everything. The other day she designed a nurse's stripper outfit." She screeched again. "It made me emotional."

"Thanks so much for offering." Here we go. I took a breath and prepared to be peacekeeper for the bridal shower war. "There is a teeny problem. Anya and JJ want to do it, too, so I need to talk to Ellie."

"What?" What a shriek. Blew my ear out. Neither Tati or Zoya holds any emotion in. None.

"No!" Tati said. "We're going to do it. For bridal shower gifts for all the ladies we're going to give them a stripper outfit. They'll *love* it."

I pictured Aunt Polina and Aunt Holly and my mother in their stripper outfits. I laughed, then tried to pretend I was coughing. "Stripper outfits?"

"Yes. Every woman needs to find the stripper within themselves."

"Even Aunt Polina?"

They hesitated.

"Yes. Uh. Yes, I think so. It's in there somewhere. Deep down," Zoya said.

"With Aunt Polina it would be deep, deep, quite deep down," Tati said, "but we could yank it out and dance with it and teach it to slither."

"You're going to find a slithering stripper outfit for Aunt Polina?"

"Uh, yes," Tati said. "She might need some Russian vodka first. . . ."

"Like a pint?"

"Yes, but we'll find that spiritual stripper. I feel a powerful pull toward it."

"So you're going to give all the bridal shower guests something to wear that is short and tantalizing with Velcro?"

Zoya said, in all sincerity, "Yes. We're family. We're the Kozlovskys. We want everyone to be together. I know that there will be other people there, too, but this is our bonding time. Kozlovsky time. When we're all together." She gasped on a sob.

"Are you crying, Zoya?"

"No." She sobbed.

"Yes, she is," Tati said. "And now I'm crying! Quit crying, Zoya! But, think of it, Toni, this is a time for the Kozlovsky women." Her voice wobbled. "Generations, as one, for a stripper bridal shower, holding hands, dancing. A pole. It's making me *feel*. Love. Gratefulness for the family. I feel lust, too."

"Lust? Right now?"

"Yes. But not for you," Tati clarified. "I need a man. Wait! I have a new boyfriend. His name is Raoul. No, Randy."

"I'll give him a week."

"Don't be negative. He's a month-er. Anyhow! Zoya and I want to do the shower. Pasties for all! Thongs for all! And we're going to get boas, too, the feathery ones. Everyone in pink." She sniffled. "We're doing the shower."

"Yes," Zoya said. "Us. The la la twins."

"La la," Tati sang, then sniffled again.

I had four warrior women relatives wanting to host Ellie's shower.

It was not going to be bonding time, it was going to be an epic battle.

"They all want to do my shower?" Ellie asked, stricken, when I called her to see if she had an opinion on who should give it.

"Yes."

"What another nightmare."

"Another nightmare? You mean in addition to the nightmare of being engaged?"

"Forget I said that." Her voice petered out.

"I'm worried about you."

"Don't be. I'm in love." Her breath caught, as if a hook had snatched it away.

"If you were in love, you would be happy, excited, but calm, too."

"I'm happy," she wailed. "I'm excited, damn it, so damn excited. And I'm calm!" she wailed again. "Can't you tell I'm calm?"

"Not really."

"I'm calm!" Her volume went to high and hysterical. "So calm!"

It became quite quiet on her end of the phone.

Then I heard a bag inflate, deflate, inflate . . .

"I'm going to have to buy you more brown bags, Ellie."

Moscow, the Soviet Union

The black rot in the Soviet Union, in Moscow, grew like tentacles, reaching out to strangle whom it could.

It grew like the heavy clouds blanketing the city, the raindrops that drenched us, the winds that blew through, screaming a warning. It was a hard life, filled with deprivation, worry, endless work, and a soul-sucking government that would not tolerate dissent, or you would be labeled an "enemy of the people." There was mass surveillance and a systematic oppression of anyone who spoke against the government, or for democracy, capitalism, Christianity.

My father continued to lead us in prayer at every meal. My mother hid a Bible beneath the floorboards and read it to us. They taught us about God, Jesus, Mary, the disciples, the Old and New Testaments, the Apostle Paul, the stories of the Bible. They were careful, because of us.

But my uncle Leonid, fun, bright, funny, was not being careful.

"Leonid," my mother whispered to my father one night, "is getting too loud, Alexei. He is writing articles for two underground newspapers now."

"I know, Svetlana. I talked to him. I told him to stop, to hide, to leave."

"Each week he gets more bold."

My father put his head in his hands.

"What is it, Alexei?"

"Svetlana." He reached for her. "Leonid wrote an article yesterday where he said that the KGB is a band of thugs, dangerous and out of control, violent and protected by an invasive, inept government that stole from the people. He said they had infiltrated Russian life, turning father against son, daughter against mother, neighbor against neighbor."

My mother covered her mouth. "Oh, my Lord, protect him."

"He will need it. He will go to prison if he does not leave the Soviet Union."

My mother bowed her head to pray. "God, may Leonid's enemies' feet be infected by gangrene. May their ears be packed with worms. May you strike them in the head with a serpent. Bless you, Mary, mother of God, for your sacrifice and help us against our enemies. Keep the Kozlovskys safe. We are good people. Amen."

Even as a child I heard about the prisons in the Soviet Union, most of which were labor camps. Run by the devil, his boss Communism and the KGB. The prisoners, many of whom were not criminals but political protestors, worked all day in incredibly harsh conditions, some in Siberia. They were starved. They were beaten. If they did not get enough work done on one day, they were given less food the next day. The prisons were overcrowded, and the prisoners often turned on one another, the guards sadistically turning on the prisoners. They slept on wood planks, shivering through the night, their clothing nothing against the wind and pounding cold, their bodies withering.

When Elvira's friend Lena's father was taken in the middle of the night, my father said to my mother, "We must make plans to leave. We will drag Leonid with us."

She nodded.

When I spotted Lena's father's body floating down the Moskva River and I told my parents, the planning ramped up.

My father's brothers, Yuri and Sasho, started to plan, too. None of us were allowed to simply leave the Soviet Union. Uncle Vladan was offering to help and sponsor us from the States, where his landscaping company could offer them jobs. They all begged my uncle Leonid to leave the Soviet Union immediately.

He resisted everyone's entreaties. He wanted to change life from within, to help the people.

My parents told me, never tell what you hear here around this table, Antonia.

I never did. But someone did, and the tentacles started to reach for us in the dark, waiting for the perfect time to wrap themselves around our family, and strangle us.

8

"Too many clients."

"Gee, Lindy. I can see why that would be a problem."

"I'm raising my rates. They don't like it, they can go."

"Supply and demand."

"They demand me, they can supply more money."

Lindy, high-priced call girl, said Nick never came to her place. She said he was polite to her but did not try to initiate conversations. "He knows what I do. He's not stupid. He's known since the week I moved in three years ago, I could tell. But we're neighbors, and he's a smart guy. He's DEA. He's after the big guns. The drug dealers. The murderers. Some woman, with no pimp, who is keeping all the money for herself to sleep with men with whom she has made a business transaction? Eh."

It was surprising to me when I first moved in that no one complained about Lindy's business, although her place was a little off of our dock, so we didn't see much, plus she has only two customers a day, weekends and holidays off. It wasn't like there were strange men in and out, twelve a day, all hours.

Her white Queen Anne home was charming with pots of flowers and that wraparound purple wisteria. Plus, Lindy's kind. She takes Daisy to the grocery store once a week. She was an English major, so she helps Vanessa grade her students' papers, and she, Jayla, and Beth do yoga together on her back deck. Lindy and I are friends and love talking about books. It's Portland. It's Oregon. Live, let live, don't get uptight.

"How's your job, Toni?"

"I hate it." She asked more questions, she listened. Lindy is interested in other people, and she's an excellent friend. Her clients feel the same way. She says she has many clients who buy two hours of her time. "One hour and forty five minutes of talking and eating lunch together. Fifteen minutes of woo-woo, and that's it."

"And how are the wedding plans going for your sister?"

I groaned. "Well, my mother can't stand that he's a nonrusseman."

"Nonrusseman?" Her brow furrowed. "Is that one word?"

"Yes, she made it up. She wanted to be efficient."

Daisy knocked on Lindy's door, then opened it up.

"Hello, hooker, hello, kayak lady," she said to us, smiling, happy. She was wearing a blue coat with yellow daisies, red pants, and yellow daisy cowgirl boots. I recognized the brand. Her sons spare no expense for their mother to make sure her feet are warm and safe.

"Hello, Daisy." Lindy smiled and stood up, led her to the couch.

"I brought you two girls a cake. Champagne cake, pink peppermint cream icing. I made one for the black and white couple, and for the lesbians, and I brought that sexy man a cake, too, and made a heart out of red hots for him on the top. He has a pistol in his pants. Cannonballs. You would know, Toni. Sits in the kayak on her deck. Not crying today, right?"

"No, I'm fine today, thanks, Daisy. I like your boots."

Daisy's face scrunched up, then the tears ran. "It makes me sad to see you cry."

"Daisy . . ." I hugged her, and in a few minutes she was better.

"Let's have cake together," Lindy said. "I made coffee."

"Thank you, hooker Lindy."

We chatted with Daisy, ate her cake, which was so delicious I could eat it every day, and then she left. "Time for the Daisy concert. I have to sing now."

We heard her singing at the end of the dock. She sang songs by Neil Diamond, Elton John, and Liza Minnelli.

"It's like being at a concert," Lindy said.

"She's fading. Seems like every week I see her mind shutting down a little more."

"She'll hate a nursing home. She walks everywhere. She loves the woods down by the river, loves the city. Hates to be confined. When I met her three years ago she said she was claustrophobic. Her father used to lock her in a closet when he went on drinking benders, and she hates when she's in small places."

"That would explain her houseboat. No walls."

"She had all the walls taken down for that exact reason. It's also why she lives on the river. She said she has to have a view, to not feel locked in, trapped."

"A nursing home will kill her," I said. "She'll feel locked in and trapped. She can't do it. She'll be totally miserable."

"Skippy and Georgie know it, too, so that's why they're trying to let her stay here as long as they can. Skippy was over here. He tips really well, and he cries about his mother. Did you know he worries about her feet getting cold? When he was a kid she always had cold feet. Anyhow, later on she had him weeding her daisy planters on her deck, then sweeping it, then I heard the vacuum running. He came outside in an apron. I asked him what he was doing, and he said he was cooking pasta primavera and bread with his mother because she likes to cook with him."

We listened to Daisy sing a love song.

"That song makes me feel romantic," Lindy said.

"It makes me want to cry."

Lindy stretched out her hand and I took it.

"It's too bad we're not gay, Toni."

I laughed. "Yes, it is." I thought about Nick.

"You're thinking about the man with the pistol in his pants, aren't you?"

Lindy reads minds.

We laughed.

My stories on the family who had saved their kid from a gang and the women's shelter had gone to print. They'd been received well. I had recently won an award for a story I had written on meth. I had highlighted two addicts and an addict who was currently sober, but only because he had been arrested and jailed. I had statistics and numbers, interviews with two meth dealers, doctors on the front lines, rehab people, law enforcement, etc.

Normally the award would have made me happy, but now I simply wanted out of the gruesome details of some people's sordid and sad lives.

I had my resignation letter up on e-mail. I had entered all the addresses to all of the people who would receive it. Today was the day. The letter was polite, succinct, thanking them for the job, blah blah blah. I did not mention that I felt a nervous breakdown coming on like a freight train off its tracks.

"Toni, how are ya?"

"Ricki. Great. Fine. How are you?" I pushed my chair away from my desk and stood up. Ricki had been a reporter at the *Oregon Standard* for thirty years. Knew everyone in the newsroom, knew everyone in town, knew the names of their pets. And she knew secrets. Tons of them.

Ricki could drink anyone under the table. She often won at a once-a-month *Oregon Standard* poker game and smoked cigars. If you smelled a cigar, it was Ricki, sneaking one in.

"How am I? I think I'm drying up down there. Something to do with menopause. Other than that I'm doing well. You got the friggin' job, Toni."

Relief, sweet and warm, rushed through my body. I would not have to quit. I would not be jobless. I would possibly not have a nervous breakdown. "I did?"

"Yes. Surprised you applied."

"Had enough blood and carnage for the time being."

She nodded. "Yeah, you've had more than your fair share. I've hired Kim to be the garden writer. Shantay and Zoe to work as copy editors. Penny and Jessie for graphics and design. A bucket of other people." She waved a hand. "You for homes and home décor, occasional garden if it hits you in the gut. You walk by one and think, 'That's going to blow my mind off,' then you do it. Otherwise, stick to homes.

"Congratulations on your latest award, by the way. Is this going to be exciting enough for you? I've always seen you as a gal who would wear a holster and gun and would swing a sword if it were legal."

"I don't like guns. I can see myself with a sword."

"Swords are powerful, aren't they? I'd like one myself. We're having a meeting today down at Butch's Bar. Three o'clock. We'll talk shop." She crossed her arms. "You know that a lot of the boring stuff has already been decided, right? Here's the history of the magazine up to date. It's so exciting your estrogen levels will shoot up. *Homes and Gardens of Oregon* started with a committee. I hate committees—they make me drink whiskey—but it had to be done. Shantay and I and a bunch of upstairs drivel mongers talked a lot. We talked to the newsroom people, marketing, circulation, those irritating people in advertising. Met for several months in more brain-bouncing meetings to explore the viability." She tapped her red nails together.

"What should *Homes and Gardens of Oregon* look like? That was the first question. We decided it had to be local homes and gardens. Local, useful, entertaining, educating, beautiful. I wanted there to be a section at the end where men could see my dating profile and call it in, but that's not going to work."

I laughed.

"Anyhow, the focus groups are done, they loved it, got a kick to their butts about it. Another group thought the prototype was finer than sherry wine on a sweet autumn day. Had a huge survey that we sent to advertisers asking if they would advertise in it. Most of them said yes or maybe. Publisher had to decide, and she said yes, and the prigs on the top floor said yes, too. Boom boom boom, we were a go. So now we gotta get this magazine up and shooting from the hip."

"I'm ready to shoot from the hip." I was so happy. I thought I was going to have to quit the paper, but now I wouldn't have to. I could write about homes. No one would die or be shot.

"Everyone's got to get copy in freakin' pronto. I've been planning this for months longer than I can possibly stand, I can feel my womanhood drying up like the Sahara desert, but now we're launching *Homes and Gardens of Oregon* and you are our home lady. Remodels. Renovations. Redecorations. Remarkable crap, stuff like that."

"Thank you, Ricki." Whew.

"Hell, no. Thank you. Soon as I had your application in my ever-lovin' hands I knew I was going to hire you, but I had to get through all the bull, giving everyone a fair shot, blow blow blow. Anyhow, finish up whatever wreaking havoc stories you're working on by the end of the week, and we're all moving to the west side of the building, in the corner, third floor, lots of windows so we don't lose our flippin' minds."

"Can't wait. Police scanners, crime, racing out of the house at two in the morning have lost their shiny luster."

"You and I have been in the trenches for too long. We need to do something else. See you at three. I know you're Russian, so you know how to drink vodka." She turned away, then turned back. "That's a stereotype. I hate stereotypes. Sorry. I'll assume that you're deleting that resignation letter that's on your computer screen?"

I smiled. "You're quick."

"You have no idea." She winked, teetered out on those heels.

"How do you walk in those?"

"I walk like I mean it, as all women should, that's how I walk in these suckers. Walk like you mean it, Toni."

I left Butch's that night feeling a heck of a lot better. I walked like I meant it out to the curb.

Ricki and I and the other Hooters of Homes and Gobblers of Gardens, as we nicknamed ourselves, brainstormed story ideas for the magazine. It was not going to be a large magazine at first—we'd need ad revenue to drive it—but we would feature at least one home a week.

I told them my ideas: beach houses, city condos, houses from across the state, mountain retreats, tiny houses on wheels, houses decorated on a budget, high-end homes, homes filled with do-it-yourself types of projects, odd and original décor, etc.

We would also feature artists and writers in their homes, their studios, and offices. We would have themes—how to decorate a master bedroom, how to redecorate a room with before and after shots, bathroom and kitchen remodels, kid friendly family rooms, etc. We would feature how-to stuff—how to decorate a porch for fall, how to decorate a home for Christmas, how to fix a dull patio, etc.

People seemed to like my ideas, and we clinked our glasses together.

Ricki asked me to write a column for the last page of the magazine each week, too. "Write something about homes. Make it personal, about you or another homeowner. Try not to be a sap. Try not to be cold. We want some bleepin' heart and soul in this rag. Don't yakkety-yak your mouth. God help me if you do. Six hundred words. Tops."

"I'm never a sap. I think I'm cold sometimes so I'll have to tone it down. I'll find my soul and dump it in. I won't yak my mouth."

"I like you, Toni. You're a kick buttocks reporter and I like your heels. You're tough. I've seen you rip apart sanctimonious editors with a computer mouse stuck up their yin yang and stand up to arrogant, ego-driven men and their glass balls. Glad you're here fighting in the fort with me."

"Thank you." I was so happy. My nervous breakdown was inching away, I could feel it. "Seen the same with you. And I like you, too."

"Now you're getting sappy."

"You started it, Ricki. Let's see if you're a real woman. Another vodka?"

She was a real woman. We took cabs home after I walked like I meant it to the curb. Lucky I didn't fall in the river off my dock. That would have been embarrassing, to haul myself up off the dock like a drowned rat.

I told Nick I got the job later that night. I had told him exactly why I wanted the job and what I was going to do—quit and become a hippie beach bum—if I didn't get it.

"You got the job?"

"Yes." I was so thrilled I almost clicked my heels together like a Russian American Dorothy from *The Wizard of Oz*.

Nick picked me up, hugged me, and spun me around. "Congratulations, baby. That's great."

I kissed him, he kissed me back, and we had a celebratory romp in his bedroom.

The next day there was a huge vase of flowers—irises, daffodils, roses—by my front door, a box of chocolates, and a stack of three new books I'd told him I was going to read next. One was a book we had planned to read together.

That man.

He knows me. And that is so romantic.

About two months after I moved into my tugboat, Nick and I met in the parking lot one night, about one o'clock in the morning. I'd had a long evening. There was an attack in northeast Portland and I'd covered it. Nick was getting out of his truck. He had a bruise under his eye.

"Hi, Toni. Late night."

"For you, too."

"Yes."

"Did you have a nice evening?"

"I wouldn't call it nice," he drawled, and flashed me that grin that was *invitational* and yet . . . kind. "And you?"

"I wouldn't call it nice, either." I told him about the call.

"Hard job you have."

"I'm not the one who comes home with bruises and cuts." It made me feel sad, and worried, that he had been hit. Then it made me sad and worried that I was sad and worried. More chaos in my emotional department.

"True. I hope you never do. I would find that upsetting if you did."

"You would?" That was interesting.

"Yes."

"What happened to your cheek?"

"Had a slight altercation with a drug dealer who didn't want to go to prison."

"Darn them. They won't agree to consequences, will they? How rude."

"Yes, rude."

Under the moon we smiled at each other. He was tall like a tree. A tight and muscled redwood.

"Come on, I'll walk you home."

I smiled. I liked his humor. "I'll take you up on your offer."

He took my elbow when we headed down the stairs to the dock, as it had rained earlier and he didn't want me to slip. Marty always did protective things like that, too.

We chatted. He was circumspect about his work, but he did tell me they were running surveillance on a drug ring here in town.

We stopped in front of my tugboat. "Thanks for walking me home."

"Anytime. Next time you're coming in late, call me and I'll walk you in."

"That's chivalrous. Will you gallop in on a white horse?"

"I think the white horse would bust through the dock, but I'll be there. I'll be the white horse."

"Thanks." Maybe I would ride that white horse. *What?* Why did I think that?

"Take my number down. And please call me, especially if you're coming in late at night. The parking lot is deserted. Not safe."

"Okay." He told me his number and I put it into my phone. Nick was so masculine. I've always liked men who are men. I liked his light blue eyes, the way he focused on me. And those cheekbones, slanted, sort of harsh, I wanted to . . . no, I didn't want to *kiss* them. I couldn't. But that mouth . . . I wanted to . . . no, *I couldn't*. It was easy, in a way, to miss his mouth, because the rest of his face was so compelling, but that lower lip, I wanted to . . . no!

As I was embarrassing myself, grinning like a lusty fool, Nick leaned in and kissed me. First on the cheek, his hand light on my waist. I didn't move, but I took a deep breath. His mouth was warm. He smelled delicious. I felt protected.

It was on instinct. Utter instinct and utter desire boinging about. I turned my head, put my hand on his shoulder, and that man needed no other encouragement. His lips came down on mine, both arms went around me, and he pulled me close into that wide and hard chest. It was like being cuddled and set on fire at the same darn time.

I could hardly breathe. Seduction had whirled and twirled and landed.

I pulled away only when the vague, distant part of my brain knew that I was going to rip off my clothes in front of my tugboat's door in about thirty seconds.

I couldn't even meet his eyes, so I looked down, his arms still around me, my hands and my forehead on his chest. I could feel his heart thunking, mine racing at full speed.

"That was the best kiss of my entire life," Nick said.

I started to laugh. I couldn't help it.

"And that's the absolute best thing you could have said to me, Nick."

"It's true."

With all my willpower, as I wanted to do a naked straddle with him, I turned and opened the door.

"Now will you go out with me?" I heard the laughter in his voice.

"Maybe." I turned and smiled at him.

"Please?"

"I'll think about it."

"How about Friday?"

"I'll call you. I have your number."

I shut the door, then leaned against it. Whew. He was going to be impossible to handle.

Maybe you shouldn't try to handle him then, a voice inside my head said. *Just let go.*

After that kiss, though I fought it, I started to really like Nick Sanchez.

Rancher. Cowboy. DEA man. Neighbor.

And he liked books.

I was done for, and I knew it.

* * *

The next day I gently told William Lopez, the man who hired me years ago, that I was going to work at *Homes and Gardens of Oregon.*

"The *hell* you are," he said, jabbing a finger at me.

"I can't do it anymore, William."

"The *hell* you can't." He leaned back in his chair. We had a staring war. He sighed. "Will you come back when you get bored writing about kitchen faucets and fancy ovens and"—he waved a hand in the air—"other mundane and useless home-maker trivia?"

"I will."

He sighed again. "You're my favorite reporter, Kozlovsky."

"I can still be your favorite reporter."

"No. Now you're on my bad side."

I smiled. "I've loved working for you."

"You're making me emotional, Kozlovsky. Get out. Right now."

I gave him a hug. I pretended not to hear him sniffle.

"When are you coming home?" I asked him, holding the phone in my hand. I was up in the wheelhouse, on the bench, the pillows from all over the world crowded around me, soft and silky.

"I'll be back for the wedding."

"And then?"

"Travel. Wandering. Walking."

"Will you ever stop?" It was dark out, the stars hidden, the clouds churning.

"When I can get her, and the blood, and the blood in her hair, out of my head. When I know what happened and when I know if my memories are real or if I'm losing my mind. When I know where I'm from. When I'm at peace. When I'm done."

"Are you anywhere near peace?"

"No. It's further away than ever. I'm seeing the white dog again."

Shoot. White Dog flashback was back again. I leaned my head back on my deck chair, feeling unbearably sad for him. White Dog flashback was upsetting.

"I heard that scream. I saw the dog crash into a wall. He's dead. I think it might be me screaming, but I don't know, I don't know who did it, I think it was him. That shadow, that man. Maybe my father . . . I don't know." He stopped. I knew he was fighting for control. "I don't know if it's real or if it's my imagination."

"I think it's real, I do."

"What are they hiding from me? I know there's something."

"I don't know."

We talked for another half hour. He wanted to know how I *really* was. "Tell me the truth," he said, so I told him.

"I can't wait to see you."

"You, too. Night, Toni. I love you."

"Love you, too." When I hung up I felt the guilt again, brick hard, lying on my chest, stomping on me like a thousand Communist boots.

The lie started when I was ten. Right before we left Moscow. I lied to him by omission. By not telling him what I knew.

My parents told him they adopted him from an orphanage in Moscow the night before we left.

It's a lie.

I know it because of the blood.

I popped in on Valerie's murder trial. I sat with Ellie, two rows behind Valerie, stern and authoritative in her blue suit and white blouse. She did have on some women-power high blue heels. Shamira Connell, my colleague from the *Oregon Standard,* was writing about the trial. She was one of my favorites. Shamira wasn't that friendly. She wasn't that social. She took herself, and her work, seriously, and she was an awesome reporter.

We studied the Barton family gang. Valerie was right. They hated her. Their attention on her so intense, the way they wouldn't stop glaring at her, how they shifted when she spoke, was positively frightening.

I felt that chill again, like a warning.

"They want to kill her," Ellie said.

"They do. They would if they could get away with it."

She nodded. "Listen for her carefully."

Yes. I would listen for the Sabonis family gift, completely scientifically inexplicable, but there. I would listen for Valerie in my head.

I actually shivered, the snake back, cruising up and down my spine, the gun-toting, weasel-trapping, tobacco-spitting Barton family reverberating with hate and violence.

Ellie squeezed my hand. "I have a feeling we're going to hear from her."

"Me too."

"Good God," Ellie murmured.

Ellie and I went to Valerie's house for dinner, at her invitation. "I need my sisters," she told us. I could see why after the Barton family freak show.

Valerie's house is like a rainbow. Color everywhere. Stuff everywhere.

We walked in, pulled out the wine and flowers we brought, and Kai and the kids arrived with pizza.

"We ordered your favorites, Aunt Toni and Aunt Ellie," Ailani said, her braids flying as she ran in.

"Pep e zonni," Koa said, jumping up and down. He was wearing a monster hat with red horns. It's fun to be three years old. "And we got big salamis."

"You got us some big salamis?" I asked.

"Yes!" Koa jumped again. "I got a big salami! Daddy got a big salami. See?" He pointed at the salami on the pizza. "We got big salamis."

Kai grinned. He was wearing a red flowered Hawaiian shirt. I was always struck by the difference to his captain's uniform. "Why does this kid tell all my secrets?" He pulled Valerie straight into his arms and kissed her. "Want to see my big salami, sweetheart?"

Koa clapped his hands. "You eat the big salami, Momma, eat it!"

Too, too funny.

"Yum," my sister said. "This big salami is delicious." Kai laughed and kissed her again.

We poured wine and milk and we all clinked our glasses together. "To Family," we cheered. "To the Kozlovskys." Bottoms up.

During dinner Ailani whined to Ellie and me, "Mom said I can't come to watch her trial."

"That's something you can skip," I said. "It's boring. Plus, you have school." What I was really thinking was, *Heck, no. You are not going anywhere near the Barton family. They do not need to know Valerie has a kid.*

Ailani sighed and flipped back her black braids, so dramatic. Then she fiddled with her widow's peak, like her mother does. "But school is boring. Math. Reading. Writing. I want to learn about forensics."

Forensics? From any other ten-year-old kid, that would be an impressive word, but I wasn't surprised with Ailani.

"I am also working on an important project," she said.

"What is your project?" Ellie asked.

Ailani opened a blue folder. "I'm taking the fingerprints of every kid in the fifth grade. See? The fingerprints are right there, and Mom gave me a camera. Old camera. You snap the picture and out comes the photo. After I do their fingerprints, I put their picture above it." She scowled. "Some of these kids, like Caleb, see, he didn't take the picture part seriously. That's why he's making a funny face." She turned the page and her face scowled further. "And see this girl, Annalise? I don't like her. She had to brush her hair and put on lipstick before I took her picture. People should take crimes seriously. It's not a beauty competition."

"But your friends haven't committed a crime, have they?" Ellie asked.

"No, *not yet*," she stressed, contemplating that boring fact. "But they *could* in the future, and that's why I need them to be serious when I take their picture for the mug shot."

"This kid looks serious." I tapped a boy's picture.

"That's Alex!" She stomped her foot. So irritating! "He's always smiling and laughing, and when he made a frowny face for his picture everyone thought it was funny. It's not funny. Crime isn't funny."

"I think you're going to make an excellent detective or attorney or forensic scientist, Ailani," Ellie said.

"Me too," she said. "And I take crime seriously!" She made a *humph* sound. "I need to take your fingerprints, Aunt Toni. You too, Aunt Ellie. Anyone can be pushed to commit a crime at any time. You never know. Squish your fingers into the ink. . . ."

We let her take our fingerprints and our photos. Ellie and I did our best to take our crime seriously. Later that night, when everyone else was in bed, Valerie, Ellie, and I sat on the back deck, on the stairs, together. We held hands.

Listen for me.

"We will," Ellie and I told Valerie.

A week later the Hooters of Homes and Gobblers of Gardens team moved to a corner of the building, third floor, wraparound windows. We put a long table in the center, where many of us worked together, our desks around the edges. The light was better, it was quieter, we laughed a lot. We put a table out for coffee, tea, treats. We added plants and flowers, and the area was soon taken up with photos of homes and gardens, the pages of the magazine, paperwork, and the rest of the mess one makes when working for a newspaper.

I liked it.

For the first time in a long time I felt happy about going to work.

I resisted going out with my husband, Marty, at first, even after he karate chopped my stalker, but he was getting increasingly irresistible.

Marty read my work in the alternative newspaper, then he read my work in the *Oregon Standard* when I changed papers. He commented on it. Asked me questions. Told me about his work, his patients. He was funny. I always, always laughed with Marty.

About a foot taller than me, he made me feel dwarfed, but not in an intimidating way. As my mother said, there was some resemblance to a blue heron in his strength, confidence, and elegance.

When he asked me to go with him to a play, I said no.

A concert? No again.

Dinner? Lunch?

No, no.

A hike?

Nope.

A kayak ride?

He got me there.

I said yes.

Marty loved kayaking. He had kayaked all over the country. It was his one hobby. I had never kayaked. We went on a tame kayak ride in the Willamette River. I was scared. He was confident. I fretted. He smiled. I told him I didn't think I could do it. He said, I bet you can. I said, I'm afraid I'll drown like a rat. He said, that's what the life jacket's for. I said, I'm afraid I'll end up alone, downriver. He said, I'll be right beside you. I said, this boat wobbles. He said, let me show you how to paddle.

I loved it. I loved being in the water.

That first day we pulled our kayaks ashore, laughing, and had a picnic. I had tipped mine over only once, right after we'd pushed off. I was soaked, and he was soaked, as he'd done what he'd said he would do and he'd jumped in and helped me.

At the picnic, he made me laugh. I made him laugh. We talked and talked.

He kept smiling that smile at me, and I smiled right back.

After our first kayaking date, Marty sent a bouquet of flowers with a small kayak stuck in the middle. We went kayaking again. And again.

I know now that one of the reasons I pushed Marty away was because my self-esteem was somewhere around floor level. I had anger, grief, and fear issues trailing after me like an axe-wielding ghost from Moscow. I saw myself as someone who still didn't fit in, a Russian immigrant, so I faked it behind my armor of stylish clothes and my career. I didn't like myself a whole lot and I continued to make mistakes, in particular with partying and men, which kept my self-esteem at floor level.

Marty was, in my mind, so much better than me. He had been born in the United States, in Oregon, and he had always felt like he fit in. He had gone to a prestigious college and med school. He was an oncologist. He was gregarious and funny. Everyone liked him.

I was quieter, and I liked to be alone to think, to wrestle with the ghost from Moscow. Too many people around for too long, too much noise, and I had to back away and hide. I had a rougher edge. I was sarcastic and would not back down from a fight.

But Marty made me feel special. He made me think I was an equal to him, when I didn't feel that way at all. He made me laugh. He made me put aside that rampant toughness. I learned to trust him. I didn't see him anymore as an intimidating, dedicated, and brilliant doctor, though I knew he was. I saw him as Marty.

I said, "I think you're too smart for me."

He said, "I was thinking the same about you, for me. Not sure if I can keep up with you, Toni. I read everything you write. Your last story on those kids whose parents were arrested and their journey through foster care was one of the best articles I have read in my life. Probably the best. It made me cry."

I said, "I don't go to church willingly. Only when my parents guilt me into going."

He said, "I find God in nature. I think God can be found in how we treat other people. How we live, how we give. Right now I would like to give you a date where we could go to dinner."

I said, "I'm moody. I need my space."

He said, "I like people with emotions. I like complicated people. I'll give you space. I like your independence. Just don't get so independent you don't want to go kayaking with me."

I said, "I don't trust people easily."

He said, "Give me time, Toni. Please. I am trustworthy, and I will earn your trust, if you let me."

I said, finally, "A lot happened in Russia to us. I still think about it. It's hard to get past."

He said, "You've made it clear that you don't want to talk about it, but I'd like to hear about it when you want to tell me. I would like to help you get past it."

"I'm not a kind person like you."

He laughed. "You are one of the kindest people I know. I see kindness in how you treat your parents. I see kindness in your friendship with your sisters. I see kindness in your writing. I see kindness when you let me hang out with you. Which, I hope, will be more often. Do you take chocolate bribes?"

It was then that I thought . . . yes. Yes to Marty.

9

"I take a platter off the wall when I need it for dinner."

I looked around Bevvie Kearns's home. I was featuring it for *Homes and Gardens of Oregon* because of her extensive collection of painted, ceramic platters. The home was about 1,500 square feet and had been built in 1940.

There was a distinct and charming resemblance to Snow White's house, only the roof was not thatched and there were no dwarves. There was an arc separating the dining and family room, built-in shelves, a built-in desk, wide white trim, stained glass windows on either side of the brick fireplace, and old wood floors that had felt many generations of feet.

Bevvie was about fifty. She'd told me she was half Japanese and half African American, "with a smattering of Dutch." Glasses. Smart.

"You take the ceramic platters off the wall," I clarified, "use them to serve meals, then you hang them back up." I knew the photographer from *Homes and Gardens of Oregon* would have a field day. The platters were hand-painted with English villages, elegant gardens, Scottish clansmen in kilts, landscapes, farms, charming cottages, bridges and rivers, bouquets, etc. So refined. So genteel.

"Yes. As you can see I have a tiny obsession here."

"Not obsessive." The platters were floor to ceiling in some places. "Okay, I'll agree. But it's an attractive obsession."

Bevvie then began to regale me with stories about each platter. Where she got it, who painted it, how old it was, etc. I was so filled with platter information, my brain was combusting as my hand flew across my notebook.

"You have to keep a hand out, don't you?" Bevvie asked.

"I'm sorry?"

"We keep a hand out to help others. That's why we had Da here."

"Da?" We were off topic. Had I missed something under the deluge of platter information?

"Yes, this platter"—Bevvie stood and took a platter off the wall—"was given to me by a woman who ran the international medical foster care program at the local hospital. She knew I loved platters from other countries. This one is of a village in Vietnam.

"My husband and I are international medical foster parents. Kids come here from all over the world to get treatment. We volunteer to take care of them when they're in and out of the hospital, take them to their appointments to see the doctors, then help them recover and recuperate after the operations. Da was from Vietnam. A land mine blew the lower half of his right leg clear off. I'm sure he was within an inch of death. He was here to get a new prosthetic at the hospital on the hill."

"How old was Da?"

"Eight. A precious and precocious child. Here's a photo of him with my husband and me."

I saw a smiling Vietnamese child. Bevvie blinked her eyes and two tears fell on the photo, which she brushed away quickly. "Silly me. Getting so upset still."

"He's a handsome boy."

"Yes, he is. So sweet." Her hands tightened on the photo. "Who does things like this? Who manufactures land mines? Who lays them out? They know the mines will blow people apart. Pure evil. Billions made every year on weapons designed to kill people. So many people, making money blowing off the legs of children like Da."

"It's tragic. It's hard to even get your mind around it, isn't it?"

"Oh, I can't. I know what a child who is missing half a leg looks like. I know their struggles."

"How long was Da here?"

"Six months. He had an infection, so he ended up here longer. We loved Da." Her eyes filled with tears. "Da loved the platters. He wanted to draw them so he could remember us, so we bought him three drawing pads and he drew every day. He drew most of the platters that I have, one on each sheet of paper. That child never complained about his life.

"He asked to live with us forever. I will tell you, Toni, it broke my heart when we had to return him. We gave him three platters to take home. He had the platters in front of him, clutched in his little hands when he left. I'll never forget his tears hitting the platters. Plink, plink, plink, that's how it went.

"When the kids are here, getting their treatment, every night, they can choose which platter to take off the wall to eat off of. Believe it or not, they love it."

"I'm sure they do." I dabbed at my eyes with a napkin. I am a sap.

"These platters have so many memories for me."

She reached out and held my hand and we studied her platters, together, as she thought of the kids she'd held out a hand to. Undoubtedly, they had held her hand as firmly as she was now holding mine.

Ricki called me later that night after I'd e-mailed her the story. "Read the story on Da. Shoot and blither blather. Made me cry. Why do you do stuff like that?"

"I like to smear your makeup."

"You're doing it." She hung up after a honking sniffle.

"You are now the hosting... the hosty... what the word? I forget. Wait. I know it!" My mother snapped her fingers. "You are the ho." She pulled out red and yellow mixing bowls from her kitchen cabinets. "You are the bossy of Elvira's bridal bath shower. I don't want no shower at all, but if there is one, you do it, Antonia. You the ho."

"I'm the what?" I'm the ho? I had to push my laughter down to my toes. My mother does not like to be laughed at when she uses the wrong English words.

I picked up my coffee mug off the train station table. Whew. Strong enough to dissolve my intestines, but delicious. I popped a miniature chocolate fudge cookie into my mouth. My mother always serves coffee with her chocolate fudge cookies. She does this at the restaurant, too. People love it. They sit at the bar and instead of ordering martinis and vodka tonics they order "Svetlana's Bitter Russian Coffee and Sweet Chocolate Cookies."

"You have the shower party," my mother said, pointing at me. She turned and grabbed flour and brown sugar from her blue armoire. "For Elvira. For the family and the friends. The womens only. I cannot believe this." She crossed herself. "Mary, mother of God, who did not get enough credit for her sacrifice, how this happen? My daughter, she be marrying a nonrusseman. You remember I make that word up myself?"

"I remember. Mama, about the bridal shower. You know Aunt Holly and Aunt Polina don't like each other currently."

"Yes. I know this. I live it. It is like keeping two, how you say it, dragons apart. Dragons. With too many hormonies. In them. Hormonies."

"They do have hormones."

"Menopausie. They have it. They both sweat like this." She mimicked rain running down her face. "Night time they tell me, sleeping in a pool of the sweat. I never have that because your papa and I . . ." She banged her fists together. "You see, if you have lots of that love make then you don't have the hormonies and the hottie flashes."

"I don't need to hear about you and Papa, Mama." I ate another chocolate fudge cookie in one bite.

"What? Not wrong have the love make with your husband. All the time you can do it, God says so. In the Bible, He says it. I tell Holly and Polina when they say they have the hormonies, go home and do the bang bang with your husband more and get rid of it. See here." She swept her hand down her body, from the white streak down to her legs. "He cannot stay away and I have no menopausie."

"And Anya and JJ aren't speaking. Again."

"Ack. What now, I ask. What problem is there? But no!" She put both hands up. "Don't tell me. I no want to know."

I wouldn't tell her that Anya was mad at JJ for trying to "take over the bridal shower in her pushy, shovy way. Like a disease," and JJ was mad at Anya for "thinking she could do Ellie's bridal shower. What are we going to do if Anya does it? Play Trivial Pursuit—the hypochondriac's version? Maybe we could talk about strange African sicknesses? Will we have to sanitize the cake with hand sanitizer?"

Tati and Zoya were so mad at JJ and Anya for wanting to do the bridal shower, they said they would never give them lingerie again. That was a low blow, we all agreed.

"Mama, you want me to have the bridal shower on my tugboat?"

"Yes. You do it. You have wide deck. Ladies get too upset, they can jump in river. Or I shove them. Like this." She mimed a shove. "I know, my honey, this hard for you." She took hold of my face and kissed both cheeks. "I kiss your cheekies with my love. Please? For your Mama. Then, all the fighty stop."

"Okay, Mama. I'll do it." My heart twisted up, tight and lonely. I tried to block out another memory.

"It hurts you, I see this, but you see, Elvira, your Ellie, she love you, and Valeria, your Valerie, two kids, and she not . . . uh uh uh. She not right woman to plan bridal bath shower. You know. She take out wallet, say meet at this bar, and I buy the drinkies and food. No!" My mother made the sign with both hands that all umpires make when a player is safe. "We use china. Silver. Proper bridal bath shower for my Elvira, even though he a nonrusseman."

"Silver. China. Sounds like Ellie."

"She no want any wild stuff. She not like that Zoya and Tati, bless them God, wearing lingerie for the shirties. No bars. No loud parties, no strip man. That no. And no drunk peoples. You are best friend to Elvira, so you do it, you hear her in your head, her words and the thoughts, then there peace."

"I'm happy to do it." I loved Ellie. "I'll make it perfect."

"Yes, I know. You be the ho at the party. That not right word, I think. The hosty. Everyone love you in the family. When it time, I see your invitation to the Elvira party by the mail, not the e-mail, not classy that e-mail, by the paper mail where the post-man, he brings it to you. I not happy about that nonrusseman but I help you with food. And I like game."

"Game?"

"Yes. I at bridal bath shower for Linda's daughter, Abigail." My mother clapped her hands. "We play silly game. With prizes. Me, I won apron with flowers. That right for my cooking. See? I wear it now. So game at the party bridal. A lot of game. And the prizes. You do this, Antonia." She hugged me close. "You my angel, Antonia. You always been my angel. We been through the bad times together, bad times." Her eyes flooded with tears, so mine did, too. We both knew what she was talking about, but we didn't talk about it. "You and I, daughter and mother, we have our love."

"I know, Mama."

"Now. You not cry." She wiped my tears. "My brave girl. My dear and courage wolf girl. No, not wolf girl. Werewolves, I tell you about those werewolves in the Soviet Union."

"Human werewolves."

"Yes. Them. From the prison." Her expression changed, soft-ness to hellfire in a second. "I hope they rot for what they did to my Alexei, my love."

"Yes, Mama, me too."

She inhaled, a full breath, bosom rising and falling. "I leave those bad werewolves in the past. The past is past. We not talk about it." She waved a hand, *swish swish*, Moscow go away. "Your papa home soon. You stay for dinner."

I had dinner with my parents that night. My father hugged me tight. "Tell me everything, Antonia. I have not seen you for a week. So, you start on Thursday. What you do at work on Thursday . . . okay, now Friday? You went out to *The Barber of*

Seville? With Boris? Beautiful opera. He steal car on way home? No. I like hear that. No need you in the jail. Now, Saturday. What you do?"

My parents listened intently, day by day. My father once said, "No detail in my daughters' lives is too small for me to hear." I asked them about their lives, too, repeatedly. They always turned it back to me.

"And what about that scary man on the dock?" my mother said. "You know, I think he sell the drugs."

"I told you, he doesn't sell drugs, Mama. I've told you that he arrests people who sell drugs. He does not do drugs."

"He not scary," my father said, patting my mother's hand. "I talk to him. I like him."

"He rough man. I know. I live in Soviet Union."

"Svetlana, I tell you," my father said. "I like Nick Sanchez. I know the men. How they are here." He tapped his head. "And here." He tapped his heart. "And he the winner. He a man. Man for you, Antonia?"

I about choked on yet another chocolate fudge cookie.

Before I could answer, my mother reached across the table and held my hand. "I believe my Alexei. He so smart. Don't be scared, Antonia. We here for you always."

"I'm not scared." *Oh, yes, I was. Many things scared me.*

"No. You not scared," my parents said together.

"I'm fine." *Sure I am.*

"Yes, yes, you fine," my parents said again, reassuring. "You fine."

I wasn't so fine and they knew it. That's why they gave me extra-long hugs and my mother sent me home with a box of leftovers and a bag of her chocolate fudge cookies, which I ate later in my bathtub. If she didn't, in her mind, the possibility of my starving to death by noon tomorrow was high.

Later that night I went out to my deck, slung my feet over the side, and watched my blue heron take off. I rarely see her at night. Dixie was alone.

"*You the ho!*" I said out loud. I had to laugh. I am the bridal shower ho. What an honor.

"Stay the night, Toni."

I snuggled back in, naked back to Nick's naked chest in his king-sized bed. Tempting. It was Saturday night. I could sleep in here.

"Five minutes," I told him, my voice quiet in the darkness of his bedroom, the river hugging his houseboat.

"How about nine hours?"

"No."

His arm was heavy over me. Nick is a muscled man. He was warm. He was comforting. He was protective. When I was with him, I could forget. Until the guilt hit and sent me into a tail-spin.

I had brought my mother's meat and vegetable pie over. On the Specials board it was listed as "You Eat, Trust Me." Meat and vegetable pie sounds terrible, but as soon as customers try it, they love it. I also brought chocolate cake. My mother called it "Alexei Sexy Chocolate Cake." I knew I'd get calls about my sexy father the next day.

"I'll make you an omelet in the morning if you stay."

"I can't."

"You won't."

"Don't bug me about this, Nick. I've told you, from the start, that I don't want this to be anything more than what it is." Man, I sounded cold.

"You did tell me that."

"So live with it." Freezing.

"I'm trying. It's tough."

"You're a tough man. You can do it." Hypothermic.

I moved to get up, though I didn't want to. He flexed and held me down, then lifted his arm when I pushed again, and sighed. I am not modest and I did not care that he was watching me, that I was naked, and I was getting dressed in front of him.

I bit down on my lip so I didn't cry. I pulled on my jeans, my knee-high black boots, a black tank top, and my lacy, black hippie style blouse over it.

I looked down at Nick before I left. He was sitting up in bed, his hands together. He stared back at me.

I blinked, then left. I heard him get out of bed and pull on jeans.

"You don't have to walk me home."

"Yes, I do."

I walked down the dock. I heard Nick behind me. I kept my footsteps quiet, though I knew the neighbors knew that I slept with Nick. I didn't care that they knew. I have been through too much to care what anyone thinks of me, ever, but I didn't want to wake people up, either.

"Good night, Toni."

I didn't answer. I was mad at him. Mad because Nick was pushing me to a place I couldn't go.

I took a shower, showering off Nick, while I thought of Marty.

Then Nick's and Marty's faces blurred, and Nick's became clear and Marty's faded, which made me feel awful.

I wrapped myself in a towel and went outside, in the rain, opened the kayak house, and sat in our two-seater. I listened to the water hit the roof.

"This dress looks like toilet paper." Ellie lifted the skirt of the fluffy white wedding dress.

"Yes, it does," Valerie said. "Unraveled toilet paper."

"It's not quite you," I said.

"I can't believe," my mother whispered, *loudly,* sitting beside me in a blue lacy dress and pearls. "She marry a Italian. Not a Russian. She marry nonrusseman. I make that word up. I make this word up, too: badchoicey. It one word." She held up one finger. "More efficient."

The four of us were in a bridal salon in downtown Portland. It was lush. Whites and pinks. Mirrors everywhere so brides could lose their frazzled minds while staring at themselves from three directions.

"It looks like you could take it apart sheet by sheet and use it in the bathroom," Valerie said.

"Do you have to be so blunt, Valerie?" I asked.

"I like honesty."

"Honesty can be combined with kindness, creepo."

"What about this one? Mermaid style, satin train." The shop assistant, a woman in her twenties, held up a dress. She looked exhausted, hair falling out of her bun, shirt slightly untucked, mascara smearing. We'd been there for two hours.

"I don't think so . . ." Ellie said. She took a paper bag out of her purse and blew into it.

My mother threw up her hands. "What? You no like that one, either, Elvira?"

"What about the silky one you tried on earlier, sewn by La-Toine, with the scalloped hem?" the assistant asked, only slightly pale. "You looked like a princess."

"That was a gorgeous dress," Valerie said. "But you looked bad in it."

"Valerie. Come on," I said, getting ticked. "You're not helping."

"I help," my mother whispered, again, *loudly*. "I take her away. Morning of wedding. Kidnap Elvira. You come, too, Antonia. You be quickie at kidnapping, that what I think."

"No," Valerie said. "I meant that the expression on Ellie's face was bad, like this." Valerie rolled her blue eyes back in her head, her body went slack, her tongue slipped out of her mouth and she made gagging noises. "You didn't look happy in it."

"I wasn't happy in it. I'm not a princess," Ellie said, semi-gasping. "I think it's ridiculous for women to want to resemble a spoiled, entitled, elitist princess on their wedding day, happy to have a man whisk her and her flighty brain off to a drafty castle and slay the dragons. I can slay the dragons myself."

"We were never princesses growing up," I said. "I admired the witches more. Clever and temperamental."

"Pickpocketers weren't allowed in the princess category," Valerie said.

My mother cringed. I cringed. I don't like the word "pickpocketers" used near my mother. It brings up a riptide of pain and yet another family secret.

"I refuse to buy into this whole fairy tale idea," Ellie said. "I do not want a prince to ride up on his white horse, or a Porsche, and rescue me. I can rescue myself. I don't want his castle. I have my own. It's a home by the river." She stopped to wheeze into the bag. "I don't need protection from him, I have a gun. I am not a mindless princess, grateful to be entering into a relationship of sexism and servitude. I'm a woman who can stand for herself."

The shop assistant, poor thing, not expecting such an anti-princess tirade, halfheartedly held up another white dress, plunging neckline. "This elegant design is by Perunia. Beading hand sewn. Not princess-y at all. Modern. Sleek. For a woman who knows her own power."

"You've got the figure for that one," Valerie said. "I wish I had your body, Ellie, I do. Boobs and butt and a skinny waist. I would kill you but I won't because I know how much time you have to spend in jail nowadays for murder."

"Do we have to talk about murder when she's trying to find a wedding dress?" I pulled on Valerie's hair, lightly. I didn't try to yank it out of her head.

"My daughters!" my mother said, disapproving, mouth tight. "Valeria be with the criminals and throws them in the jail and always talks blood. Another one marries a Italian and cannot breathe without bag. And the oldest one, she live on a tugboat. Like she a sailor. Too skinny sailor!" She eyed my disappointing figure. "I always say to you three: Put on the lipstick and earrings before you leave the house unless the house on fire. But no! Sometimes, no lipstick, no earrings. That's not right for lady."

"Okay, Ellie," I said, ignoring my mother because I needed out of that shop. "Of all the dresses you tried on, narrow it to three that you like."

She couldn't think of even one she liked.

"What about this one?" the assistant said, picking up one

dress, then another, eyes glazed. "Or this one . . . you seemed to like the Italian lace on the skirt here, it adds a whimsical flair . . . this exquisite strapless gown with the satin piping enhances the bustline . . . the glittering rhinestone belt offers a touch of glitter and glam . . ."

"No . . ." Ellie said. "No . . . not that one . . . too fluffy . . . too loud . . . too intricate . . . I'm too fat for that one . . . don't like the neckline . . . not that one, either." She took another drag on her bag and flopped down, like a rag doll. Anxiety attacks are exhausting.

"What is it, Ellie?" I asked.

"I am having a hard time envisioning myself walking down an aisle, clinging to Papa's arm because, by tradition, he is giving me away. I can't stand that concept. No one gives me away. I won't give myself away. What I'm doing is getting married, not handing myself over like a cow to its new owner. I'm supposed to squish myself into a white dress, which traditionally is supposed to symbolize virginity, though I am not a virgin, and I think it's ridiculous that society would value virginity anyhow. We should always value women on their character and personality, not on their hymen. So the color white is bugging me."

"Maybe you should wear another color," Valerie said.

"If I wore what I wanted to wear, it would be purple, as that is my favorite color."

"Wear purple," Valerie and I said.

"*Purple?*" My mother threw her hands in the air, eyes wide, oh, the horrors of it all. "For the wedding dress?"

"Gino would have a fit." Ellie put the bag back to her mouth.

"That's a bad sign right there," I said.

"Man, I need a shot of vodka," Valerie said. "At home. Not here. I have my car. You three should come to my house and get drunk after this. We could have so much fun."

"I don't like hangovers," I said. "I find them depressing."

"Brave it, Toni. So, Ellie, what'll it be? You have to tell us before our saleslady hides in the back room and starts slamming straight shots."

"I won't—" The saleslady's expression changed. "Well, I might...."

"I don't like any of them," Ellie said. "I'm sorry. I don't." She lay down on the floor of the shop with her bag and closed her eyes. "Reach within yourself for your personal truth, Ellie," she singsonged. "Be with your body, not your mind...go to a meadow, a lake...breathe a gentle spirit into your true self and be one with nature and your organic identity..."

"How about be honest with yourself, smart one?" Valerie said.

My mother, in a state, stood up, marched over to her prone and chanting daughter, and put one leg on either side of her. "See? What I say?" She bent down to make her point with Ellie. "I have daughter with bag on face. What I done wrong? What happen? This black magic curse because of the Italian stallion."

"This isn't about the dress," I muttered.

"Duh, Sherlock," Valerie said. "It's about the nonrusseman."

"She made that word up," I said.

"I know. Impressive," Valerie said. "More efficient."

My mother unceremoniously flipped Ellie over and smacked her on the butt. Twice.

"Ow!" Ellie said. "Ow!"

"You get yourself together, bag daughter. I not leave Soviet Union so you marry Italian who you no can breathe around."

I slipped the saleslady a large tip and we left, Ellie leaning heavily on my arm.

"If you can't breathe around a wedding dress, it's probably a sign," Valerie said.

"Shut up, Valerie," Ellie said. Bag inflated, bag deflated....

"Hello, Daisy." I fell into step beside my neighbor on the dock. "You're off early this morning."

"That I am. I saw you crying in your kayak. Poor lady. Sad. I'm going duck hunting. I'll bring you home a duck so you'll feel better." Her white curls bopped about under a green hat with a yellow duck on it. A necklace of fake white daisies hung to her waist.

"Duck hunting?" Oh, that was bad, bad, bad. She was not carrying a visible rifle, though.

"Yes. I've got my duck hat on and my duck galoshes."

Her galoshes were pink with white ducks, and she did have a hat on with a yellow plastic duckie on the brim. The hat had fake pink daisies stapled to it.

"And I'm wearing duck underwear. I had Georgie find them for me. He had to order them on the computer thingie." She pulled up her skirt. Indeed, there were two yellow duckies on her bottom, which she let me see by bending over.

"Those are friendly ducks, Daisy." I pictured Georgie, tall and menacing, searching for duck panties for his mother online. I tried not to laugh.

"I can have him get you some, if you'd like."

"Thank you. I appreciate that." I had to say yes. The thought of Georgie, aka Slash, buying me duck panties was too precious to give up.

"Quack and quack. How's your shot? Mine is ducking perfect. It's from the Bad Years." She pointed a fake rifle at the sky and shot it off. "I had to kick Georgie and Skippy's dad out when they were little ducklings. He beat me with his wings. Walked in the door one time, drunk as a snake on snake oil, and I pulled up my rifle and pointed it at his ducking head. I told him, 'You son of a female dog. I didn't get married so I could get beaten up twice a week. Now take your sagging butt and your orangutan face and get out.'"

Daisy's memories of the past are often much more clear than those of today or yesterday. "What did he do?"

"He argued. Said he would change. I'd heard that before, so I told him he had had seven years to change, then I shot at him."

"Did you hit him?" I could see her burying the body.

"No, I missed on purpose. Couldn't go to jail, what about my two small ducklings? Skippy and Georgie, what would they do without me? He took off running, quacking. We never saw him again. But I needed money, needed a business, or I'd lose our home. In those days, women were supposed to stay home and take care of ducklings. But not me. I started buying the moon, the sun, and the earth, and I was in business."

"How much was the moon?"

"Expensive. But I had money squirreled away in a hole in the wall, like nuts. So I bought the moon, then got the sun at half price, and the earth I bought from a friend when he had to get out of town fast on account of a killer chasing him down. He owed the head duck a lot of money, but I didn't."

She pulled out a pink, plastic toy gun from her purse, aimed at a duck in the sky, and pulled the trigger. Then she searched the sky, twirling in a circle, to see if a duck was falling through the clouds. No duck. "Bad shot. I'll try again."

"Bye, Daisy."

"Bye, honey." She shot off her gun again.

The next morning I had a cake—white frosting, with a yellow duck—on my front porch. Daisy might call herself Crazy Daisy, but she still had the same generous heart she'd had forever.

Putting together a magazine, inside a newspaper, once a week, is a ton of work. Everyone has to get their stories in on time, written right. The stories are checked and rechecked by the copy editors and Ricki. The photographer has to get photo shoot assignments, and the photos have to come in with the right lighting and composition. The design people have to lay it all out, headlines must be written, the ads have to be added in, and the cover has to be designed, with the "tempting titles," as I call them, on the cover so people will want to open the magazine.

"We want to inform, educate, and entertain," Ricki said to all of us in a short meeting. "Don't screw this up. It's gotta be friggin' beautiful. Write like your butt is on fire."

I felt myself smile more the longer I was away from crime, criminals, and the justice system. Writing about homes, home décor, and remodeling projects is simply . . . more joyful. Easier. I liked the group of ladies I was working with. Yes, all women, except for the photographer. Ricki said, "Someone could smash my ass for only hiring women, but hell, men did it for hundreds of years. Who are they to whine? Besides, the women were all far better candidates than the men. Bring on the estrogen, leave home the testosterone."

We moved fast, without ego. We worked together, efficiently, friendly.

We worked long hours.

Our meetings were quick. We e-mailed extensively.

I actually started to get excited. I was helping to launch a homes and gardens magazine.

It was fun.

That work could now be slotted into the "fun" category was a revelation. Amazing what happens when bullets and knife wounds are no longer a part of your daily life.

I wrote my first column, on my tugboat, in bed, starting at ten one night. It was my goal to have at least five in the pipeline before we launched. I didn't know what the title would be, so I wrote, "What will the title be?"

What Will the Title Be?

BY TONI KOZLOVSKY

I live on a yellow tugboat in the Willamette River.

My tugboat, in its former life, used to haul barges filled with timber, grain, sand, gravel, and larger boats. I bought it from a friend of my father, Captain Petey, who used to own it.

It's about a thousand square feet total, three stories. I had the whole thing remodeled. I kept the original interior where I could, but some was rotted out and some had mold, and those parts had to go.

From my back deck, I watch Dixie, my blue heron, as she soars and glides. Anonymous, a bald eagle, visits, but not often enough, hence the name. A golden eagle named Maxie makes an appearance now and then. There are two beavers, Big Teeth and Big Tooth, who are building a new home, and a number of river otter swim around, so I call all of them Sergeant Ott.

I've added a bedroom next to the second-floor crew quarters. The crew quarters are now my closet. I've added a kitchen with blue cabinets and a bathroom with a claw-foot tub. The previous bathroom looked like, well, like men had been living on the tugboat for twenty-five years.

I had a bench built in the wheelhouse so I can search for shooting stars at night and watch the moon change color during fall. Chairs and tables on my decks let me live outside as much as possible.

I moved to my tugboat after a hard time in my life. I needed new, different. I needed change. I'm glad I moved, especially when the sun comes up, wrapped in hazy purples and blues, and when I return from my chaotic job in the city, I can sit and watch the river. Pizza tastes better eating it by a river.

Do I think I'll stay here forever? No, I don't.

But I love it for now. I love living in nature. I love living on the river and drinking coffee from my decks.

Some people stay in the same home for years, decades even. Others move every few years. Some homes call to us; some homes don't ever seem to fit and we're glad when we move.

Sometimes a home is suffused with memories, by the neighbors and friends we meet, by the children we have who run down the hallway and tackle the dog. Sometimes we're simply passing through, a waiting spot, until we get our life back together and we move on.

I think a home, though, no matter what phase of life we're in, should be a place of peace. A place of joy, a place where you can hide out and be alone and think, a place for you and your spouse or partner, your kids and the pets. A place for lasagna, beer, or ice-cream sundaes. A place where there's color and light, organization and cleanliness, your favorite treasures next to your favorite mixing bowls.

Welcome to *Homes and Gardens of Oregon,* where we'll be talking about homes and how to make them beautiful and peaceful, true to you and your life.

And welcome to this column, which I will be writing from my yellow tugboat.

We hope you like it.

Ricki called me the next morning. I was on my way out to interview two sisters who had designed their home to look like a hobbit home. I had caught a glimpse of two Sergeant Otts swimming by. They stared right at me and I waved. I had also seen, on the far bank, Big Tooth the beaver. Lucky morning.

"I am bustin' my mind, lovin' your first column. Personal, lets the reader get to know you, to know us, we're not a corporation, we're fun, high-heel-wearing women and we have someone quirky and odd who lives on a tugboat. Zippy awesome job, Toni, and I love all the photos of the tugboat that Stefano took. We'll have you write the captions when we get it laid out."

"Thank you."

"Did Stefano take your head shot? We'll put it in the corner of each column. What's the title of your home column?"

"I don't know."

"Think quickly. Kim's calling her column 'Gardener's Delight.'"

"How about 'Living on a Tugboat, Talking About Homes.'"

"Wet. Strange. Doesn't Fit. It's fantastic. We'll use it. See ya tomorrow. Ten o'clock meeting. Meetings will never be before ten. I don't want to see anyone before nine. It should be illegal to start working before nine. Too early for sanity. Bye."

She hung up.

* * *

The dad, mom, and kids were inside the garage of the white house with the red door. The boys were jumping up and down, tossing a ball over the kayak; the mother was sanding it; and the dad had a hammer.

They were a happy family with a kayak.

I tried to buck up before my tears blinded me.

"She's pr—"

"What?" Ellie, Valerie, and I asked at the same time.

"My daughter is . . ." Our cousin JJ clutched her throat.

"Here, wine," Valerie said, filling her glass and pushing it across my dining room table. Outside it was raining, the drops slashing against the windows of my tugboat, the wind whipping around the corners.

"She's pregnant!" JJ howled, then covered her mouth with both hands, as if she wanted to shove the words back inside. She opened up her hands, like a book. "Pregnant. Knocked up." She closed her hands, opened them again. "A bun in the oven." Tears streamed from her eyes.

My sisters and I didn't move. We were three shocked sister statues.

JJ opened her hands/book again. "A baby." Hands closed, keep those words in.

We three sister statues were speechless.

"She's expecting." JJ's voice cracked. She was losing it. "She's in a family way."

JJ's mascara was smeared down her cheeks.

"I'm sorry, JJ," I finally stuttered out. I thought of her daughter, Chelsea. Black dyed hair. Black eye shadow. Black fingernails. Black clothes, black leather. Drummer in a rock band with other teenagers. She snuck into clubs. She snuck out of the house at night. She snuck into bars. She hid joints in her jewelry box.

As JJ had told me, "Chelsea needs a chastity belt and a leash. The leash needs to be wrapped around her neck and locked to a load-bearing wall in my house so she can't escape at night."

"That is bad news," Valerie finally said.

"I know, I know!" JJ drank an entire glass of wine, head slung

back. "Give me another glass of wine. Get the scotch out, Toni."
I gave her a straight shot of scotch. She tossed that back, too.

"How are you doing?" Ellie asked, which was a bit inane, because JJ was breaking down piece by piece, her hair a mess. If someone walked into her salon like that, she would shout at them, "Did you deliberately put your head in a weed whacker?"

"How am I doing?" she snapped. "I have a pregnant daughter. She is not out of high school. She is not married. She is a teenager. I am out of my head, that's how I'm doing." She slammed both hands on my table. "I am panicked. I am pissed. I am worried about her."

My sisters and I adored Chelsea. She was a rock-and-rolling rebel, but she was charming and smart and musical and loved us right back. She hugged us all the time. When she was a little girl, she would cry when we left and beg us to live with her.

"How is she feeling?" Ellie asked.

"She's hysterical. Scared to death. I thought I might kill her. I thought Jax was going to have a heart attack. He put ghosts to shame, he was so white. Jax and I have had two more dates where we pretend we don't know each other and meet at a bar and pick each other up, and things have been all hot and heavy again. I even wore a blond wig last time and now this! This! We are going to be grandparents. How do you pick up a grandfather at a bar?"

"I'll call Chelsea and tell her I love her," I said. As soon as I could get my mind around this.

"Me too," Valerie said. "I love Chelsea, that wildflower child."

"We'll support her," Ellie said. "Kozlovsky family, lots of love."

"Oh. My. God," JJ said. She put her refilled wineglass down too hard. I was surprised it didn't break. "Does no one listen to me? It's not Chelsea who's pregnant!"

"What are you talking about then?" I asked. "Who's pregnant?"

"Are you pregnant?" Ellie asked.

"You're pregnant again?" Valerie said, incredulous. "Now

that is a slip-up. You're pushing middle age and you're knocked up. Haven't Jax's sperm wings been clipped?"

"It's all those dates that she and Jax have been going on when they pretend they don't know each other and shack up for the night," I said, happy for JJ. "You got carried away and voila. A new Kozlovsky. Congratulations!" I held up my glass.

"It's not me!" JJ shouted. "It's *Hope*. Hope is pregnant."

What? *Hope?* My sisters and I were stunned down to our bones. Straight A student. AP classes. Played volleyball, basketball, ran track. The rain lashed the windows, streaming down.

"Yes. Hope. The academic star. The athlete. She's pregnant." JJ covered her head with her arms.

"You're kidding," I said.

"That can't be," Valerie said.

"How?" Ellie said.

"If you have to ask how Hope got pregnant, Ellie," JJ said, "you should not be getting married."

"I meant—"

"She meant," Valerie said. "Well, hell's bells, we were not expecting it to be Hope."

"No one did. But, she is, she is." JJ put her hands over her mouth, once again.

"Is she keeping the baby?" Valerie asked.

"Yes. She's keeping the baby," JJ said. "She's about six weeks along. She told me she already loves it."

We sat in that for a while. Teenagers should not be pregnant. It was a disaster. But there it was.

"Well, we all love Hope and we're all going to love the baby," I said.

"Yes, we are," Ellie and Valerie said.

"I wanted college for Hope, travel, a career. And now..." JJ cried and we hugged her, a four-way hug.

"She can still go to college," I said.

"It will be so much harder," JJ said.

"She can still travel," Ellie said.

"How? With a baby in her backpack?" JJ said.

"She can still have an exciting career," Valerie said.

"Let's be realistic. She's a teenager having a baby," JJ said. She rubbed her face. Exhausted. Devastated. "She's a mother. She has no husband. It's a wreck. The whole thing. A wreck."

Why pretend? Why be sickeningly positive, how irritating. Why try to gloss over it? We loved Hope, we would love the baby, but teenagers should not be pregnant.

"Here, have another straight shot, JJ," Ellie said. "I'll drive you home."

Off in the distance I heard thunder. Of all nights, thunder, as if on cue.

There was a lot of talk about Hope that next week within the Kozlovsky family. Tearful phone calls with JJ. Phone calls with other members of our family. Shock. Disappointment. More tears.

Jax was beside himself. "First he had to get his mind around his daughter having sex, his *little girl* having sex," JJ said, slamming down a shot of whiskey at the bar at Svetlana's Kitchen, "and now he has to get his mind around her being pregnant. His mind can't get around that, so it's about to combust."

My uncle Yuri and aunt Polina went to bed for the weekend, rocked off their feet. "First," Uncle Yuri said to me, calling me from bed, "it is the friendship, Antonia. You have to be the friends. Then you ask the parents, can we date? If the parents say yes, then the date. Parents come, too. No kissing. Then the kissing if the person is right for you. Then you ask the parents, can I marry your daughter? If they say yes, then the engagement. Only kissing. Then the wedding. Families come together as one family. Then the babies. Everyone happy. This not right order."

My aunt Polina took the phone from Uncle Yuri. "Baby in the baker, that's what they say here, right? A baby in the bun. She's knock-knock, right? This baby too soon in the bun. I cannot believe. Antonia, how this happen?"

But, as my father said at our next family gathering, a birthday party for my aunt Holly, where people were still reeling from the pregnancy, "All the babies—gifts. Some come earlier than we expect, no? But in this family, we love all the babies. We love Hope and we love the baby." He clasped his hands to-gether, then switched to Russian. "This is my final word for the family—for everyone—on this subject."

And so it was.

Poor Hope, she of the excellent grades and a bright future, she who had followed all the rules except for when it came to her boyfriend, Macky Talbot, sitting right next to her. She burst into tears.

Then the cousins started fighting over who was going to give her a baby shower.

And so it was.

We stopped the talking. Stopped the chatter. Let the shock go. These things happen. We are the Kozlovskys. We are a family. We are not perfect, have never tried to be, have never pretended to be.

10

Nick calls me about once a day. He wants to chat, say hello, see how I'm doing. Or he'll text. Sometimes he'll ask what I'm doing that night, or he'll now and then suggest meeting downtown for a date, which I don't accept, or he'll ask about an article I'm writing, see how a meeting went that I had previously mentioned.

I like talking to Nick. I like hearing what he's doing—as much as he can tell me. Most of the time he's the top guy running the undercover drug operation, which sounds mind-numbingly stressful to me, especially when he's working to bring down the big guns where the busts end up in the paper.

Sometimes he's asked to help with a coworker's operation. He buys, sells, and moves drugs and helps to facilitate, transport, and launder money to build cases against the drug dealers he works with. He's on the ground working and sometimes in trucks and airplanes.

Nick initially works with the smaller dealers, through a contact and introduction, often through an informer, then finds out who is above them, and above them. The goal is to get to the top of the drug pyramid and bring down the whole cartel, gang, or organization and send the whole lot to jail without any drug enforcement agents getting discovered, hurt, or killed beforehand.

"They deal in misery," Nick had told me. "That's what they

bring to everyone whose lives they ruin and to their families. My job is to break up the misery train."

When I think about the dangers inherent in his job I feel cold and sick, nauseated, and tired.

But we like talking about other things in life, too—the weather, the dock and our friends there, what funny thing the Quackenbusches did that morning. We talk about movies. We talk about social and political issues, national and international issues. The conversations are interesting, challenging to my tired brain. He makes me think, because he's so, so smart, quick, open-minded. He listens to me, he asks my opinion.

And still, I push back, and don't commit to him, to us.

The first time that Nick and I got naked together, three months after I moved in, it didn't go well. I was holding an ice pack to my face. He was coming out of his houseboat, I was walking into my tugboat.

"What the hell happened?" He was ticked. He pulled off the ice pack and sucked in his breath when he saw the swelling and the bruise.

"Nothing much. I went to a car accident, two jerks chasing each other, a couple shots fired. One car slammed into a tree, another into the side of a building downtown. I was there quick, as it happened right down the street and I was finishing up with a tiny shopping spree. Anyhow, one of the guys went running and ran smack into me and knocked me over."

"Damn, Toni." He was upset, I could tell.

"It's nothing. My bags scattered, but I managed to save my new blue heels."

"It's not nothing. That . . . damn." His jaw clenched.

"It feels a lot better than it did before."

He shook his head. "Here, come to my house, please? I have soup from Katie's Kitchen."

"Soup from Katie's? What kind?"

"Broccoli cheese. Potato with bacon. Clam chowder."

"Yum."

"Please, Toni. Come over."

It was hard to admit it, but having Nick take care of me was worth getting run into by a criminal. We ate the soup, the bread, the salad. We sat on his couch and watched a movie. It was a thriller, but no violence, about space and astronauts.

When the movie was over, he turned and kissed me. I put my hand behind his head and pulled him closer. He was warm. He was sexy. He was a heck of a kisser.

I had been lonely. I had been ruined. I had been in I'm-Trying-Hard-Not-To-Want-To-Die mode for almost two years, and Nick was the sexiest man I'd ever met. He had been kind from day one. He had been attentive, he had smiled that Nick smile, he had seemed interested in who I was as a woman and how I thought.

I could not resist. I ran my hands up his shirt, and he took things from there. Everything was going well. My silky shirt was off, my lacy bra was off, I'd whipped off his T-shirt, and he was lying on top of me on his wide couch, kissing me until I couldn't think, my chest against his. I wrapped my legs around his, and the tears came at that inopportune second. I didn't even know what was on my face at first. A tight sob pierced the room. He lifted his head from my arched breast.

"Baby, what's wrong?"

I couldn't speak. I could only cry.

I put my hands over my face. He pulled my hands away, gently, oh so gentle, kissed my mouth, and pulled me up and onto his lap while I cried. We did not have sex.

I woke up at two in the morning, in his bedroom, my arms wrapped around him. I was absolutely mortified and humiliated. I peeled myself away and snuck into his family room. I found my pants, but not my underwear, and pulled them on. I found my shirt but could not find my bra, and pulled that on, too. I was on all fours searching under the coffee table for both when he walked in.

"What are you doing?"

"I'm trying to find my bra."

"Here it is." He reached behind a couch cushion.

"Thank you." I turned and peered under a side table, rear in the air.

"What are you looking for?"

"My underwear."

He found it under a pillow and handed it to me. The red lace looked tiny and overly feminine in his hands.

I turned to leave.

"Where are you going?"

"Home."

"Why? Stay here. Let's go back to bed."

"No. Thank you." My voice sounded prim. Proper.

"I'd like you to stay."

"I can't, not tonight." Formal. Tight.

"Why can't you stay? We don't need to make love. I understand, Toni, I do. But I'd love to sleep with you, love to wake up with you."

"I'm cranky in the morning."

"I'll make you coffee. You'll feel better."

"I'll have morning breath."

"Everyone does. Stay here, please."

"Nick, no. I'm a wreck and a mess and I can't do this. I'm sorry about what happened."

"Don't be. I'm sure not. I liked it." He smiled that Nick smile, sure and friendly. "Until you cried, I meant."

"I don't know what happened. I shouldn't have cried. I . . ." I threw my hands up. "I'm a head case."

"You're not at all."

"I have to go. I'm sorry, Nick. I truly am."

He studied me. He wasn't mad, I could tell. He was sad. "Okay, Toni. I'll walk you home."

"I'm two doors down. You don't need to do that."

"Yes, I do."

And he did.

The next day I found chocolates on my doorstep.

My first thought: He's a kind man. My next thought: Daaaanngg. I'm in trouble.

*   *   *

Nick called me on my lunch break. I had snuck out to buy Lace, Satin, and Baubles lingerie. I told him what I bought.

"Can't wait to see it," he said.

"I'll bring wine."

"I'll make dinner. Let's have dessert first."

"Always a smart move."

When I got home from work, on my front porch were ten pairs of duck panties. I laughed, then went to Daisy's houseboat to thank her. Cracked me up thinking of Georgie, aka Slash, buying them for me. Maybe I'd model those for Nick, too.

"There's something I keep trying to remember, Toni," he said.

I juggled the phone. It was Sunday evening and I was in my bathtub eating peanut butter out of the jar with chocolate sticks. Nick had worn me out the night before.

"It's there. It's right there, and I can't bring it up."

"Is it the shadows again?" I put the chocolate sticks down.

"Yes, the shadows, but it's the screaming, too. I can hear it, but I can't, too. It's like . . . it's an echo. Everything is dark. I'm scared. I'm watching it, but I can only see it on the wall. It's like it's a movie, only I can't see the movie. I am making no sense."

"Who was there? Do you remember anyone?"

"I don't know, Toni, but I think it was two people. I also think I knew someone named Lu Lu."

"Can you picture her?" I heard his anguish, his pain.

"I don't think so, but the name . . . Maybe it was a dream. A very bad dream, but . . ."

"But what?"

"But it doesn't explain the other memories. The wood ducks, the blue box with the fancy lady on it, the garden, red toy trucks. Last night, in my dreams, a blue door kept opening. I think I lived in a house. I do. But then, what happened?"

Never tell, Antonia, never, ever tell.

"I had a home, so somehow my parents or whoever was raising me, my mother, they must have died or given me away to the orphanage."

"I'm so sorry, Dmitry." In so many ways, I'm sorry, and I will fix this.

My adopted brother, Dmitry, the brother who is haunted by memories he can't latch onto, is twenty-eight years old, give or take a few months, or a year, and has blond curls. He is the only one of us with blond hair.

He has light green eyes and he's built like a cement truck. He played football in high school and made at least one touchdown each game.

I heard my father say to my mother during one football game where Dmitry made two touchdowns, "That one fast kid we have, Svetlana."

My mother said, "Runs like the devil is after him."

"I think the devil after me, not him."

"Perhaps the devil after you and me, Alexei."

"We will have to run fast, too, Svetlana."

Maybe the devil was after me, too. That's how a secret feels when you're hiding it from someone else, when you know that you should tell the truth but you can't or won't.

Long ago I had promised I wouldn't. I would break that promise, but I would not do it now. Dmitry had to be home. He would feel as if he'd been run over by a bulldozer when I told him.

I had only a piece of his truth, but it was enough to pull out the first string of the secret, which would start to unravel the rest. My parents would have to pull the rest of the strings.

They adored Dmitry, but when we were growing up there was sometimes this inexplicable tension between Dmitry and my father. Dmitry, especially as a young boy, seemed to be afraid of him, he'd pull away, or he would see my father and then hide. It translated into some anger issues between them when he was a teen, though my father was unfailingly kind and loving.

I thought, though, that how Dmitry felt about my father was rooted in the deep mystery of his past. It had to be. I could tell he was spiraling into that pervading sadness and aloneness again.

"When are you coming home?"

"Not yet, Toni. But soon. Did you get the embroidered shirt I sent you? I sent shirts to Valerie and Ellie, too."

"I did. We did. Thank you. We all wore them to our Pillow Talk night. Mama loved the paper flowers and Papa loved the Mexican wallet."

"Miss you. Love you."

"Love you, too. Try to sleep more, Dmitry, please."

"I'm trying. If the wood ducks, the blood, and the rocking horse that rocks on its own would get out of my head and my bed, it would be easier."

I didn't have all the answers for him, but I knew about the blood, and I knew that Dmitry was struggling again with the depression that had followed him from Russia.

I am a secret keeper. It's wrong. I'm wrong. I was trying to outrun the devil and it wasn't working.

"We need to do something daring, shake things up," Ellie said. "It will help me get control of my nerves."

"But let's not get arrested," Valerie said. "Bad for my job."

"That only happened twice," Ellie said, waving a hand. "Charges dropped."

"Three times," I corrected her. It was the three of us at one of Ellie's long tables for Pillow Talk. Around us were Ellie's fabrics—silk, cotton, taffeta, velvet, satins. Lace was in colorful bins, and glass jelly jars and boxes of buttons and trinkets, ruffles and ribbons, sequins and beads, fabric paints and paintbrushes, were stacked on shelves.

"Charges dropped," Ellie repeated. "We were young. High school. College."

We were caught with alcohol, twice, underage. Perhaps once we were on the roof of the high school at two in the morning singing. Perhaps we were drinking with friends in the middle of a football field another time, streaking naked across the goal line at midnight. Our parents were not amused.

"Although that one time I was twenty-one," Ellie said.

I rolled my eyes. All the Kozlovskys had been rounded up for a bar fight. What were we supposed to do? A drunk man hit on JJ, grabbed her, and she shattered a bottle against the bar and threatened him with the jagged edge. Things went from there. "What do you want to do?"

"Something that will help me to feel how I used to feel," Ellie said. "Something so that I feel courageous and strong, and not weak and gutless like I do when I have to use paper bags to breathe."

"I want to do something fun," Valerie said. "I'm prosecuting a serial killer. His sick, scraggly relatives sit right behind him and want to put me on a stick and cook me over a fire. His brother has a bald head that is covered in tattoos. His uncle has a nose ring and looks like King Kong. His mother has a strong resemblance to a gargoyle. May they all disintegrate like dust and fly away."

"Are you worried about Ailani and Koa?" I asked, suddenly feeling cold, as I always did when she talked about this trial. Was it foreboding?

Valerie stopped sewing. "The risk to them is small. It's me they want, and when this trial is over, they'll go away. Plus, different people—a cop, a detective—have talked to them. Made them know that they're watching them, that we know who they are and we know they're gunning for me."

"Awful," Ellie said. "Is anyone else cold?"

My hands shook, a freezing chill blasting through my body. This trial was not right. Something was off. "I'm cold."

"I'm cold, too," Valerie said. "I get cold every time I think about those bat catchers."

To distract myself I studied the owl pillow I was working on. I was using seven different fabrics for the feathers. The owl's face and body were made of felt. I'd attach googly eyes and sequins when I was done. A kid, in the hospital for whatever reason, would love it—I hoped.

Valerie was making a pillow for a boy, with a rowboat in the center, with a kid reeling in an oversized green and yellow fish.

She, too, would attach googly eyes and sequins. Ellie was making a pillow for a little girl, pinks and yellow, a ballerina in the center. She would attach pink and white gauze for the skirt.

"So, what's fun to do?" Valerie said.

"It's hot," I said. It wasn't actually that hot outside. Rather cool.

"Way too hot," Ellie said.

"I'm burning up," Valerie said.

"I'm boiling," I said.

"I feel like my skin is coming off," Ellie said.

We knew what to do.

There is a pool of water, a tiny bay, in the Willamette River near Ellie's house. It's pretty and private. We call it Pool Paradise for Fun Russians. Kozlovsky cousins come here to play. There's a rope over a tree branch that sails you right on out to the water, and grass to sit on. My sisters and I drove down a quiet street, then another, seeing no one. We stripped off our clothes and dove into the Pool Paradise for Fun Russians. Yes, we skinny-dipped.

We laughed, we pretended we were dolphins, we drank our wine.

I flipped over on my back and thought about Nick. Ellie started singing a song and twirling. Valerie swam out a bit, then back, out a bit, then back. She likes exercise.

When I was having a particularly vivid daydream about Nick, I heard, *"Toni! Toni!"* in my head.

I stood up and didn't see Valerie out in the river. I tried to stuff the immediate panic back inside of me so I could think. Ellie stopped twirling, too, and searched the river.

"Where is she?" Ellie asked.

"Valerie!" I shouted into the dark. Her name echoed back to me.

"Valerie! Where are you?" Ellie yelled. "Valerie!"

I turned when I heard her gasp. She was flailing in the water, out farther than she should have been, stuck in a current, going downstream fast.

"Oh no," Ellie moaned.

For a second I had a vision of another river, another time, a different sister's near drowning, then it was gone, and Ellie and I both raced out of the water, and sprinted down the river bank. Valerie was fighting the current, which gave us time to grab a long branch off the ground. At a curve in the river, we stuck it out to her. I would give this one shot. If she couldn't grab it, I was going in to help her. I could tell she was tiring.

"She doesn't get this, I'm in," Ellie said.

"I'll be with you."

Ellie anchored the base of the branch, and I grabbed the other end and stretched an arm out, my feet not touching the bottom.

"Come on, Valerie! Swim to me!"

"Valerie, three feet!" Ellie yelled.

Valerie went under again and I went out farther, holding the ends of the branch. Her fingers brushed mine, then pulled away. I stuck my leg out, and that stopped her enough so she could reach back her hand, kick, and grab my hand. She went down and came up sputtering.

Kick, Valerie, Kick.

She started to kick, as did I.

Pull, Ellie, pull!

Ellie immediately pulled the branch in, I held on to Valerie's hand, and we both kicked as if we were being chased by the KGB. Again, another time, another river, another near tragedy, popped into my mind, but I shoved it right back out to Moscow. I needed no more fear.

Within a minute we were all standing in the river, near the bank, leaning over, gasping for breath, spitting out river water. I latched an arm around Valerie, Ellie on the other side, and we dragged her through the water to land.

She was sputtering, coughing up water. "Glad you heard me."

"Yes," Ellie said, panting. "You were loud enough to wake my brain cells."

"I got the message," I said, hitting her on the back to get more water out, my body starting to shake.

"I am so glad you grabbed that branch." Valerie made some

gross gagging sounds. "Can you imagine? I would have had to get out of the river, downstream, totally naked, and walk all the way back up."

"The newspapers would have loved it." I gave her one more whack. She gagged and spit more river water out. "Headline: Prosecutor found jiggling as she jogged naked."

"Naked prosecutor walking by the river at midnight," Ellie said, trying not to cry.

Sometimes we use droll humor to get by disasters that make our brains shake with fright in our family. It's how we cope.

"I want to hug both of you," Valerie said, still struggling for breath from her exertions but also from what almost happened. "But I don't want to hug naked sisters."

"Me either. Boob to boob is not my thing." I put my trembling arm around her shoulders.

"I do not want you pressed up against me, Valerie," Ellie said, "but I'm thinking of hugging you in my head."

"Glad you're alive," I said. I heaved another breath, then bent over and got rid of the Willamette River and a whole bunch of fear.

"Me too," Ellie said. She lost her cookies, too, followed by Valerie. It was rather disgusting, we agreed.

We scrambled up the bank.

"Thanks, sisters."

"You're welcome," Ellie and I said.

We headed back to Pool Paradise for Fun Russians. We hugged the edge of the river, ducked down when a car went by on the street above, skittered behind trees when we heard voices. At one point we started to laugh and had to stop and cross our legs so our bladders wouldn't betray us.

Now, it would have made sense for us to call it a night, get dressed, and go home. We Kozlovsky sisters are not known for making sense.

"I have to jump in the river, one more time, to get rid of the fear I now have," Valerie said. "If I don't get back in now, I won't again."

I grabbed the rope. "Same here." I gave a Tarzan cry and plunged in, followed by Valerie and Ellie.

It was insane to get back in the river, but Valerie was right. We would never return to this spot if we didn't have fun.

"Tarzanna!" I cried out, on my second jump.

"Tarzanna!" Ellie and Valerie cried, on their second jump.

Then we stopped crying "Tarzanna" and simply cried.

"That was so scary," Ellie said.

"Thank you again and I love you, sisters," Valerie said. "More than Mama's Russian tea cakes."

That night I had to spend an hour in my bathtub, trying to chase away the near drowning. Valerie's is fine, I told myself, as I rocked back and forth in the hot water, lights off, candles lit, trying to control the images that kept crawling through my mind. *It didn't happen.* Don't dwell in the fear. Move forward. I ate popcorn. Then a donut. I chased it down with sweet tart snakes.

She's fine.

Nick brought me a bouquet of cotton candy pink tulips.

There is something earthly sexy about a man who looks like Nick, broad, a few scars, a hard jaw, eyes that don't give much away, holding tulips in his hand.

"Thank you."

"You're welcome." He held up a bag. "I bought Chinese. Have dinner with me?"

I love Chinese food. "Yes."

"Here?"

"No."

His eyes hide much of what he's thinking, but I caught it. Nick wants me to invite him over. He wants to hang out in my tugboat and on my deck. He wants to tilt his head up to the sky and marvel at Anonymous with me. He wants to say hello to Mr. and Mrs. Quackenbusch, and to catch a glimpse of the Sergeant Otts as they swim on by, their fur shining.

He wants to eat dinner in my bed, as we eat in his sometimes. He wants to go up to the captain's wheelhouse and sit on my bench with the red pillows made from fabric from all over the world and have a view of the stars.

I know this is what he wants, but I can't have a man in my tugboat. I can't have a man in my home. I had a man in my home, our home, he's not there anymore, and I can't have a new one there yet. It's wrong.

It is.

Isn't it?

"Come on down, then, babe." He linked an arm around my waist, pulled me to him, and kissed me on the lips. I melted right on in because he is like chocolate. Delicious. He is my guilty chocolate.

I knew we wouldn't have Chinese food for about an hour, and I was right.

Nick has a huge tub. It fits two people and looks straight out on the river.

"On one hand, I think I know you, Toni. You're brainy smart."

I snuggled into Nick in his bed and ate another pot sticker. I love pot stickers. "Thanks, Nick."

"You're so quick on everything. You're a gifted reporter. The awards you've won are well deserved. You're a deep person, too. I can talk to you as I have talked to no one else in my life. I like being with you. You're funny. I'd call it sarcastic funny. You see things in a different way. I respect you. I even respect your love of raw cookie dough."

I laughed, couldn't help it.

"And I like the way you choose to live on a tugboat and how you've named all the animals, like Dixie, your blue heron. I know you love your family, though they're complicated, and I love how you watch out for Daisy and how you don't judge Lindy. You're sexy as hell and gorgeous, too."

"Ah. Glad to be that." I reached for another pot sticker.

"But you're a mystery, too. I know you're thinking all the time, and you don't share everything. In fact, I don't think you share much. There's a lot I don't know. I've asked you about your life in Russia as a kid, and you don't want to talk about it. I've asked about your brother, and you don't want to talk much about him, either. I know you don't want to talk about Marty, even though he's between us."

"No, he's not between us."

"He is."

I put my pot sticker down, back in the Chinese food box. I didn't know what to say to that, but I knew I didn't want to be naked, in bed, with a pot sticker, next to Nick, talking about Marty.

"I have to go." I got up out of bed.

"Please don't. I didn't mean to hurt you. I didn't mean to make you mad."

"If you know I don't want to talk about certain subjects, Nick, why do you bring them up?"

"Because I want to know *you*. I want you to trust me. I want you to talk to me. I want to work things out between us. Why are you running away like this? Why can't we talk this out?"

"There's nothing to talk out. I told you what I wanted from this relationship already. You agreed to it. I had a long day, to-morrow's going to be a long day."

"We both have long days, Toni. Stay, okay? You're not ready to open up and discuss any of this, it's fine. I'll wait."

"You don't need to wait. I don't want to talk about it at all. Now or later."

I headed for the hallway, where my clothes had come off in wild, lusty abandon, and put them on. I was now tired, frus-trated, and felt invaded and blindsided.

I had wanted to hang out with Nick and eat pot stickers be-fore I went back to my tugboat, but now he'd ruined it. He pulled on his jeans. He was ticked, I could tell. I was ticked that he was ticked.

"Don't walk me home, Nick."

He walked out his front door, and he waited until I was in my tugboat.

I shut the door and did not say good-bye.

I drove to work still mad at Nick for pushing me. I had been honest with him from the start in terms of what I wanted and didn't want in our relationship.

About a week after I was on all fours trying to find my underwear and bra in the middle of the night in Nick's family room after crying during almost-sex, we talked.

It had been awkward, at least for me, after that night. I avoided Nick. He knew I was avoiding him. He gave me a week to be alone, then he said hello and asked if we could talk.

We were in front of my tugboat and the sun was going down. I decided on blunt honesty. "I'm so embarrassed and I don't know what to say to you or how to say it or what to do from here."

"I know what to say," Nick said. "I'm sorry. I shouldn't have moved so fast."

"You didn't." It was true. He hadn't. I wanted that man badly.

"I did. And the whole night ended up being painful for you, and I feel awful about that."

"Please don't. Nick, I'm not together here. My head is not . . . functioning like a normal person's. You're hanging out with a woman who's half-cocked, easily confused, and running along the edges of crazy. I'm also moody and irrational. I want to warn you away from myself."

He smiled, so sweet. "I don't find you half-cocked, confused, crazy, moody, or irrational at all. There's no need for a warning. Let's back this up, Toni, okay? Slow things down."

I nodded. He was charming. He was understanding. We went back to chatting. He was friendly. He was kind. And soon I was right back where I started with him, like he was the flame and I was a dizzy, passion driven, out-of-control, moody, and irrational moth.

I had dinner with Nick on his houseboat one night and I

pulled him toward me and kissed him. I shouldn't have, but I couldn't resist him. The kiss was a gush of lust. A rush of rampant desire. My shirt went flying and my bra after that. I had his shirt unbuttoned and opened, my hands running up . . . and I froze. I pulled away, my hands pushing on his chest, breathing way too embarrassingly hard.

"Nick, stop, I'm sorry, I have to talk to you."

"Now?" He was breathing hard, too. I thought it was sexy.

"Yes. No. Yes, yes. Now."

"Damn. Okay." He took a deep breath, we disentangled, and he stepped back a few inches, though he had one hand on the counter to the left, one to the right, and I was between them.

"I have to tell you something. You might not like it. You might like it. But I have to say it and then you can decide what you want to do. Hang on, I'm going to put my shirt on when I say this. Where is it? Never mind." I shook my head. I could do this half-dressed.

"What is it?" His chest was heaving. He looked adorable, all riled up and blond, but I had to say what I had to say so he could choose to have me leave.

"I don't want a relationship with you."

His head pulled back as if I'd swiped him, and his eyes narrowed.

"I mean." My hands fluttered. "I don't want a relationship with anyone. I don't want you to think that if we sleep together that we're . . . together."

I could tell that I'd hurt his feelings. It was a flash in those light blue eyes. A few rapid blinks. A hardening jaw.

"I can't do it, Nick. I don't have the confidence to be with you. I don't have the strength for any turmoil or problems that relationships always have. I would not be a fun girlfriend, anyhow. Not that I'm presuming that you want me as a girlfriend."

"I do."

"You do?"

"Yes."

"I can't do it. I can't. I only want . . ." I waved a hand. "This."

"You want to make love."

"No. I want sex."

"Then we have a problem." He pulled back and crossed his arms. His muscles were so grippable. "Because I don't want just sex, I want to make love."

"Well. You can make love, I'll have sex."

"I would prefer we were both making love."

"Nick—"

"What?"

"You're already making this hard. This is exactly what I don't want, stress and problems, emotions, and that's what I've been trying to tell you. I want easy. I want uncomplicated. I want a reprieve from life." I tried to find my bra. "I'm leaving. This was a bad idea." My bra had landed on Nick's toaster. He stepped in front of me. Man, he was quick.

"Toni." He tipped my head up with one warm, gentle hand.

"I don't want to talk about this." I was going to cry. Dang. "I want to go."

"You're free to go, but I'd like to talk."

I blinked, and the tears fell down my cheeks.

"I'm sorry, babe. I don't ever want to make you cry."

"It's not you. I'm a half-cocked crazy lady. Don't call me babe."

"Listen, Toni. You told me what you wanted. You want to have sex. You don't want to be my girlfriend or anything else. I heard you. I understand. And I'm telling you what I want. I want a relationship. I want you. I want us. I want to make love. If you want a relationship in the future, I'm here."

"But then it isn't fair."

"Fair?"

"You want something I don't."

"I'll risk it." He kissed me gently. "You're worth it, babe, so I'll go for what you're offering."

"Only sex. Nothing more."

"I can't help it if I feel more, Toni, but I won't crowd you, I won't push you, I'll respect where you are now."

I cried. The tears ran, he kissed them, but then I met his kisses with my own, and that gush and rush came back like a firestorm, and I went for his belt as he yanked my skirt down.

We had sex/made love, depending on whose perspective, that night.

Nick was magic in bed.

It was like being sex transported. Orgasmic fantasy land.

I had to make sure I didn't scream, or groan too loud, or moan like a maniac. Sounds carry over the water, and I knew the river would not hide my noises for me.

I did not spend the night.

When I flipped the covers off to leave, he said, "Please stay, Toni."

"No. That I cannot do."

He linked an arm around my waist and pulled me back down to him. "What if I promise not to speak at all? It'll be a sleep-over. I'll make popcorn."

"No, no sleepovers." I started feeling emotional and my voice cracked.

I heard the silence between us, then Nick said, "Okay, babe."

I got up and dressed, and so did he.

"What are you doing?"

"I'm walking you to your door."

"You don't need to."

"It's late. And yes, I need to."

So he did.

He always does. As if something could happen to me. I have to admit that I like it.

Even after sleeping with Nick Sanchez for the last almost four months, I still find him intimidating. A little scary.

Hard to handle.

Scratch that, a man like Nick could never be "handled."

But he's so hot, and he's kind and protective, and I look at him and lust, and when we're naked I lose my mind, which is what I want to do—lose my mind and forget everything that has happened, and, truthfully, I simply can't stay away from him, head case that I am.

11

~

A week after Valerie nearly drowned in the Willamette River I had one of the most vivid nightmares of my life. I dreamed of the time when Ellie almost drowned when we were living in Moscow. The Moskva River was filled with snow and ice, snaking through the city.

Our mother had heard there was bread at one of the shops, so she went to stand in line. She had been gone for three hours.

Valeria and I were sitting on the couch together, each sewing a pillow. I was embroidering a picture of a cottage in the country. She was embroidering roses. Our grandmother Ekaterina had helped us with our designs. With my hand posed above my cottage's red door, I heard Elvira in my head. One word: *River*.

I looked at Valeria and she was frozen, too, needle in hand above a pink rose.

I gasped for breath the same time that Valeria did.

"Where is Elvira?" I choked out.

"River," Valeria said. "She said river."

Elvira had gone over to play with her friend, Lena. Lena lived closer to the river than we did. We sprinted down the stairs of the apartment complex, to the street, our boots sliding against the ice, the snow drifting down. I tripped over the back of a bike and went flying. Valeria ran into a teenage boy and they both crashed to the ground in a heap of arms and legs. She shouted her apology, and we kept running to the river.

When we arrived at the river, Lena ran toward us, hysterical.

"Help! We were playing and Elvira fell in the river and the water took her! She's in the river! She's in the river!"

We couldn't even see her. The Moskva River was freezing, a wet line of death.

"Elvira! Elvira!" we shouted.

"Go get help!" I yelled at Lena, who took off, running and crying.

Valeria and I sprinted along the bank, following the river down.

"I can't see her," I panted.

"I can't, either. Look for her red hat."

I heard Elvira in my head. *Monster building.*

"Monster building," Valeria said.

We called a huge, looming, scary government building the monster building. It sat down river like a cement lump. We sprinted. We screamed her name.

In my head, two more words. *Rock place.*

"Rock place," Valeria said.

The rock place was after the monster building. There were rocks on one end that we liked to throw and break.

We kept running, screaming Elvira's name, out loud and in our heads. People heard, and they started following us, running along the river. Suddenly, Elvira's red hat poked up. She was clinging to a log.

"There she is!" Valeria and I both took off our shoes and our coats and clambered over a concrete wall along the river and jumped in. Vaguely we heard people behind us yelling for us to stop, stop, stop, don't go in, but we didn't listen.

Elvira was crying when we got to her, our little bodies quickly freezing, shaking. I have no idea, to this day, other than sheer determination and sisterly love, how we made it to Elvira. The log was small and slick, and the three of us wrapped our arms all the way around it.

"It's okay, Elvira," I said to her. "We're here, you're fine."

"Hang on tight," Valeria said, spitting water out of her mouth. "No one let go."

We were going numb, the frost of the river slicing into our

bodies, the water dragging us down, our small fingers stiff, legs tingling.

"Kick," I cried, and we kicked, but a log in a current doesn't move as you want it to, and I knew we would have to swim soon.

"Right there," Valeria said, still kicking. She nodded to a slight curve in the river, where the land stuck out. The current felt like a steel force, the water an icy grave, but we could make it.

"Elvira, you have to swim. We'll be with you, but you have to swim," I told her. I looked at her white face and I knew she couldn't swim. She was too cold, too spent, too scared. Her eyes had a dead expression, vacant.

When we were as close to the bank as we would become, our hands slipping off the log, Valeria and I grabbed Elvira at the same time, one arm each, and lay on our backs, kicking as hard as we could, our bodies sinking into the rolling, merciless river, then back up, the snowy, icy water pooling over our faces. We struggled to breathe, to stay afloat, to not panic.

We kicked and kicked, the bank closer, then farther, then closer. I looked at Elvira, whose eyes were closing, and across at Valeria, whose eyes were nearing hysteria.

"*Kick, Valeria, kick,*" I told her, not having the energy to speak aloud, using the Sabonis family gift.

"*I'm trying. The water's killing me,*" Valeria said, her broken voice in my head.

"*I can't breathe,*" Elvira said. "*Too cold.*"

We kicked harder, until we couldn't, gasping, struggling, the river pulling us down, swirling us down to its black depths. Valeria cried out, Elvira closed her eyes, I kicked one more time, frozen.

"*I love you,*" Elvira said, her voice weak, her mouth closed against the water.

"*I love you, too,*" I said, as did Valeria, their words a good-bye in my chilled, slowing mind.

"*I'm sorry,*" Elvira said, her head almost completely under the water. I tried to pull her back up, a sob in my chest.

"*Grab my hand. Please, Elvira, grab my hand.*"

"I can't. Too cold. Help Valeria."

Valeria was hardly moving, the river taking her away. *"Valeria! Don't give up. Keep going."*

"I can't, Antonia, I can't move my legs."

Crushed, choppy ice hit us, and soon we were going in three different directions. I screamed, terrified, my sisters' heads sinking under the water, their arms flailing about. I could feel their panic alongside mine, their desperation.

We heard splashing beside us, yelling.

Hands reached out to grab us.

We were carried out of the churning river by many people, then dragged up to the sidewalk to a crowd. One man picked Elvira up, completely limp, in his arms. He put his hand on her chest to make sure she was still breathing. "Where do you live?"

Two women and two men pulled Valeria and me along, our feet barely touching the sidewalk. They admonished us as only people of the Soviet Union can. "What was that all about? Why were you in the river? Good girls do not jump in the river in the middle of winter. Where are your parents? Did they know you were here? Your mother will beat your ears . . . your father will get the belt . . . your poor parents, wait until they see you. Are you all right? You'll be fine. Keep breathing. You're a bit blue, breathe in with me, come now, dear. Breathe."

We burst through our front door. My mother's face drained of all color as she stared at Elvira, head back, unmoving, Valeria and I half drowned, mostly frozen. "Oh, my Mother of God, help me."

My father, white as the snow in the Moskva, leaped over to Elvira. Explanations were hurried, as were the actions. All three of us found ourselves unceremoniously stripped by my parents and five strangers. We were dumped in the tub—we had hot water that day—tea was made, soup was heated, the women later toweling us try, quite vigorously, all while continuing to tell us that what we had done was "silly . . . dangerous . . . you'll be in such trouble . . . there now . . . all will be well . . . soup is almost done . . ."

My father asked us, later that night, all of us tucked into bed,

Elvira coming back to us, her eyes not filled with the hallows of death, "How did you know, about Elvira?"

My mother didn't ask. She shook her head. She knew what had happened, she knew.

Valeria answered for us. "Elvira told us."

"You heard it in your . . ." My father paused. "Your mind?" We nodded.

"We talk through our brains sometimes," Elvira whispered.

"Once again, the language of sisters," my mother said proudly. "The language of the Sabonises. It comes down the line, like genes, and our widow's peaks. Mother to daughter. Father to son. Then the sisters and brothers, we hear each other. It comes through right here." She pointed to her widow's peak.

My father patted my mama's hand. "It is God's gift, girls. A gift. You can talk to each other without talking."

"We are Kozlovskys and Sabonises." My mother sighed. "We are odd. Mother of God, help us all."

"Let us pray," my father said. "Thank you, God . . ." It was a long, long prayer of thanks that his daughters were still alive. We were asleep long before he was done.

I went to Svetlana's Kitchen on my lunch break, about two o'clock.

My mother and father joined me for lunch. The waiters and waitresses only came over to say hello. My mother had already ordered what she wanted me to eat.

Charlie was playing Tchaikovsky, staring at the ceiling, in his own world, and Ralph came over, said hello, saluted, and went back upstairs.

"You too thin, Antonia." My mother glared at me, then patted my hand and said, "I give you some fattening up. Lunch coming."

"Antonia!" my father said. "I no see you for six days. What you do? Start on Sunday . . . yes? Okay, now Monday, what you do? Tuesday . . ." This went on as they asked about my new job and how the bridal shower planning was going for Ellie. Which was: It wasn't. I was not going to plan a bridal shower unless I knew this wedding was going to take place, and I had my doubts, as I had faith that soon Ellie would recover her full brain power and shut this thing down.

Then we came to the matter that I needed to talk to them about. "Dmitry will be coming home for the wedding."

"He tell me last night! I be so happy to see my son." My mother smiled at me, sitting straight up in her wraparound black dress and heels. Her hair was back in a bun, her white streak so elegant.

"I cannot wait one more day," my father declared. "I want to hug my son, hold him in my arms, tell him I love him. I tell him on the phone, but that not enough."

My mother shook her head. "That right. Not enough. We want him here, in our arms."

I put my hands together on the table and took a deep breath. "You need to tell him the truth about how he arrived in our home that night. Where he came from, who his parents were, anything and everything that you know."

My father's face fell.

My mother's shoulders caved in.

They both slumped, as if on cue. My mother never slumps.

"I know he didn't come from an orphanage. He arrived in the middle of the night. He had blood on him. Was it your blood, Papa? Someone else's? You were beaten up again."

"No," my father said, switching into Russian, as if we were there, in Moscow, in our freezing cold apartment. "We told you then, we're telling you now, *never tell, Antonia, never, ever tell.* It is best for Dmitry to believe what we have already told him. He came from an orphanage."

"There are some pasts that are best left, forever, in the past. His is one of them," my mother said, also switching into Russian.

"Dmitry does not need his truth." My father choked up. "Trust me, Dmitry doesn't want to know. He is better off without it."

"The truth is that he is our son," my mother said, her voice cracking. "We love him as we love you and your sisters."

I pressed again, though I knew I had caused my parents, especially my father, deep pain. "Dmitry needs to know. It's hurting him not to know. He knows there's a secret about him and his life. He can't move forward because he doesn't know who he is, where he came from. His memories from the past used to come up only now and then, rarely, and now they're coming up more and more, in dreams, nightmares, flashbacks, even during the day."

My mother rubbed her temples.

My father ran a hand over his face.

"Maybe it's because he's older and feels safe," I said. "His mind isn't traumatized anymore, so it's opening up the door that was shut down when he was a child. Maybe it's because he keeps digging for the truth, trying to remember what he saw as a kid."

"That door should never be opened," my father said.

My mother swore in French, then went back to Russian. "Antonia, he will have to live with these"—she waved a hand—"memories. Let it lie. Let the past lie."

"By not telling him what you know, you're denying him his own reality, his own life."

"It is better that Dmitry is denied his own reality than to know what I know," my father said, slapping the table with his hand. "If he ever finds out, he will be devastated. It will hurt worse than what he believes about himself now. It will be more than most men could stand."

That made my throat constrict. What was in Dmitry's past? "Papa, please."

"No. That is my final word."

And that was that.

My favorite waitress, Dez, brought our meals. My mother had ordered me soup with meat, sausage, and cabbage; a salad with tomatoes and vinaigrette; and chicken Kiev with rye bread. Later, I knew, I would be drinking her bitter coffee, strong enough to grow hairs on my chest, and chocolate fudge cookies. I would have relished the meal if my parents didn't look as if they'd aged five years during our conversation.

"I'm sorry for hurting you," I said as I left, hugging them both.

"Antonia, you are not hurting us," my father said, still in Russian. "The past has hurt this family, the KGB hurt this family, the Communists hurt this family, but you are a loving sister who wants to help her brother."

My mother kissed my cheek. "Eat more. You are too thin."

Lindy and I watched about twenty women in a dragon boat row down the river from the bedroom deck of my tugboat. Their ferocious dragon's red mouth was wide open, white teeth ready to bite. The purple and blue tail rose like a rainbow off the back.

"I can't believe Tweedle Dee Dum and Tweedle Dum Dee want to dismantle the dock and kick us off," I said. "I'd like to tweedle their necks with my bare hands."

"I can believe it." Lindy was wearing a blue skirt to her knees, tennis shoes, and a pink blouse buttoned to the top button. Her hair was back in a ball, her glasses perched on her nose.

"Men take what men want," she said. "If they have to run over someone to do it, a hand tucked around their own balls for protection, they'll do it. They're interested in money, power, and sex. Not in that order always. And with this dock, they think they can make more money if they transform this whole area into condos. The sewer system is having problems and they don't want to fix it. Same with the electricity lines. Men are like containers of sweat and body fluids with brains that only limp toward competence."

"You don't like men, do you?"

"I find them silly. Ridiculous. Sometimes dangerous and violent, but a species that has not evolved at the same pace as women."

"Given your career, how do you hide your disdain?"

She rolled her eyes. "Seriously? I smile and stand in a negligee. They can't see past that because their dick is straight out."

"Business seems good."

"It is. I have a long waiting list. One man offered six hundred dollars an hour. He's at the top of the list now. I'm kicking out one of my clients tomorrow."

"He probably won't be happy, will he?"

"I'm going to tell him that I'm going back to school to become a librarian."

"Will he believe it?"

"It doesn't matter. He's too fat."

"Ah. I'm always worried you'll get hurt, but I wonder if you ever worry you'll be arrested."

She laughed. "My dear friend, Toni. You've heard of a little black book? Let's just say I have a little black computer with a long list. If I'm arrested, five names come out a day until I'm out of jail, charges dropped. Too many high-powered men have been on my houseboat for hanky-panky-spanky for me to be arrested."

The dragon boat flew by, the women laughing and chatting. We waved. They waved back. Lindy opened the lid of a pink box. Two huge cupcakes were inside. "I went out to that bakery in Trillium River for these. Bommarito's Bakery. Best cupcakes on the planet."

"Oh, yum. Sometimes I drive all the way out there for their cupcakes, too. Pretty drive."

We ate in silence. The cupcakes were oversized. Mine had huge daisies on it and Lindy's had a dalmatian.

"I do not want to lose my home, this dock." I didn't want to lose Nick.

"You won't, Toni."

"How do you know?"

"Because I know." She licked her fingers.

"You're not worried about this at all?"

"Nah. Here, let me have a bite of your cupcake and I'll let you have a bite of mine."

We leaned over and took a bite of each other's cupcake.

Lindy's a true friend.

"I love cupcakes and I love books, Toni. You know I visit different libraries in town and hang out among the stacks."

"Yes, you strange book nerd."

"I love the feel of books and the smell of them. I'm rereading *East of Eden* now. Want to read it together?"

"Sure."

Lindy had to leave at two o'clock for her appointment.

"See you at the meeting Thursday, Toni, where I will tell people we don't need to do anything, because I can save the dock, and they won't listen and will immediately go back to their useless plotting."

"Got it. See ya then."

That night I opened the door to the kayak house and dragged out our double seater and sat in it on the deck. I pretended to row, like the oddity that I am.

Marty said to me, after our fourth kayaking date, on the Rogue River, "I love kayaking with you, Toni, I do. But how about dinner? I'd like to take you out. Now, don't say no again. Not right away. Think about it."

I thought about it at home, called him, and said yes. "This doesn't mean we're dating, Marty."

"No, it doesn't. If we were dating, our parents would have a huge and embarrassing party. They would make an announcement at church and ask for a group blessing. Your father would offer up a long prayer of thanks. Your mother would make a dessert called 'I Want Toni and Marty To Get Married,' and put it on the Specials board at the restaurant. No, we'll keep this between us."

"Exactly. I'll be harangued until I'm forced to move to Australia and live with kangaroos."

"That sounds appealing. Can I come? I like kangaroos."

Marty took me to dinner at elegant restaurants. One day we went hiking. Day trips to the beach and mountains. We went to plays and the symphony, things I had never done. I loved both. That surprised me. And in some inexplicable way it made me feel better about myself. In the audience, in the theatre, I listened to the characters' problems and grief, their tears and aloneness, and it touched me. I could relate to their loss, their fear, their love.

I lost myself in Bach, Beethoven, Mozart. I always thought

people who went to the symphony were snobs. I wasn't a snob, but I could feel the music.

When my parents dragged me to church, and Marty was there, too, with his parents, we were polite to each other, not giving out a single hint that we were friends.

My mother would admonish me, finger in the air. "That Marty! He for you. He a Russian. He make you happy. In the life and under the sheeties. What that bird called, Alexei, that Marty remind me of?"

"A blue heron. I think you make mistake, Antonia. Marty a true man. Loyal. Faithful. Please. Give that man a talking to, eh? I want what is best for you, he is the best for you, okay?"

When they weren't looking, Marty would wink at me.

Marty finally said to me, after five months of patience and kindness, of smiles and talk, of his waiting for me to come around, to want to be more than a friend, against my rigid resistance, "Toni, I want to thank you for the friendship."

We both laughed. We were in my loft downtown. I'd made dinner. Italian.

"You are my best friend."

I sniffled, all emotional. I stared out the windows at the city lights, then back to him. "You're mine, too, Marty. And Valerie and Ellie."

He had such an endearing smile. "Always, your sisters. But we have a problem."

"What is the problem?" *What? A problem?*

"The problem is that I am in love with you."

I swear my heart flipped over and danced a jig. "Ah, that."

"Yes, that." His face sobered. "But you have said to me, a hundred times, spear to my heart"—he mimicked spearing himself—"that you only want to be friends with me."

I took a deep, shaky breath.

"And Toni, I want both. I want friendship and I want the forever."

My hands started to shake. He wanted more. I had always known it, felt it. He had been hoping I would change my mind.

"I need to know how you feel, honey."

Breathe, Toni, I told myself, *before you pass out and make a fool of yourself and your tongue lolls out of your head and you wet your pants when you're unconscious. Figure this out.*

"I want to be with you for the rest of my life, Toni."

"You do?" *Oh. My. Goodness.* "We've been friends all this time. . . ."

"Friends, but then I think lusty thoughts about you." He wriggled his eyebrows up and down and made me laugh. "Toni, I can't have this relationship as it is anymore. It hurts to know that we're not together and may not ever be together. Lately, it's gotten worse. I want to get married, I want children, and if I am not right for you, I need to know."

"And then that's it?" I felt an enormous sense of loss. Of breathtaking sadness. "We're done? No friendship?"

"Toni, see it from my perspective. I have met the love of my life, funny enough, through my parents, and yours. But I can't keep seeing you if you will never see me as the love of your life. If I'll always be only a friend."

"You've never even kissed me. How would you know if we would be . . ."

"Compatible?"

I nodded.

"We are. I'll show you."

And he kissed me. It felt so . . . natural, for a second. So safe. So comfortable, so right.

For about five seconds.

Then the passion flared up in me like I'd caught on fire, flames shooting toward the ceiling. I had never felt a wave of passion like that in my life. I actually gasped. He took it from there. He led. I followed, panting, responding. He was seductive. He was sexy. He knew how to make love even better than he could kayak or operate on people.

Darned if Marty wasn't amazing.

It was a tumble of uncontrollable heat and passion, as if it had all been bottled up from the second I'd met him, and I stomped it down because I wasn't ready for it, and it came barreling on out. I was naked before I knew it, my bra off, my panties gone. He pulled me on top of him, and skin to skin, body to body, we were smokin' smooth velvet. He kissed me as he entered me, and we locked eyes.

"I love you, Toni," he whispered.

"I love you, too, Marty." The words were automatic. Easy. True.

I closed my eyes because I could not keep them open anymore, my legs around his hips, our rhythm perfect, my orgasm blasting through my body, followed by another and another, and his, too, all mingled up together, seductive and loving, and trusting.

And there we were. Panting, all tangled up.

When we were done panting, our hearts slowing back to normal, we smiled, we laughed. Three hours later, we were at it again. And that was us. We had a sex life that wouldn't quit, because it was based in love and laughter and enduring, eternal friendship.

They want to kill me.

I heard Valerie's voice in my head in the morning, about ten o'clock. I called her from work. I was at my desk reviewing an article I'd written about a couple who had left city life to move to the country. They couldn't stand the stress of their jobs, the commute, the time they didn't have with their kids. The father became a high school teacher and a coach, the mother started a candle-making company from home. They restored their house; bought chickens, two horses, three dogs; and they were happy. Ta-da!

Valerie was not happy, and I was flat-out frightened.

"The Barton family is psychotic."

"What's going on?"

"Still snarling at me with their semi-toothless mouths, their skeleton tattoos taunting me as I know they would like me to be a skeleton."

I rubbed my forehead, right on my widow's peak. I figured she was doing the same. This whole situation was making me nervous. "Did something new happen?"

"Yes."

"What? I thought you got a security system and cameras at your house."

"I did. I do."

"Then what?"

"Taped to my car windshield at work was a note."

"And the note said?"

" 'You're going to die, sister.' "

That freezing-cold snake wound around and up my spine. "You called the police?"

"Yes. They have the note. They spelled 'you're' wrong. No comma between the word 'die' and 'sister.' "

"They have poor grammar, then." Black humor. Kozlovskys have to use it.

"Yes. Psychotics who don't know how to write. Often psychotics are incredibly bright people, but often not, so this is not peculiar."

"I'm worried about you." I put my hand to my throat, frozen cold now, chilled.

"I'm not. I'll be fine. But be listening for me. I'll tell you where I am in my head if things go south with those tobacco-spitting sickos."

We chuckled. It was forced, but it was chuckle or break down into pathetic semihysterical sobs, which would annoy both of us.

"May the Bartons be burned in their trailers," my sister said, "run over by stampeding horses, and pounded into dust."

"Still so creative in your curses. Love you."

"Love you more than Mama's Russian tea cakes."

"I am not leaving," Jayla said, her stethoscope from work still around her neck. "They will have to explode the dock before I will hook up my houseboat and move it down the river."

My dock neighbors, not the whole dock this time, only those of us from the six houseboats, were at Jayla and Beth's, the nurse and the doctor's, to discuss our mutual problem of losing our home for our floating homes.

I wanted to see Nick, but he was working late. He had been working long hours. It had given me a breather from the guilt I felt sleeping with him, but I missed him, which made me feel guilty, too. I wanted space, because I didn't want the stress of fighting this relationship, and yet all I wanted to do was curl up next to that warm body and lose myself for a while.

I was an emotional mess. I felt like I had a tornado in my brain.

Beth had made paella for everyone. We chatted first, and poured a lot of wine, then got down to the business of the dock shutting down because of Tweedle Dee Dum and Tweedle Dum Dee.

"Those damn pink cocks," Daisy announced, the white daisy in her purple hat flying around. "I want to whip up their insides with my mixer, then dump them in the oven and cook them with no salt."

"I'm going to lose my appetite if you talk like that," Charles said. He smiled at Daisy. I liked Charles. Wise, measured, elegant man. He had won Professor of the Year at the university where he taught, voted on by the students.

"Dagnabbit, Charles," Daisy said, slamming a hand down and leaning forward at the table. "You're right. I won't talk about cooking people without salt."

"I appreciate that."

"But can I talk about boiling them?"

"Let's skip the cauldron image," Vanessa said. "Too witchy."

"Cauldrons! I'm not a witch. Except!" Daisy pointed a finger up. "On Wednesdays." Daisy was wearing a necklace with a tiny stuffed bear over her pink sweater with red cats. Her black boots came up to her knees and had silver studs on them.

"We need an attorney," Vanessa said. "You all have heard of Cherie Poitras? We've been friends for years. She has a colleague she recommended for us. Cherie said the woman is a ninja warrior in high heels. Her name is Heather Dackson. She'll fight for us, and this will give us a head start."

"Head start! I know how to make a head start," Daisy said. "We'll put their heads on a pick. That's a start."

"I think that's too violent," Vanessa said. "But, Daisy, I think we all want to thank you for bringing the blueberry pies tonight. These are scrumptious."

"Ya. I know how to make blueberry pies. My momma taught me. She could shoot a fly's whisker off, toss a rattlesnake without getting bit, and bake pies. She escaped from prison once, too."

"Awesome," Lindy said.

"Shot a man's private part clean off," Daisy said, proud, pointing at her crotch.

We sat in that vision for a second.

"Shot another one in the buttocks." Daisy spanked her own butt.

"So, the attorney?" Jayla said, getting us back on track.

We all agreed to hire Heather. We also agreed to put up $500 each.

"Nah," Lindy said. "Don't do it. The dock will not close. I promise."

"How do you know, Lindy?" Vanessa said. "We've already received notice."

Lindy waved a hand. "We're all safe. Make no plans to move. Don't get an attorney. I'll have it handled."

"What do you mean, you'll have it handled?" Charles asked. "We need to keep this legal."

"Legal?" Lindy said, arching an eyebrow.

"What he means is . . ." I didn't know what Charles meant, but I didn't want Lindy offended.

"Charles simply meant . . ." Vanessa said, fumbling. "Well . . . hmm . . . he didn't intend—"

"No offense, Lindy," Charles said. "Please. I didn't mean to hurt you."

"We know that you would, uh, uh, uh . . ." Jayla said. "Keep it legal."

"Absolutely," Beth said, so earnest. "We trust you."

Lindy shook her head back and forth. "Please. Come on. Do you think this is how big business works? Legally? No, we'll fight this on their level. The level of the Tweedle Dees who are scum. Don't worry. This will all stop soon. Could you please pass the paella again? This is delicious, Jayla and Beth."

"I think we have to worry about this," Vanessa said.

"We can't sit and do nothing," Charles added.

"Listen to me," Daisy said, her stuffed bear swinging from side to side. "All this talk about attorneys. Attorneys are like vultures. They peck away at you and tear your flesh out. I'll just shoot them." She pulled a tiny gun out from between her breasts and pointed it at the ceiling.

We weren't fazed.

"Please don't shoot, Daisy," Jayla said. "The cat sleeps upstairs, right above you."

"The kitty sleeps right there?" Daisy smiled, then tucked the gun back between her boobs. "I will not shoot a furry animal. Never. Or a hairy animal. No animals with flippers. No animals with whiskers." She shook her head, and the daisy on her hat bobbed. "Only humans."

"That's comforting to me," I said.

"I feel comfortable now," Charles said.

"Good enough," Jayla said. "Who wants more blueberry pie?"

We all did. Daisy went upstairs to get the cat and held it on her lap. "I would never shoot you," she whispered to it. "Don't you worry."

I heard Daisy singing at the edge of the dock that night. Her haunting, melodious voice is a complete dichotomy from her shoot-'em-up personality.

Skippy and Georgie told me that she used to sing at the bars she owned. The bar would be packed.

"I saw my momma, many times, drag drunks out of her bars like she was haulin' coal out, swearin' like a son of a gun," Skippy told me. "I can't even count how many men she smashed in the face with this huge skillet she had. *Boom.* They'd hit the ground like dead ducks. She drank like a sailor, smoked like a chimney, she fought, and she ran the businesses with a fist full of iron. But when we were home at night, the three of us, she would sing like a bird. She could sing opera, the blues, lullabies." He wiped his eyes. I noticed his knuckles were scraped, so it made me wonder who he had beaten up.

"At night she sang us to sleep," Georgie said. He had a bruise on the side of his face. They had probably been together. "When Skippy and I were teenagers, she'd come in and sing even if we'd been up to no good and she'd paddled both of us a minute before."

"I still call her for a song," Skippy said, his eyes watering. "I'm not embarrassed to say that as a man. Life's rough, right, Toni? Gets me in the mood to sleep, what with all the stuff I have to deal with. I bought her some new boots. Warm ones. I worry about her feet gettin' cold."

I did not mention that I saw Arthur/Skippy, aka Slugger, and George/Georgie, aka Slash, in the paper again and that they had, once again, slithered out of charges filed against them for money laundering of what appeared to be, but was not proven to be, illegal gambling money, loan sharking, etc.

So it was almost funny when Skippy said, "I wanted to talk to you about somethin', so did Georgie, Toni, and, uh, we know you're a crime and justice reporter for the paper and, uh, don't believe everything you hear, okay? I mean, it's embarrassin'. We're embarrassed that you, uh, heard this stuff and we don't want no trouble with you, we know you're a friend to our ma."

"Don't worry, Skippy. To be honest, as soon as I met you I was then unable to write about you, so another reporter always covers your . . . shall we say, business challenges?"

"Yeah, yeah. That's it. Our business challenges. Hey! I like that."

I did not mention the dock closing to Skippy or Georgie. That was for Daisy to do, and she told me she hadn't done it because "if my boys find out that Tweedle Dee Dum and Tweedle Dum Dee are kicking me off the dock and into the river to sing with the whales, then they'll send those two wankers off a bridge and then my boys will be in the slammer. They been in the slammer before and they didn't like it, so I'm not saying nothing to them until I check with the whales."

I decided to keep quiet, too. I did not need the Tweedles' deaths on my head, and I wouldn't put it past Georgie or Skippy.

Daisy's voice carried over the water. She was singing about a woman who had lost her man.

It broke my heart.

12

〜

"How was your day?" I asked Nick, my voice wobbling like a teeter-totter in his kitchen. I was tossing a salad, trying not to look at him. I had seen enough. He had a bandage on his shoulder under his black tank top, a long bruise on his arm, and a cut on his neck. It made me nervous and upset. Another reason not to be in a serious relationship with Nick: He could get killed.

"Not as productive as the day before."

I felt like crying when I saw that shoulder. I turned away as the tears came and rubbed my hands over my cheeks. He came up behind me and wrapped his arms around me.

I swallowed hard, and snuffled, and wiped my tears with a dish towel. "What happened?"

"Someone didn't like me arresting him."

I tried to pull away.

"Toni."

I tried to pull away again.

"Babe, please. I need a hug."

"And I need—" I choked. "Not to see you getting beat up."

"Doesn't happen that often."

"Happens enough, and I don't like seeing you like this. It's upsetting. I don't like knowing that you could get hurt worse...."

"It's good to know you care."

"I care. What do you mean by that?" I snapped, angry.

"Babe, I can't even get you to go out on a date with me. You pull away every time we're together, you go home—"

I tried to push his arms away from me as I always do when he puts pressure on me.

He cupped my face with one gentle hand. "Look at me."

"No. I don't want to."

"Please, baby." He tilted my chin up. "Come on, look at me."

"No." I finally did, then my eyes shifted to the bandage on his shoulder and to that bruise on his arm, that cut on his neck, that someone did to him, some dirtbag criminal hurt Nick . . . my Nick. Who shouldn't be my Nick. There was no Nick and Toni, but he was still my Nick, even if I wouldn't go on a date. He pulled me close and held me tight.

I put my head under his chin while I trembled like some sappy lady who couldn't get it together. "I don't want to sleep with someone who gets hurt."

"I'll try not to get hurt again."

"Try harder, you big oaf."

"Okay." He kissed me and I was a sloppy kisser because I kept crying. He lifted me up, I wrapped my legs around his hips, and he carried me into his bedroom. It took my mind off things for a while, but when I stopped panting, and I was lying underneath him, I laid eyes on that bandage and bruise and started crying all over again. I pushed him to get him off of me.

He rolled and pulled me down on top of him again when I, the sloppy crier, tried to get away. He stroked my back and I settled down, about how a cat would. I was so tired from all that emotion that I fell asleep on him, and when I woke up it was two in the morning.

I got out of bed.

"One night, Toni. Please. Call it a pity night because of my shoulder. Call it a night when you give in one time. Come on, honey. We're so comfortable."

"No. You're making me cry. I didn't come here to cry and get scared about you and worry about you and I am not here to feel like that again and I don't like your job."

"I like you."

"I don't like you. You are bad for my, for my . . ." I struggled to think of something. "For my face."

"I'm bad for your face?"

"Yes. It's all puffy now and swollen and my tear ducts are tired."

"Then close your eyes and go to sleep with me, and I will rub your back."

Tempting. I loved when he rubbed my back, but no.

I left. I do not spend the night. He's my lover, my Nick. That's what he is: lover.

He trailed after me and walked me to my door and kissed me on the cheek. I hugged him, then pulled myself out of his arms when the kiss became all sizzly again and shut the door behind me after I said, "I'm mad at you, Nick," because I was mad at him for getting hurt. "Really mad."

I did not miss his sigh and one short swear word.

Living on a Tugboat, Talking About Homes

BY TONI KOZLOVSKY

I visited a woman this week who was born in the home she lives in now. Mabel Stiva is eighty-four years old. Her light blue front porch, the one that is almost invisible because of the overflowing flower boxes, is one of three front porches we featured this week because it's so welcoming.

"My home is me," Stiva told me. "It's my family. My parents and grandparents. It's us. It's the Stivas. I made strudel with my grandma in this kitchen. My father taught me how to clean a gun in the family room. My grandfather taught me how to ride a horse out back, where there is now a line of homes. They're all gone, but the home retains our memories between the walls. That's why I'll stay here until I die. My family is here."

I talked with a man named Marv DeSota, who

said that his modern home, about four blocks away, was the pinnacle of a hard-working life, a goal he had long held. "I grew up poor. We had nothing. I had two jobs by the time I was fourteen, delivering newspapers and working in a restaurant washing dishes. I used to look at people who had nice homes and think, I want that. I want that life. I want to have a roof that doesn't leak, a place that doesn't have rats, a floor that is not so broken in places we can see the ground. This home, for me, is the culmination of decades of work. No one helped me, I did it myself."

I also talked with an artist, Lucianne Micah, who has painted every wall of her home several times, depending on her mood and where she is in her life. "My home, to me, is my canvas. And my canvas, my art, is my life. That's why it's special. When I get tired of what I've painted, I paint it white, live with the white until I know what I'm going to do, then I paint a mural. It's mental therapy for a few hard knocks I've had to deal with in my life."

My own special home? I will always remember a small, tight, shabby apartment I lived in with my family in Moscow, Russia, then called the Soviet Union.

Do I want to live there again? I don't. Too many things happened I want to forget. Too many dangers, too many whispers in the night, too much of the KGB. It was cold, it was poor, it was desperate. Life as an American is much better in every way.

But I can see my mother making syrniki there, with jam and sour cream, and my grandmother Ekaterina making my sisters and me dolls out of cloth, and my grandfather carving me toys out of wood. I can see my father grading his students' papers, his brow furrowed. I can see my sisters and myself playing games in the small bedroom/closet we shared, one bed, all piled in together at night. I can see my uncles and aunts playing cards, laughing, shouting, an argument here and there.

I can remember Christmas, how we had to hide our small, homemade Christmas tree in our bedroom because being Christian was illegal. I remember the dollhouse my parents built us out of wood one year, wearing mittens as the apartment was freezing, the hot water off for weeks at a time.

I will never forget that apartment, our lives there, the laughter, the happy times.

Wishing you much laughter and happy times in your own home.

I saw my ex-editor, William Lopez. "Bored yet, Kozlovsky?"

"Not yet, William."

"I'm bored thinking about what you're doing. It makes me lose brain cells. I can hardly stand it."

I laughed. I bought him a box of cookies to "sweeten his sour disposition," which is what I wrote on the card.

He wrote back, "It'll never work, Kozlovsky."

"I no understand," my uncle Sasho moaned, head in his hands. "I no understand. How this happen? How this happen to me?"

"Sasho, all will be well," my mother said, patting his shoulder.

"Woe on my life, these things happen," Uncle Vladan said. "I don't know how."

"This not so bad," my uncle Yuri muttered, casting a glance at his pregnant granddaughter, Hope, who was outside in the backyard.

All of the Kozlovskys were at Uncle Sasho's house to celebrate his son Pavel's birthday.

Ellie was there with Gino, who hugged me, friendly as ever, and said, "I wish Ellie wasn't so worried about the wedding. I'm trying to help her, but she keeps telling me she has everything organized already, that you and your mom and Valerie are doing it."

I told him we were doing everything that Ellie asked us to do, and we chatted from there. There was a serious communication problem between those two, but I didn't say that, as that would have been a poor choice and Gino would have lost his marbles.

Valerie gave me a hug and said, "The Barton psychos haven't gotten me yet," Kai hugged me and said he missed seeing me on crime scenes, and Ailani told me she was studying DNA for a class project. "Can I put a cotton swab in your mouth and rub the inside of your cheek, Aunt Toni? I'm practicing taking DNA. Also, can I pull out one of your hairs?" Koa was wearing a King Kong outfit. He wielded a wooden spatula and tapped me on the rear with it.

JJ had circles under her eyes, and Jax had a stunned expression on his face. JJ told me that Jax was almost to the point where he could understand that his little girl had had sex, but her growing stomach still stopped him in his tracks. "He'll see it, then he feels faint and has to sit down."

Hope looked seasick from her pregnancy, and she told me she was "scared out of my mind, and sick in the toilet." I gave her a hug.

Chelsea arrived wearing all black and a second nose ring. "Mom and Dad are so upset about Hope getting pregnant, they didn't even say anything about the new nose ring. It was disappointing," she mused. "Not what I thought their reaction would be at all."

Boris insisted he was not stealing cars, and Tati and Zoya proudly showed us their new stripper clothes line for Tati and Zoya's Light and Lacy Delights.

Anya told me that she was worried about contracting Ebola the next time it "came around town."

The kids and teenagers were all outside in the backyard as Uncle Sasho continued to moan.

"Pavel, my Pavel, he want to be dancer. Ballet! Ballerina. For the boy."

"So he want to be dancer," my aunt Polina said, patting Uncle Sasho's left shoulder. "It okay. We no have any dancers in these families."

"A dancer? A dancer?" Uncle Sasho shook his big head, then put a hand to his face, over that nose that had been broken one too many times boxing in the Soviet Union. "No. I want him to be doctor. Engineer. Attorney. But he say dancer!" His bushy eyebrows shot up.

My father patted his other shoulder.

My aunt Holly said, "I like ballet."

Tati, ever the business owner, said, "Maybe he can introduce us to his dance teachers and we can make the outfits for their next recital."

"Tati!" Zoya gushed. "That gave me the shivers. See my arm? Shiver bumps. We should make up some samples and bring them to his school."

"I don't think that the high school will appreciate stripper outfits for their dancers," JJ said.

"I'll take a stripper outfit for my wife," Kai said.

Valerie slugged him, lightly. "Sweetie, I bet you'd like that." She paused, then turned toward Tati and Zoya, "Actually, could I get one from you? I need to get my sexiness back. I don't feel sexy. And I need one that covers my stomach. Two pregnancies have reduced it to cottage cheese with stretch marks."

"I like cottage cheese," Kai said. Valerie smiled at him. They are so in love, it's nauseating.

"I don't feel sexy, either," Anya said. "With all these diseases you can catch anywhere. I was studying African diseases during rehearsal and how they can travel on planes, spread themselves in the bathroom—"

"Let's get back to Sasho and Pavel," Aunt Holly said.

"I only want to know this: Why the little pink shoes?" Uncle Sasho said, distraught, his eyebrows rising up, down, up. "My boy. He *boy*. He want to wear the ribbon on his ankles? Pink ribbon on a boy? No. Not normal. I send him to this school, it say the school for peoples who want the art and science. Pavel say he like chemistry. So chemistry. This news I like. Chemistry for a doctor. But no. He like chemistry but he like ballerina-ing more. I not even know. It a secret. Ack. I raise boy ballet dancer!

How this happen? This America? They say you be what you want be, but now my son want be ballerina."

"We should design a stripper outfit line called 'The Ballerina,'" Zoya whispered to Tati.

"That's genius!" Tati whispered back. "Zoya, you always think of the best ideas."

"Oh no, stop. You do. You were the one who thought of the police officer stripper outfit. So popular. . . ."

"Go and get your brother," Uncle Sasho said to Tati. "I need to talk to Pavel."

We argued that it wasn't the time, or the place. It was Pavel's birthday! He insisted. Pavel was brought in. I hugged him, so did Ellie, Boris, and Zoya. Kozlovskys often solve family conflicts as a group, even when it's only between two people.

"Pavel, my son," Uncle Sasho said, sitting across from Pavel in the family room. "You are ballet dancer."

"Yes, Dad, I am." Pavel's voice was soft, but resolute. "I love ballet."

"Why, son?"

"I love to dance. I love the music, the rhythm." Pavel's hands were shaking. He was trying to be brave. "I love to tell a story through dance, to make people feel the emotion that the choreographer or the writer wanted the audience to feel. I love making something, a production, a show, and being a part of it. I like the people who dance, Dad. I feel like I'm a part of something, that I'm accepted, that people know I'm alive."

His words hung heavy in that room. We heard the loneliness. We heard the love for ballet.

"But you lie to me, son. You say you're after school for the classes in the chemistry."

"I know." Pavel's voice caught. "I'm sorry I lied. I knew you wouldn't approve. You want me to be a doctor or an engineer or an attorney. I can't do it, Dad, I'm sorry."

"What else? What else do you have to tell me? Are there more lies? Tell me now," Uncle Sasho said.

Pavel glanced at me, and I nodded. We had had many emotional calls.

Pavel studied his feet, then studied the ceiling, his eyes filling with tears. "Dad, I'm gay."

"What?" My uncle Sasho wrung his hands, his eyebrows shooting up again. "Gay?"

"Dad, I'm sorry. I know you don't want me to be gay, but I am. I can't help it. I remember liking boys in kindergarten. I know you're disappointed, I know you hate me, I know you probably want me to move out. . . ."

"No!" Uncle Sasho stood up. My father rushed to his side, as did my uncle Vladan and Uncle Yuri.

"Sasho!" my father reprimanded. "Sit down. Listen to your son."

"Be kind, Sasho," my uncle Vladan said. "It is love between a father and son."

"Brother," Uncle Yuri said. "Wait. Still your mouth. No hurtful words."

"No!" Uncle Sasho said.

"Uncle Sasho," my sisters and I said together, standing in front of him. Uncle Sasho had been a doting father—he was mother and father to his children since my aunt Yelena ran off with the plumber—but the shock was making him angry.

"Dad, I'm sorry." Pavel jumped up, too, in tears, his face red, crushed. "I'm sorry. I love you, Dad."

"No!" Uncle Sasho said again, his huge fists clenched.

"Uncle Sasho," I said. "This is who your son is—"

"Uncle Sasho," Boris said. "Pavel's a fine son to you—"

"Stop," Aunt Polina said. "You must not react like this, Sasho—"

"Please," Aunt Holly said. "Please sit down. He loves you, Sasho!"

"Uncle Sasho," Ellie said. "It's about love. It doesn't matter if he's gay—"

"Stop!" Uncle Sasho said, hands up.

"Dad, I can't change. I tried. I prayed. I told myself to stop it. I tried to make myself like girls when I was younger. Nothing changed—"

"I say no!" Uncle Sasho said.

Pavel's whole body slumped, and I blinked rapidly, furious with Uncle Sasho. Maybe I would hit him.

"That not what I meant, Pavel, when I say no." Sasho placed his heavy hands on Pavel's shoulders. "Son. I don't know about you being . . . being the gay. Being the homosexual. I don't know. You ballet dancer, too. I am confused. So much confuse. But this I know." He pointed a finger in the air as he raised his voice, booming again. "I love you. I love you with all my whole heart and my Russian and my American soul. You are a caring and loving son to me. If you want to be ballet dancer, then you be ballet dancer."

"Really, Dad?" Pavel's voice cracked. "It's okay?"

"No!" Uncle Sasho shouted. "It not okay."

Pavel's body seemed to pull in on itself again. I *would* hit Uncle Sasho soon.

"It better than okay." Uncle Sasho's voice softened. "I know what it like to live sad. To live with no hope. To live when people, what the word? Discriminate. When they don't like you for who you are. You honest. You ballet dancer. I come see you. I cheer for my son. I say, 'That my son up there.' I proud of you. You talented ballerina?"

"I hope. I'm trying." Pavel stood straighter, but the tears flowed. "Dad, thanks—"

"Then, my son, you be the ballet dancer. And you say you gay? So, you like the men?"

Pavel nodded. "But only one . . . man. My friend Danny."

"Danny? That Danny." Uncle Sasho sighed, shook his head again. "So much today for old man like me to hear. To understand. I try understand. This new life, all these years here in America." His shoulders stooped, and he paused. He thought. His eyebrows went up, down. We all held our breath. For once, all Kozlovskys were quiet.

"Well. Danny polite. I like that Danny. He come from good family. Not Russian American, though. That too bad." Sasho pushed his ham like fists together. "So you my gay son and you ballerina on your toes with pink ribbons. Okay. I take it. I take you. What I want, son, is happy son. That what I want. We have much sad in these families. In Kozlovsky family. In Sabonis family." He nodded at my mother, "Terrible things happen to us! But you happy, Pavel?"

"Yes, Dad, I am," Pavel said, his face a flood of emotions.

"Then this is well. I love you, my son. I always love you."

"Life is short," my father said, in Russian. "Love who you love. We accept and love Pavel as he is. He is a Kozlovsky. We are a family no matter what. Everyone needs to be happy. He is happy, and we will leave this as it is. This is my final word."

And so it was.

"Will you come to my show then, Dad?" Pavel asked. "The one I'm in? I have the star role. It's called *Bennie and the Music*."

"What? My son?" Uncle Sasho's mouth dropped. "You have star role? I can't believe. This big news. Yes. I come. We want everyone to be together. All the Kozlovskys. Who else come to the show with my gay ballerina love son?"

"I'm coming!" we all said.

Uncle Sasho hugged Pavel.

"See? We have love, right?" my mother said, hands out. "Kozlovsky love. Now, please. I make my coulibiac with salmon and eggs, and the loaf I made in shape of smile for all the bodies. Who want that?"

We all did. It had been a very emotional event. Many of us wiped tears off our cheeks. We're tough, we Kozlovskys, but we cry easily.

Boris the car stealer, definitely not gay, women in and out of his bed all the time, wiped his tears and followed my mother to the kitchen to help serve, followed by Zoya and Tati, who whispered to each other, "I don't care what they say. We can still make modest outfits and take them to Pavel's school . . . another business opportunity . . . costumes for school plays . . . we need to go to Vegas this year . . . they *need* us . . ."

There was only one person missing.

Come home, Dmitry.

Dmitry is a wanderer. He always has been.

He wandered away for the first time in kindergarten. When

the frantic principal finally found him, in a tree, almost at the top, and asked what he was doing up there, Dmitry said he was trying to find a red and purple butterfly.

He wandered away from home in first grade and was found sitting in the middle of a woman's vegetable garden.

He wandered in second grade onto a city bus because he said he wanted to find a blue door.

Third grade he wandered to the woods a half mile from our house and found a trail. He was brought back by hikers, stunned to see a small child alone.

Fourth grade he wandered to a duck pond and watched the ducks for hours.

In fifth grade he was found in the backyard of a neighbor playing with a white dog.

Dmitry was popular in school. Sports came easy to him. He was angry, often, and he took it out on every field, every court he came across. He got in fights with the opponent. He was the center on the basketball team and fouled out almost every game for being too aggressive. He hit baseballs out of the park.

Dmitry also loved art, music, and writing, particularly poetry. Math was a nonstarter.

Sometimes he wouldn't go to school. He would be gone all day and the school would call home, and my parents would go looking for him, until he was about thirteen, and then they gave up. They knew he was walking, wandering, exploring, *searching,* and he was fine, or as fine as Dmitry could be, and there was nothing they could do short of locking him up.

He was always vague about where he went, but mostly he headed into nature. He hiked. He backpacked. He camped. He fished. When my parents gave him a camera, that was it. He loved taking photos. Then they gave him a journal so he could write down information about the photos. He had found his calling.

After high school, at the beginning of summer, he left. He had saved his money from working at the restaurant, and he literally walked out the door with a tent, sleeping bag, and his laptop in a backpack. He started walking and camping and meeting people.

He created a blog called *We Need To Know Each Other* and

wrote down what he did, who he met, and their problems and concerns. He wrote about traveling. He wrote about solitude, being alone, but not lonely, and about being lonely while with others.

He wrote poems about not knowing who you were, who you came from, who you could be in the future. He wrote about emotions. He wrote about nature, preserving nature, and tied that back into his feelings.

One of his poems is called "Screaming." Others, "If Mountains Cried," "Rivers Who Call Your Name," and "Coyote Lonely."

He shared his day and his life and his thoughts. He took photos of people, arching bridges, barren deserts, soaring mountains, thriving cities, destitute slums, tragic situations, victorious celebrations, poverty and extreme wealth, art and books, bookstores and museums.

He walked from Oregon to New York City—in a roundabout way—over the course of two years. A small press saw his blog and photos, and picked it up. Dmitry titled it *The Loneliest Walk Together*. They were hoping to sell 3,000 copies. It became a cult classic type of book. He has sold over a million copies. His blog gets endless hits a month, and people walk the same trail he walked—Oregon to New York.

After the U.S. wandering, he started wandering the world, and he started volunteering his time, and his well-read blog, to raise money to preserve and protect forest land, meadows, mountains, and rivers. Because, as he said, "A wanderer needs a natural place to wander." He also started volunteering in poverty-stricken areas of the word, in orphanages, schools, and villages, because "we need people healthy enough, and safe enough, to wander."

His readers lived through him, vicariously, on the beaches in Mexico and the jungles of Vietnam and in the mountains of Spain. They read about living the simple life in Thailand and the isolated life in the northern wilds of Canada. They were with him roughing it in Montana or with a backpack in Guatemala. India. Pakistan. Kenya. South Africa. Remote islands.

He has posted photos of migrant workers, young girls rescued from the sex trade, drug traffickers, desperate immigrants, war victims.

When he's been in one place long enough, and it is unpredictable how long "long enough" will be, he "moves on." His next book is coming out soon.

His wandering has not cured him of his depression, though, that comes and goes, the nightmares and flashbacks scraping at him, reminding him of something, but not enough, shadows flitting in and out, never giving him enough to hold on to.

I called Dmitry on a Saturday afternoon from my tugboat, the river choppy that day, rushing faster than usual, the clouds gray and white, full, ready to burst.

He asked how I was, and how everyone else was. "How are you, Dmitry?"

"Fine. But I had another blond woman episode happen to me. I was on the beach, late. It was quiet, no one else on the beach, and I swear I felt my mother around me. Or that blond woman, whoever she was to me. I felt her presence again. Soft. Loving. Like she was hugging me."

This happened now and then to him. Dmitry said he could feel "her" around him.

It started to rain, but I didn't go in. Maybe the rain could help ease my pervading guilt.

"The Garden is back, too. I can't stop thinking about it."

Ah. The Garden. Usually The Garden was a cheerful image he had, but he had at least one terrifying image of the garden being demolished by some invisible force and him screaming, a dark shadow hanging over it. "What are you seeing in The Garden?"

"I see beets and potatoes, and they make me feel almost ill. Why do I hate them? Why have I never been able to eat either? I swear it has something to do with my childhood, but then sometimes I think I'm imagining the whole thing."

"I believe you, Dmitry, and I think it's all from your past, too. I'm so sorry." I'm sorry I've kept the secret. I shouldn't have. I tilted my head back and the raindrops slid down my face, cool, wet, blaming me.

"I'm sorry I talk about this all the time now, Toni. The visions this last year are getting stronger, more detailed. I feel like they're trying to tell me something, which makes me feel like I'm possessed or something. "

"You're not possessed." The skies opened up. The rain poured. I was drenched. I didn't move.

"Part of me thinks it's all in my head. That it's something I've dreamed up. That I'm not mentally healthy."

I heard his anguish, his confusion. "You are mentally healthy. Your memories are real. They're too specific. They evoke too many emotions not to be. What you're seeing has to be a part of your childhood. You asked for your mother when you were a little boy. Come home soon, Dmitry. Please. We can talk it out more." I was worried about him. He was sinking into his depression, I could tell.

"I'm headed that way. And I'm going to ask Mama and Papa some questions. But enough about me. What story are you writing now, Toni . . . how are you really doing? Tell me, please . . . and how is Valerie with that case . . . what about Ellie? She's still hyperventilating, isn't she . . . why is she getting married when she can't breathe when she thinks about Gino and a wedding dress . . . I asked her that the other night . . . and Mama and Papa?"

I was soaked by the time I finally went back into my tugboat. Whoever has said that rain is emotionally cleansing has clearly not been a guilty secret keeper.

It was not a happy sisters night.

We decided to meet on my tugboat for dinner. Ellie arrived wearing jeans and tennis shoes, her hair in a ponytail. I knew she'd been crying, because her eyes were more green than blue. Valerie stomped in, tense and tight, still in her suit and heels from the trial.

I had done two interviews that day for home articles I was writing. One home had rooms decorated with "world themes." There was an African giraffe living room, a Paris boudoir for a bedroom, a Chinese-themed family room, etc.

The other home was owned by a couple who had six kids and had remodeled their home to be kid friendly. The four-year-old twin boys had eardrum-busting temper tantrums when I was there. The fourteen-year-old told her mother that she was "ruining her life," and the sixteen-year-old boy took off with the car after being told no. They definitely needed more friendliness in that house. I would not be mentioning that in the article.

We sat down to eat on my deck, at the table, all stressed and tired. I hoped the gentle sway of the river would infuse us with some peace. If not, I hoped the vodka would work.

I had made pancakes, eggs, and bacon.

Valerie said she thought the Bartons were going to kidnap her, then she said, "Why have you been crying, Ellie? Maybe it's because you're tired of wearing a paper bag over your face?"

I threw a piece of bacon at her. "That's enough, Valerie."

Ellie threw a piece of bacon at her, too. "Shut up, Valerie."

But Valerie wouldn't stop yakking her mouth about how Ellie should call off the wedding.

"Valerie," I said. "She's not on the witness stand. Stop attacking."

Ellie shoved her chair back and stood up, beyond frustrated. She stalked toward the edge of the deck, about an inch from the river, then spun around, her face red and furious. "You know what, Valerie? You are the most arrogant person I know. You think you know everything. You don't. You're bull-headed. You're Type A for asshole. And you lost your gentleness and kindness a long time ago. You're like a human shark, do you know that?"

Oh. My. Gosh. That was Ellie. Finally fighting back.

"I would rather be a human shark than a wimp." Valerie threw down her napkin, her high heels tapping on the deck as she stood within a foot of Ellie.

"I am not a wimp. You're an overly ambitious, cold robot, Valerie. You like filleting people. You like the power. No one else can breathe around you. You suck the air out of the room. You're always talking about your job and murder and crime.

You hardly ever ask anyone else what they're doing, and you get bored easily with their answers because it's all about you."

Valerie's mouth open and shut, like a fish. "No, it's not."

"I'm getting married, and I'm happy, and you can't be happy for me." Ellie dragged in a ragged, rumbling breath. There was that "married" word again, which always triggered her. "I celebrated your wedding, the births of your kids, I go to all the parties, and now when it's my turn, all I get is you criticizing Gino, criticizing me."

"That's because I'm worried about you because you can't even pick out a wedding dress without lying on the floor of the shop. You can't even set a date. You can't even talk to Aunt Polina about the flowers without bending over to vomit, yes, she told me that happened."

"Damn it, Valerie. I am going"—*gasp, gasp*—"to get a wedding dress, and set a date, and order stupid flowers from Aunt Polina and get married!" She bent over and muttered to herself, "Calm down, heart, be still, go to your island of calm . . . embrace your strength and courage and . . . and . . . rainbows and daffodils and . . . breathe, please . . ."

"Open your eyes, Ellie. You're making a mistake."

Ellie flipped back up. She was angrier than I've seen her in a long time. "You want me to open my eyes?"

"Yes."

"They're open. Now close yours."

"What?"

"Close your eyes."

Valerie closed her eyes. Dumb thing to do.

Ellie pushed Valerie right over the edge of the deck. She tumbled into the water. Luckily the Sergeant Otts were not swimming by at the time.

"She's going to lose her heels," I said to Ellie.

"I could not care less. Thanks for the pancakes." She turned and left, grabbing her last pancake to take with her, as Valerie bobbed sputtering to the surface, shoving hair out of her eyes.

"Wow," Valerie said, treading water. "She is pissed."

"Yep, she is." I dropped a hand down to Valerie and helped her out.

"I hope I gave her something to think about."

"I think you did."

"I lost my heels."

"Yep."

"That was one of the best things that Ellie has ever done." She pushed her soaking hair out of her face.

"I was glad to see it. Surprised that you didn't see that coming."

"I saw it." She twisted her silk shirt up and rung water out of it. "I wanted to see if she would do it, and she did." She peered into the river, murky now, gray, blue, and black. "I'm going to miss those heels."

13

We had two weeks before the launch of *Homes and Gardens of Oregon*. There were ads, but not a lot. Companies were waiting to see the magazine before they invested in it. They wanted to know we had readers and they wouldn't lose money. But the ads were Ricki's and the *Oregon Standard*'s advertisers' problem. My problem was content.

I was writing two to three stories a week, interviewing people, checking out homes to see if they were beautiful/interesting enough to feature, writing my column, setting up photo shoots, and working with Ricki and the rest of the Hooters of Homes and Gobblers of Gardens.

An architect asked me out after I interviewed him about his own home. He gave me a list of 10 Reasons Why You Should Work With an Architect to Build Your Dream Home. Then he asked me to dinner. I said no.

He said, "Damn. Any chance you'll change your mind?"

I thought of Nick. "No, but thank you for asking."

"Sure. But damn. You're beautiful."

"Thanks."

"Damn."

Later, in the car, I thought how curious it was that I thought of Nick, not Marty, when I declined the architect's offer of dinner.

It gave me a sense of hope.

It made me feel guilty.

It turned my stomach upside down, but then my heart gave a pitter-patter.

I am emotionally screwed up, but I put on a front and fake it so I can function. Sometimes I wonder how many other people are doing the same thing.

I went to the mall afterward to practice Keeping The Monsters At Bay: Shopping Defensive Strategies.

I bought a red skirt with a side slit, a new pair of jeans, three bangle bracelets, and two dresses—one black, one patterned—for work.

I had a brief memory of feeling like a starving street urchin in Moscow. Then I remembered the bone-rattling chill of the winters, and the time that my shoes had a hole and the snow kept coming in until I stuffed it with a newspaper.

I bought a pair of warm boots, with faux fur, to remind myself I was not living in poverty anymore, slipping my hand around other people's wallets.

It was ridiculous.

My parents had picked my husband out for me. *Marty's parents* had picked him his wife.

As my mother said later, after Marty had asked me to marry him, in a river, in our kayak, "I knew he be perfect for you, my darling daughter, and that what I want for you. I want perfect. I want a Marty for you. He remind me of, what the bird, Alexei? That right, the blue heron. He excite in bed, isn't he? Like your papa. He excite in bed. It makes lots of babies. I want the little babies, you know. Any in there now?" She leaned down and patted my stomach, staring at it as if she could see through my skin. It wouldn't have surprised me if my mother had that talent.

"No, Mama."

"Humph. You no wait long time." She shook her finger. "I want be grandmother."

I rolled my eyes, and she laughed, and whispered, "His mama and I already planning wedding. You like it, I know you like. We do everything you like. She love you, too, like Grandmother love me. Mother-in-law, daughter-in-law, get along. Life better. I love you, my Antonia."

My father hugged me, then cried. "Antonia, I want for you happiness. That what I want. And here, with Marty, you have. I am happy now."

Being in love with Marty was peace. It was "excite," like my mother said. It was the happiest time of my life.

And then it wasn't.

The neighborhood gang met at my tugboat to strategize how we were going to save our home.

"Heather Dackson is going to represent us," Jayla said. "I gave her the deposit money and she's working on it."

"I don't want to leave. I go from the hospital, tending to sick and hurt people," Beth said, "to this dock, living in nature."

"I leave the college, and my students, and my old brain is fried and here"—Charles swept a hand up—"I recharge."

"Being on my tugboat has made me find a peace I didn't think I'd find again," I said, then was surprised that I'd said something so personal.

They nodded, smiled at me.

"Ya," Daisy said, a purple daisy in her purple hat, "I love it here, too. But you know what I love? I love you. You're my family on the dock. My family on the river. I'm getting crazy. Crazy Daisy, I call myself. Eighty-five years old, I think, and up here"—she tapped her head—"I get forgetful and confused, but I always know how to find my way home. I follow the river and I listen to the whales and they tell me where to go."

"It is home," Vanessa said. "And you make the dock special for all of us, Daisy."

"Really?" Daisy's voice caught.

"Yes."

"We love to listen to you sing," Charles said.

"You do?"

"I look forward to it every day."

"I can't help these dumb tears," Daisy said, waving a hand at her face. "I never used to cry, and now I do. I think it's because of this river family. Black and white couple, like vanilla ice cream and chocolate chips, two loving lesbians, a hooker who wears glasses and reads books, and a lady who sits and cries in her kayak. That's you, Toni. And the sex god. He's not here. You're family."

"You're the best, Daisy. Don't worry about being forgetful. I forget stuff all the time," Lindy said.

Daisy straightened up, her purple daisy flopping. "So we have to shoot the creepy monsters who are trying to take our home away!" She grabbed a silver gun from between her boobs and held it straight up. "If they take one step on this dock—*ka-boom*. They're gone. I'll disappear them. I know how to do that, you know."

"We know," we said together.

The thing was, we figured she probably did.

Daisy sang on the dock that night. The notes sailed around, like a song gift, then out to the rolling river, toward the thunder of the ocean waves. This time it was "Ave Maria," followed by Elvis Presley's "Hound Dog," "Silent Night," and "I Will Always Love You."

Valerie, Ellie, and I met at the restaurant about ten on Wednesday night. We sat upstairs, near a window, and prepared to eat what our mother decided we should eat. No arguing, no requests, no complaining. Ralph saluted us and smiled; Charlie saw us and started playing Beethoven's Fifth. He knows I love that one.

"I'm sorry I pushed you into the river, Valerie," Ellie said.

"I'm glad you did."

"Why?"

"I needed to cool off. You're right, Ellie. I am bull-headed. I am a human shark. I am a cold robot sometimes, and I do like the power in the courtroom over criminals. I'm sorry that no one can breathe around me and I suck the air out of the room. I'm sorry I'm not as gentle and kind as I should be. But you were wrong about one thing you said to me."

"I know. I said a lot that was wrong—"

"There was only one thing you were wrong about. You said that I don't care about anyone else. You two, Dmitry, our family, Kai, the kids, you're my whole life." Valerie teared up. "My whole life. And I do love and care about all of you, and I will listen more and shut my trap more."

"Oh, Valerie," Ellie squeaked.

We had a lovely sisters hug and, on cue, we said, "I love you more than Mama's Russian tea cakes."

"Ack!" my mother shouted, bringing our dinner in on trays. "What? You no love my Russian tea cakes?"

Ricki and I poured over the first copy of *Homes and Gardens of Oregon* on the conference table in the middle of our office, along with Kim, Shantay, Zoe, Penny, and Jessie.

The magazine would come out next week. The first home we were featuring, which was also on the cover, was a home I had found driving through an older street in Portland. It was pink. It was small. It had a black-and-white checkerboard door, and black shutters with hearts cut out of them.

I'd knocked on the door and had been delighted by what I'd found. The husband was a master carpenter, the wife was an artist, and they had transformed their tiny home.

The kitchen island was a former apothecary table with tons of drawers and a granite countertop. An ancient card catalogue from a library was painted bright red. They kept spices in it.

The walls were different bright colors, the curtain rods were made from long tree branches sprayed silver, and three metal colanders dripping with crystals, turned into light fixtures, hung over the table. Old shutters, painted lime green, formed a table with a glass top. A wagon wheel on a wall held photographs. Three small antique tables were stacked on top of each other, painted blue, and used as a bookshelf.

People would love it, especially the woman's paintings, which could only be described as color-blasting dream scenes. It was eye-catching, but there were ideas there on how to inexpensively reuse and recycle to make new décor and furnishings.

Kim had a two-page spread featuring a garden in the country, complete with a blue bridge across a wandering stream, a koi pond, and a shed that had been remade into a reading room with a red couch. There was a seven-foot-tall blue woman made of wire, a collection of birdhouses, and cement blocks that had the words LOVE, PASSION, DREAMING" carved into them.

We also had stories on how to start your own vegetable garden, the world-themed home that I wrote, and a column by Ricki introducing *Homes and Gardens of Oregon* in which she didn't swear at all or mention tequila. Kim wrote a column on gardening that was funny and amusing and informative.

My column, "Living on a Tugboat, Talking About Homes," was on the last two pages. There was a small picture of me in the corner, with a photo of my yellow tugboat, my kitchen with the glass backsplash, the wheelhouse and the red bench with the pillows, my bedroom with the French doors, my downstairs deck and view, the spiral staircase, Mr. and Mrs. Quackenbusch, and Dixie the blue heron in full flight.

We had a calendar of events, and a florist's bouquet of flowers that readers could win by signing up.

We were all exhausted. The hours had been relentless.

We stared at the pages in silence.

Finally, Ricki said, "Not bad, ladies."

We all nodded. "Not bad at all," I murmured. "Pretty dang good."

"Drinks on me," Ricki said.

We were ready for drinks on her.

Nick and I had dinner together, then we flopped into bed and talked about the book we were both reading. It felt very intimate. Book sex, I'd call it. I liked it.

I could hear Valerie in my head the next morning. One word: *Toni.*

I called her from my desk at work. I was eating a donut hole for energy and nutritional value.

"The Bartons left a dead rat underneath my car."

"Valerie," I moaned, clutching my phone, that chilly snake wrapping around my spine again.

"Right behind the front wheel."

"A dead rat."

"Yes. It's disgusting. It's sad. Poor rat."

We sat in silence, phones to ears. We both sort of whimpered.

"The police talked to all the Bartons. They all denied it. They know how to lie. They don't care about the law. The police are trying to prove it. The scary thing was that I was parked at the grocery store."

"They followed you."

"Yes."

"You need security people around you at all times."

"I'm getting it. Kai's on it. So is my boss. I'll be glad when the trial is over."

Kai was a saint. He was also a police captain, and he would be raising the roof. "How's it going?"

"Relentless evidence. Tyler's going to jail for a long time."

"If you could round up that band of merry sociopathic thieves who are following you, all the better."

"I have never felt threatened like this."

"I'm scared for you."

"I hate being scared, Toni. I hate it."

"I do, too. We had enough of that as kids."

"And I thought this type of fear was over."

"I don't think fear ever ends," I said.

"I think you're right." She paused. "But I will keep fighting. They will not scare me off this trial. I will get justice for his victims and their families."

"I know you will. Love you."

"Love you, too."

On my way home from work, I drove by the white house with the red door. It was raining, but the husband was in his garage again working on the tandem kayak. It looked like he was still sanding it down, getting rid of the chipped red paint. I saw his boys running around in front, chasing each other, their black curls bopping about. The mom walked out with glasses of lemonade.

They were a happy family. I was happy for their happiness. But it hit me in the gut, again, so I stared straight ahead and tried not to think about them and their red kayak.

My mother called Sunday afternoon. "You girls, I need you to work at restaurant. Tonight. Got reservation I forgotted about." Under her breath she swore in French.

"You forgot about a reservation?" I had to bug her about it. "You? Svetlana?"

"I forgotted. So, fifty people. Please. I beg on you, my love."

I rolled my eyes. "I'll be there in fifteen. But punish Ellie and Valerie, too."

"Ah yes. They come. No one say no to Mama, right?"

I saw my sisters thirty minutes later.

"I cannot believe I'm agreeing to do this," Valerie said. "I'm in a trial."

"I have an order to fill that will have me up all night now," Ellie said.

"I have a deadline," I said.

We headed upstairs to the private room. Fifty people. Noisy. We knew a bunch of them. When the three of us walked in, the ones who knew us shouted, repeatedly, "Kozlovsky! Kozlovsky!"

We laughed, we raked in the tips.

Afterward, my mother served us a salad that she named "Three Daughters. All Trouble." It's popular, but I often have people asking me what I did to cause my mama trouble.

My mother told us, "I know three thingies today. Three." She held up three fingers in case we were in doubt about the number three. "One, save your money. You never want to run out of the money, and then you starve to death. Two, women must be boss of their life, I knows this, I do. Don't let the man boss. Three, always put on the lipstick and earrings before you leave the house unless the house on fire. See? And three again, another three, your father. I say this to you now, when will he slow down? I don't know." She threw her hands up. "You would think, he old man, that I could get peace in the bedroom—"

"Okay, Mama," Ellie said. "Check that."

"Mama, please," Valerie said. "I'm eating."

"He's a firecracker in the bedroom, we understand," I said.

"Firecracker? In the bedroom?" My mother was baffled. "Why let a firecracker go boom boom in the bedroom when your father he already boom boom me and I so tired?" She sighed again, so dramatic. "It is this, what can I say?" She waved her hand from bust to hip. "You girls have it, too. The va va zing zing on the body, no?"

I finished my wine. So did Valerie. Ellie poured us another glass.

"I'm going to pretend," Ellie said, "once again, that I am not hearing about my parents' love life."

"Cheers to that," Valerie said.

"Ah, cheers," my mother said, holding up her wineglass. "To God. To family. To the Kozlovskys. And may those who wish us harm"—her voice rose, vengeful—"be struck by thunder and blinded by lightning and eaten by ants."

What a vision! We clinked our glasses together.

Homes and Gardens of Oregon launched. It went out on a Thursday, and by noon we had tons of names for the bouquet drawing. E-mails streamed in, people loving the magazine, a few hating it. One woman wrote, "I don't need to read about homes. I need to read about aliens." Another wrote, "I hate the home that was featured. Pink. Really? Everyone hates pink. It's menopause pink. It's little girl pink. It makes me feel like hitting someone."

But the compliments were effusive, too.

We got a call from Shirl, the advertising lady. "I've finally come up for air. You're getting reams of ads."

I told Ricki. She said, "I knew we'd kick some tail around here. How could we not with all these high heels and brainiac women running around?"

I had a story to turn in on a home that was built on stilts. I was also working on a story featuring the home of a local actor, who I knew through Anya. His home in the country was almost all glass.

But at six o'clock we closed up shop and went to O'Malley's, the whole *Homes and Gardens of Oregon* gang. Heckuva party. Ricki paid for it, and we toasted her as she yelled, "To the Hooters of Homes and Gobblers of Gardens, let's party, people."

So we did. I sang karaoke with Kim. I sounded like a frog with a seagull stuck in its throat. She sounded like an off-tune drunk nightingale. Our cohorts on the magazine about fell out of their chairs laughing. We made Ricki get onstage next. She did a Bette Midler song. She had the figure, not the voice. We about wet our pants.

About ten o'clock that night, I went over to Nick's.

He smiled, handed me a huge bouquet of pink roses, pink peonies, and baby's breath; a fancy gold pen that came in a box because "I love what you write"; and a picture of my tugboat, on a white mat, with a frame. "So you'll always remember your first column."

He is a manly and masculine cupcake.

Moscow, the Soviet Union

In our neighborhood in Moscow, there were the usual kids one finds in every neighborhood. The bullies, the quiet ones, the smart ones, the ones with wild imaginations, the leaders who organized everyone for games.

What was different there, as compared to our new neighborhood in Portland, was how grim it was. We all had so little. Few clothes, cold apartments, worn-out soles on our shoes, not much food. There were loving parents, doting parents, but vodka ran through the block, with the usual and expected problems. Drunken fathers, fathers who hit, mothers who had nowhere to go, mothers who sobbed. Families that struggled.

But kids are kids, and we played hide-and-seek and tag, horses and riders, and Cossacks and robbers.

My mother told us not to hang out with two of the neighborhood kids, Bogdan and Gavriil Bessonov. She said their father was a criminal and muttered something about the Russian Mafia, "may God have mercy on their black souls, and may He strike them down before they get to us."

We were intrigued by her warning, especially since Bogdan and Gavriil were funny and fun, daring, brave and bold. My sisters and I displayed an early attraction to the bad boys.

We watched them fight back when another kid picked on them or anyone else, we watched them wrestle, and I smiled into Bogdan's eyes. I was nine. He was eleven. I thought he was so handsome with that dark hair and green eyes. Two years of my childhood by then had been dedicated to daydreaming about Bogdan.

We disobeyed our mother and we hung out with the Bessonov boys. We walked partway to school with them, as they waited for us on the corner. We walked home with them. We played at the park together when we could arrange to, secretly, meet.

The five of us were walking home from school together one afternoon, commiserating about my strict teacher who made us memorize reams of information, especially about the Communist government. Valeria skipped ahead of us, her white bow bopping around, eager to get home because Mama had made a bread and apple pie. It was snowing, light, fluffy, but it made the gray of Moscow, the darkness of the river, the dull sheen of cement block apartment houses, less threatening. Whiter. Cleaner.

It was the beginning of winter, and we were young enough to still be excited by snowflakes. Elvira and I hung back with Bogdan and Gavriil, catching snowflakes in our mouths.

In the midst of laughing at one of handsome Bogdan's jokes, I heard Valeria scream in my head. *Help me, Antonia!*

"Where is Valeria?" I said, interrupting him, spinning around, trying to find her, people all around, buses, cars. I searched for her uniform, the same one I wore, a black dress, a white apron, a bow.

"What? Why?" Bogdan said.

"She needs help, she needs help!" I started to run toward home, knowing that was the route she would take. I dragged Elvira with me, holding her hand. Bogdan and Gavriil ran beside me, confused, but they were our friends, and they were coming with us to find Valeria.

"She said they're hurting her!" Elvira cried. "They hit her in the face. There's blood."

"How do you know that?" Bogdan hollered.

"I can hear her!" Elvira yelled back as we ran around a group of people heading to the subway, slipping on the snow. "I hear her."

Antonia! I heard her calling me again, but her voice was weak this time, tearful. *Get Bogdan and Gavriil.*

"She's telling me, run!" Elvira said. "They ripped her dress! She said to get Bogdan and Gavriil."

In my head, I said to Valeria, *Where are you? Where are you, Valeria?*

Alley. By the bakery.

"She's by the bakery," Elvira screamed.

"She's in the alley." I ran as fast as I could, but Bogdan and Gavriil were faster, whipping around the corner, their faces hot and livid.

It was three older boys. Two of them were holding Valeria back against the wall, one in front, his pants down to his ankles, his butt out. Her dress was ripped in half, her underwear down, her hair a mess. She was crying, blood on her face. One of the boys hit her and told her to shut up, shut up, shut up.

Gavriil and Bogdan had a lot of roving, raging anger in them. Their father loved them, but he was strict and could be scary. More than that, the five of us were friends. As tight as young friends can be.

Gavriil and Bogdan flew at two of the boys like hell had lit itself on fire. I flew at the third boy, the one standing to the side, egging his friend on, making fun of Valeria. That boy was bigger than me, but I caught him by surprise, and my fear for Valeria's safety sizzled through. When we fell, his head hit a rock and bled, and he didn't move for a second, which gave me the opportunity to punch him in the nose.

Valeria, sobbing, but now vengeful, pulled up her underwear, jumped between his legs behind me, and kicked him in the balls. He curled up, emitting a high-pitched scream. I took the opportunity to punch him in the nose again, blood spurting, and Elvira took the opportunity to grab a rock in her small fist and smash it in his face.

Valeria stumbled over to the other two boys, who were on the ground, straddled and being repeatedly pounded by Gavriil and Bogdan. She kicked them in the balls, too, as hard as she could, holding her dress together with one hand.

When the boys were beaten and curled up on the ground, Gavriil and Bogdan both pulled out knives. Short, sharp, jagged-edged knives. Those three boys froze, on the dirt, blood all over.

"If you ever," Gavriil said, almost calmly, "come near any one of the Kozlovskaya girls again I will kill you."

"I, too, will kill you," Bogdan said. He dug his knife into the boy's neck, enough to draw blood and make his point. He smiled, almost sweetly. "And I will enjoy it." Bogdan moved to the other boy, straddled him, knife to throat, a small cut.

The three of us sisters stood still, all of us panting with fear and fury, behind Gavriil and Bogdan. We had never seen them like that. With us, they were kind, protective, funny, always goofing off for the Kozlovskaya girls. This time, there was not an ounce of humor in them. I knew they would do what they said. Gavriil and Bogdan were capable of murder, even then, as young men.

"Do you understand?" Gavriil said, his voice steady.

The boys grunted through swollen lips. They sure understood. The Bessonovs yanked the boys up, shoved them, and the three hobbled off, two crying.

I tried to pull Valeria's dress together, my hands shaking. Her face was bleeding in two places, her hair a mess. Gavriil and Bogdan wrapped us up in their arms, and there we stood. Three crying girls, two boys who'd acted like men, in a dirty alley, in Moscow, the snow fluttering down.

"You heard Valeria in your head," Bogdan said to me.

"Yes," I said. I couldn't help but enjoy Bogdan's warmth.

"And you, Elvira?" Gavriil said.

"Yes," she said.

"Valeria told you where she was," Bogdan said.

"Yes," Elvira whimpered.

"We hear each other sometimes," Valeria said.

There was a silence.

"Okay," Gavriil said.

"Strange," Bogdan said, "but I like it."

"It's like magic," Gavriil said.

"It came down the Sabonis line," I said, "Like our genes, through our widow's peaks." I pointed to my widow's peak.

"Maybe there's a witch in your past," Bogdan said.

"Oh! I like that idea," I said.

"Me too," Bogdan said, smiling at me. I smiled back.

They hugged us closer. I enjoyed that, too.

Valeria had not been raped, but it was quite clear that she would have been within seconds.

Bogdan and Gavriil walked us home. My mother and my aunt Polina were there. They were out of their heads when they heard what happened. They cried, they shook, but they were strong women. Valeria was hugged and held. Bogdan and Gavriil were invited in and fussed over, hugged and held, too.

My father and my uncles were called. Uncle Yuri and Uncle Sasho and my aunts and cousins would soon leave for America, but they were still in Moscow at that point. Uncle Leonid came, too.

My father and my uncles, the former boxers, went to the boys' homes. It was ugly, I heard about it later from the neighborhood kids.

"They will not bother the girls again," my father said when he came home that night.

It was true.

"It was the language of sisters, wasn't it?" my mother asked. We nodded.

"Are we from witches?" Elvira asked.

My mother laughed.

I went with my mother and father, along with Valeria and Elvira the next night, to the Bessonovs, Bogdan and Gavriil's parents' home. Valeria's face was bruised and cut, and she was pale, but she wanted to come.

Stas Bessonov opened the door, Irina Bessonova behind him. She was a well-dressed and coiffed woman.

My father took one look at Bogdan and Gavriil, who each had a bruise and a cut on their face from protecting Valeria, standing behind their parents, and he could not speak. My father is a courageous, resolute, well-tempered man. He was used to the deprivations and fear in the Soviet Union. But when it came to his daughters, that heart melted.

My mother's lips trembled, her hands shook. She whispered, "Your boys, Stas, Irina, how can we ever thank them? They saved our Valeria."

"They told us they were in a fight," Irina Bessonova said. "That their friend was hurt." She turned eyes of pride to her boys. "Our boys are protective of their friends. They get it from their father."

My sisters and I each held out a pillow that we had made for their family. Irina Bessonova, made such a fuss over our "perfect stitching," our "exquisite embroidering."

"Please, come in," Stas Bessonov said.

"Oh no, we did not want to intrude!"

"Please, you must," Irina said.

We ate dinner with the Bessonovs that night and had a wonderful time. Irina put our pillows on her couch. We were so proud.

We were invited to eat beef with them—beef—spiced so well it melted in my little mouth, and Mr. Bessonov had "the best" vodka, according to my parents.

"New friends," my father said as we left.

"Yes," my mother agreed, her arm around Valeria, swaying a

bit from the vodka. "And what is a little criminal activity between friends?"

"Nothing." My father waved his hand. "And Stas kills only the bad guys."

"Certainly," my mother said. "Only the bad guys."

We were close friends with the Bessonovs from then on out, dinners at their house, and ours.

I was so relieved. Now I could marry Bogdan!

How were we to know how much that family would help us in the future?

It is not surprising that Valerie became a prosecuting attorney.

She believes that abusive/murderous, etc., men and women should be locked up to protect society. She is particularly an avenging angel when a woman or child is hurt. She has been that child.

She goes after them, in each case, as she did those boys who attacked her: with relentless ferocity and determination.

But Valerie is not blind, either. Several times she believed the "criminal" was innocent, or the charges against him had been inflated. She searched for further evidence and let him go, or charged him with a lesser crime.

There were other occasions where she believed that the police had stacked the deck against the defendant. She doesn't tolerate that and raised hell when it happened. She was ruthless in getting three cops fired and an assistant police chief forced into retirement. She also was a driving force in getting two inept, racist prosecutors pushed out. Though she believes in the law, she is also not overly punitive, especially if it's a young person who committed a nonviolent crime. She is fair.

But if you have hurt or killed someone, especially a child, or if you are a serial criminal, you are toast. Valerie will slice, dice, and lock you up.

Valeria Kozlovsky has never forgotten being that child, her dress ripped, up against a wall, in an alley, next to a bakery.

* * *

Living on a Tugboat, Talking About Homes

BY TONI KOZLOVSKY

This week I talked with Leah Dialoo about her 300-square-foot tiny house. Up on wheels, she pulls it with her 2000 blue Chevy truck. The roof is blue corrugated metal, the wood shingles give it a mini Craftsman style, the red front door is cheerful, and the many windows allow her to see all around.

A loft upstairs is peaceful for sleeping, and a blue couch against a wall is all she needs to curl up on. The galley kitchen has granite countertops that swirl like art.

White Christmas lights swoop through the rafters, two red tulip pendant lights illuminate the kitchen, and the floor-to-ceiling bookshelf is filled. Embroidered pillows from Mexico are scattered on her couch and chair.

Small, yet stylish.

Dialoo told me she has three pairs of jeans, four pairs of shoes, a handful of sweaters and sweatshirts, two coats, two pairs of shorts, about ten shirts, three pans, a strainer, and place settings for six. She has six coffee mugs and a tiny coffeemaker. She does have a scrapbook.

She has minimized her life to only what she needs.

But why a tiny house on wheels?

"I'd had enough," she told me.

"Enough of what?"

"Life. I was an investment banker in New York. I went to the right schools, had a bachelor's and an MBA from Ivy League schools, and I started climbing the ladder in the investment banking world. Then I found out what was going on. I could no longer be a part of that corruption and dishonesty, and the criminal manipulation of the markets, which led to real people losing their homes and jobs and almost sent this country into a depression.

"I worked with people who should have been jailed for what they did, and instead they danced off to their country homes.

"I paid off my parents' house, as they are taking care of my brother who has Down syndrome. I dumped money into an account to pay for his future care so that we would never have to worry. Then I took off for the first time in my life to find myself. I'd lost myself and I was deeply depressed.

"I gave away and sold almost everything I had and bought the truck and my house on wheels. Now and then I'll stop for a few weeks, often to volunteer.

"It is a tight space, but I'm outside all the time. I hike. I talk to people. I listen to the wind. I watch wildlife. I've seen deer, elk, coyote, a cougar once, bears. I canoe. I swim. I found I like painting flowers. Who would have guessed in my race toward the top that I would like painting?"

I asked her what she'd learned.

"That I need relationships. I need to help others. I need experiences."

My interview with Dialoo made me stop and think about stuff. All of our stuff. Our junk. Things clogging the attic and the basement and our drawers and closets. Some people even rent storage space for all their stuff—for years. It's economically totally impractical, but they do it.

I went home to my tugboat after I talked to Dialoo and cleaned. I threw out clothes I don't like and items that will never fit right, things I don't need. I took three bags to Goodwill, I hauled out boxes of paperwork to shred, and bags of trash, mostly from my refrigerator and pantry, which really should have been cleaned a long time ago.

It was hard. There were things in my home that brought pain to me, brought back memories, made me think of people who are no longer here.

After I threw out the "stuff," I cleaned.

When I was done, I felt lighter. My mind felt lighter. My tugboat felt lighter. My spirit was lighter, despite a few tears. Home should be relaxing, it should not be a place where we're crammed, we're squished, we're disorganized.

I doubt I'll ever go and live in a tiny home on wheels.

It's odd enough, to some people, that I live on a tugboat on the river.

But what I do want is an uncluttered life, like Dialoo's.

I want less.

I want organized.

I want efficient.

I want clean.

And I want only what I need.

The photographer had taken super photos of Leah and her tiny house on wheels. One was of the whole home, flowerpots on the porch. Others were of her loft with her fluffy comforters, her kitchen, her living space, and her flower paintings. The last photo was a picture of Leah sitting outside reading in front of her tiny home and old blue truck, a lantern nearby, the sunset spreading behind her, on fire with cotton candy pinks, tomato reds, and swirling purples.

Ricki came by the morning after she saw the photos. "Leah made me want to chuck everything and buy a small house and drive it from Alaska to Florida, like her."

"You couldn't," I told her.

"Why? I could be outdoorsy. Fish. Hunt. I could learn how to use a lantern. I could learn how to be quiet in nature."

"There would be no room for your shoes."

Ricki grimaced. "Now that would be a problem. Megaproblem. Insurmountable problem." She snapped her fingers. "Maybe I could have the tiny house, and pull it with my new bright red truck, and inside the truck I could have boxes and boxes of my shoes."

"I don't think that's the point of tiny-house-on-wheels living." I mused. "And what about your handbags?"

She puzzled that one out. She snapped her fingers again. "That guy I'm dating. He could follow me in another truck, and that truck could hold the handbags and clothes."

"I think you're set then, Ricki."

"Me too. I like being a cougar."

"You're not a cougar. Men aren't called cougars for going after younger women, so why do you have to have an animalistic label because your boyfriend is younger?"

"True. But we call men who go after much younger women lechers. Or midlife crisis creeps. Or dirty old men. Or pathetic. Or victims of young women who want them only for their money. Personally, I'd rather be called a cougar than that. Cougars are sleek, dangerous, smart. Me."

"You have me there. I'd take the cougar title over midlife crisis creep any day."

"He is chocolate chip cookie batter to me, though." She turned. "Want to get a drink after work?"

"You betcha."

14

&

The whole Kozlovsky family went to the opening night of Anya's play. It was titled *The Many Splendored Lives of Marie Bennett*. Anya was Marie. She was absolutely brilliant. Hilarious, serious, honest, raw, demanding, charismatic, flawed, lovable.

Long, long standing ovation.

No one would ever guess that the night before, gorgeous Anya had called me because she was worried she had "contracted a rare disease. I can tell by the slight pimples on my left arm . . ."

The critics adored it, the show sold out, they added three more weeks.

"I saw your *Peace Out and Head Out* blog, Dmitry." It was midnight. I was in the wheelhouse, wrapped in my white fluffy robe. I'd eaten apples dipped in melted chocolate for dinner in my bathtub. I washed it down with a blend of carrot and orange juice. Sometimes I try to be healthy.

"Hey, thanks for reading it. That blog is getting a lot of comments."

"Let's see," I said, reading his blog out loud. " 'Twelve Ways to Peace Out,' by Dmitry Kozlovsky. One, dude, get rid of the people in your life who are mean or sink your spirit or crush your courage. Two, let go of the crap people have done to you that hurts you. Three, go see a shrink. I've been to two women shrinks and they helped me sort through a lot of messed-up stuff.

" 'Four, get outside, camp by a river, fish. Five, have some wine at the beach and sit and be with those waves. Just be. Six, learn how to cook. Nourish the body, man, and you'll nourish the soul. Seven, volunteer. You need to share your generosity with other people. Eight, get a dog from the pound or a cat. Or both. They'll learn to like each other. Probably. Nine, listen to music, all types, and think about life while you're listening. Ten, read a bunch of books. Eleven, hang with people who reach your soul. Twelve, make someone's day better every day.'

"I like the ending." I read it aloud. " 'I don't want anyone thinking the way to peace is easy. I'm not even on that road today. Peace seems like it's somewhere off in the distance, beyond a desert, over a mountain range, through a thunderstorm, so don't think I've got it all together, man, I don't.

" 'Be truthful about your life to other people so we all don't get the impression that everyone's happy except us. Here's the truth of my life: Some days are better than others for me. I'm trying to work things out that happened when I was a kid in Russia that I don't understand. The past keeps snatching me back. I have problems. I have memories and flashbacks and nightmares that I don't understand that are all jumbled together. I get angry sometimes, and it's like, man, Dmitry, cool off. What are you so angry for? And I've got a problem I'm trying to solve right now that is not going away, it's only getting worse.

" 'I move from place to place and camp and couch surf and wander the world. I can't settle down, I can't be in one place for long, I can't commit to a woman because I'm not whole enough to be someone else's "whole," do you know what I mean? So, I've got my own stuff to deal with and have to follow my own advice. But if my advice helps anyone else, I'm glad of it. Peace everybody. Peace.' "

I leaned back in my chair. "Dmitry, that's an honest blog. I like it."

"Thanks, Toni." We chatted about the usual things, mostly about our crazy family, then I asked how he was sleeping.

"Better the last few nights. I don't know why. It comes and goes. But it was strange the other night, too. Right before I went to sleep, I saw a necklace, a gold locket. It was a heart and I saw two pictures in it, but I couldn't see their faces."

"A locket?"

"Yes. It was old. It was engraved with flowers, I think. It was on a white tablecloth."

"And you've never see it before?"

"No."

"I haven't, either."

"One more object in my head. I don't know if it's me losing my mind or if there's truth behind the object."

"I think there's truth behind the object."

"You've said that before, Toni, and I appreciate it. It makes me feel better. As if the things I'm seeing are truth, not the figments of a brain that is cracking or I've got some crazy neurological disease."

"I think everything you're seeing is in your past." You are not losing your mind, Dmitry, but that I have kept a secret that could have helped you to understand your past, without you thinking you were cracking up, makes me a terrible sister. Terrible.

"I think they are, too. I don't know, however, if I'll ever be able to put them altogether."

"I don't know, either." That would depend on two people and what they knew and didn't know and what they were willing to share.

Never tell, Antonia, never, ever tell.

All the Kozlovskys were at my uncle Yuri's and aunt Polina's to celebrate their anniversary. It was at their home, about a half mile from ours, brick, stone, traditional colonial style, built about forty years ago. The event was catered, and we were having French food, French wine, and Russian-made vodka. "For the fancy," my aunt Polina told me. Aunt Polina had done the flowers, of course, from her shop.

My father gave a long, long prayer before we ate to "bless this marriage, and all other marriages and the children and grandchildren, protect us, we Kozlovskys. Thank you Lord for . . ." and he went on and on.

My mother was resplendent in a red dress. She hugged me tight when I walked in, kissed both my cheeks. "Ack, Antonia. I could barely leave. Your papa." She sighed, poor woman. "He cannot resist me in this color, this red. I almost late. I put on my lipstick, see my lipstick, match the dress, but then your papa"— she glared at me—"he kissed me and I have to do it."

"Mama, please."

She rolled her eyes. "You old enough, Antonia."

"No. No, I'm not. I will never be old enough to hear what you and Papa . . ."

"How that saying go? He a lover, not a biter."

"Uh, no. It's 'He's a lover, not a fighter.' "

"He a nibbler. You know that word, Antonia? Nibbler. He take a nibbler, but he no take a bite of me."

"Oh, my Lord." I put my head in my hands.

"Yes, he a man of the Lord," my mother said, crossing herself. "But the Lord gave your papa lot of the passion in the bedroom. I tell the Lord, give me break, but no! No break from your papa. The Nibbler."

"Mama!"

She laughed and tapped my shoulder. "I think you a prune, Antonia."

"A prune?"

"Yes. I hear that on TV. Husband say to wife, 'I think you prune.' "

"No, Mama. He must have said, " 'I think you're a prude.' "

"No." She wagged her finger. "It *prune*. You eat the prune for the, what the word? Contraception? No. Not that. Constellation? No. I have it. Constipation."

"That makes sense to me now. I'm a prune for constipation."

"I know. I right." Victorious! "Give me hug and kiss, Antonia. You have no hug and kiss for Mama?"

I hugged and kissed my mama.

She whispered in my ear, "I bring you some lymonnyk, the

lemon pie you likie. Same with Elvira and Valeria. In my car. You need eat-y more, too thin, I tell you. Eat-y more."

My next conversation was with Tati and Zoya, the naughty twins, they of the stripper clothing business. They were dressed in high heels, shiny shirts, sequins, tight jeans.

"No dates tonight? I thought you both had a boyfriend."

"Two boyfriends," Zoya said, kicking up a silver heel. "Right now."

"You have three," Tati said.

"No, two. No." Zoya put her hand up, fingers counting. "You're right. Three."

"Aren't you exhausted?" I asked.

"No." They smiled.

"It does wonders for your skin," Tati said.

"Yes, and for your blood pressure." Zoya took a drink of champagne.

"I read the other day," Tati said, "that sex loosens up your bowels."

Was this happening? Constipation and loose bowels in one evening's conversation?

Zoya peered at me. "Your skin is porcelain, Toni."

"It is. Always has been," Tati said. "Must be the Jolly Green Giant Sex God we've heard about."

"Please don't tell my parents. They'll name a special after Nick at the restaurant, make an announcement in church, start calling him their future son-in-law..."

"We know," they said together.

"That's why we haven't told our father, either," Zoya said.

"We kept it to our twin-self," Tati said. "One brain."

Zoya handed me a box. Red. Gold ribbon, as all their stripper/sexy lingerie clothes are wrapped. "This is for you. It's to make you feel womanly again."

"Thank you."

It was red, lacy, flowing. I sniffled. "It's the most beautiful lingerie I've ever seen."

"Don't cry, Toni, or I'll cry! It was Zoya's design," Tati said. "She's so clever."

"No, it wasn't. I drew a rough outline and Tati did all the rest. She's the smart one."

"Give Zoya the credit . . . no, give Tati the credit . . . We love you so much, Toni." They sniffled.

"Love you both, too." Three-way hug. I love my cousins.

The Jolly Green Giant Sex God would love the lingerie.

I visited with JJ, who said, "I'm going to fix your hair, Toni. Didn't you brush it today? Did you lose your brush?"

"It looks fine."

"No," JJ snapped. "It does not."

She put her hand on my back and pushed. We went to her parents' huge bathroom, and JJ had my hair up in a ball with a couple of braids in minutes.

"Much better. It doesn't look like you walked through an Iowa windstorm. You're so pretty, Toni."

"Thanks. How's Chelsea and Hope?"

JJ wrapped her brown hair into a French twist, rather ferociously. "Chelsea continues to wear black all the time, which is unflattering with her coloring. She pierced her eyebrow again last week and looks like she has a pincushion on her face. She still wears black eye shadow and resembles a ghoul. She won't let me fix her hair, which is, currently, pink and scraggly. She bought black combat boots last week, so she looks like a biker gang member, and she won't come in on Friday and Saturday nights until two. She is sneaking into clubs downtown via, get this, the ceiling. Yes, she crawls in through the roof. However, she did sit down with me the other night, and we had a serious conversation about college because she has decided she wants to study chemistry."

"Chemistry?"

"Yes, she is apparently part witch and likes to mix things up. She is taking three science classes this year because she loves it. On the other hand, Hope is getting more and more pregnant by the day. My teenage daughter has morning sickness." JJ started to cry and perched on the rim of the two person bathtub. "I can't believe this."

"I'm sorry, JJ. I don't know what to say that won't sound inane. I love Hope and I love the baby and you and I'm sorry, all at the same time."

"Yes." She rubbed her temples. "I get it."

Valerie walked in. We knew she would be late because of the trial.

"What? You have a mop on top of your head, Valerie!" JJ screeched. "What did you do, run it through a leaf blower and then cut it yourself with a hatchet?"

Valerie peered in the mirror. "Wow. It does seem I've been in contact with a leaf blower."

"Sit down right this minute." JJ fixed her hair. "Valerie, don't go out in public like that again. You're disgracing my salon."

Valerie nodded, smiled, but she was worried, tight. We would talk later. I knew what it was about.

"How's the musical?" I asked Pavel.

He smiled, ear to ear. That kid has a beaming smile. "It's so much fun, Aunt Toni. I can't wait until the opening night. But I'm scared, too. I'm glad Dad knows. Now I don't have to lie and have a secret. I hate secrets."

"I hate them, too." Oh boy, did I hate secrets. "Your dad took it pretty well."

"Yeah, I know. Want to see my ballet number for *Bennie and the Music*?" I did. I clapped.

"I like what JJ did to your hair, Aunt Toni."

"Thanks." Interesting that he knew JJ did it and not me . . .

Hope gave me a hug. "I can't believe I'm pregnant." She burst into tears. I took her to Aunt Polina's bathroom, and we talked on the rim of the tub. I was spending a lot of time in there.

Chelsea came up to visit later. She was carrying a mug. I'd bet it was vodka and Coke. She was dressed in a black dress and black combat boots. Her face did not look like a pincushion. Her hair was pink.

"You have another piercing," I said.

"Yes. Mom and Dad hate it." She frowned. "But not that much. I'm not the problem daughter anymore."

I could see that troubled her, poor thing. "I hear you like chemistry?"

"Yes. I accidentally started a small fire in the lab on Thursday. It made this loud booming noise . . ."

Kai gave me a hug. He was holding Koa, who leaned over for me to hold him. "Aunt Woni!" he said, resplendent in a blue cookie monster outfit. "I yove you."

"I yove you, too, Koa." I talked to Kai about his job. "I've had enough of arresting people and rolling around in the dirt or on the street downtown. I don't want to get shot at again. I'm retiring as soon as I can and Valerie and I are going to Hawaii where we can surf all day. She's going to wear a bikini and I'm wearing Hawaiian flower shirts."

"That'll be when?"

He knocked his fists together. "As soon as the kids are through college."

"You do know that Koa is three?"

His shoulders slumped. "It'll never happen will it? Will it? Will it?"

Ailani bounced up, hung on her father, and said, "Aunt Toni, I'm studying Jack the Ripper and I'm writing my book report on him."

"You are?" I slammed my teeth together so I wouldn't chuckle. "Well, that's almost criminal."

She seemed confused. She brushed hair back from her widow's peak. "It's not criminal to write a report on Jack the Ripper. I'm reading a biography on him. Four hundred pages. I'm going to get one of those five feet by three feet bulletin board thingies and I'm going to make a time line of the murders with all the photos I can find. Then I'm going to draw a huge picture of Jack the Ripper from the back because they don't know who he was, not exactly, and I'm going to paint the edges red. Do you know why red?"

"For the blood?"

"No." She was baffled by my ignorance. "Because then the picture will pop out way better. It's important to consider color."

"Your teacher will be surprised."

"By what?" She was, once again, confounded by my question. "I like what Aunt JJ did with your braids." She skipped off to give my mother a hug.

My father gave me a hug and a kiss. "Ah, Antonia. You are movie star. JJ did pretty job with your hair. Now, you tell me everything. I haven't seen you since Monday. So. Start at the beginning. What you do on Tuesday? Ah, I see . . . what about Wednesday . . . Now you tell me, Thursday?"

"I think, I do truly think," Anya whispered to me over veal ragout, served on white plates, with crystal glasses nearby filled with wine, "that I have chips of bones in my neck. I think my spine is deteriorating. That can happen. I studied it on the Internet. Listen to my neck when I move my head. Are you ready? Lean in, lean in closer . . ."

"I'm so close I could kiss your neck."

"Take this seriously, Toni. Did you hear it crack? It crackles, pops, scratches. What do you think that is?"

"I think it's normal."

"It's not normal. I think I'm going to go to the emergency room."

"Don't go for a disintegrating neck. Go to the doctor's in the morning."

"My doctor said I'm a hypochondriac."

"Do you think he's right?"

She crossed her arms and rolled her eyes. "No. Duh. I think he's sick in the head. I told him that. I told him that I was seeing signs of dementia in him."

"And what did he say?"

"He said he was going to forget I had come in for another appointment."

I laughed.

She glared. "I do have a disintegrating neck, Toni. That is not in dispute."

Of course it wasn't.

"I like what JJ did to your hair."

"Why do you think JJ did it? Maybe I did it."

She made a no-one-believes-that sound in her throat.

"How's the play going, Anya?"

Boris swooped on in, hugging everyone. He saw me and made a beeline.

"How's the car stealing going?"

"I don't steal cars, I fix them. And if I do steal them to fix them, it's only from the spoiled and the wealthy. You're going to lose your head over this one, Toni." He flashed two tickets, underneath his coat, grinning like a banshee. "I have two tickets to *Carmen*. Will you go with me? Please? You're the only one in the family who won't laugh at me when I cry at the opera."

"Happy to go, thanks, Boris. But don't steal a car to get to the opera. If you were arrested, it would be embarrassing."

He was appalled. "I don't steal cars, but that would be my nightmare. Missing 'La Fleur Que Tu M'avais Jetée.'" He shivered. "Don't even suggest such a thing." He studied my hair. "Man, JJ can do anything with hair, can't she?"

I asked Uncle Sasho how he was and he said, his short, frizzy hair seeming to move on its own accord, "Two daughters, make clothes for the stripper, can't believe it. But—" He paused, raising his bushy eyebrows in acceptance. "It a business. They make the money. And I have one boy, dancer. Gay." He paused again, the eyebrows shot back up. "But, he talented. No sign of wife who left me. She no call. Maybe, soon, I get another wife. You think someone have me? I don't know. I not handsome. But"— those eyebrows shot up once more—"I be a right husband. How are you, my Antonia? Pretty hair. My niece, JJ, she knows the hair."

I asked Uncle Vladan how he was, and he said, "Woe on my life. My daughter. Anya. Actress. No husband. No babies. Thinks she sick all the time. Last time, she say I have to listen to her knees. Thinks a bee in there or something. Tonight she think her neck disappearing. Boris, his mechanic business, it thriving. Many cars. What you doing, Antonia? So beautiful with your hairs like that. JJ can fix any hairs."

I asked Aunt Holly how she was. "I'm fine. Remember, I teach kindergarteners. Two boys had a squirting war in the bathroom on Friday. One girl asked me what it was like to have dinosaurs around when I was younger."

"What did you tell her?"

"I told her I liked to ride on their backs. I had a number of them as pets and I put leashes on them."

"Did she believe you?"

"Those little sweethearts believe everything. One girl told me that her mommy said she got a baby in her stomach because she drank too much wine. But how are you, Toni? Love your hair, by the way. I have to go and see JJ again soon, too."

Why did everyone assume I hadn't done my own hair? Okay. I knew that answer.

Ellie, Valerie, and I met on the rim of the bathtub with our wine for a few minutes away from the Kozlovsky cacophony. Ellie needed a break from Gino, too. He was by her side, attentive. She was nearly nonbreathing, her bag to her face.

"One of Tyler Barton's cousins was obnoxious in court today and the judge kicked him out." Valerie took a long drink of wine.

"What did he do?" Ellie asked.

"When I walked up to question a witness, he whispered, 'Dead woman walking.' Security was all over it, hauled him up and out. Then he shouted, 'Dead woman walking,' three times. He smirked at me. He went to jail. Threatening a prosecutor."

"Geez, Valerie." The chilly, squirming snake of fear wound around my spinal cord again.

"What about the other Bartons?" Ellie asked, bag away from her face for ten seconds.

"They're allowed to stay. They didn't do anything."

"When I went the other day I couldn't believe it. Police, security, suits," I said.

"They're on it. The Bartons are rabid. Thanks again for coming down. You, too, Ellie. I liked having you both there."

"I'm worried," I said.

"So am I," Ellie said.

"The trial has me up at night, I'll tell you that," Valerie said. "This is a whole different breed of human."

"Let's have a bath hug," I said. The tub was huge, the three of us lay in it, arms around each other.

Our mama walked in. She was not surprised to find us in the bath together. "*Tsk.* I cannot have tub like this, because I never be able to work. Your papa"—she pointed a finger upward—"he would—"

"Mama!" we shouted.

Uncle Yuri and Aunt Polina stood in front of all of us, straight shots of Russian vodka in hand. Uncle Yuri made a speech, in English, following the Kozlovsky family's motto, "Speaky the English," and ended it with, "Polina is the love of my life. My life be nothing without Polina."

And Aunt Polina ended her speech with, "Yuri, we not divorce because I have patience of saint, thank you Lord. Many times, I want to hit you in face with pan. My silver pan, not the special new pan from JJ. I like that red pan. Don't want no damage. You drive me crazy in the head"—she tapped her head in case we had forgotten where her head was—"but I love you, old man."

"Ack! What? Am I not good husband, Polina?" Poor Uncle Yuri!

"You okay, old horse. You could be worse, could be better." She kissed him. "So, next two decades before you die like old rat, you be nicer to me. More flowers. You buy me nicer car, too. I want car that goes zoom, like on the commercials on the TV, you cheap skater. Is that the word, cheap skater? And you no give me bad time when I buy the new dresses. You get it now, old man?"

Yuri nodded. "Ya. Okay, Polina."

Well now! That was romantic enough for the Kozlovsky gang! We cheered, "To Yuri, to Polina...to family...to the Kozlovskys..." Bottoms up.

My cousins/spouses, etc., and I ended up at a bar later.

As Boris said, "We're all going out. We want everyone to be together."

We were noisy, laughing, playing a light drinking game once we were all crammed around a table together.

There should not have been a bar fight, but a man was too aggressive with Zoya and she swung her purse at his head and conked him. That pissed him off, and he charged Zoya, but Boris, who is not unfamiliar with street fighting, and Jax, who has a tough side, jumped in, along with Tati, who screeched in outrage and jumped on the offender's back. One of the conked guy's friends joined in, and Kai tried to break it up, along with Gino, who is sweet but no wimp. Another of the conked guy's friends jumped in and so, too, did the rest of us Kozlovsky women.

The police came. We knew a bunch of them, but we scooted on out, laughing so hard I wet my pants, a tiny trickle.

We called taxis and the Kozlovskys scattered into the night.

"Are you going to invite me to your sister's wedding, Toni?"

"No."

Nick was not pleased. I couldn't blame him. I blamed myself. We were naked, in his bed. I had brought dinner. Pasta with chicken and parmesan. Hot bread. Beer. We ate dinner on his deck, we talked about our days, Nick kept kissing me, I kept laughing, and we ended up in his bath, then his bed, by nine.

"Why?"

"Because. My family is loud and noisy and nosy and I can't bring you yet."

"We can sleep together but I can't meet your family?"

"Right." I am a cold piranha-like human. "I'm sorry."

"So am I, Toni. We need to talk about this."

"There's nothing to say. I'm not ready to introduce you to my family."

"You're not ready for anything."

I got up to go, anger flashing right through me, along with guilt and a dose of deep sadness. I did not need this. I didn't need the stress or the pressure.

He caught my wrist. "Why don't you quit running and talk to me?"

"Because we don't need to talk about anything, and why did you have to spoil a fun night?"

"I didn't want to spoil it, and yes, we do have to talk."

"Why? Things are fine. We like to sleep together now and then."

"Now and then, Toni?" I didn't miss the incredulous tone. "Most nights. We also like talking, being outside on the deck, and reading together in bed, to name a few things."

"That's enough."

"It's not enough for me, babe."

"It's all I can give."

The silence was a zinging, tight cord between us. Yank, yank, yank.

"I know what you're doing, Nick."

"What am I doing?"

"You're trying to figure out how best to handle me, and I don't appreciate it. You're trying to figure out how to get what you want, how to make me change my mind, how to make me see things your way in our relationship."

"You're a brilliant woman, and that's one of the things I like best about you, but you're also making me sound manipulative."

"Aren't you being manipulative?"

"No, I'm not. I'm trying to change where we are in this relationship. I like you, Toni. You are the most remarkable woman I have ever met, and I know you've been through a hard time."

I felt the tears. The tears always seemed to start in my heart. "Everyone's been through a hard time."

He nodded. "Yes. But you have been through a particularly hard time."

"You're making my brain tired. I don't like it."

"What do you mean?"

"I mean, Nick, that I can't take the tired. I can't take more stress. I don't want either in my life. I want a relationship that's only for us. I want you to be an island. That sounds stupid, but I want you to be the place I can go to where everything is smooth. Peaceful. I don't want to tell you all my problems. I don't want to delve deep into your life, because I can't handle the job that you do and the threat to your life and how you sometimes get in fights and get cuts and bruises, and I don't want to have to worry about you, and care, and be at home wondering if some drug addict has attacked you. It's too much. And I don't want anything serious, because I would feel overwhelmed."

"I don't want to make you feel overwhelmed. I don't want to make you tired. I don't want to cause you stress. I don't want you to worry about me when I'm at work. That's not my intention at all."

"But I do worry about you already, and I'm ticked off about that." Super-ticked off. How dare he make me worry?

"I'm sorry, Toni."

"You should be, Nick." I knew my tone was angry. I knew it sounded silly to get angry at Nick because his job made me worry. "I told you from the start what I wanted, and you agreed to it."

"I have agreed to it. And now I need to change this. What about what I want? Is that not relevant to you at all?"

"I want you to be happy, Nick. If you're not happy with me, then we'll quit seeing each other."

"That easy for you, is it?"

Oh, that triggered him right on up the temper ladder. "It's not easy for me to say that we'll quit seeing each other, but I'm also not going to get in a deeper relationship than what I want, what I can do."

"Shit," he muttered. "You really know how to make me feel like I am nothing in your life."

"I don't mean to—"

"Yes, you do. You're clear on that. You could walk away from us, from this, easily." He stood up and yanked on his boxers. "You just said so. You said we could quit seeing each other, as if it wouldn't matter to you at all. As if I don't matter to you at all."

"I don't want to walk away from us, Nick. I thought you and I had an understanding. I thought you wanted what I want."

"What I want is a committed relationship with you. I have always wanted that. I was clear about it. I thought, I hoped, we could move in that direction."

"I told you from the start we couldn't. I was up-front and honest. Now you want to change my mind."

"Can't I?" His eyes were soft, and sad, but still truly pissed.

"You can't." But he could. And I couldn't let that happen. "I'm not ready and you have a bad job that I am not going to deal with."

"I have a job that I love, Toni. It's what I've always wanted to do. I believe in what I do. We take down drug dealers, we break up drug rings. It's relentless, but I know what I'm doing is right."

"It's not right for me."

"I would never ask you to quit your job, Toni. Even when you were working crime and justice and you were in dangerous places sometimes, I never said quit."

"If you had, I would have been even madder than I am now." I threw a pillow across the room.

"Feel better?"

"No."

I threw another pillow.

"Feel better now?"

"No." I threw one more, then laughed, couldn't help it.

I saw a smile tip a corner of his mouth.

"Nick, I know you love your job, but I don't want to be so

wrapped up in you that I have to"—I stroked my throat, suddenly tight, as if despair was shutting it down—"have to lose . . ."

"You're not going to lose me. I'm careful." He stared out his window at the river, then turned back to me, his shoulders not as straight as they had been before. "Okay, Toni. Here's where I am. I want to be with you, but I need more between us. You don't. You know where I am, and when you're ready, I'm here, if you want to change things. I'm not going to wait forever, but I will wait now."

Why do I cry so easily? I put my arms over my head. I wanted to hide. Nick wrapped his arms around me, and I cried on that chest of his. "I am so screwed up."

"You aren't screwed up, babe."

"I'm sorry I threw your pillows. That wasn't nice."

"It's okay. Don't cry. Come here. No, don't pull away, come here, baby. I'm sorry. I didn't mean to upset you. . . . I bought chocolates for you. Want a chocolate?"

I did.

Nick deserves more than me, more than this.

I loved Marty's parents, they loved me.

It was ridiculous. Everything was butterflies and rainbows and puppies that didn't slobber.

I didn't know a thing about planning a wedding, but it didn't matter. My mother and Marty's mother, Raina, sat down with me one day, after they had had lunch to discuss "our children's wedding."

They asked me ten questions about what I wanted. Flowers, colors, bridesmaids, invitation design, etc. My head spun. But, first question they asked—when did I want the wedding?

I told them to ask Marty. They said they had. Marty wanted to get married as soon as possible, preferably "next weekend." The mothers were in a mighty stew about that one. They "could not possibly" get it together that quickly. They both wagged their fingers at me, as only Russian mothers can do. "No. That is no. *Tsk!*"

"The wedding must be perfect," my mother said. "For our children."

Raina nodded. "It is a gift, from us to you, our son and daughter. We will plan this for you, okay?" She cupped my face, kissed my cheeks and said, "You are now my daughter, Antonia. I love you." And then she peered down at my stomach, her face hopeful. "Is there a baby in there yet? I want to be a grandmother."

My mother sat up straight. Yes to being a grandmother! "You do it, Toni. You do a quickie. We want the baby."

The reception would be at the restaurant, that was a given.

I hear nightmares about mothers-in-law. My mother-in-law was, is, beautiful, as is Marty's father, who is so like him.

Marty and I let the mothers do their thing. They were delighted to do it. The fathers got together to "help" and ended up in our garage, my father's man cave, where they watched football. They also "helped" by going golfing together.

Both Marty and I were working long hours and the mothers had the wedding in hand, so we decided to spend more time in bed together. It was more relaxing and exciting.

I decided to keep my last name. I know Marty would have liked it if I changed it, but I couldn't. Maybe it was because of what the Kozlovskys went through in Moscow. Maybe it was my independent streak. But I was a Kozlovsky forever, and so in love I could hardly think.

As for my bridal shower, fiery fight on who got to do that, but JJ ended up doing it because she got all bossy and promised cool hair products from her salon. Bachelorette party, another fiery fight on who got to do that, but Zoya and Tati did it because they promised everyone a packet of stripper panties. A bridal brunch, fiery fight again, my aunt Polina won because she put her foot down and threatened to "let my temper run around and about like Russian Mafia!"

The rehearsal dinner, for eighty, as no one could be left out, Marty's parents hosted at their home.

Then the-day-after-the-wedding brunch. Another fiery fight. Anya and Aunt Holly took charge. Forcefully.

Miraculously, at the end of planning the wedding, the mothers were best friends, as were the fathers. You want fairy tale. Marty and I had a freaking fairy tale.

We loved the bridal shower, the bachelor and bachelorette parties, the bridal brunch, the rehearsal dinner, and the day-after brunch. The wedding was spectacular because all of our family and friends were there. Two hundred people, about half of Russian descent.

It was too perfect.

Perhaps that was the problem.

It was too sparkly and shiny and bright to be true, so it was taken away.

15

"I'm worried about Dmitry," Valerie said.

"Me too," Ellie said.

"What? What wrong my Dmitry?" my mother asked, dropping her fork, her voice low. We were at my parents' house for Sunday dinner. Valerie's family begged out as Ailani was writing an essay on how to become a homicide detective, and Gino was going to his niece's birthday party.

Gino was not pleased that Ellie wasn't with him at the niece's birthday party, which made Ellie put a bag to her face when she told us. "I can't stand his family," she said.

"What is this? Why the worry?" my father asked, his head swiveling back and forth, daughter to daughter. "What is happening with my son now?"

"His sadness is back," I said.

"My Dmitry." My mother's lips trembled.

"No," my father said, his shoulders hunching. "No. Not again."

"When is he coming home?" Valerie asked.

"Soon, he said." I poured a glass of wine for my mother, who was now saying the Our Father and crossing herself.

"How soon?" Ellie asked.

"For the wedding." There was still no set date for Ellie's wedding. I poured a glass of wine for my father.

"Please, God," my father said, tilting his head up. "Bring my son back home to me."

"All this . . ." My mother threw her hands in the air. "Always walking, searching. Wandering, he calls it, on that bloggy that he writes." She put a hand to her lips as the tears spilled.

"But no wandering to Russia," Valerie said. She looked exhausted.

"Russia!" my father spat out. "Was Soviet Union. Dangerous government. Dangerous men. He does not need to go to Russia. Not safe."

"When he comes home, he wants answers, Papa." I leaned forward. "The truth."

"The truth?" My father suddenly stood up and slammed his fists on the table. We all jumped. "I tell this family the truth many times. Many times! The truth is Dmitry is my son, your mother's son. He is your brother." He stabbed a finger at us. "That is truth! He comes to us a little boy, a gift from God, and we raise him as a Kozlovsky. But still. Not enough, never enough!

"You want more truth? The truth is we hardly, by an inch, not even two inch, made it out of the Soviet Union alive. I barely lived in that prison. Your uncle Leonid, gone. My father, gone." He didn't bother to wipe his tears. "Curse that man who tormented my father. He has been in hell, all these years, where he belongs. Your mother, so ill when I return. Our names on The List. Do you not remember, you girls, do you not remember? Antonia? Valeria? Elvira?"

We all nodded.

"So there. The truth is we take Dmitry with us when we leave. Yes. It was like that. We hide. We leave it behind. All behind!" My father slammed his fists on the table again.

He gets angry when Dmitry is unhappy. It makes him unhappy, so it brings on anger. "Dmitry should leave it behind. Be happy. Grateful that no men come in the middle of the night, drag us off, beat us, starve us . . . but no, he not. He walk around this earth. He should come home, marry nice Russian girl. Have the babies."

We were silent. My father did this now and then, a proclamation. He would stand at the table, or hit it with both hands. Then he would settle down.

He settled back down, sighed. "Never enough for my boy."

"He says it's hard to move forward in your own life when you don't know who you are and where you came from," Ellie said.

"He says he knows you two have kept something from his past from him," Valerie said. "Have you? What do you know?"

"Ack," my father said, rolling his head in his hands.

"*Tsk, tsk,*" my mother said. "We keep the past in Moscow, where it belongs, but how we make Dmitry happy, Alexei?"

My father's eyes widened. "I have answer!"

"What Alexei?" my mother said, touching his arm. "What the answer?"

"We plant a vegetable garden together." He grinned. He knew the answer!

A vegetable garden? Ellie, Valerie, and I exchanged a glance.

"Yes. Vegetable garden," my father said. "Then maybe he stop walking. Stop trying to find something, someone, who not there, who he will not find again. Stay home. Grow carrots. Radish. Tomatoes. He tell me in high school, he remember a vegetable garden. He say it to me many times, but he no like potatoes or beets. So no potatoes and beets. We buy land, and he work the land and we use vegetables in restaurant. What you think, Svetlana?"

"Yes! You are smart, Alexei," my mother gushed. "You think of everything." She tapped her head with her finger. "Right there."

My father smiled, proud. Proud his wife was proud of him.

My mother stood up, leaned over, and kissed him on the lips. He hugged her, kissed her back. She wrapped her arms around his neck.

"I'm trying to eat," Valerie said. "That's enough."

They laughed together. My mother kissed him again. "You solve this problem, Alexei. Now you call our son, say come home, no?"

"Yes, I do it once again. Tomorrow. I had enough of this," my father said. "Now is time I tell him. Dmitry come home. Gets a wife and the babies. And a garden. No beets. No potatoes."

He kissed her cheek. She smiled at him with such seduction, I rolled my eyes.

"I'm but an innocent child," I said. "I should not have to see this."

My father lifted my mother onto his lap. She *giggled*. Yes, it was a giggle.

"Mama!" Ellie said. "Papa!"

"Stop," Valerie drawled. "I'm still drinking wine."

My mother shrugged.

"Your mother is very tired," my father told us.

Mama didn't look tired. In fact, she giggled *again*.

My sisters and I made our excuses, got up to leave. Our parents gave each of us a hug, kissed both of our cheeks, and as soon as we were a millimeter out the door, it slammed shut.

"Sheesh," Valerie said, moving her heel away quick as could be so as not to get it smashed.

"Who was the architect who built your home?"

"The architect? Jer Engleton. I slept with him."

Now that was an interesting factoid. My pen paused above my yellow writing pad. "You did?"

"Yes."

The woman I was interviewing for an article for *Homes and Gardens of Oregon,* Liza Pennington, was massively hung over. It was eleven o'clock in the morning. Her blouse was open one too many buttons, and her mascara was smeared. She didn't know, wouldn't have cared. She was too thin. Her cleaning lady had just left. I had the impression that the cleaning lady had hauled Liza out of bed.

We were at her dining room table staring out at the panoramic view of Portland from her 4,500-square-foot home in the hills. Liza and her husband, Eddy, a technology CEO, lived in a steel, glass, and wood wonder. Jer Engleton was a talented architect. "My husband doesn't know it."

"Ah." As a reporter, I hear a lot. It never ceases to amaze me how people open up to me. Anything they say can and will be held against them, so to speak, and I've had some doozer quotes in the past. But this was an article about Liza's home, not her hangover or the affair, so I wouldn't be using it.

"I couldn't resist Jer."

"Why not?" That was me being voyeuristic. Shame on me.

"Jer is attractive enough, but basically it was his butt."

"His butt made you cheat?"

"Yes. My husband has a skinny butt. My butt's bigger than his. But Jer. Nice big butt. Not fat. But hips. And my husband works all the time. I pay attention to my husband when he gets home. I talk to him, listen, give him massages, sex whenever he wants, but he hardly knows me. He thinks everything is fine between us because he's happy, ergo I must be happy, and that ticks me off."

"That would make me mad, too."

"He'll say, 'How are you, Liza,' and before I can answer he'll say, 'I'm hungry, what's for dinner?' So he doesn't truly care."

"How are you, then?" I knew how she was. It was blatantly obvious. She was depressed. Searching for light. Struggling with a cloying sadness that could not be shaken away and using alcohol to self-medicate.

"I'm lonely. Alone. I love my husband, and it hurts me every single day that he doesn't really see me. But Jer, the architect, saw me from the start. He listened to me. Not only about the house but about who I was. Jer knew more about me in one day than my husband and we've been married fifteen years. So, it wasn't actually about Jer's butt. It was about the brain a few feet above the butt."

"Why don't you leave your husband?"

"Because I love him. We've been together a long time. We met in college. I already said that." She had not said that. Liza lit a cigarette, impatient, efficient. I truly hate cigarette smoke, but I couldn't say anything. It was her house.

"Are you still with Jer?"

"Yes. I'll be with Jer until my husband pays attention to me. I can't live like I'm dying. That was a stupid thing to say. Sorry. I hate clichés." She puffed out smoke in a *smoke ring*. I was impressed.

"Why don't you tell your husband how you feel?"

"I did. I have. Several times." She tapped her cigarette on a glass ash tray. "He was gobsmacked each time. He changed for about two weeks, then went back to who he was."

"So why do you love a man who doesn't pay attention to you? Who doesn't want to know you?"

"I don't know. Prodding question I can't answer. Are you sure you don't want wine? I had this stuff flown in from France." She poured a glass.

"No, thanks."

She poured me a glass and handed it to me. She almost fell out of her blouse. I thought she was going to cry and run more mascara down her face, so I steered the questions back to her home.

"Tell me about your goals for the home when you were first designing it."

"Are you married, Toni?"

"No." The question still hurt.

"Ever been married?"

"Yes."

"Got rid of him, huh? I understand. I can't do that to my husband. When you love him, you love 'em, right?"

"Right." I stayed calm. She blew another smoke ring.

The front door opened and a man walked through. Tall, skinny, smiling. "Hi, honey."

"Hi, Eddy, how are you?"

"Fine. How are you, Liza? I'm hungry. What's for lunch? Who do we have here?"

I stood and shook his hand, we chatted. Eddy was a nice, bland man, but I could see what Liza meant. Loving, thought all was well, would never hurt her; in fact he was obviously indulgent, but dense like a tree trunk.

For a woman who wanted a husband who would delve deep through life with her, who was in touch with his emotions, and hers, who was interested in her as a woman, who dreamed and worried and cried with her, who paid attention and was thoughtful and insightful, it would be an unending, emotionally degrading problem. The relationship was hollow. One person knew it. The other didn't have the capacity to recognize it. Hard to work through.

"It's a pleasure to meet you, Toni. I'm hungry," Eddy the dense husband said again. "What's for lunch? Will it be ready soon? Did you pick up my dry cleaning? You know my mother's coming for lunch on Saturday?"

"Yes. Yes. And yes." Liza got up and got him his lunch, then returned.

Liza's shirt was undone almost to mid-boob. She had mascara down her face from tears. She was clearly hung over. Her husband was absolutely blind to that blatant call for help or was narcissistic or thoughtless enough not to care.

"See what I mean?" Liza said.

"I think I'm hungry," I said to her. "When's lunch?"

We laughed and she filled her wineglass and blew another smoke ring.

"Jer, the architect, is awesome in bed. Don't put that in the article."

I went out to the kayak house and stared at my red kayak, then Marty's, and our tandem. I swallowed hard and brushed my tears away. I pulled my kayak out and sat in it. I held the row across me.

Marty and I kayaked in Oregon, Alaska, the San Juan Islands, Florida, Montana, and Mexico.

We laughed. We met new people. We saw sheared cliffs, towering mountains, fascinating geological formations, sunsets and sunrises that were surely hand-painted, twisting rivers, sandy beaches, bears, herds of deer, elk, beavers, coyote, and one wolf. We kayaked in the sun, the rain, and twice the snow.

When we were done kayaking for the day, we set up our tent, or headed to our hotel, had dinner and wine, and when we were recharged, we had wild and rolling and loving sex.

Then we fell asleep and did the whole thing the next day.

"Toni, look at that." He would point at an eagle, a carving in a ridge, a purple line across the sky.

"There's something about nature that makes you feel alive, yet tiny, grateful, like your whole city life is not real life, don't you think, Toni?"

"I love feeling like I'm part of the river, but more than that, I love feeling that we're part of the river together, Toni. . . ."

"You're my river, Toni. . . ."

"I feel like a new person after that trip. Do you? Do you feel different? How? Where do you want to go for our next trip, Toni? Tell me and I'll get it planned. . . ."

We laughed. We talked. Nothing I said was too small for him to listen to and comment on.

He held my hand. He made me feel like the sexiest woman in the world. He looked at me and I knew he wanted me naked.

We kayaked, we traveled, we built memories.

I am so grateful now, for all those memories.

Marty was popular in our Russian community, not only because he was kind and interesting and always asked people how they were doing, but because he helped them with their medical concerns.

We would go to parties, to church, to dinners and celebrations, and members of the Russian community would come up and talk to him, in English and Russian. One elderly man spoke in Russian and Hebrew, sometimes changing midsentence.

"My heart goes thump thump, then it goes thump thump thump, quick, like a damn coyote. Why does it do that?"

"I have a problem with my gooser, Dr. Marty. Yes. My gooser. Here." A woman smacked Marty's butt, then turned around to show him her butt. She leaned in and whispered, "I have to talk to you privately."

"Can you take a peek at my titties, Dr. Romanowsky? I think one is a lot bigger than the other. Is that normal?" Marty was flashed by a seventy-two-year-old woman. "Do you see the problem?"

He listened. He was compassionate. He referred people he thought had true problems. They brought us meals, treats, sent flowers, hugged him.

Everyone loved Marty. I loved him, too.

"You all received the notice of eviction?" Charles asked, leaning back on his couch. He was worn out. Charles and Vanessa had worked hard for our dock to stay open, as had many other people. I'd done what I could through the newspaper and donated extra to pay the attorney. Heather Dackson had sent letters, worked with the courts, filed this and that.

But Tweedle Dee Dum and Tweedle Dum Dee, Portland slumlords, had hired their own attorneys. A counterattack was now being launched. Whether they could actually kick us off with a suit filed, that was another question. Maybe there would be an injunction, a hold, until the courts could settle it out.

"Yes," I said, along with Nick, Lindy, Beth, Jayla, Daisy, and other houseboat owners on the dock.

"I received it right after a nine-hour operation." Beth was worn out, too.

"Ninety days," Vanessa said, "and we're supposed to be off and out."

Everyone groaned.

Nick sat by me. I could feel his hotness. I was upset about the dock closing, but I also wanted to go to his houseboat, modern and clean, and roll around in his king-sized bed.

Nick had tried to help. He knew the governor from when the governor worked in law enforcement. The governor called his contacts. No go.

"Cannibals, both of them!" Daisy stood up and announced. She was wearing a green daisy the size of a saucer in her black felt hat and a purple dress with a white-haired woman holding a white feather in her teeth painted on the front. She was also wearing vintage, shiny red heels.

"Daisy, you told your sons that you have to leave, right?" Jayla asked.

"No, the f-word, I haven't told them. They are very bad boys. I'll tell them once I sail my houseboat away on the open ocean and visit the whales."

"Now, now," Charles said, worried, sitting back up. "Let's not do that, Daisy. Don't try to sail your house."

"That wouldn't be safe, Daisy," Jayla said, patting her hand. "We'll tell your sons and they'll move you to a better place."

"No, I don't want a better place. I'm staying here on the river, with my river family! We're all together. I'm not going to live in a place with sick and old people. I'm not sick. I'm not old. I'll jump in the ocean with the fish and ride the whales before I live in a place without my river family. I love you! I want to live with you."

Nick sighed, sad. Jayla dropped her head. Beth seemed to sink into her chair. Vanessa said, "We'll always be a family, Daisy," so gently, "but we might have to move. How about if I call your sons?"

"I'm mad at my boys." Daisy was suddenly angry. "They took my nunchucks. I know it. They took my sword, too. From China. Stealers. Burglars. Sometimes they're well-behaved boys, sometimes they're naughty. They tossed a man into this river, right here, under our feetsies, when it was snowing like a snow cone a few years ago, another one they made fly like a bird off a bridge. That man didn't have wings. How could he fly? There were two men gone with bang and bang, they shot with water guns, a long time ago, but they were mean to their wives, slime balls. Bang!"

Nick rolled his eyes. He was an officer of the law. I knew he could not let that go.

"I told you, you don't have to worry," Lindy said, waving a dismissive hand. She was dressed in a white blouse, a brown skirt to her knees, and flats. Her blond hair was back in a pony-tail, no makeup. Earlier she had regaled me with her opinion of Dostoyevsky. "We'll call it You Are Toast Day, and Tweedle Dee Dum and Tweedle Dum Dee will back off and no one will have to leave the dock."

"And what's that? What's 'You Are Toast Day'?" Nick asked. I felt him tense a bit. "You are toast" is not a phrase a DEA agent likes to hear.

"It means I have them handled." She smiled at everyone. "Guess what I brought for dinner? Italiano!" She kissed her fingers. "Delizioso!"

We did cheer up over the pasta primavera, gelato and hot bread. Hard not to.

It was also hard not to stare at Nick.

I tried, tried hard, but his natural seductiveness reached out and stroked me and prodded my naked thoughts. I glanced away every single time he caught me staring at him. I might have even blushed. He smiled at me. I smiled back.

I blew him a kiss. I didn't think anyone saw the flying kiss until Daisy announced, "Aha! I see it! A kiss between crying kayak woman Toni and Pistol Man. It's love. I know it is." She hugged me and said, "Now I'm going to sing you a love song," and she did.

We do all love Daisy.

"This cake is enough to make me orgasm," Valerie said.

"Please don't," I said.

She mimicked one, short and sweet.

Ellie laughed.

"My daughters! I cannot believe you talk this way. Tsk." My mother poked Valerie in the arm with a fork. "Mary, mother of Jesus, help me—"

I interrupted. "Mama, what do you think of the lemon cream?"

"I think it not made by Russian, but I like." She winked at Juliet, a friend of ours since high school.

Juliet owned Juliet's Cakes, a pink-and-white bakery. Her cakes were like eating cake heaven. Ellie was trying to pick a flavor for her wedding cake, and we were tasting bites of each one—a difficult job but someone has to do it.

"I'm a boring and faithful married woman," Valerie said. "You're going to be a boring and faithful married woman soon, Ellie. How does it feel?"

"Delightful." Ellie smiled, teeth gritted, lips pulled back like a scary mask.

"Geez, that smile," I said. "Gave me a fright."

"I'd have to agree, Ellie," Valerie said. "That was a freaky smile if I ever saw one."

"It is because of the Italian stallion," my mother said, waving her fork. "Elvira, I want to see you smiling for this, and I no see a right smile. See that smile? I think you ate a alligator."

Ellie stopped smiling. She put her hand right over her widow's peak. The worry spot.

"What is it?" I asked.

"It's nothing . . . but last night I was thinking of our vows and other . . . thoughts . . ."

"What thought?" my mother said. "You tell me the thought, I tell you don't marry Gino the Italian."

"It's not that. . . ." Ellie paused. "It's not that I want to be with a bunch of men in my life, I don't. You know me, I am not promiscuous."

"You're one step away from being Pollyanna," Valerie drawled. "All you need is the blue dress and the white bow at your back."

"But . . ." Ellie fiddled with her hair. "One man? For decades? Forever?"

"That would be marriage," Valerie said.

"Yes, that what it is," my mother said, tapping her fork on Ellie's plate. "It forever. Like me and your papa. We together forever. You ready for that, Elvira? I ask this, I think no."

I thought of Marty. I had wanted him for forever. Then I thought of Nick. Nick. Ah, Nick. "You don't like the forever part?"

"Gino is a sweet and caring man. The other day he brought me flowers. He makes me laugh. He loves me. He's smart. He's protective. But . . ."

"See, I fix this problem," my mother said. "You want wedding cake, Elvira? I buy you wedding cake, right now, we eat after dinner, but not at wedding. How about it? We take pink one, Juliet. Let's go."

Ellie shook her head, pulled her paper bag out of her purse. "Juliet?"

"So, of the cakes before you," Juliet said, taking her cue. "The vanilla cake with lemon cream icing, the pink champagne with coconut icing, the chocolate cake with mocha butter cream, the chocolate cake with salted caramel icing, and the white cake with raspberry butter cream, which is your favorite, Ellie?" She smiled. Juliet is calming and encouraging. She has a black belt in karate and I've seen her knock a grown man onto his back.

Ellie said, "They're all delicious. I can't decide. Can we get five cakes?"

Juliet's eyes opened wide. "Five?"

"Yes. Five medium cakes."

"We could do that," Juliet said. "It's not traditional, but I love the idea. It would be splendid for my business, too, if everyone started ordering five different cakes for their wedding."

"I'm not that traditional. All the traditional stuff with this wedding is making me feel..." Ellie waved a hand in the air, then pressed her fingers to her widow's peak, the worry center. "Like I can't breathe."

"It's not the traditional that's taking your breath away," Valerie muttered.

Ellie breathed into her paper bag. "I'm supposed to be with one man for the rest of my life. I'm supposed to take a vow, saying I will stay with him, forever." Her voice pitched, higher and higher. "We are both going to change. We will become different people. Even if things go bad, go wrong, and I don't like him anymore—"

"Which they will, trust me," Valerie said.

"I'm supposed to stay," Ellie said. "Trapped. Stuck. Unhappy."

"That is right," my mother said. "You stay until you're dead. You stay with that Italian Gino until he is old man. Wrinkled. You stay with him when his bladder not work. You stay when that other thing not work. When he makes the farties, you stay with him. You want that, Elvira? Do you? I say no."

Ellie, the jittery bride, who was getting closer and closer to running, I could feel it, attached the bag to her face again. The bag scrunched in, blew out.

"I'm keeping my mouth shut so I don't get tossed in the river again," Valerie said.

Ellie stood up. "I'll take one of each, Juliet, thanks." She walked, swaying from one side to the other, her air gone, out of the bakery.

What? After all that? I leaned back in my chair. When would she end this?

"We buy cake and I have daughter who go down the aisle with paper bag on face," my mother said, patience for this mess gone. "We call her bride bag lady, no? Maybe we give brown bags out to guests for presents, huh? Everyone use when they see Elvira."

I envisioned that. All the wedding guests with bags to their faces. I laughed.

In order not to lose my skills at Keeping The Monsters At Bay: Shopping Defensive Strategies, I dropped into a store nearby and bought new panties by Lace, Satin, and Baubles. All lacy and silky. Nick would like them, I was sure of it.

"Can I take you on a ride in my boat, Toni?"

I thought about it for only one second. Nick had invited me out on his boat before, but it felt like a date, and a date I could not do, and a boat was like a kayak, in that they both floated, so I said no.

But it was Saturday afternoon. I'd finished a story about a woman named Grenadine Scotch Wild, who made ten-foot-by-eight-foot paintings, then added collage items like sticks, birds' nests, beads, and sequins. Her art was exquisite. I was tired. I love the water and I hadn't been out on it in too long.

"It's not a date," Nick said, smiling, as if he could read my mind.

"No, it's not." His blondish, I-like-running-my-hands-through-that-hair was feathering back in the wind. "Why do you have to be so hot?"

Nick blinked a couple of times. My comment had caught him off guard.

"It would be a lot easier for me to resist you if you resembled a boar."

"A boar?" He thought about that. "They're scary when they run straight at you."

"You're scary enough."

His face gentled. "I don't want to scare you, Toni. Ever."

"I know, but you do."

"I'm sorry." He smiled again.

"Why do you have to have a smile like that?"

He laughed. "Like what?"

"A smiley smile. Handsome smile. Irresistible smile. Turn it off. Please."

He stopped smiling. He glowered. Sheesh. "Now you're scaring me again."

"I'm trying to do the right thing, here, babe. Come on, Toni. Will you go out on my boat with me? I bought chocolate chip cookies for you from that bakery you like downtown."

"Yes, I will. I'll be brave on this non-date."

"I'll hold your hand."

I almost said, "Why do you have to have such sexy hands that know exactly what to do and where to go?" I refrained. I held my hand out, he took it.

I loved Nick's boat, *Sanchez One*. Two stories, as I like to say. Newish. Handled well. Clean. We anchored and had a late lunch of turkey sandwiches and the chocolate chip cookies.

We were in a quiet spot, the wind rustling through, a flock of geese flying overhead before landing on a nearby sandbar. We talked about what we often talk about: work; the book we were reading together; history, which we were both interested in; Ellie's wedding plans; my concerns for Valerie; his parents and my "unique" family and how they were all doing. There was the usual flirtation and laughing.

It was normal.
It was fun.
It was almost too normal, and too fun.
I really liked Nick.

Marty had a cough that wouldn't quit.
Go to the doctor, I told him.
It's nothing, he told me.
His cold clung.
Go to the doctor, Marty.
I'm fine. I'm tired. Long hours. Come here, honey.
He was weak, run down. He actually took a nap on Sunday.
Go to the doctor, please.
He went to the doctor because I called two of his doctor friends and they examined Marty, almost by force, and ran tests. When all the tests were back, Marty said to me, "Be brave, Toni. You have to be brave."
He told me. He caught me as I collapsed.
I was not so brave.

16

~

Moscow, the Soviet Union

"Girls, I am sorry to tell you this," my mother said, pushing her black hair back with a hand that shook like it was being electrified, "but your uncle Leonid has disappeared."

We couldn't speak. Uncle Leonid, our mother's only sibling, a happy and cheerful man who brought us candy and talked to us as if we were adults, who made us listen to Rachmaninoff's Concerto No. 2 in C Minor because it was his favorite, was missing.

My father took my mother's hand in his and kissed it. Her face crumbled, her blue eyes desolate.

"Mama," I cried. Valeria's lip trembled, and Elvira burst into tears.

"Where did he disappear to?" Valeria asked.

"The KGB came to get him." My mother's face was as white as the snow that dumped on Moscow as if it would bury us. She swore in French.

"The bad men?" Valeria stomped her foot.

"What is KGD?" Elvira clung to her doll. "Where is Uncle Leonid?"

"When?" I asked.

"Last night."

"How do you know?" I was devastated. We were devastated.

"I heard him in my head when they came for him. He spoke

to me. He said, 'They're taking me away, Svetlana.' " My mother started to weep. She turned to my father, "He said, 'Get out of the Soviet Union.' "

"Are we getting out of here?" Valeria asked.

My mother and father held hands. They didn't answer, but I saw my father nod at my mother.

Over the next month, my mother continued her work as a popular professor at the university, lost weight, and spent her spare time staring out the window as Moscow became colder and more desolate than before.

"Have you heard from Uncle Leonid in your head?" I asked her after school one day.

She nodded. "He told me where he had hidden my marbles when we were children." She laughed, sad laughter. "Behind our father's bookcase. I kept throwing the marbles at him when he would not look up from studying and talk to me."

I held my mother's hands as she bent over, in half, the weight of grief forcing her down.

Three days later, as we sewed our miniature pillows, our father at a meeting at the university, she said, "Uncle Leonid came to me when I was making coffee this morning. He told me that inside of a wooden box, under his bed in his room at the dormitory, there was a carved white swan. He had made it for me, for my birthday. I went to get it today." She held out the swan. It was glorious. Every feather carved so intricately, no detail lost. Underneath it Leonid had carved, I LOVE YOU, SVETLANA. MAY YOUR TROUBLES BE FEW. LEONID.

"I'm glad he told you where the swan was."

"Me too." She ran her hands over it, her tears soaking straight into the wood.

Two weeks later my parents sat us down again, after school, on our couch that sunk in the middle. My mother's eyes were puffy, my father's shoulders were stooped. "Girls," my mother said, "I am very sorry to tell you this, but Uncle Leonid is dead. The Communists have killed him."

"How do you know?" Valeria said.

"Who told you?" I said.

"What?" Elvira cried. "What?"

"Uncle Leonid came to me last night. He woke me up." She leaned heavily on my father, and he kissed her cheek. "I thought I was dying. My throat closed. The air was gone. I could feel myself being pulled away."

"He talked to you, Mama?" Elvira asked.

"Yes. The Sabonis gift, the gift from God." She tapped her widow's peak. "He said for me to tell you that he loves all of you. That he hopes you keep reading books and to listen to Rachmaninoff's Concerto No. 2 in C Minor and think of him. He told me he would not last the night."

"I'm sorry, Mama." We all cried, even my father, who rarely cried. Leonid was one of his best friends.

"He is in heaven now," my mother said, sobbing, then turned to my father. "He said we need to leave, Alexei, right away, we need to go."

My father nodded. He did not question his wife's and her brother's invisible language. He knew it to be true. Plus, he knew that our family tie to Leonid, an "enemy of the people," as the Communists had labeled him, would automatically put us in grave danger.

I envisioned holding Uncle Leonid, hugging him, but then he pulled away, farther and farther until only our palms were touching, then our fingers, then our fingertips, then the swan flew between us and carried him off. I cried for Uncle Leonid with my family.

Ten minutes later I saw my mother straighten her backbone, put her chin up. Her face hardened, more furious than I'd ever seen her.

"Those bastards. Those KGB vermin. Those Communist criminals. They will never tell us the truth. They will never give us his body to bless and bury and pray over. When he first disappeared, your father, me, Uncle Yuri, Uncle Sasho, we all went to the police station. They laughed. They refused to help. Protect the people." She pretended to spit. "They protect no one."

"Svetlana," my father soothed.

My mother was not done with her rant. "I curse them all and I hope their intestines break free, wrap themselves around their necks, and strangle them inch by inch, blessed be Mary mother of God, I hope they suffer."

"Svetlana," my father said, gently, patting her back.

"I hope they all die," I said.

"Me too," Elvira said, hugging her doll.

"I hope that, too, Mama," Valeria said. "I hope that hawks peck at their eyes when they're still living and a snake bites their toes off. I hope that a cougar's claws rip their bodies open. I hope that worms crawl through their ears and ants fill their mouths. I hope that a vulture eats their bones."

My mother, father, and I all gaped at Valeria, her braids wrapped around her head, her bow bopping on top.

"I hope that, Mama," Valeria said, and a vengeful prosecuting attorney was born.

"I'm scared," Elvira said, shivering.

"Me too," my father muttered, staring at Valeria.

Uncle Yuri and his family soon left the Soviet Union, sneaking out through the shadows. Uncle Sasho and his family left, too, quietly, stealthily, off to a new life in America.

I knew we would leave soon, too.

My father lost his job as a physics professor at the university on a Tuesday.

On Wednesday my mother lost her job as a Russian Literature professor at the same university.

The reason was clear: They had been found out. The meetings at our home where people discussed democracy, free elections, capitalism, freedom of press, religion, speech, etc., made them, officially, enemies of the people.

In addition, they were Christians, not Motherland Communists. They did not talk about their faith at the university. My mother herself even said that faith does not belong in an academic setting, or in politics, that the separation was important. But in our home, they were Christian. That was not allowed.

When we returned from school, my parents were huddled together on the couch. White. Worn out. Sick with worry. We sat with them and didn't say a thing. We knew to be quiet. We felt their insidious fear.

The whispering, the intensity of the conversations, the late-night visits from our family's best friends increased. I heard words here and there. "Get out of the Soviet Union . . . they'll take your housing away from you soon . . . no jobs except at the factory for Christians . . . dangerous . . . you're a threat . . . political revolution . . . you could be jailed . . . think of the children, their safety . . ." There were long hugs and tears.

"Why are they hugging us, saying good-bye?" I asked.

My mother and father brought us in close, all on our couch. "We are leaving Moscow in two days," my father said. "You must not tell anyone. Do you understand? No one."

"Girls, there is no greater secret for you to keep than this one," my mother said.

"Are we going to Uncle Vladan and Uncle Yuri and Uncle Sasho in America?" I asked.

"Yes."

"Do not tell *anyone* we're leaving."

We said we wouldn't, we didn't. Not even Gavriil and Bog-dan, though my young heart beat sadly for the loss of the handsome and heroic Bogdan.

On Tuesday night at two in the morning, they came for my father.

Three men, in uniform, one with a long gray coat, all with knee-high black boots, pounded on the door, then they kicked it down. My father was in pajamas. He fought, his boxing skills coming out, but it was three on one. My mother jumped in to help him, and one of the men backhanded her so hard, she flew into the wall and passed out, blood splattering.

Elvira ran to my mother, sobbing, holding her against her chest.

Enraged at what they had done to our mother, what they were doing to our father, Valeria and I leaped on their shoulders, yelling at them to let go of our father. The soldiers did not hesitate. They tossed us—*children*—across the room. Valeria knocked clean out, exactly like my mother.

"Valeria, Valeria!" I crawled to her, my body splintering in pain, while my father fought and Elvira screamed. He gave in when one of the men put a knife to his throat and said, so calm, as if he were asking for tea, "Continue struggling, comrade, and I will slice open your neck and you can die before your family."

"Let me check on my wife, my daughter!" he shouted, and the man dug the knife into my father's neck. Blood spurted out like a fountain.

"Arguing does nothing now, does it? Come with me, Professor, and we will get this straightened out. Perhaps your Jesus will help you." He glanced over at my mother, my beautiful, black-haired mother, collapsed against the wall. "And do not worry, friend, I will look after your wife for you."

My father took a swing at the man and clipped him, hard, on the chin. He stumbled back, and the other two jumped him, beat him, then dragged his limp body toward the door.

We were traumatized, stunned. I glared at the soldiers from my place, against the wall, holding Valeria, dizzy and sick and broken, then spat on the ground. "I hate you."

They laughed again, as if our family's misery was the most amusing thing that had ever happened to them.

"You will be a sexy young woman," he said. "In a few years I will return for you. Would you like that, Professor? I will come and visit with your wife and your daughters."

My father swore, something we rarely heard, and the soldiers threw him through the open door of our apartment. I heard him smash against the wall.

My grandfather, my father's father, Konstantin, was arrested the same night we learned later. My grandmother, Ekaterina, had died suddenly, the year before, of a brain aneurism. My mother said later that it was a blessing that it happened, as our sweet grandmother would not have been able to live through the sheer agony of our loss. "She will be their angel," my mother said.

Father and son, jailed together. Tortured together. They would need more than an angel.

"I saw your blog today, Dmitry. I liked it. As always." I was in my wheelhouse watching the sun go down, propped up against the red pillows.

"Thanks, Toni. I thought people might like to know what it looks like to be jammin' and singin' with people on a Mexican beach at night."

"I liked the song you wrote along with it." Dmitry had a . . . well, how to describe his voice? It was low, baritone, husky.

Was his singing always in tune?

No.

Always at full force?

No.

He admitted it. He wrote about it, wrote about how he couldn't sing well, that he could think of a "billion" people off the top of his head who sang better, but that he wanted to sing, so he did.

What people responded to was the combination of his singing, his guitar playing, his poetry, and how he would talk, before and after, and sometimes during, a song. "It's storytelling with music and poetry and an occasional note that's in tune," he wrote.

He also never hid his tears. Tall, tanned, blond-haired Dmitry—100 percent raw, American male—and there he is, tearing up when he's singing and playing his guitar in front of an ancient ruin, or reading his poetry from a mountaintop, or talking about destitute people in a poor village in Guatemala and how they are struggling to make it. When he was in front of waterfalls or forests or a hidden mountain lake and he became emotional about the beauty of the earth, he told people to embrace their emotions and share them with others.

The number of people following his blog had ballooned again, I noticed, and his insightful, introspective, and funny book continued to sell.

We chatted about Mexico, the people he'd met, the poverty

he'd seen, and his volunteer work in the schools while the sun sunk further on the horizon, like gold candy, stretching its wings out in magentas, purples, azure blues.

"Last night I saw a house in my dreams, Toni, with a blue door."

"Did you recognize the house?" A flock of geese flew in front of the sun, almost down now, the clouds turning pink, a touch of yellow.

"No. Yes. Maybe. I think so. I don't know."

"How did you feel about the door?"

"It felt like it was open, like I was supposed to walk through it, and I wanted to, but I was scared, too, as if I didn't want to see what was behind it."

We talked more. He wanted to know how I was doing, if I had kayaked, how I was feeling. What was I working on for *Homes and Gardens of Oregon*?

"I love you, Toni."

"Love you, too. Can't wait to see you." The sun was a semi-circle now, a last good-bye.

We hung up, and I went back to watching the sunset through the windows of the wheelhouse.

When Dmitry knew the truth, knew what I had kept from him, would he still want to talk to me? Ever?

I had never told. The secret keeper had kept the secret. And the price was going to be astronomical.

I saw my blue heron fly through the shadows. The sun set. It was dark now. So dark.

"We're freakin' killin' it."

"What?"

"We have ads selling left and right and behind my butt," Ricki said, hands on her hips. She was wearing a zebra print dress and a flowing pink scarf to her knees. "I have to give most of the credit to you, Toni. I am loving your home stories and your column. We're getting calls and e-mails, we even received letters—letters—about how spectacular and fantastic-o your stories are."

"Ricki, I'll take a bit of credit because I've just eaten a candy bar for breakfast and I'm high on sugar, but the garden stories by Kim make even me want to garden and the other articles on—"

She waved her hand. "All bodacious. But you, Toni, you have this down, and I have a date tonight and I think I'm going to get laid."

"Who with?"

"A man I met in my hiking club."

"What happened to the other boyfriend?"

"Dumped him. Boring. This one is younger than me by ten years, or maybe a little more. I think he's forty-eight. I told him I wasn't sure he could keep up with me."

"Do you think he can?"

She tapped her red nails together. "Tough question. Maybe. Doubtful. We went on a climb this weekend and I beat him to the top, but we'll see. I don't like men my own age or older. So dull. A lot of them are retired. Honestly, I could not handle having a man home all the time. You wake up, there he is. You come home from work, there he is. Weekends, all day, there he is. Like slugs that you can't get rid of with slug killer.

"Plus, a lot of them have health issues, and for some reason they think I'm going to be fascinated by their aching shoulder, their arthritis, their urinary problems. They want someone to take care of them. I don't want to be a caregiver, I want to be a woman. I want a man who is younger than me who has stamina and vigor and is interesting and can do sexual gymnastics."

"Wow. Sexual gymnastics." I thought of Nick. It's important to be nimble.

"Yes. He has to be flexible."

"This one is a flexer, then? Like Gumby?" I linked and twisted my arms and legs together.

"I am exploding with hope. How's your column coming along?"

"Haven't written it yet."

"You friggin' kidding me? It's due in two hours."

"I'll write it."

"I'm getting out of your way. E-mail me that column in two hours or I'll fry you alive myself."

Living on a Tugboat, Talking About Homes

BY TONI KOZLOVSKY

I met a girl yesterday named Serenity.

Her real name, she told me, was Carole. She had been named after her grandma. "Carole didn't seem to fit and I'm trying to find serenity, so I changed my name."

We met in a coffee shop. I was trying to hide in the corner so I could write, and so was she. We shared the corner and started talking. I asked her about her backpack. It was green, stuffed, with two tennis shoes tied to the outside and a water bottle.

She flipped her dreadlocks back and said, "My backpack is my home."

Serenity decided, after going to a famous East Coast prep school, that she was burned out. She graduated, and instead of heading off to college, she headed out the door.

"It blew my mother's mind. Kaboom and boom. My father was so freaked out I didn't want to go to college, I don't think he closed his mouth during our entire conversation. But I had to get out. I had to figure out what I wanted to do. I don't even know if I want to go to college, but what I do know is that I can't live in a small and wealthy and entitled world anymore."

I asked her where she'd been. She started off in Boston and was working her way, by bus, by train, on foot, around the country. "I've explored twenty states, and I'm going to explore all fifty."

How long had she been traveling and working? "Eighteen months. I work, live cheap, then move on with my house on my back."

"What's in the house?" I asked her.

Surprisingly, not a lot of clothes. What Serenity cherished were her books and notebooks, the gifts that had been given to her by people she met, beaded bracelets, an owl necklace, a knitted shawl, a pair of thick socks with peacocks on them. She had a small collection of rocks from a Florida beach, a totem pole from a reservation, and earrings made of wood from a national park.

"I have a jacket, two sweatshirts, jeans, T-shirts, but what I've tried to do is pare down to what's valuable to me. What I want to have around me.

"Months ago I threw out three shirts that I wore when I was battling anorexia. Now I eat when I'm hungry and don't worry. I threw out a picture of a boyfriend who was mean to me. I don't know why I stayed with him, but I know now I shouldn't have. I gave the pearl earrings he gave me to a homeless girl in Baltimore. I tossed out my red tennis shoes that I wore out from so much walking, but I kept one red shoelace to remind me of my journey. Every day I wear a flowered brooch my dead grandma Carole gave me, because I love her and miss her and I feel like I'm walking with her.

"People might see junk, but it's not junk to me."

Serenity has pared down her home to a backpack.

When I asked her if I could write about her for this column, she flipped back her dread locks, said yes, sure, and told me to tell you all one thing, "Find your own home. Find yourself."

So there it is, friends.

From Serenity.

*   *   *

I called and got a photographer to the coffee shop. He took photos of a smiling Serenity, her backpack, and her treasures.

I bought her a coffee card to take with her, and she took off. She was catching a train to Montana.

It had a lot of appeal. . . .

I had dinner with Charles and Vanessa, spaghetti and meatballs, then we headed out to the dock when we heard Daisy singing as the sun went down, the rays casting white sparkles over the ruffles of the river. She sang "Think of Me" and "All I Ask of You" from *The Phantom of the Opera*.

"Her voice," Vanessa marveled.

"Pitch perfect," Charles said.

Lindy stood in front of her houseboat, and Jayla came out and sat in one of her chairs.

"I do not want to leave here," Vanessa said.

"I don't either," I said. "The river. The animals. The blue heron. Daisy and her free concerts. You all."

"I feel the same," Charles said. "We have a mix. And we all get along. This is home."

"Yes," Vanessa said, wrapping an arm around Charles and tilting her head up at her husband. "This is home."

Though I knew Vanessa loved their houseboat, I knew she wasn't talking about the houseboat when she talked about home. She kissed her husband on the cheek. He smiled, gentle, sweet, the smile of a husband in love with his wife of many decades.

Nick wasn't home. He was at work busting who knows what kind of scary, dangerous people.

Be safe, Nick. Please be careful, watch out, don't get hurt.

Don't die. Don't die. Don't die.

Daisy's voice rose and rose . . . the crystal clear notes swirling all around us, the whole dock, before they landed on the tips of the waves of the blue-gray river and were pulled toward the mysteries of an endless ocean.

No one clapped when she was done. She doesn't like people to clap. She sat down on the dock and kicked her feet in the water as the sun went down, golden globe, swishing purple, flowing orange, dashes of pink. "Hello, whales," she called out. "Sing to me, sing to me, whales!"

The sun continued its journey down, the rays casting white sparkles over the ruffles of the river. The whales didn't sing.

So Daisy sang Elvis Presley's "Hound Dog."

I sat in my two-seater kayak that night, in the river. I rowed it out so that I was in front of my tugboat. I knew I could never have anyone else in that kayak with me.

I heard Nick's footsteps. He saw me in my kayak and walked aboard my tugboat to my back deck.

"How are you doing, Toni?" He was concerned. He was sweet. I bet he got it from his mother.

"Better now that you're home." The river didn't feel so lonely.

He smiled. I rowed back in, attached my kayak to my tugboat, and Nick leaned down, pulled me up, and gave me a cuddly bear hug.

Of all things. Marty, an oncologist, was diagnosed with bone cancer.

Cancer in his bones.

We cried as if our eyes were made of faucets turned all the way on.

We told his parents, gently. His father crumbled and had to be taken to the hospital, Marty riding in the back of the ambulance with him. He had passed out, his blood pressure sky high. His mother had a heart attack within the week. My parents, for once, were silent, tears streaming down their faces.

My sisters heard me in their heads when I said, *Marty is sick.* They called. They cried.

I told Dmitry. We told no one else in the family until we had to. When did we "have" to tell them? Chemo time, as Marty's hair would fall out like everyone else's.

My family went into overdrive to help us and to give support to Marty's parents, as did our church, which we had not attended for a while. They had a nightly meal rotation done within hours for us and Marty's parents.

They did yard work for us and for Marty's parents. They came and cleaned our homes when we were at the hospital.

They made three quilts. One for Marty, one for his parents, one for my parents.

Prayers were said in church.

I hugged Marty every day, all night. I never wanted to let go.

I have learned that what we want from life, and what we get, are often two very different things.

"Hi, Toni."

"Valerie, hi." I was drinking coffee on my deck. Third cup. Seven o'clock. I'd been up since five. I watched Dixie, my great blue heron, fly by. A second later, Mr. and Mrs. Quackenbusch climbed up on my deck, quacked a hello, and settled in. Was that Anonymous soaring overhead? I squinted in the sun. "How are you and how's the trial?"

"Trial is going my way. Even the defense attorney knows. Hey, Bill Kortrand isn't stupid. He knows his client is as guilty as a possum caught in your trash can. There's no way out."

"And the Barton family?"

"Let's put it this way. Last week the judge called my team and me back to his chambers, along with the defense team, and questioned the security that had been provided for us."

"Even the judge thinks there's a problem." I shivered.

"He knows he's got a psycho on his hands, and the psycho's DNA is sitting on the benches in his courtroom."

"You have to be careful."

"I am. We're all a little freaked out, but I will not, *I will not,* allow this family, this killer, to intimidate me. I will do my job, which is to make sure that Tyler never, ever gets out of jail and hurts anyone else. I've got the families of three of the victims in the courthouse, every day, watching. I will not let them down."

"I know you won't, Valerie. I haven't told you in a while that I truly admire your courage and your dedication and your hard work. You are one heckuva warrior woman."

"Same to you from me. I love you."

"Love you, too. Watch out, Valerie."

The stepped-up security did not prevent the Barton family from tossing a dead cat on Kai's truck at the grocery store. They must have known about the new security cameras at Valerie's house and waited until Kai left home and followed him. They were following a captain on the police force. It was absolutely sick.

They were absolutely sick.

Lindy came over the next night to sit on my deck with me and drink wine and talk books.

I asked her how her day was.

"Fine. Two clients. My vagina is a little tired. The second guy is overly enthusiastic."

"What does he do for a living?" I was always amused by her answers.

"He's an Oregon state senator."

"I'll bet I can guess who it is. Chad Tucker."

She smiled. "I never reveal my clients' names unless you guess it right on the nail the first time."

"I don't like him. Sanctimonious. Always quoting God. Family values."

"He has no family values, trust me. He's a pig. He wants me to wear black leather all the time and do this dominatrix stuff. He has all the gear—handcuffs, a whip he makes me use, fishnets in a black briefcase he brings."

"He can get all that stuff in there?"

"He's an excellent packer."

"You need a photo of that guy."

"Oh, honey. I have better." She paused, for dramatic effect. "I have—wait for it—videos."

"Really?" I laughed.

"Yep. They're on my computer, in my safety deposit box at the bank, and with my attorney."

"And why do you have the videos?"

"For safety."

"What do you mean?"

"I mean a working girl has to do what a working girl has to do." She would not say more, but I got it. "And how are you doing, Toni?"

I told her about work, the articles I was working on.

"What about Nick?"

I closed my eyes. I was so confused. Nick. Marty. Nick. Marty. "I'm screwed up."

"Because you're in love with Nick?"

"Yes. No. Trying not to. It feels wrong."

"It's not wrong, friend."

"I don't know what I want. I don't know what I should and should not feel."

"When I don't know what I want, I read."

"When I don't know what I want, I get in my bathtub and eat junky sweets, like licorice. Last night."

"I hope you can fix this with Nick. I do, friend. He's a superb human being. Other men aren't like Nick, super stud with character."

"I'm a wreck."

"We're all a wreck. We're all a mess sometimes. I like you, Toni."

"Thank you. You too."

"You're honest. You're always thinking. You have morals. You don't judge me."

"If I judged you, I'd have to judge myself and I'd hang myself way lower than you."

We sat on the deck and watched the waves. I like having a friend who agrees we don't need to talk all the time.

"Life. Darn near breaks your heart, doesn't it?" Lindy said. "Have you read *Slaughterhouse-Five*? You have? Let's discuss it while slugging down another glass of wine. I would also like your opinion on John Steinbeck."

Another glass of wine couldn't hurt.

*   *   *

Dmitry called, and we ended up talking about our father.

"We don't always get along, but I do love him, Toni."

"I know you do."

He choked up. "It's always been like this. Even as a kid, I sensed something between us. It was like a rock. And sometimes I didn't want to be with him, I pulled away, I was scared of him. I remember hiding from him so many times.

"And then that anger, in my teens toward him. I didn't get it. I still don't get it. It would come out of nowhere. He was always kind to me. He came to all of my games. He was the one who bought the camera for me. He taught me how to cook in the restaurant. But why was I afraid of him? He knows, I know he knows."

I was sure he did, too.

"Why won't he tell me?"

"He doesn't want you to know."

"That's the obvious answer, but why? In my dream last night I saw that gold locket again, but this time I opened it up, and nothing was there. It was empty."

"No pictures?"

"No. But then the locket disappeared and I saw a knife and it slashed through the air and I saw blood. It was on me, warm, sticky. The dark shadow was there. Looming. I heard screaming."

"Geez, Dmitry. No wonder you can't sleep."

"My dreams can be a problem. I wrote a poem about it. I titled it 'Nightmares in a Locket.' Want to hear it?"

I did. It was on his blog the next day. He played his guitar while he read the poem. People loved it, though it was dark, piercing, the arching shadow of death ever present.

The locket represented love gone forever.

17

What I learned when Marty was dying is that you discover a lot about a person's true character when they're on their way out.

Marty worked until two months before the end. He had the most advanced medical care the world had to offer. He had friends, specialists, all over the country, who wanted to help him. They flew in, they studied his charts, they held conferences with each other and with Marty's doctors here.

No one could save him.

It was not to be.

They cried.

I cried.

His parents cried all the time.

Amidst the tests, treatments, procedures, Marty still worked at the hospital with his patients. He wanted to help them as long as he could. He lived for that job, to help others in the worst times of their lives. In some sad way, it helped that he was bald, that he was going through chemo. Marty would cry with his patients. They knew he understood them.

Now and then he would get chemo right next to them, and they would play chess or Monopoly, talk.

"I have to work, Toni, as long as I can. I cannot abandon my patients. Being a doctor was what I was born to do. Helping people is what I was born to do."

"But, Marty, you need to rest."

"Rest? I have not lived my life resting, and I won't start now." He hugged me close, then said, "Toni, there is no changing the end here. I'm an oncologist. I know. I want my life to matter to my patients, to me, so I need to work. Please, Toni. Please understand."

He was anguished. Torn. Dying. "I understand, Marty. I do." I did. I understood his passion, his dedication, I understood how he felt about his patients. I was not going to stand in the way of him doing what he wanted and needed to do.

"I love you, and you have a nice butt, Toni. Have I told you that lately?"

"Last night." I sniffled.

"And your breasts, they're so . . . full. Full and seductive. See, even now, I want those breasts in my hands. Come here, sweetheart."

I laughed through the tears.

Though he worked, Marty spent time with me, too. He always made me feel important, special. He looked at me with love and lust.

One night he sprayed whip cream and a squirt of chocolate sauce on my stomach in bed, then said as he licked it off, "You sure took a long time agreeing to date me."

"I did."

"I was in hell. I thought you'd meet someone else and run off to the wilds of Montana and my life would be over."

"And here we are. Whip cream and chocolate sauce."

"Here we are. That smile of yours. See how you're doing that? Smiling? That turns me on."

"Let's see how turned on you are."

He flipped over. He was mightily turned on. I sprayed whip cream on him.

One day we took a drive and watched the sunset. "My favorite thing to do is be with you, Toni."

"Me too, Marty."

"You're smart, but you're not smart enough to know what I want now."

I laughed. We were parked alone on a hill, in the dark. "I think I know."

"No, you don't."

"Yes, I do." I unsnapped my bra and threw it at him.

"I want chocolate mint ice cream."

"Ah. Not this then." I pulled my shirt open and flashed him.

"Well." He pretended to think. Ponder. Analyze. "I'll have that first, then chocolate mint ice cream."

And that's what we did. I jumped the poor, bald man fighting for his life in the back of our car.

Marty loved it.

Me too.

Then we bought chocolate mint ice cream.

As a joke, I made Ellie a wedding dress out of paper bags for Pillow Talk night. I stapled them together and created a long paper bag train. Valerie and I presented it to her one night at ten o'clock, the soonest that Valerie could meet because of the trial.

"Very funny," Ellie said, then put it on. We took pictures. Valerie and I stood beside her as her bridesmaids dressed in black plastic trash bags. We held pillows in front of us as flowers. We are ridiculous, we know this.

Ellie took one of the bags off to breathe into. "Gino and I had a fight."

"What about?" We settled in with our wine and our pillows. I was making a purple peacock pillow. I had made the body of the peacock in green and blue fabric squares, then had gone to the craft store and bought fake peacock feathers.

Ellie was painting a sunflower in about ten different shades of yellow and gold on a yellow background. Valerie's pillow was in the shape of a white cat. She would add a multitude of sparkly, shiny buttons for the collar.

"We fought about a lot, a whole list of problems. He wants to move in with me before the wedding or he wants me to move in with him."

"You don't want to?" Valerie asked.

"No." Ellie fiddled with her paper bag dress. Then she started taking the dress apart, bag by bag, and throwing the bags to the ground. I'm not even sure she knew what she was doing. "I don't mind spending a weekend with him or going on vacation together, but I don't want him around all the time."

"Sheesh, Ellie," Valerie said. "You're going to be married. That means you live together."

Ellie put a bag over her face. Inhaled. Exhaled.

"Why don't you want to live with him?" I put my peacock pillow on my lap. *Come on, Ellie. Talk it out. Be brave. See this through. Come to the answer you know is there.*

"Because I'll feel smothered."

Then shut this down. "Do you think you would feel this way with any man?"

"Probably. I think I'd feel smothered with anyone around all the time, except for you two. I like being alone, a lot. I like working on my pillows, my business. I like going downtown by myself. I like going to movies by myself. That was the other reason for a fight. Gino asked me to go see this action movie and I said I had already seen it and he got his panties in a twist because he wanted to see it with me. That makes me feel as if I can't even walk out the door and go see a movie without checking with him first. I don't want, or need, that kind of control in my life, and I won't ask anyone for *permission* to do anything."

She blew into her bag. "Except, sometimes, Mama . . ."

"What else did you fight about?" Valerie asked.

"He wants us to live closer to the city to make his commute shorter. I don't want to move. I have my house and my business in one place, on the river. I like it here. I have a five-second commute. He wants to vacation in America only, saying that we have enough to see here. I want to travel all over the world, as I already have. That his mind is so closed to travel, to other cultures, other people, bothers me. It says something about him that I don't like."

She blew into the bag.

"Gino loves me. He's honest, he works hard, he's reliable, he's smart and thoughtful."

"Seems a little controlling to me," I said.

"Maybe he's just not for you," Valerie said.

"He should be, though," she wailed. "What's wrong with me?"

"Nothing's wrong with you," I said. "Nothing."

It is truly hard to break up with people sometimes. It's emotional chaos wrapped up in a mental hurricane. And you can't push anyone else to do it, either. They have to get there themselves.

Valerie and I sewed as we watched Ellie take the wedding dress apart bag by bag.

We met at Daisy's houseboat for a meeting on the possible closure of our dock. I wished that Nick were there and not working. I tried not to worry about him. I hoped he was safe. I hoped he wasn't getting beat up again. I hoped I wasn't madly and wildly in love with him, because that would be a betrayal.

Daisy's light purple houseboat is two stories tall, no interior walls except for bathrooms so that she won't be reminded of her drunken father who locked her in a closet. Her sons have a housekeeper coming in once a week to clean and organize so it's immaculate.

I had had a conversation with Daisy the day before at the end of the dock.

"Bang, clang, crash, pop, smatter. It's all"—she made a twirly motion with her pointer finger next to her ear—"noisy. Lots of things going on in there. Like the sea. Mermaids. Mermen. Talking whales. Undersea castles. Fighting sharks."

Daisy told me she had walked to downtown Portland that day, and said, "I saw a lot of black people, Africans; brown people, Mexicanos; Yellow people, Japs; Pink people, white trash; and white people, ghosts. They were all nice to me. Nice." She was wearing a white-and-yellow bikini top under her blue-and-white daisy coat, and when she became hot at Pioneer Square, in the center of town, she took her coat off.

"Lucky I had my Wednesday bikini on," she told me.

It was Tuesday. "That was a stroke of luck."

She also told me she had seen a cougar in the trees on the way home from Portland. "He talked to me, but I don't like cougars, so I threw three rocks at him."

Daisy greeted everyone at her home wearing a hat like Marie Antoinette might wear. It was about two feet tall, covered in flowers. The hat tied in a red, fluffy bow under her chin. She was also wearing a sweatshirt with a gray, grinning cat on it. The cat had human teeth.

Our attorney for the Dock Fight, Heather Dackson, was there. She is a bulldog, complete with a loud mouth and the admirable ability to file and send a mountain of paperwork. It did not appear to be working. Tweedle Dee Dum and Tweedle Dum Dee's attorneys fired back, and we all received another notice reminding us that we needed to make arrangements to have our houseboats towed.

"I'll be honest with you again, as I've been before," Heather said. "I'm fighting for you. I am on your side, but I can't guarantee a win. This is a neighborhood, but it's also a private dock. This land was bought decades ago, and the dock was built under different rules and laws then. The Shrocks can choose to not pay for the repairs that are needed, which would render this place unsafe, and it would be closed down for them."

Charles and Vanessa had been quoted, and pictured, in the story in the *Oregon Standard*. They sounded educated, reasonable, and persuasive. The paper had also quoted Beth, who said that it was wrong to destroy someone's neighborhood. Unfortunately, the reporter had also run into Daisy, who said, "Those (expletive) developers. They want to ruin (expletive) everything. I hope they turn into (expletive) whales and drown in the ocean."

Tweedle Dee Dum and Tweedle Dum Dee had been quoted as saying that there were extensive structural, plumbing, and electrical repairs that needed to be made that they could not afford. They said, "We're sorry that the people in the houseboats are unhappy. We understand. Still, they are all renting slips from us.

If you own a home and you want your renters to leave, you have the right to ask them to go. It's the law. We have that right."

"I keep telling you," Lindy said, crossing her legs under her long beige skirt and pushing her glasses up her nose, "don't worry. You will not lose the dock. You will not have to move your homes down the river. Make no plans to leave. I have them handled. I'm only here for the dinner and hopefully to talk about books if anyone has read anything interesting?"

"I don't understand, Lindy," Beth said. "You keep telling us not to worry. What do you know that we don't?"

She waved her hand. "Don't worry."

"I worry," Charles said.

"I worry about hauling our houseboat down the river and it breaking in two in the middle of the Willamette," Jayla said.

"None of this will happen," Lindy said. "More wine anyone?"

Oh yes to that!

The meeting droned on with the attorney and her legalese, then Daisy stood up and announced, "I see them! Here they come! It's time to eat a cow and a lobster now!"

We exchanged confused glances until the doorbell rang and Daisy opened the door, her Marie Antoinette hat wobbling.

Four people, dressed in black, carrying huge foil containers, walked in. Caterers. They smiled.

"Lobster feed!" Daisy yelled, forming her hands into two pronged lobster claws and snapping them together. "Come and get 'em. They were alive an hour ago, but they were conked and thunked, boiled and oiled, and now we eat!"

I couldn't believe it. Charles's mouth was hanging open. Jayla said, "Oh, this is going to be delicious." Lindy said, "I can smell the butter and garlic sauce."

We ate on Daisy's deck.

She sang "Take Me Home, Country Roads" by John Denver, which we all sang along to, and "Memory" from *Cats*.

"Memory" made us all choke up. Then she taught us a drinking song, and we laughed again.

I missed Nick. I hoped he was on some back country roads and would be here soon so we could make some memories.

Fifteen minutes after I got home, Nick knocked on my door.

"Care for a houseboat date?"

"Yes."

I walked straight into his hug, then pulled back and studied him, head to foot.

"What?" he asked, smiling.

"I'm making sure you're not hurt."

"I'm not hurt, baby." We walked down to his houseboat.

Daisy pounded on the door and yelled out, "Pistol Man, are you home?"

We both laughed.

"Hello, Daisy, come on in," Nick said.

"I brought you a lobster and a cow," she said, handing him a foil-wrapped box. "Mr. Pistol in His Pants. Have you had dinner?"

"No, not yet. Come eat with us." Nick is so kind to Daisy.

"I can't," Daisy said, adjusting her Marie Antoinette hat. "I have to make another hat. It's going to be a hat with a whale on it, the one I'm going to wear when I ride with the whales, and hello to you again, Toni, kayak lady. I'll sing to you when you cry in your kayak again."

I gave Daisy a hug, feeling so emotional. This would not end well for Daisy. She was losing her mind, but not her heart.

"What?" Daisy shouted. "Why are you crying? Cheer her up, Mr. Pistol in His Pants. Take out your pistol and whip it around."

She turned and left, singing a song unfamiliar to me about pistol-packing, ball-racking barroom-brawling buddies.

"Would you like me to take my pistol out now and whip it around?"

"You bet, Pistol Man."

"Did Dmitry talk to you about the locket he saw in his dream?"

My parents, seated across from me at an upstairs table at Svetlana's Kitchen, froze.

"A locket?" My mother swore under her breath in French.

My father put a hand to the bridge of his crooked nose, then sunk back in his seat.

I let them sit in the locket problem for a while, exchanging troubled glances.

Charlie was playing Tchaikovsky downstairs, but he had come upstairs to give me a hug. Ralph came over to say hello, then saluted me and went back to his room. I could tell he was upset. Ralph was not having an easy day, my mother told me. He'd heard a car backfire and he'd hidden under a table, after grabbing two waitresses and pulling them down with him. They were truly flattered that he had, in his own mind, risked his life to save theirs. Ralph and Charlie are very endearing people.

"Do you have a gold, heart-shaped locket, Mama?"

"No." Her hands twisted in her lap. She switched to Russian. "I do not."

"Dmitry thinks it's from his past." I switched to Russian, too. "He's going to ask you about it."

"I never meant harm," my father whispered, also speaking in Russian.

"I know, my love." My mother patted his hand. "I know you didn't."

"He has never rested," my father said. "Never. Even as a boy. Walking away. Leaving. Searching. Lost."

"You have to tell Dmitry what you know about his past," I said. "You must."

"Dmitry and I, we have always had tension, stress, distrust between us." My father laced his fingers together, blinking rapidly. "From the time he was a little boy, he has not liked me. I don't blame him. I know why. He remembers more than he knows. He knows who I am. Deep in his soul, he knows what I did."

What? What was all this? "Papa, what are you talking about?"

"I am talking about a tragedy. His tragedy. A crime on top of other crimes. Revenge and punishment. Evil."

"Papa, please, you've lost me."

"I have lost myself. I love Dmitry. He is my son." He pounded his chest. "Mine. Ours. I love him. His past will never be erased though, will it, Svetlana? I thought it would, but no, it won't. It will be worse when he knows."

"Healing will come from this, Alexei."

"He's blocked it out," my father continued, lost in the misery of the past. "A wall. But brick by brick, the wall is coming down. Crumble by crumble. The locket now. Already the rocking horse, the blue door, a vegetable garden, a white dog. Soon the wall will open, like his mind, wider and wider still."

"Then help him, Papa," I begged. "Tell him what happened. Tell me how you got Dmitry. You said it was an orphanage. I know that's not true."

He shook his head. "Not an orphanage."

"Then where, Papa? Where did Dmitry come from?"

"I cannot say. Not yet. I will tell him, you are right, Antonia, he should know. When Dmitry is here, after the wedding, we will tell him his own life story. It will cause him deep pain and anguish. He will wish he could go back to not knowing. He will hate me."

"He will not hate you," my mother said.

"He will. He remembers, somewhere. In that head of his, he is brilliant. He was young, but it's there. He talks about a shadow. The shadow comes out and plays with him, teases him mercilessly, then it hides away, waiting. I know who that shadow is."

My mother reached for my father, both arms around him. "You did what you had to do, Alexei. There was no choice. We had no choice."

"I chose what I thought was best for him at that time. We didn't have much time, do you remember, Svetlana?"

She shook her head. "No time at all."

"What Dmitry saw has never left him. It has followed him from Moscow, hanging on to him, haunting him, hurting him. But it is time. Time for the truth. Time to tell my son why he entered this family with blood on him."

I sat back in my chair, weak.

Charlie had moved on to Mozart. Ralph smiled and went downstairs to clean the kitchen.

What other secrets were my parents hiding?

When Marty couldn't work anymore, we settled in at home, and I took a leave away from the paper. We kayaked, so gently, and at the end with friends, because Marty needed help getting in and out of the kayak. On our last kayak trip, he laughed and said to them, all doctors, "Good thing you boys are finally doing something worthwhile" and "I've always wanted you guys to carry me, as if I'm your King. I finally got my wish. If only I had my crown with me."

His poker group came once a week, not once a month. He spent time with his parents. Both of them looked close to dissolving from pain. He hugged my parents, my sisters and brother, who had flown in several times from around the world to see Marty. He hugged my uncles and aunts and cousins, and they blubbered and cried all over him. We had his best friends over, from high school, college, medical school. Who he wanted, I called, they came. We laughed and sang songs.

He invited the Kozlovsky family, and his parents, over for dinner. My parents brought his favorite Russian dishes. After dinner, Marty said, "I want all of you to know that I love you."

He was bald and thin, weak, but still smiling, so brave.

"We love you, too, Marty." Everyone said it, some with ragged voices.

"I would like you all to do one very important thing for me."

"Anything . . . name it, son . . . I'll do it . . . Yes."

He put his arm around me. "Take care of Toni."

I don't think there was anyone in that room who didn't cry.

And then, at the end, it was only us, and his parents.

Marty and I cried, but he was never angry. Never bitter and furious and scared, like me, as he had warned me not to become, though his life was ending so much sooner than it should have.

One morning, as we watched the sun come up, because Marty told me he wanted to watch sunrises and sunsets as much as possible, he said, "I will miss you, honey. I already do."

I tried to be brave. I was falling apart. "That's how I feel. I already miss you, Marty. I'm so sorry this happened to you. To us. To your parents . . ."

"Me too, but I wouldn't wish it on anyone else in place of me."

"I love you so much, Marty."

"And I, you, Toni. You are my life. You are the best thing that has ever happened to me."

There was no hope then. He had done surgery. Chemo. Radiation. Two failed clinical trials. He was on hospice care.

"Toni, you must kayak again. You love the river, the animals, nature, the wind, the rapids. Do what you love, my love."

"No. I can't. Not without you."

"Please, honey. Live when I'm gone. I want to know that you'll be on the river again."

"No."

The sun came up, the light blues and butter yellows and sweet pinks blurred, that fuzzy light grew to golden light, and we went back to sleep, arms entwined, my head against his bald head.

Another night, sitting on our deck, the sun sinking, prophetic, an ending, we held hands, a berry pie off to the side that we'd eaten earlier with his parents. Marty pointed out the bright and shining tunnel from the ground through the puffy white clouds to the sun. "It's a stairway into heaven."

"I hate that stairway."

He kissed my cheek and I turned, put my hands on his bald head, and kissed him back.

"Thank you for marrying me, Toni. This has been the happiest time of my life."

"I don't know what to do. I don't," I said. "I was lost when I met you, Marty, and now I feel lost again, and I don't know how to live without you. I don't know why this is happening. I don't know how I can ever be happy again. I feel like I'm falling down a pit and here I am telling you my problems and it's me who should be listening to you, but I need you. I need you to help me. Marty, please. I don't want you to die, I don't want you to die, I don't want you to die."

I started getting hysterical, drowning in the type of crying you do when you are all broken up inside and you can't take it anymore and nothing seems right because nothing is right and you are losing a person who is your heart and you will not see them again in this lifetime, you will live on and they will go and the world looks absolutely impossible and bleak and scary to live in and you wish you were going together. Together through that golden staircase into the clouds.

"Honey . . ." He held me close, those arms that had been so strong, now weak. That body that had been so healthy, now brittle, but his voice was still there, and his love. "You can do this. It will be hard, but you are a strong, brave woman . . . I will always be in your heart and you in mine. I want you to be happy again, honey, I want that for you. Remember I said that. Please."

"I will not be happy without you, Marty."

"Try, honey. You must try. Don't give up, don't give in. Don't quit." His eyes filled. "Toni, honey, there's something else we need to talk about." His face crumbled, so I cried more.

"What is it?"

"I want you to get married again."

I moved back as if he'd hit me. "No."

"I want you to fall in love. But only with a man who will treat you with respect and kindness and love all day long, as you are an incredible and beautiful woman and you deserve it. When you find him, marry him, and know that I'm happy for you, and I want it for you. I don't want you to be alone, Toni. I want love for you."

"I will never marry again, Marty." It was ridiculous. It was sheer pain. The thought repelled me. "There isn't going to be anyone else."

He tipped my head up and kissed me, and our tears mixed. "I

want there to be someone else, Toni. There needs to be. I know you want kids. I wish we'd had them. We waited too long, we had so much fun, we thought there was time, but you can correct that. Have a bunch of them."

"Not without you, not without you, not without you." That soul-crushing crying was back, and he held me until I could catch my breath again.

"Yes, without me. I will be the angel who looks out for you and your kids." He kissed my forehead. "But remember how awesome I am in bed."

"Why do you make me laugh when I'm crying? And I'll never forget how awesome you are in bed."

"Nothing compared to you, sweet cheeks. You turn me on." He wriggled his eyebrows at me—or where his eyebrows were as they were now gone. "You have done that for me since the very first time I saw you."

I was falling apart from the inside. The love of my whole life was pale, gaunt, his eyes shadowed. He was too thin, his chest concave, his cheeks hollow, despite the food that my family kept bringing, all of Marty's favorites.

My mother even learned to cook Chinese and Japanese food for Marty. Ellie was making fruit drinks for him. Valerie was making vegetable smoothies. The vegetable smoothies weren't very tasty.

"You are the best wife a man could have, Toni. The very best." He turned to me. "But you have set the kitchen on fire twice. . . ."

"Not bad fires, though." I sniffled. "Small ones."

"I think when the fire department came the second time, the captain called you by your first name. . . ."

We laughed again. Laughter, tears, back around.

The golden staircase waited.

Two weeks later we sat together in our two-person kayak, in our living room, pretending to be on a river, near sunset. Marty was breathing hard, the effort to get up at that point a strain, but this was what he wanted. We rowed, but I rowed backward so I could see him. We talked about our trips, the rapids, the times we flipped over, the beavers we saw, the wolf, the golden and bald eagles, Montana, Mexico, the Rogue River, Alaska. We talked about the food we ate, the campfires on the side of the river, the people we met, the shooting stars we marveled at, the moon that shone, the sun that warmed our shoulders.

We talked about our lives together, how we dated, our wedding, our love life.

We laughed, we drank wine.

I got him back into bed, and we watched the sun go down together, the golden staircase glowing again, from the hills, through the sky, to the white puffy clouds, up to heaven, an omen, a sign.

"I love you, Toni."

"I love you, too, Marty. I love you so much."

I waited until Marty was asleep, then hugged him closer. About two in the morning I finally went to sleep myself, ragged, grieving.

Sometime during the night, his heart stopped. Just like that. A last breath. A whisper of good-bye. A soul leaving.

I hugged him all night long, and when I finally woke up, he was cold.

My own husband was cold.

He was gone, up the golden staircase.

He was dead.

I was dead, too.

When I see golden staircases climbing into the sky, through puffy white clouds, up to heaven, I turn away. Every time.

I told my sisters, in my head, that Marty was dead.

They both called. I didn't answer. They waited and didn't call me again. They respected the time and the quiet I needed with Marty. They gave me space, to cry until my body ached, my head throbbed. We are close sisters, we are not invasive.

They were with me in spirit, and I knew it.

I called Marty's parents first, and they came over, hardly able to walk. They had lost their son. Their only child. Inconceivable.

Two hours later, after the funeral home came and Marty's parents were back at their house, collapsing, I called my sisters. I didn't need to say a thing. Both of them said immediately, "I am coming."

They came. My parents came. Dmitry flew out. We cried together, for my husband, Marty Romanowsky, my life and my love, gone.

18

⌒

"I started working in clay when I was sixteen. I had to create. I had to make something. School had no interest for me at all. Art was, is, my destiny. It's my life's work. I want to bring beauty to people's lives."

Zelly Ostrander was a well-known ceramic artist. I was sure readers of *Homes and Gardens of Oregon* would love her, her home, and her art.

Zelly had white, curly, long hair. She was "seventy-five and proud of my wisdom," thin and almost six feet tall. Her art studio was in her backyard—one room, a pitched roof, two sinks, and filled with clay, a hundred different paint colors, brushes, drop cloths, equipment, and two pottery wheels. She made her own art and taught at the university.

Zelly Ostrander's art was stunning. Think of blue flames, mixed with a rainbow, swirled up with a magical spoon, and you had her work. Her specialty was bowls. Bowls for cereal, bowls for fruit, bowls for salads, bowls that you would build a glass fronted armoire for and display as art.

But Zelly's bowls weren't . . . normal. Some tilted at an angle. Others had an almost lacy rim. She had a blue and pink bowl with three dragonflies perched on the edge; bowls with a green and blue swirling design with a ruffly edge. She painted butterflies on bowls so detailed they looked as if they'd flown in from the window.

Zelly told me about her life growing up with her parents in

an apartment in San Francisco. Her mother owned a gun shop, her father worked on the docks. "They loved me, but glory be, they were tough people. My father fought for the union. Those men didn't mess around, they got the job done, and if a few skulls were cracked, that was the way it had to be. My mother was not above a fight, either, but I was their soft spot."

How she came to art? "I didn't speak until I was six. Until then, I drew pictures to show how I was feeling. That's where it started."

On her day-to-day life, "I create art. I read. I see friends. I have a whiskey every night, like my mother. She had a cigar, I don't. I travel the world twice a year. I must see this planet before I die."

On her home? "I've only had it for three years, but I feel like I've been looking for it my whole life. A home isn't only wood and concrete, is it? It's . . ." She spread her arms out. "A bowl. A colorful, clean, safe bowl with a roof where you live your life."

"I love your work," I said. "I have two of your bowls. One is white lattice with snowflakes painted along the side and another is an ocean wave."

"Ah. You bought during my freezing year and my drowning year. My mother died during the freezing year, the snowflake year. I still miss her. The ocean bowls I made when I felt like I was drowning. I suffer from bipolar depression. I'm not embarrassed for you to print that, either. Please do. Others need to know they are not alone.

"It comes in like an invisible, bio-chemical avalanche. A wave, hence the ocean. As I get older, I know how to handle it better, but it's never easy. It's like living with a tsunami. Sometimes it comes and gets you and you have to swim to the surface and not let it get you thinking that you'd rather die than deal with the swimming for one more day. It's a hard-fought battle every time."

"I love these." I pointed to rows of flowered bowls. The bowls simply opened up like flowers: roses, camellias, tulips, daffodils, lilies, violets, orchids.

"I'm in a flowery time of life, so I make flowers."

Made sense to me. I bought a set for Marty's parents.

Maybe I needed to work on embracing flowers again. Maybe.

The next day, in my head, I heard Valerie say, *They scare me.* I called, got her voice mail. She was in trial. She called about eleven that night. Nick and I were reading in bed, a new book, discussing it as we went.

"What are the Bartons doing now?"

"They're furious, naturally, that I'm trying to put their murdering son/brother/cousin in jail and insist he's innocent."

"Do they not know him? Are they not listening to the evidence?"

"What people don't want to believe, they won't. To them it's a conspiracy. We're out to get them. We're on the side of a corrupt government. The evidence is a lie, manufactured. They glare. They snicker when I'm in front of them. Today the judge told them to be quiet or they would be escorted from the courthouse. He then put two guards there, either side of the row, to glare at them."

"Did it quiet them down?"

"No. They were removed from the courtroom."

"Tough lot."

"Yes."

"There's something more. I can tell." I felt that chill of a snake winding around my spine yet again. "What is it, Valerie?"

"There was a dead possum on my back porch today."

I was speechless for long and stunned seconds.

"I thought there were security cameras. You've called the police?"

"They came in through the shadows, hoodies on. The police can't identify them."

"I thought the police were also driving by?"

"They are. They snuck like lice over the back fence."

"I'm sorry."

"Don't be. This guy has to go to jail."

"We'll be scared together. You're carrying a gun?"

"I am now. Love you."

"Love you, too, more than Mama's Russian tea cakes."

I hung up the phone and leaned back against Nick. He held me while I shook.

The cold spine snake slithered, head poised, ready to bite.

Moscow, the Soviet Union

Things went rapidly downhill for our family after our father and grandfather were arrested. Valeria was in bed for days, aching from being thrown against the wall, clutching her head. My mother, also with a splitting headache that lasted a week, as did the nausea, pulled herself together, attended to Valeria, and went to the police station. She demanded to see her husband and her father-in-law, Konstantin. They refused. They pretended they didn't know where either one of them was.

By then, we were all alone. Uncle Vladan, Uncle Yuri, Uncle Sasho and their families—all gone. Uncle Leonid dead, though the Communist Party would not confirm it. Friends volunteered money for gas, and my mother drove hours to a prison that she thought my father and grandfather might have been taken to. She demanded to see them. They put her in a cell for three days. Told her not to come back and said she was lucky not to be locked up, too, for being an enemy of the people. "Pray to your God now," they mocked my mother, exhausted, starving, as she hobbled out.

Valeria, Elvira, and I were so relieved to see her after three days alone, we cried and clung to her.

My parents had always saved what little they could, but life in Moscow was rough and it would not last for long at all. In addition, my mother was worried that we would be taken away from her, now that she had been exposed for being a Christian.

My mother started sewing for people, a skill her mother, Lada, an expert seamstress, had taught her. She had put it aside as a college professor and a mother.

She went to the people she knew, professors, colleagues, students who came from wealthy families. She offered her services. My mother, a woman with a PhD in Russian Literature, a college professor, scrambling for work to mend someone's torn pants.

She put her pride aside, and she did it, though I heard her swearing in French now and then. Many of the people were too scared to give her work, but some did, quietly, secretively. She picked up the work late at night, at their back doors, and they handed her the money. Some people took advantage of her desperation. "I hated Professor Gerasmiov when I worked with him, and I hate him more now, may he die in pain, alone with no one but cackling hyenas to watch him writhe." He negotiated the work down to a pittance in payment, because he could, knowing she needed every ruble.

Others were fair, a few generous. "One of my students, Vada Utkina, comes from a wealthy family. They pay more than I ask."

My mother quickly decided that the way to make more money was to start selling fancy gowns for wealthy women—all wives to high ranking Communist Party members, of course. It worked. The money started to come in, but we still struggled, the pantry often bare, the refrigerator not much better.

Bogdan and Gavriil's father, Stas Bessonov, came down one night, and offered my mother money. My mother told us to go to bed when Stas arrived. We did but, as usual, I snuck out, along with Valeria, and listened.

"I cannot accept it," our mother said. "But thank you, Stas."

"Svetlana, you must. I hear you are making gowns for the enemy."

My mother bent her head. "I hate them, too. I have no choice."

"I do not blame you at all, Svetlana. It is for food, it is for the girls' survival, but take this. It's what I have now. Pay me back when you can."

"Stas, it is wrong to take this money. I can provide for my family." She bent her head, covered her face, her shoulders shook.

"Svetlana, please, don't cry. I don't know what to do when women cry. It makes me nervous."

"I cannot take it. I doubt I will ever be able to pay you back."

"Then don't. It's yours. Here. A tissue. No more tears now. Don't make me nervous."

Stas put the money on the kitchen table, tapped it with his finger. My mother, full of pride, integrity, a woman who had been fired from her university position, a husband and father in law in jail, no living parents nor brother, a mother with three girls to feed, took it. She hugged him.

"Svetlana, your husband has always treated me with respect, as have you. I am a man from nothing. You know my business. I have appreciated the friendship. Plus the children are friends. I am helping many families now. It is a horrible time, and I will do what I can for you."

This gentleness from a man who regularly whacked people and dumped them in the river.

"I am trying to get Alexei released. It takes time, it takes bribes, it takes the right person signing off." He cracked his knuckles.

"Thank you, Stas." My mother was close to breaking, but she wouldn't, because that's not what a Kozlovskaya woman did. She had told me often, "We stand strong, always, Antonia. Don't you forget that."

There was more help coming from the Bessonov family, which Valeria and I found out later that week.

"Do you want me to show you how to get some money, Antonia?" Bogdan asked.

I had witnessed my mother crying the night before. I was hungry all the time, my stomach eating itself, growling, but I didn't want to tell my mother.

Hunger is a scary thing. It hits at the root of your life: You get too hungry, and you'll die. Worse, the people you love will die. You can't think, you can't plan, you can't dream if you're hungry. Elvira resembled a walking sheet. Valeria was moving slowly. My mother was down to bone.

"Antonia?" Bogdan said again. "Do you want money?"

"Yes." I did.

Bogdan showed me. It wasn't that hard, and I was trained by the boy who was trained by the best, his father.

Bogdan and Gavriil trained Valeria and me how to pick-pocket and Elvira how to be a distraction. They trained us using their own pockets. The boys were competent teachers. They were patient, skilled, and they helped us with every movement. Gavriil told us how to study people, to watch for the signs that indicated they were wealthy, that they would actually have something to steal.

In that time of stagnation in the Soviet Union, the Cold War an economic icicle, it was easy to see who had what. Most people had nothing. We were not after them. We were after the ones who did.

I was scared to death the first time I pickpocketed. I felt as low as the sidewalk under my feet. I had been taught not to steal, yet there I was.

My first victim was a well-dressed woman in a fur coat and hat who I saw walking through Red Square, St. Basil's Cathedral, with its ice-cream tops, in front of her. Bogdan and Gavriil said to me, "She has money. See her purse. See her rings? Diamonds. She could sell one and we could live off of it for six months."

My stomach rumbled. I thought of my mother that morning, sewing at the table, swearing in French when a stitch went wrong, working, working, working.

I followed the woman, Valeria beside me, Elvira behind her. We skipped along, singing, our bows on the tops of our heads bouncing around. I accidentally bumped into her. I slipped my hand in and out of the woman's purse. She had forgotten to zip it, which was why we targeted her.

"Excuse me." I smiled. Valeria smiled, too. The woman smiled back, went on her way.

Guilt, and fear, hit hard. I cried over the wallet I held in my hands. I knew I was now going to hell and the devil would burn me with his tail, so help me God, forgive me. We rushed around a corner, then another, and hid in an alley, making sure that no one was following, as Bogdan and Gavriil had taught us, then we hurried to the meeting place.

At the meeting place, between two buildings, outside of Red Square, I sat down and covered my head, a dancing devil with a burning tail skipping through my mind.

"Antonia," Bogdan said, getting to eye level with me. "I know you're upset. You don't have to do this. You can go home. I understand."

I sniffled, wiped my sleeve. Beside me, Valeria stared straight ahead, stricken. Elvira, only six, snuggled into me.

"But your family's broke. Your papa's gone. He's in jail with your grandfather, our father told us. We don't know if, or when, they're coming back."

"They're coming back," I cried.

"They'll be back soon. You're stupid." Valeria tried to kick Bogdan. He dodged. She tried to kick him again, and he dodged again. So she ran after Gavriil, fists up. "Stop running. I hope your eyes fall out of your head, Gavriil. I hope your legs run you into a wall, Bogdan, and your brains squish out."

To their credit, neither brother hit back, despite her swinging fists. They simply ducked, put up their arms to protect themselves, then circled back to us when Valeria's anger petered out. We were three miserable Kozlovskaya girls in a heap.

"There are wealthy people here," Gavriil said, "all in the party. They have houses and cars and jewelry and vacations that you can't believe. They take all the money. They make all the money. It all goes to them. My father told us. That's not the way it was supposed to work. They're the wealthy, we're the poor. They took your papa and grandfather for what? Because they talked about a new kind of government. They talked about being able to say what they wanted, and write what they wanted. And they took them because they're Christians. I don't believe in your God but it's okay if you do. We're taking back what they have taken from us."

"Who do you think put your papa and grandfather in jail?" Bogdan said. "That's right. They did. The wealthy. The people who are running this country. The KGB. The government. Communists." He spit on the ground. "My father hates them."

I thought of my father and grandfather, suffering in jail, for doing nothing wrong. I nodded. "I want to take back what they took from us."

"Smart girl." Gavriil helped me up.

Bogdan smoothed my hair down with his hands. "There."

I smiled at him. He smiled back. He was so handsome.

"Me too," Valeria said. "I'll steal from the people who took my papa."

Gavriil approached Valeria again, and she didn't hit him. He patted her on the back. Elvira stopped crying, and we got back to work.

Picking pockets. Stealing rubles.

Soon I was talented at pickpocketing.

I knew how to slip my fingers in, soft and smooth, like moving silk. I was lightning quick, a sleight of hand, a twist of the wrist. I was adept at disappearing, at hiding, at waiting, until it was safe to run, to escape.

I was a whisper, drifting smoke, a breeze.

I was a little girl, in the frigid cold of Moscow, under the looming shadow of the Soviet Union, my coat too small, my shoes too tight, my stomach an empty shell.

I was desperate. We were desperate.

Survival stealing, my sisters and I called it.

Had we not stolen, we might not have survived.

"Monster creeps."

"Who is?" I asked Daisy as we sat on her deck and watched a motorboat cruise by.

"My sons." She wiped her hands together as if wiping her hands clean of her sons. "I am rid of them now!"

"Why do you say that?"

"They took my ammo."

"Ah. That. Yes, uh . . . that's too bad. . . ."

"They took it all. Thieves! Thieves! They even took my bullet treasures from my negligee drawers!"

Drawers? Plural? "Sorry to hear that." I so wasn't sorry to hear that.

"How am I going to shoot without ammo?"

"Who did you want to shoot?"

"Spiders."

"Maybe you can simply smash them with your foot?"

"I hate spiders."

"Spiders are irritating."

"And slugs. I want to shoot slugs. There was a slug on my hosta the other day. Where it came from, I don't know. I went to get my gun and I shot it, but no ammo. Monster creep sons."

"They love you a lot."

"Oh, piss off. I love them, too, but they shouldn't interfere with my bullet shots."

Daisy sang that night, her voice carrying down the river. She sang "Over the Rainbow" and "We're Off to See the Wizard" and "The Sound of Music."

Jayla and Beth, Vanessa and Charles, and Lindy and I sat behind her as she stood on the edge of the dock, a white daisy in her purple hat. No one said a word. We listened. We closed our eyes.

I was not the only one tearing up that night.

I sat in my and Marty's tandem kayak in the river by my tugboat the next afternoon, the sun warm, the wind soft. I knew exactly what he would say to me if he were here, "Come on, Toni. You can do it."

I did not turn around and look. There would be no Marty there. None. I tried to breathe, my eyes shut.

For the first couple weeks after Marty died, my family would come to our house—I later learned they had a schedule—and help me get up. They all knew where the hidden key was, and they'd use it and put it back.

They would get in bed with me and I'd cry and they'd cry, too. My cousin Boris and my cousin Zoya were particularly weepy. Poor Uncle Vladan. He could hardly control himself. Somehow it felt better to cry with someone than cry alone.

They would force me to get up, literally pushing me into the shower. None of the men stripped me down, but my sisters and female cousins and my mother had no qualms about standing me up in the bedroom and stripping off my clothes before manhandling me into the shower.

"Don't forget to wash your hair," JJ would say. "You wash it, I'll fix it."

"I feel bad for you being alone in there," Tati would wail. "Do you want me to shower with you?"

"When you're done we can draw pictures of monsters being arrested," Ailani called to me through the door. "And you can use my new crayons."

I thought about never going back to work. Marty had left me a life insurance policy, and I didn't have to work. I thought about shutting down, cutting out. It took all my strength to get through every single day, but I did it.

I am a different person in many ways than I was before Marty died. I am more compassionate. I understand the anger and bitterness that people experience when someone they love more than the universe dies.

I'm stronger than I used to be. I appreciate laughter more, and the love and friendship of my family and my friends, who were there for me. The people who were not there for Marty and me when Marty was ill, I simply don't see anymore. Either you are a friend, good times and bad, or you aren't.

On the other hand, people can irritate me much more quickly than they used to, though I have always been on the snippy side. I have little patience for listening to inane problems and people whining over them. I am acutely aware of what is a problem and what isn't.

I'm a better person than I was when Marty died, and I'm worse.

Both.

Sometimes life asks for too much. It knocks you down, and when you try to get up it kicks you in the teeth again. It gets so tiring, trying to get up. Sometimes it seems easier to give in, but that's an emotional train wreck, too, to stay that far down in the trenches of excruciating pain.

Tough place.

Mr. and Mrs. Quackenbusch, always together, quacked at me and headed up to my deck. In the distance I could see the new home Big Teeth and Big Tooth were building for their new life.

I wanted to kayak. I wanted to be on the rivers again.

I didn't want to live like this anymore. I didn't want to be locked into the knocked-down place.

I wanted to change. I had to change because I wanted to live, I knew that.

Knowing something and acting bravely on it can be two different things. I wasn't feeling brave.

I tilted my head back to the sun. It was warm, the wind soft. Maybe I would try to be brave.

I went to a grief group for widows one time. I had to. I was reeling from grief, rage, loneliness, aloneness, and the utter unfairness that Marty had died. All of them said that the first time they made love to a man who wasn't their husband, they cried.

Some cried because they missed their husbands.

Others cried because they felt guilty.

And a few cried because they were so happy to be having sex and they didn't miss their mean, belittling, difficult husbands at all.

Sitting on Nick's dock, as the sun went down on a Saturday night, I talked about Marty. Maybe it was because I was feeling closer and closer to Nick. Maybe it was because I trusted him. Maybe it was because of something I didn't want to admit yet.

I told him how Marty and I met, how I didn't want to date a man my parents picked out for me, how I gave in. I talked about kayaking. Our friendship. Our love. Our wedding.

I talked about how I had felt so overwhelmed with grief, I could hardly function.

I paused now and then, to make sure it wasn't too much for him, too much emotion, too much loss, too pathetic, but it wasn't.

I told him how guilty I felt for sleeping with him and how it made me feel like a bad wife. That it was too soon, that I had betrayed Marty and our vows. I didn't talk on and on and on. I told Nick what I thought he needed to know, what I knew he wanted to know.

I studied Nick's light blue eyes when I was done. That hard face with a couple of scars. The huge shoulders. He looked like a dangerous man, but he wasn't. He wasn't dangerous at all except to my heart and my guilt level.

Nick pulled me into his arms, I actually saw tears, and he whispered, "I am so, so sorry, Toni. I am."

We did not have sex that night. Nick would have called it making love, but I couldn't. Marty was between us. Nick held me until I left, then walked me to the door of my tugboat.

I kissed his cheek and shut the door.

Nick.

Marty.

Nick.

Ellie and I were at Svetlana's, back corner, grateful not to have been called into waitressing by our mother. The waitresses came by to say hello, but they did not take our order. We all knew our mother would be bringing us what she wanted us to eat.

It was a full house, as usual. Charlie had decided he was going to play Mozart all night. Ralph came downstairs, the subdued lighting shadowing the dent in his head, saw Ellie and I, saluted, and went to the kitchen to clean.

Tonight, up on the Specials board the dessert of the night was named "No More Wearing Black, Chelsea." It was carrot cake. I laughed.

"How are you, Ellie?" I picked up my wineglass. Yum. My father knew how to pick 'em.

"Gino wants four kids, maybe five." She rubbed her widow's peak. Stressed.

That one hurt. Four or five kids sounded like a fine number to me. Six was not out of the realm. I pushed my own feelings down. "Do you not want four or five kids?"

Ellie brought the brown paper bag out. Inflate. Deflate.

"Breathe, Ellie. And try this wine. It takes like Italy and hot bread and purple grapes."

She drank the wine, hand unsteady. "I don't know if I can say it out loud."

"Try. Please." She didn't want kids, I knew it.

She whispered, so low I couldn't hear her. "What?"

"I don't think . . . I don't think I want kids."

I took another sip of wine.

"You're not surprised, Toni."

"No. But if you don't think you want kids, and Gino does, you have an unsolvable problem."

"I know. We talked about it." She fluffed her face with the bag. "I like kids. I like being an aunt to Valerie's kids, JJ's kids, and I feel like an aunt to Pavel because he's so young, but to have my own kids? I don't think I'm that maternal. Does that make me a bad woman?"

"Not at all. It makes you honest. If you don't want kids, you should not have them."

"I remember a lot of scary things that happened to us as kids, Toni, so maybe I'm projecting. Maybe I don't want to inflict that on a child even though my rational mind says that's silly. But though I love holding a baby and toddlers are cute, I get bored when I'm with them too long. Like in thirty minutes. And JJ's teenagers . . . hearing about Chelsea and Hope is enough to make my uterus shrivel. Plus, I know I would have to stop working so much. I know I would have to give up my free time. I know I would hardly sleep for years. Motherhood"—she breathed into the bag, back out—"doesn't appeal to me at all."

"What did you say to Gino when he said he wanted four or five kids?"

"I said, 'How will we have four kids when I have a business?' And he said that since I work at home, I could run the business while raising the kids, or I could give up the business and be a full-time mom. He told me he made enough for our family, and this would be his preference.

"I almost threw a pillow at his face. I said, 'Gino, why don't you work from home and I'll move my business out of the house and you run your business while looking after four or five noisy, temper-tantrum-throwing kids?' And he said, getting all uptight, 'I can't do that. I have an office, downtown, I have clients to meet, calls, e-mails, projects . . .' and I said, 'I have the same, Gino, do you not realize that? You want me to give up my business, but you won't give up yours. Is that fair?' "

How infuriating. "What did he say?"

"He said that he hadn't thought of it that way, that he assumed we would be like his parents and I would be at home with the kids and I said, 'You want me to stay at home with four or five kids, drowning in housework and laundry and making macaroni and cheese while you get to build your career? You want me to give up the business that I love, that I built from nothing, in favor of burping babies and changing diapers? Do you not know and appreciate how much my pillow business means to me?'

"Toni, the expression on his face while we were fighting. It was like I'd hit him with a sewing machine. He said, 'Ellie, I didn't think about it like that,' and I said, 'Well, you better start thinking.' "

"Here, have some more wine."

She downed the whole glass. "It was so frustrating, Toni. I said to him, 'Gino, you clearly don't know me at all. You have no idea how hard I've worked to build this business and how much it means to me. How interesting it is to me, how intellectually stimulating it is, how I love it. How I love to design and make pillows and market and sell them.' And he said, 'I do know!' and I said, 'Then, Gino, what you have asked me to do is even worse. At first I thought you were simply dense and selfish in asking me to give up my business, but now I think you're an asshole. Knowing how much I love my pillow business you would still ask me to give it up? Don't you want me to be happy? Your solution is for me to run my company while taking care of four or five children. Do you want me to die of exhaustion? Don't you care that that would be too much for one person?' "

"I want to strangle him." I drummed my fingers on the table. "It's like he's got a brick in his head."

"We kept fighting, and I screamed at him to get out."

"Did he get out?"

"No, he started backing way up. He said that we could work it out, but I said how, and I really pressed him for answers, and all he said was that we needed to calm down and find a solution. Men will often say, 'We can work it out,' but really what they're doing is waiting until you give in, until you make the sacrifice that they want you to make, and then they act all thankful, but really that was the goal from the start. To make you give in and they make no concessions. The 'solution' is for the woman to give up part of herself."

"How did it end with Gino?"

"He paced, we argued, he cried, but what I said made an impact on him. He finally said, 'How do you see it? I don't want my kids in daycare.'"

"I told him that they would be *our* kids, not his, that I would financially support the family while he raised the children. He was floored, said he could never be a full-time dad, it would be too boring, that he needed his career, and I said I can't be a full-time mother, I love my career, too, and I told him I was not going to be the sacrificial lamb and work two full-time jobs."

"I think you have to tell him the whole truth, that you want no lambs at all."

"If I tell him that, it will end it."

I waited. Strangely, when she said that, she put the bag down and took a deep breath.

"You seem calmer now, Ellie."

She closed her eyes. "I am."

Our parents sat down with us. My mother was wearing a silky red dress, my father in a dress shirt and tie.

My mother said, "I make food delicious tonight, no? You like the 'Why Marry So Young, Elvira'? It on the Specials board. Everyone like. I make for you." To me, she said, "You too thin. But I happy you no hanging around with criminals no more, Toni. Right, Alexei?"

"That right," my father said. "Our daughter writes about kitchens and homes and decorations. I see your articles. I like them. But how about coming here to work for us at Svetlana's? We pay you high salary. Okay?"

"Thank you, Papa, but no."

"And health insurance. And!" My mother held up her finger. "My cuisine, I like that word, free to you. All you want of my cuisine." She raised her eyebrows, as in, "Can you believe it?"

"Thank you, Mama, but no."

"Ah. Yes, I understand," my father said. "You a writer. So, my daughters. I no see you this week. Tell me what you do. Start with Monday . . . okay, now Tuesday . . . what about the Wednesday . . ."

Our parents grilled us on our lives, with love and laughter, then they stood up and announced to the restaurant that we were all going to sing a Russian drinking song together. That was met with enthusiasm. There were a lot of Russians in there. The rest pretended to sing, swinging their wineglasses and beer mugs back and forth.

Keeping The Monsters At Bay: Shopping Defensive Strategies allowed me to buy a pair of tight jeans that were staring at me, begging me to buy them, from a display window downtown.

I wondered how fast Nick could get them off.

19

I read about Tyler Barton's trial in the paper again. My sister was quoted as saying that justice would be served. She was circumspect and professional, as usual.

Shamira Connell continued to report on the trial, and the evidence from the crime scenes was nauseating.

I called Valerie. "One of the reasons I quit my crime and justice job was because of the gruesomeness I'm seeing in this trial, Valerie."

"I know. This trial is pushing it for me. I'm thinking I should go and work for Mama and Papa and make desserts all day."

"You sound tired."

"I am. I need to see the kids. The other night Ailani told me that even though she liked that I put bad guys in jail, she felt as if she didn't have a mom. And Koa hugged me so tight, he wouldn't let go. I carried him around for much of the night."

"How's Kai?"

"Kai's my man. He works, he takes the kids to school and day care and picks them up. He makes dinner. He leaves dinner for me."

"Anything else going on?"

"Why?"

"Because I could hear your silence in my head."

"That's new. Hearing my silence."

I waited in our silence.

She sighed, teeny tiny. "One of the Bartons recently swore to kill me. I heard about it an hour ago. It was Leroy, a cousin. They've locked him up."

"Valerie—" Cold and slithery snake wound around my spine.

"I know."

"I'm worried about you and the kids."

"Helps to have a Portland police captain to sleep with each night."

We talked, then she had to run off.

Shamira texted me that night. "Leroy Barton threatened to kill your sister. She knows. Will be in paper tomorrow. When is your mother making those lamb shish kabob things again, do you know?"

I called my mama, asked her.

"Tell Shamira I make for her on Saturday."

I told Shamira.

"I can't wait. Thanks, Toni. Sorry about the death threat for Valerie."

"My parents are coming to visit this weekend. I'd like you to meet them."

"What? No." I dropped my fork. *Hell no.*

"No?" Nick placed his fork down, too, rather slowly, then put his forearms, tight and musclely, on the table and leaned forward.

We were eating the taco salad Nick and I had made, together, on his deck. The river wandered by. Dixie the blue heron took off. Mr. and Mrs. Quackenbusch had found me and climbed up on Nick's deck. The sun was headed down.

"No, Nick." I avoided his eyes. He waited for me to get the courage to look at him. I finally made an I-Give-Up sound in my throat, and did, capitulation to the blond giant, whose hair was longer now for his current undercover assignment.

Meeting parents was too serious, too much. I am not in that type of a relationship with Nick. I still love Marty. I am already betraying Marty by sleeping with Nick. I am sleeping with Nick because I can't resist him and need sex and he takes away the loneliness and aloneness and I can breathe again and he is kind and interesting and protective and smart and I like him.

"They're nice people, Toni."

"I don't want to meet them. All I want to do is eat this taco salad." He was silent. I tried to eat. Couldn't. I put my fork down again. "You're mad."

"Yes, I am. It would be a dinner, that's it."

"It's more than that." I went from nervous and feeling cornered by the invitation to ticked off. "Hey, Nick, don't push me."

"Don't push you? We've been sleeping together for months. Whether or not you want to admit it, we're together—"

"No, we're not."

That one hurt. I could see it in his blue eyes, and I castigated myself for being a mean and gross monster of a woman.

"We're not together? We sleep together. We talk. We laugh. We have dinner, but we're not together." He leaned back in his chair, jaw tight, shoulders back. "Thanks, Toni. You know how to make me feel special."

"I told you from the start what I wanted, and it was not to be a couple. Not a serious relationship."

Silence. Cold and simmering.

"Think about it for five minutes, Toni."

"You are really pissing me off, Nick. I said no and you're not accepting it. Accept no." I couldn't meet Nick's parents, I loved Marty's parents. They still came over, they called to check up on me, I went to their home, too. They were friends with my parents. They loved the set of bowls I brought them from Zelly Ostrander. I stood up.

"Really? That's it? Don't go, Toni."

"I will if I want to. Don't ever tell me what to do."

"You're going to run off? You don't like the conversation, so you take off? Fine. We'll talk about this later."

"There you go again." I threw my napkin down. I tried to throw it to the table, but the wind picked it up and I had to run and chase it down before it went in the water. "Listen to me. I don't want to talk about it later. I don't want to talk about it at all."

"Damn it, Toni." He stood up, too.

"Damn it what?" He was frustrated with me. "I don't need the stress of any man being frustrated or angry with me. I have been clear about this relationship from the start. You agreed. Now you're ticked because you thought you could change this around, change me, and have me meet your parents. I was honest, you weren't."

"I have always been honest with you. Always. And I honestly want you to meet my parents. You said no. Okay. You won't meet them."

"But you're mad about it."

"It's one dinner." He spread his arms out. Exasperated. Pained.

And I am not that brave. Not yet. "It's not one dinner to me. It means I'm dating someone. It means I'm in a relationship when I'm not." I thought I was going to cry. "My husband has only been dead for . . ."

Nick towered over me and put his warm hands on my shoulders. "More than two years, babe."

"That's right!" I flung his hands off of me. *More than two years already?* "It's only been more than two years!" When I said it out loud, it didn't sound rational. I decided to bypass that.

"It's a long time, honey."

"It's not a long enough long time. I am not dating you, I am not dating anyone. I am not meeting your parents."

"You aren't betraying Marty."

I sucked in my breath. He got it. He nailed it. "I am. I'm a terrible, disloyal wife."

"You aren't a terrible wife. You aren't a disloyal wife."

"What do you know, Nick?" Fury rose, destructive, out of control, the fury that I had felt for so long. The unfairness of Marty's death. The loss. The endless grief. "You've never been married. You've never had a spouse die on you. You've never watched them get sicker and sicker, thinner and thinner, weaker and weaker, their hair falling out from chemo.

"You've never taken a spouse to the hospital for appointments and treatments and the news is bad at first and it gets worse and worse and they become gray and white and skinny but smile when you're in the room to be brave and then they start to sleep more and more and they hold your hand and tell you what to do when they're gone and then someone says you need hospice and you know you don't need hospice because the person you love more than anyone is going to get better but then he doesn't and hospice comes in to help because you can't lift them anymore, can't turn them, can't take care of all the horrible stuff that happens when someone is dying, and then they can't get out of bed, and you cry and laugh together and say I love you and then they die.

"They die and they die forever. You, Nick, have never been through that, but I have and that is why I am not going to meet your parents because you and I are not dating."

"Toni—"

"Don't Toni me!" I raged. "And don't follow me home." I put my hands on his chest and I shoved him to make sure he knew what I was talking about. He is built like steel, so he didn't move. "Don't follow me." I burst into tears. "Don't come after me. Don't call me."

"Toni." His face softened. I thought there were tears in those light blue eyes, but I couldn't see through mine. "Babe, please stay, I'm sorry. I don't want to hurt you, ever. I never want to make you cry—"

"Screw it, Nick. I don't need this, and I don't need you."

I swear I could see the color running straight out of his face, but because I'm an awful monster of a person, I didn't stay around to find out. I turned and left and I slammed his door, then I slammed mine and I went up to the wheelhouse and I curled up on my red bench and I cried until my insides turned inside out.

* * *

I saw Nick's parents on the dock when they came to visit Nick that weekend. His father was a tall, solidly built Mexican American man with black and white hair. He wore jeans and cowboy boots. His Italian American mother was smaller, curvy, lots of black hair, a colorful dress, a huge smile. I watched them from inside of my tugboat, still as a rock, my sneaky binoculars up.

They hugged Nick. They were happy together. I heard them out on his back deck, chatting, laughing. They went out together on *Sanchez One* while I was alone in my tugboat, alone on this lonely blue-and-gray river, except for Dixie the blue heron, who seemed to stare at me from across the water.

I did not go and have dinner with Nick's father and mother.

That would have been wrong.

Right? I asked myself. *Right?*

Three days later Nick left for work. He had mentioned that he was going on a "trip." I didn't know where he was going, but I had the impression it was Mexico.

Good, I told myself, sniffling, when I heard his footsteps on the dock. I'm glad he's gone. I don't need someone pressuring me. I don't need Nick telling me to meet his parents. I don't need Nick trying to change me or us. Not that there is an us anymore. No, there was not a Nick and Toni, and there never was.

When Nick comes back, I told myself, I'm going to break up with him. Not that we have a relationship that needs to be "broken up," but I'm going to tell him that we're not sleeping together anymore, no sitting on his deck, no dinners, no reading the same book and talking about it, nothing. I blew my nose.

I would ignore him, and we were all getting kicked off the dock anyhow, so I wouldn't have to see him anymore. I wouldn't have to "talk about it later" when he mentioned meeting his parents or going on "real" dates.

I wiped my eyes.

I wouldn't have to see all that blond hair and those light blue eyes and that mouth. And I wouldn't have to get naked with that overgrown body at night or walk home at one in the morning or talk to him about our jobs or why he likes boating or my mixed-up family or watch him make homemade pizza or grill me a steak or kiss him good-bye or laugh or get closer and closer to him.

It would be a relief.

We would be all done and I wouldn't have to think about being brave.

I couldn't sleep that night until the sun came up.

"Sister," Dmitry drawled.

"Brother," I said back, holding my phone. It was early, seven o'clock, but I had decided to go to bed because I was miserable. I pulled my white comforter up to my chin.

He sang a few lines from a song he wrote about a brother with three sisters. It was funny, loving, filled with rhymes.

"I've been thinking about you, Toni."

"That translates into, 'I'm worried about you,' and I know it, Dmitry."

"True. I do worry about you. How are you feeling about Marty?"

"Miss him. Always will."

"And the new man?"

"Disaster."

"Tell me."

Dmitry listens. He listens so well. He's compassionate, thoughtful. But *emotional*. I could hear him quietly crying.

"Okay, I can't talk about him anymore, Dmitry. This is too upsetting, for you and for me."

"I'm sorry for crying, Toni. I can't help it. I can't stand when you're upset. I'm sorry about Marty, I'm sorry about Nick. Okay. Getting control of myself. Did you get the baskets I sent you?"

"I did. Thank you so much." They were colorful wicker baskets from Mexico. I loved them. I love baskets for organizing things in my closet, and he knew it. I like to have my socks, underwear, bras, all in the right place. I like to see them in their piles so I know I don't have only four pairs of socks and six underwear, like in Moscow.

"I sent Ellie fabric, you the baskets, and Valerie a purse."

"You know us too well, Dmitry."

"I also wrote a poem about sisters and I put it on my blog."

"I saw it and I loved it." The poem was titled "The Loves Of My Life Are My Sisters." "You know Mama named a dessert special after it. She made Bird's Milk Cake with these huge melted marshmallows and the whole thing was smothered in chocolate. It was called 'My Dmitry Loves His Sisters.' She put the poem on everyone's table. Everyone loved the poem and the dessert, line out the door. I had two servings."

"I miss Mama's cooking."

Dmitry asked about the whole family—how was everyone?

Dmitry traveled the world, but in his head he never left our family.

"I love you so much, Toni."

"You too."

I fielded several calls over the next week. They all had the same question. "I heard about the 'My Dmitry Loves His Sisters' dessert. Do you know when your mother's going to make that again? I heard it's so delicious that people cry."

The next neighborhood meeting was on my tugboat. There were many neighbors there, so we spilled out onto the dock. Nick was not there. He was still gone. I tried not to think of Nick working with creepy and dangerous drug dealers and getting hurt, because we were broken up anyhow and I did not want to cry again.

I served beef pies wrapped in light, puffy pastries that my mother made at the restaurant. She calls them Beefy Russians. I also brought her Moscow Mushroom soup, bread, and peppermint ice cream because I felt like eating peppermint. I served beer and wine to loosen everyone up.

We ate first, chatted, and laughed.

Heather Dackson arrived and presented. She talked about the meetings she'd had, the lawsuit she'd filed, the city's response, and Tweedle Dee Dum and Tweedle Dum Dee, who she called "Orangutans. No brains. Greed running through their veins."

Daisy stood up and said, in all seriousness, "I think we're going to have to hire a killer."

"Uh, no." I reached over and patted her arm. She was wearing pink pants, red cowboy boots, and a red tunic with daisies. She was also wearing a yellow hat with a rim of pink daisies. In the middle of the hat was a blue plastic frog. "Herbie," she told us when she walked in, pointing at the frog. "He talks too much."

It was sad, truly, when she started talking about Herbie. I saw Charles's and Vanessa's faces. I saw Lindy, Beth, and Jayla's. Daisy's mind was slipping, a tiny slice more, each day. It was excruciating to watch.

"My sons know a lot of criminals," Daisy said. "I'll tell them. They're coming for dinner tomorrow night and we'll be eating frogs. But not Herbie." She pointed to Herbie again. "He talks too much."

"I don't think we should hire a killer at this point," I said. "Let's wait on that."

"Don't wait too long. The best killers have a long frog waiting list."

"We won't, but for right now, we'll sit on it," I said.

Jayla asked what we could do in terms of a protest. "Refuse to leave? Block the dock?"

Beth, who had her white doctor's coat on and a stethoscope around her neck, suggested we start protesting in front of Randall Properties with pickets.

That sounded like a splendid idea. We agreed to meet the next Saturday.

"We'll call it a Picket Party Against The Pricks And Portland Slumlords," Vanessa said.

"Leave it to an English teacher to get the words right," Lindy said. "Hemingway would be proud. And I dare say Sylvia Plath."

"Do you think so, Lindy?" Vanessa said, pleased. "I do think, though, that Hemingway's boring sometimes. I lean more toward Dickens and Austen, but still. Thank you."

I knew Nick wouldn't go even if he were back. I didn't think you could have a DEA agent with a picket in his hand, but I would go.

"I am telling you all," Lindy said, glasses on, "Do not worry. I have Tweedle Dee Dum and Tweedle Dum Dee handled." She was wearing a flowered skirt and a red T-shirt. "You need to trust me."

"I can't trust you," Heather said. "I appreciate what you're saying, but I'm being paid to iron out this neighborhood brouhaha, and I'm swinging my hatchet in order to do so. If you have another hatchet to swing, let me know."

"I have a hatchet. These Beefy Russians are delicious, Toni."

"Where is the hatchet?" Charles asked. "Lindy, I think if we had a few specifics . . ."

"If you could tell us what you have planned," Vanessa said. "it would make us feel better."

"I can't tell you, exactly," Lindy said, "because I don't want to implicate you. But I will let you know when it happens."

"Ooooh!" I said. "I like the sound of you telling us when it happens. Exciting. When's the day?"

"So it's on a certain day?" Beth asked, bopping in her seat. "Hopefully it will be on a day I don't work."

"It'll be during the day," Lindy said. "For maximum impact."

"Soon?" Jayla said. "I swing to the night shift next Sunday. Can you remember not to do it then?"

"I don't quit teaching until four," Vanessa said. "I hope I don't miss out on the fun."

"Are you trying to protect all of us legally, Lindy?" Heather asked. "Is that why you're not telling us what's going on? So we don't get sued for being a part of your scheme?"

"No one will get sued," Lindy said. "Not even me."

"I'm working hard so Tweedle Dee Dum and Tweedle Dum Dee, the dock dicks, don't take my house," Daisy said. "I'm going to find killers to take care of this."

"No!" we all shouted. "No killers."

"I can't go picket with you all, for reasons you'll later understand, but let's all meet for dinner at Svetlana's afterward, shall we?" Lindy said.

"Oh, I'd like that," Vanessa said, turning to me. "I love your mama's Russian Pizza."

I tried not to roll my eyes. Russian pizza? And yet it was one of the most popular items we had. No one questioned Russian Pizza. It was always served with a shot of vodka.

"I had crepes with lamb and chicken and some special sauce for lunch last week there. They were delicious," Beth said. "But they were named 'Chelsea, No More Piercings.' Something about a teenager? A niece?"

I threw my hands up. "My mother uses the Specials board in a creative way."

"We're coming," Charles said.

"Jayla and I will come," Beth said. "Is Charlie going to be there playing the piano? He plays Beethoven's Seventh with such finesse."

"I'm coming," Daisy said. "I'll eat a Beefy Russian. I'll eat two Beefy Russians if they're handsome, but I won't eat a frog." She swung her hat off and waved. "I'm still waiting for the whales and I'm making my whale hat."

The next day we all had sugar cookies on our front porches in the shapes of whales. Daisy's mind is being trapped by dementia, but her heart is young and pure.

My rant at Nick traipsed through my miserable mind. I couldn't sleep. Couldn't concentrate at work. I told myself that this was better, to break up now with that demanding blond giant who was trying to change our relationship rules and I didn't need him or his demands or his smile or his lasagna and I didn't need to read beside him in bed. I was better off without him and his frightening job, but somehow I also decided I should try extremely hard to run into him when he returned from his trip.

There was a lack of logic that I acknowledged.

I got ready early in the morning to go to work because Nick often goes in early, unless he's out late the night before. I wanted to "by chance" run into him. I admitted to myself that I wanted him to give in. I wanted to be irresistible so he would change his mind about our relationship and not insist I meet his parents or be his girlfriend.

I acknowledged this lack of logic, too.

Every day I dressed in my best jeans and heels, or knee-high boots and tights and skirts, or dresses that fluttered. I washed my hair, I wore it down, I wore it up, I braided a few strands, as JJ had taught me. I put on dangly earrings. I checked my lipstick.

Next, I waited in my tiny entry, scrunched down below the photos of my river pets, listening for his voice or his footsteps, hoping I could pop up and pretend that we were unexpectedly meeting as we both trudged off for another day of work. By the time I stood up, when I truly had to go to work and could wait for Nick no longer, my legs were all cramped up like twisted bread sticks and my butt was asleep.

I did this morning after morning after morning. Cramped. Pained. Sleepy butt. No Nick.

I started getting worried. He had come home from his last trip. Was he on another one?

Or had he found someone else and he was shacking up at her house? That enflamed me. How could he do that to me? How could he cheat on me like that?

At night, like a deranged stalker, I sat out on my deck, listening. I heard nothing.

Now and then I saw a light go on late at night on his houseboat. I used my sneaky binoculars from the wheelhouse to spy on him, but I couldn't actually see him.

Every night, when I couldn't "accidentally on purpose run into Nick" during the day, I gave up and dipped bananas in melted chocolate chips and ate them in my bathtub.

I missed Nick so much and wanted him back.

I acknowledged this lack of logic, too.

I'm a mess.

By Thursday evening, dusk coming down, there had not been a single sighting of Nick for way too long and I'd been around my tugboat as much as possible, with my sneaky binoculars, except when I was at work or went to a birthday party for Uncle Vladan, "Woe is me I am so old."

I also had dinner with Chelsea, who was fighting with JJ. She said, "You are a cool aunt who doesn't have a fit about my black clothes and my tattoos and my piercings and if Mom keeps bugging me about my personal choices, I'm going to pierce my privates. Yes, I will do that. I will pierce my private V. I told her that. Aunt Toni, I said, 'You can't stop me, Mom, oh no, you can't!' "

Where the heck was Nick?

I wasn't sleeping. Except for the bananas and melted chocolate chips that I ate in the bathtub like a lovesick fool, I could hardly eat. I was falling into a depression I was too familiar with, my emotions shriveled and fried.

I, yet again, pathetically, folded myself into a ball below my entryway window and held up my sneaky binoculars. I spied, up and down the dock, hoping to see him. I lay in wait for my prey. Was Nick working out of town busting drug dealers or waking up in the arms of some blonde?

I'd taken care with my outfit again in case I could entice Nick with lust. Tight skinny jeans that almost cut off my circulation. Heels that wrapped around my ankles with leather straps. Stretchy white tight top. Chain necklaces with tiny crystals. Lipstick in place, red and luscious. He would see my lips and want me to kiss him.

He would see my skinny jeans and want to take them off.

He would see my clingy white shirt and want to take it off, too.

Right? Then we could get back together. I leaned my spinning and sad head against the door of my tugboat. It was exhausting and demoralizing spying on Nick.

I heard footsteps on the dock and automatically poked my hopeful head up so I could see out the window and . . .

"Oh, shoot!" I popped right back down.

Nick.

He was coming down the dock. Jeans. White flannel shirt.

Oh no. *Oh no.*

He had seen me. Our eyes had met. How humiliating. I had popped up like a jack-in-the-box, then back down. I couldn't face him. I couldn't. Now he would know I was spying on him. I felt my whole face go hot and sweaty. I sat down, knees up, head on knees, arms over my head. I wanted to die. Has anyone actually died of embarrassment? I could. I knew I could.

I waited until he had to be at his own houseboat, then leaned my self-pitying head back and stared up at the photos of my river pets, who never would have humiliated themselves like this.

"Hello, Toni."

Oh, shoot!

Nick was outside my door. He was looking in at me through one of the square windows.

"Hello, Nick." I am an idiot.

"Avoiding me?" he asked.

"No, no." That was the truth. I was trying to run into him. "No. I'm not avoiding you."

"That's nice to hear. How are you?"

"Fine. How are you, Nick?" I put my sneaky binoculars beneath my butt, slowly.

"I'm not doing well."

"What? You're not?" My voice pitched high, a mini screech, and I shot up so fast I stumbled, my right ankle asleep. What was wrong? Was he hurt? Had he been shot? Was he sick? Did he have cancer? I struggled to the door. My sleeping ankle caught on the plant table in the corner. The plant crashed to the floor, the table toppled.

"Are you all right, Toni?" he called through the door.

I ripped the door open, trying not to stand on my tingling foot. "What's wrong, Nick? Why are you not doing well? Are you hurt? Did you get beat up?" The wind blew that blond hair, those light blue eyes right on mine.

"I miss you."

"Is that it? Nothing else?" My voice was still piercingly high. "You're not sick? You don't have cancer? You're not bleeding?"

"I'm not sick. No cancer. I'm not hurt."

I felt myself go weak, so relieved. I hated his job. Hated the worry it caused me. Hated my past that made me leap to disasters automatically. I leaned on my door jam, studying him, head to toe. No cuts. No bruises. No casts. His head wasn't wrapped in a white bandage.

"Are you all right, babe?"

"Yes." I hopped forward on one leg and hugged him. I wrapped my arms around his neck and leaned into his chest. He was warm. Snuggly. Solid. My Nick. I hugged him tighter.

His arms came around me.

I moved my head and kissed his neck. I could see his temple pulsing, so I stood on tiptoe on one foot and pulled his head down and kissed him there, then his forehead and he gave in and his mouth dropped to mine.

The kiss was steamy and emotional, and I wanted to strip off my clothes and jump in his bed and cling to him.

He stopped. "Toni, we have to talk first."

"Let's talk second." I pulled him into my tugboat, and he kicked the door shut.

For a second, I thought we were going to have sex in my tiny entry, as my shirt was off, my bra tossed, my tight jeans unzipped, and I'd sent his shirt flying into the hallway. What stopped us was the broken plant pot and the dirt. I was on his zipper when he picked me up and carried me in, sideways, as my hallway is small, to my couch.

Nick is a take-charge sort of man. Masculine. Almost always when we had sex I followed his lead. I asked him about it once, asked if he wanted me to take charge, and he said, "Baby, you can do whatever you please. Lead away."

Now and then I wanted to lead, but the truth was that Nick led so well ... with such talent and warmth and this totally wild passion. It was like going along for a sex ride, although he would have called it a making love ride.

He laid me on the couch, followed me down, and we stripped off the rest of our clothes, my jeans taking longer because they were way too tight. I wrapped my legs around his hips and took that naked ride for multiple orgasms and a hundred kisses.

This time, afterward, when we talked, and he kissed me, gently, tenderly, then with more passion, and we ended up in my bed, upstairs, I curled into him and went to sleep.

I hadn't slept right since I'd last seen Nick, and when I woke up, he was still there, warm and strong, asleep, and I flung my arm across his waist, his fingers curled around mine, and I went back to sleep. In my tugboat, not his. Mine.

For the whole night.

The next morning I woke up, wrapped around Nick, warm and cozy, and I didn't feel guilty at all. I started to sniffle and tried to hide it from him, I was so happy he was back, but he woke up and said, "What's wrong, honey?" And I said, because I couldn't hide my honesty, "I missed you so much, Nick."

"I missed you, too, Toni. Every day. Every night."

We took a tumble again, soft and loving at first, then on full throttle.

Afterward, on the pretense of making coffee, I grabbed my sneaky binoculars and hid them in the back of my pan cupboard.

20

Moscow, the Soviet Union

We were talented pickpocketers, the three of us sisters. Lightning quick, whispers, drifting smoke, a breeze.

Bogdan and Gavriil's training was excellent.

Valeria would fake tripping, fake being lost, cry in front of a wealthy man or woman. They would move to help her, and I would move to remove their wallets. Valeria would stop crying, thank them, and before they knew they'd been robbed, we would disappear.

The problem came in explaining to our mother where the money came from. The solution came through sewing pillows. We sewed pillows, often using fabrics from our late grandmothers' dresses, as we couldn't afford new fabric, or find it to buy, even on the black market, to sell to my mother's customers. When we dropped off the mending, we showed the clients our pillows, our stitches tight and precise, the pillows pretty with lace, rickrack, ruffles, embroidery. We told her we sold them for more than we did.

It was a secret between the three of us.

Pillows and pickpocketing.

For survival.

In the dead of winter, our windows frozen with ice, the heat in the building paltry and sporadic, the hot water gone for weeks at a time, my mother, sewing at all hours, became sick. A cold morphed into the flu, which morphed into pneumonia.

We went to school, then we raced home to our apartment building to take care of our mother, finish and deliver the mending, sew and sell pillows, stand in line for food, and pick pockets on the days we needed to.

"Is Mama dying?" Elvira asked, her face crumpling up.

"No," I said.

"Are you sure?" Valeria asked, her hands twisting together.

"Yes." No. I wasn't sure. She was burning up with fever, she was listless, she coughed as if her lungs were being ripped, shredded, and coming up.

We were feeding her, spoon to mouth, putting cool cloths on her sweating forehead and making sure she ate and drank. The chills made her fragile body rock back and forth in bed. We couldn't get her to the doctor, she was too weak. In addition, she was scared to go. She was, officially, an enemy of the people of the Soviet Union.

It was dangerous, picking pockets. The punishment for getting caught was nauseating.

We would never have picked pockets had we not been so hungry.

Had I known what would happen, I would have starved instead.

The pickpocketing in Moscow continued until I slipped my hand into the pocket of the wrong man on a snowy evening. We—Bogdan, Gavriil, Valeria, and I—always scoped out our victims carefully. We wanted them to be distracted, out of shape so they couldn't chase after us, and affluent. Fur coats. Fur hats. Shiny boots. Well dressed. Jewelry. We did not pick the pockets of anyone who appeared dangerous, and there were a number who did, nor did we pick the pockets of the poor, the old, or frail.

Valeria and I felt guilty for stealing, as if the weight of the Moskva River were drowning us, but our mother was still sick with pneumonia, her lungs filled, her fever continual, her chills head to toe. She insisted on sewing from bed until the coughing became too much, or she passed out from exhaustion.

My goal was to get money, get a doctor we could trust to the apartment, get medicine.

I slipped my hand into the pocket of the wrong man's coat right in front of the State Historical Museum, smooth as silk, as Valeria tripped in front of him. He grabbed my hand, twisted it around, twirled me in a half circle, and smacked me. Everything went black, then sparkly, and nausea overwhelmed me.

Valeria fought to get me away from him, but he backhanded her and she went spinning into the snow. He dragged me to the police station, my feet sliding on the ice, and demanded they arrest me. I lied and said I had not done it, no one believed me, and after being thrown into a cell, hitting my head, and having no food for six hours, I admitted it.

They called my mother. She hobbled in coughing, weak, but she had managed to do her hair, get dressed. She was a beautiful woman. She had had me when she was twenty-two. She was only thirty-two then. She cried when she saw me, blood on my forehead, sick from vomiting from fear. A policeman with a scary glint in his eye linked an arm around my mother's shoulders and pulled her out of the room. He smiled at her, rapacious, hungry. I vomited again.

When she came back to me, an hour later, her face was stained with tears, puffy. Her black hair was a mess and undone down her back, the buttons on her blouse buttoned wrong.

She grabbed my arm and pulled me out, swaying, awkward in her gait. The policeman laughed and said, "See you soon, darling. Thank you. I have not seen a woman with a figure like yours for a long, long time. Get rid of that cough, though, Mrs. Kozlovskaya. It's disgusting."

My mother was now hacking, feverish, and sweating. She leaned hard against me as we hobbled home through Red Square, a blizzard of snow coming down, covering our shoulders.

"Stealing is wrong, Antonia," she wheezed.

"I know, Mama, but you're sick, you need a doctor."

"Stealing is wrong unless you are starving to death."

"We are starving to death, Mama. You need help."

She sighed, then stopped, leaned over, hand against the wall of a building, and coughed until I thought her stomach would come up. We trudged toward home. On the way, we went to see a friend of hers, a pharmacist, at my insistence. He took one look at my mother and surreptitiously handed her a bottle and pills in a bag.

"Svetlana, I will come and check on you." He turned to me. "Make sure she takes that medication, Antonia. Four times a day."

I nodded. I half carried my rapidly weakening mother home, hardly able to see through the snow, then climbed the stairs of the apartment building, the elevator broken. My sisters were in a panic thinking of me in jail, of Mama going to get me. We put Mama to bed and gave her the medicine, toast, and a bowl of watered-down stew.

The back of her dress had a red stain.

Mama closed her eyes, then collapsed back on the pillows, ghastly pale.

"Is that what a monthly looks like?" Valeria whispered.

"I guess so." But I didn't really think that. I had a vague idea of what a monthly was, not much, but why was it all over the back of her dress?

"What happened to Mama at the police station?" Valeria asked.

"Her shirt was on wrong, her hair was messed up," Elvira whimpered.

"I don't know."

We were children. We could not have conceived what happened to her. Later, older, we understood her sacrifice.

But the next day, after school, in our uniforms, Valeria and I were out pickpocketing again. We didn't have a choice, and stealing is wrong unless you are starving to death.

Elvira took care of our mother and gave her the medication.

We used the money to stand in line for hours and buy food in the freezing wind, and sewed pillows that night.

I would later learn where the blood came from.

The medicine from the pharmacist started to work. He knocked late at night, clearly scared of being seen with an enemy of the people, and brought another bottle of coughing syrup.

In five days she could sit up. In two weeks she was up and walking around, but dead tired, as if her bones had softened. She sewed for most of the day. Her cough was less frequent, not so deep. What changed was her attitude, her personality. When she was sick she still had a smile for us, gave us hugs, tried to be brave.

It was as if she weren't home in her own mind anymore. She was hollowed out. I found her sobbing, wrenching, raw sobs emanating from that tiny, exhausted body many times, as did Valeria and Elvira. She would say she missed our papa, but we knew it was something else, too. Her hands trembled. She was frightened by loud noises. She woke up screaming in the middle of the night and we had to race in and calm her down.

And yet, through pneumonia and her sobs, she still sewed and we delivered her mending and the fancy dresses. We smiled at the fancy women who bought the fancy dresses. We hated them, their wealth, their clothing, their cars, when we had nothing, our father imprisoned by the men they were married to, our mother ill. The bigger we smiled, the more our pillows sold.

My mother sold her mother's pans one morning. She put them in a large box and left the apartment, tears in her eyes. She came home with money and sent us out to stand in the lines for bread and chicken. We were able to get butter, too, and potatoes. The money from the pans fed us for a week. I know she missed those pans. They weren't just pans, they were her mother's pans. They were part of her history, part of her family, all dead. My sisters and I said nothing.

Our mama started throwing up in the mornings. By noon, she was fine. I asked her if she had pneumonia again and she said, lifting her head from the toilet, "No, Antonia, my love. Go and check on Elvira, I am fine."

My mother left the apartment one afternoon on her own, then came home within the hour. We asked her where she went, and she said she went out for a walk. We knew it was a lie. Our mother was too weak to walk, and it was snowing.

The next day an older woman with white hair and kind, sad eyes came to our home, holding a leather bag. She and Mama went to her bedroom.

"Do not come in, girls," my mother said, her eyes huge in a painfully thin face.

"I am a doctor," the woman said. "I am checking up on your mother's health. I heard she had pneumonia?" We nodded, she smiled. "I'll listen to her lungs. You girls start making dinner."

We grabbed potatoes and started making dinner.

I saw the bloody cloths in the woman's hands before she took them outside to the garbage bin.

The doctor returned and went back into the bedroom with my mother.

We didn't understand then what had happened, but our mother did not get out of bed for five days after that. There were more bloody cloths.

My mother's eyes went blank. She didn't smile. She did pray. I heard her one night, after I'd gone to bed. "May you kill that policeman, Lord, for what he did to me and what he has done to other women, and may he suffer badly, so help me, Jesus."

I am almost positive that my father does not know what happened to my mother.

I would never tell. It's not for me to tell. I know my mother, too. In her mind, it would be, "Why upset my Alexei? Why hurt him? Why make him so angry he wants to kill someone? After all he has been through, my poor Alexei! It would come between us, what happened in that police station, and who wants that? It is over. It is done. Let it lie in the past."

We have many secrets in our family.

I will always feel guilty about what happened to my mother. It was my fault. I was stealing for money for us, survival stealing, the intent was there to help, to take from wealthy people what they had taken from us, but she had to pay the price.

That guilt haunts me sometimes, like a ghost, in a police uniform, with a gun, following me around Red Square in my head, cackling.

Nick and I went back to being us . . . but there was something missing. I felt it. I knew what it was. Nick was coming to an end with us, as we were now. He wanted something more, I wasn't going to give it, and he was going to cut out soon.

He made love to me the same way, we had that same passion, but one time he had tears in his eyes. One morning I woke up and he was watching me. I saw the pained expression on his face, which he hid quickly. When we had dinner on his deck, he held my hand, but now and then he turned away and I could tell he was getting emotional.

I pretended not to see it, but in his own way he was saying good-bye to the relationship.

I pretended it wasn't there.

Pretending never helps.

I was hurting Nick, that was the truth, and he was going to choose not to live with it much longer. If I were him, I would not be with me much longer.

I wanted to change. I wanted to be open to more. I felt like I was defeating myself, but I couldn't make myself take a step in the direction that Nick wanted me to take. There was a dead husband between us.

He left.

I heard Ellie's voice in my head. I was on my way to an interview for *Homes and Gardens of Oregon.* The woman, Sheila, had transformed a pole barn into a Japanese-style oasis, complete with red paper cranes hanging from her ceiling, a tree trunk to sit on in the shower, Japanese letters on her kitchen's tile backsplash, and accordion screens painted with Japanese landscapes.

I called Ellie from my headset.

"Gino left?" I asked.

"Yes. We had a fight last night. He's upset because I keep waffling on the wedding date. He's upset because of all the arguments we've had about how I don't want to combine money or be told how to spend it, his critical mother moving in with us someday, kids, and how I know he hopes I'll give up my business and be a full-time mother. Gino's also mad about sex because we're not having it as often, and I told him it was because it's hard to be attracted to a sexist caveman who wants a Stepford wife with a lobotomy. He slammed his way out of my house. The door hit so hard, he knocked fabrics off one of my shelves."

"That must have triggered your temper." No one messes with Ellie's fabrics.

"Oh, I was fit to be tied in a thousand knots. It was a stack of fabrics from India and Thailand."

"How do you feel about his leaving?"

"Relieved."

"Have you had to use your paper bag since he left?"

"No. Not once."

"Okay then."

"Yes. Okay."

I knew she was smiling.

"I love breathing like a normal person, Toni, it's so much easier."

I went to picket Tweedle Dee Dum and Tweedle Dum Dee's Randall Properties on Saturday for the Picket Party Against The Pricks And Portland Slumlords. Their office is located on a well-traveled street in downtown Portland, right in the center. Almost everyone from the dock came. We held signs that read "Save our dock, Save our homes," and "Don't sink our houseboats!" and "Shrock brothers, get your hands off our neighborhood." The news stations soon sent cameras and reporters.

Tweedle Dee Dum and Tweedle Dum Dee thundered down,

along with their minions, and ordered us to leave. "This is private property...we'll have you arrested...disturbing the peace... you have no right to be here...affecting our business..."

Charles stood in front of them, crossed his arms, and glared. Charles's two brothers, both former military, stood right by him, saying nothing. The two Tweedles backed down as the news cameras closed in. The Tweedles looked like frightened, guilty, wealthy, entitled men screwing yet another American.

Daisy went up to the Tweedles and whispered, "Trash eaters, home wreckers," and in a rare slice of lucidity she turned to the news cameras and said, tears in her eyes, her voice cracking and wobbling, "My name is Daisy Episcopo. I'm eighty-five years old. I've lived in my houseboat for more than thirty years. It's home to me. The people on the dock are home to me. And these greedy Shrock brothers want to take it from me. How can Randall Properties take my home? How can the Shrock brothers kick my neighbors and me out? You couldn't burn down a neighborhood in the suburbs, why can you here? I'm too old to move. I want to die on the dock. I want to watch the sunrises and the sunsets from the home I've lived in for so long. Please help me." She turned on the waterworks. "Please. Help me in my fight against Randall Properties."

The news stations loved it, loved Daisy.

As soon as she was out of sight of the cameras, Daisy walked over to me and said, "If you come to my house tonight, I'll cook the shark. He jumped up on my deck this morning. A round of ketchup and he'll be delicious. He told me to eat him."

We got a lot of publicity. No one likes sweet, old women being kicked out of their homes.

Tweedle Dee Dum and Tweedle Dum Dee, we heard through our attorney, blew up like Mount St. Helens. We laughed.

We went to Svetlana's that night and had a superb time. My parents greeted all of us. They were especially gracious to Nick when they saw us walk in with his arm around my waist. Both of my parents beamed; my mother clapped her hands. My father pumped his hand and semi shouted, "Welcome, Nick, welcome!" and my mother hugged him.

We had the back room. About forty people, all from the dock, were there.

Daisy led us in songs, mostly drinking songs, the daisies on her hat bopping about, the meal delicious. Our waitresses were pleased with their tips.

My mother's special that night, "Support The Dock," and later, a chocolate dessert named "Hello, Nick!"

Living on a Tugboat, Talking About Homes

BY TONI KOZLOVSKY

I met with a woman named Jo Jo Banks this week.

Jo Jo used to love her suburban home. It was white on the outside and gracious on the inside. Two stories, two decks, huge fireplace. She raised five kids there with her husband.

"My mother died when I was young, my father ran off, and I was handed around from relative to relative until I left at sixteen. I never felt like I had a home, and I told myself that one day I'd have one, and a nice husband, and a whole bunch of kids. I would have the love and stability I always wanted."

The dream marriage was not to be. As she described it, "I married at nineteen, too naïve to get married. He was ten years older. I was looking for a father figure. Think of a desert. That's the marriage. Think of loneliness so intense you think it will kill you. That's how I felt. Think of living with a man with a trigger temper. That's flat-out scary.

"But he went to the kids' games, coached their teams, provided, and I didn't want to break up a family and do to my kids what had been done to me."

One morning, after dropping their youngest off for his second year of college, Jo Jo woke up and studied her husband, this time with zero emotion.

"I watched him eat his cereal and listened to that crunching noise he made, then I watched him drink his coffee and listened to him slurping. I had made him his breakfast and as usual he hadn't said thank you.

"I realized then how much I hated that crunch and that slurp and how I could not live one more day of my life with it. I couldn't live one more day of my life without a thank you. He was reading the newspaper, he was holding it up in front of my face as he'd done for decades, and I'd had it. I was done.

"I went out to my garden, I loved my garden, and said good-bye. Good-bye to the oak trees I'd watched grow for twenty-five years. Good-bye to the rhododendrons I'd planted myself. To my goldenrod daisies, peonies, hostas, rose gardens, and the pathways I'd laid. Good-bye to my kitchen, which was old and dingy, but my husband wouldn't let me remodel it, though he had a boat and a whole bunch of other man toys. Good-bye to my bedroom, which was a barren place. Good-bye to the kids' rooms.

"I started packing. I didn't take much. I wanted to start over. I didn't want anything except treasures from the kids and photograph books. I realized I didn't even want my clothes anymore. They were so blah. So ugly. He came up in the middle of it and said, 'What the hell are you doing?'

"And I said, 'I'm leaving.'

"And he started to cry and get hysterical. He was down on his knees by the time I left, but it was too late. Why couldn't he have treated me well all the years we were together? I had to call the police because he was blocking me from leaving. They came, I left. I filed for divorce.

"When we were sitting with the attorneys hammering out who got what, he said, 'I want the house.' He didn't want the house, but he thought I still loved it and would fight for it, and he wanted to take it from me or force me to move back in. I said, 'It's yours.' You could have heard his jaw drop to the table.

"He said, 'But you love the house,' and I said, 'Too many bad memories in it.'

"I bought a small condo downtown in the city with cash and started over. I went back to my maiden name. New home. New clothes. New friends. New activities.

"It feels freeing. I have a view of the city. I never went to plays and concerts, because my husband didn't want to go and didn't want me to go because it was 'too expensive.' Now I go by myself or with new friends. I never traveled, because my husband said, 'It's a waste of money.' This year I've been to India, Paris, and Texas for a rodeo. I even bought a pair of purple cowgirl boots. My husband used to say that purple was the color of tramps.

"I guess I'm a happy tramp. I lost fifty pounds after I moved, and I went to a stylish store where I had never bought clothes before, because my husband said I didn't need clothes like that. I'd been buying my clothes at Goodwill and at stores that also sell bananas and diapers. No more. I've bought leather boots, new sweaters, jeans, and heels.

"People say that life is like seasons. Well, I'm in spring. My condo has changed my life. My home was old. My kitchen was old. The furniture was old. Everything was out of style. And I felt that way about myself. Old. Out of style. Dowdy. Sad. Well, I'm not old. I'm not out of style, I'm not dowdy, and I'm not sad anymore. But I had to move away from a home with negativity and loneliness in it to find myself and move on with a happier life."

*   *   *

I loved the photos the photographer took of Jo Jo and her condo. The view, the spaciousness, the clean and modern lines, the color. The readers would love it, too.

I saw my ex-editor, William, in the hallway of *The Oregon Standard*.

"Ready to come back, Kozlovsky? Dying of boredom yet?"

"No, but gee, thanks. It's hard not to be working for a grump anymore."

"I might like your columns."

"You just made my day. How does that feel?"

"Don't get all gushy with me. It's irritating."

"Got it. Nice to see you, Lopez."

"Come back when you can't stand talking about granite countertops for one more second. I'm predicting that'll be soon."

I knew it was coming.

Nick closed his eyes for a second, his chest rose and fell, then he leaned back against his kitchen counters and crossed his arms. "We need to take a break."

I was unprepared for the instant, pounding pain in my chest, the feeling of falling and hitting cement, face-first. "Why?" But I knew why.

"Because this relationship is killing me."

"Nick—" *Oh no. Oh no. Oh no.*

"Toni, I can't be a substitute for another man anymore. I can't be the stand-in."

"You're not a substitute." He wasn't. "You're not the stand-in."

"Yes, I am. Your head is with Marty. I was willing to wait. I thought if I was patient, if I was your best friend, that eventually your head would be 100 percent with me. I wasn't looking to make you forget Marty, you'll never forget him, and I accept that, but I wanted us to be together. I can't do this anymore. It's driving me, you're driving me, out of my head. It's distracting me at work. Being with you actually hurts."

"Nick, please, I don't want to hurt you, I never wanted to hurt you—"

"I know you don't, baby, I know. You are a kind and loyal person who is also stubborn and difficult, but our timing is off. We're off. You need more time to grieve."

"I'm trying to get past it. I'm trying to move on." Trying so hard.

"I know you are. You can't rush it. You can't speed through this on a timetable. On my timetable. And I can't ask you to. You can't will it away. We've been sleeping together for months. Being with you has been the best time of my life, but you're always pulling away. You keep space between us. You don't trust me, you don't trust us, you're not sure if you can handle us. You're not even sure if you want us."

"I . . . I . . . like you so much, Nick." I couldn't say the other words. I couldn't say *I love you, Nick.*

My words hurt him again, like a body blow. He didn't want to hear *I like you so much.*

"You can't commit to me on any level. I get it. I'm not mad, Toni. Okay, I am mad, but not at you. I understand. But I can't continue to be with you when all you'll agree to do is sleep with me. I need more."

"I am so sorry, Nick. I'm a wreck. I'm a mess." *I am not brave.*

"Honey, don't cry. Please. When you cry, I want to cry. This whole situation is . . . it's damn tough. That's what it is. And you need to figure out what you want, who you want, which might very well not be me, and I need to pull back until you do. I can't take it like it is anymore. I don't want to hurt you any more than you've already been hurt, but I can't do this, have us like this, with no future, no commitment."

"I know." I wiped my tears. "I know." I walked over to him, my legs actually shaking, and kissed his cheek, kissed him on the mouth, and that passion flared again, at least for me, but he pulled away. I dropped my head, then tried to hug him, but he pulled away again.

"Nick . . ." My voice faltered, cracked. "Nick . . ."

I wanted to cry on him and beg him not to do this, but I couldn't do it. I was aching, but this wasn't fair to him. He was sleeping with a woman with a head full of turbulence and emotional storms.

I wouldn't want to be with me, either. Sleeping with someone, nothing more. No future, refusal to even talk about a future. I walked out, but not before I saw that wet sheen over his blue eyes, how he was leaning heavily against his kitchen island, both hands down. He did not walk me home.

I climbed up to the wheelhouse and lay on my bench and stared at the stars.

Numb now, alone. Again. My tears slid into the pillows.

It was like falling off a cliff, arms out.

I actually had a nightmare that I had purposefully stood on a rock, on a cliff, high above a valley, and jumped.

The next morning, I could not decide what to wear to work. No, scratch that. I didn't *care* what I wore. I didn't care what I looked like. I wasn't interested. It was like going back to the first six months after Marty died. I didn't care what I wore then, either. I let myself go. I hardly brushed my hair, did not eat well. The light went out, and I lost interest.

I finally grabbed a pair of jeans, a white T-shirt, and black boots. I ran a brush through my hair. I didn't shower. I'd overslept because of the cliff jumping.

I broke my mother's rule: Always put on lipstick and earrings before you leave the house unless the house is on fire.

My house was not on fire. I left for work.

My lack of interest in clothing that day continued.

And continued.

Then came my lack of interest in washing my hair.

I lost interest in eating, too.

Soon, I did not feel well.

When Nick left for work on a Monday, two weeks later, he walked off the dock with a duffel bag. He had a scruffy beard, his hair was longer, and an earring was in his ear. Back undercover. New case. I was by the front door of my tugboat, heading out to work myself.

"Hi, Toni."

"Hi, Nick."

And that was it. As if we were strangers, nothing to each other. I watched him climb up the stairs of the marina to the parking lot, not caring if he knew I was staring, like a stalker. I wanted to race after him and hug him, kiss him, tell him to be careful, but I didn't. What if he didn't come back? What if one of the drug dealers got him? What if he was shot?

I started to shake. I went out to my back deck, grabbed a blanket along the way, and stared at the river. Dixie swooped through the sky like a blue friend. I stared across the river at the new home for Big Teeth and Big Tooth Beavers.

Mr. and Mrs. Quackenbusch climbed up. They quacked at me. I didn't even have the energy to quack back. I called in sick.

About one o'clock in the morning, about a week later, I heard Nick's footsteps on the dock. I wasn't asleep, because insomnia's claw was stuck in my throat.

Nick was home. Safe.

His footsteps did not falter in front of my tugboat.

I felt empty. Numb. All the light was gone.

Again.

I miss Marty, not Nick, I corrected myself. Marty.

Nick.

Nick.

Miserable.

The next day, at sunset, I saw a golden staircase in the distance. It touched down on the river, then tunneled to the sky, the puffy clouds a welcoming door to heaven.

I turned away.

Ailani bounced up to me at Koa's birthday party. I was sitting on the sofa, growling back at Koa, who was dressed as a furry green monster with claws.

Balloons and streamers were all over, and Valerie had made a monster cake. The green monster on top of the cake appeared stoned, the eyes super wide and slightly crossed, the smile crooked. All the Kozlovskys were there, plus neighbors and friends. It was mobbed.

"Did you know, Aunt Toni, that the human body has six quarts of blood in it and a body can bleed out in a minute, like all your blood could go flowing out?"

"You're ten years old, Ailani." I tried not to laugh. "Do you really want to think about stuff like that?"

She seemed confused. She put her hands on my knees and leaned in, her black braids swinging. "What else am I supposed to think about?"

"Books. Sports. Cooking with Grandma. A body bleeding out is not a vision I want you to go to sleep with."

More confusion, then aha! Her face lit up. "Okay. I have something else to talk about."

"Super." I put my hands on hers, then growled back at Koa. "Let's have it."

"I heard my mother talking last night on the phone. Did you know that one out of three murders are never solved? That means someone gets away with it. A whole bunch of people. What do you think of that?"

"I think it's depressing. Do you want another hot dog?"

"No. There are a lot of mysterious murders. Some people die because of guns, a whole lot, but some are from knives and some are"—she put her hands around her neck and squeezed and stuck her tongue out to the side—"because they get strangled, but I like DNA evidence. That'll catch 'em."

"I bet you know all about DNA."

"I do!" She jumped up and down and grinned. DNA was so exciting! "Did you know that the crime analysts can pick up a hair at a crime scene and identify the person? They can identify the murderer if he's in the computers. You know, like if his blood is already in there or his fingerprints or his . . ." She pointed to her crotch. "That part."

"Oh, my gosh." Valeria talked to her about *that?* I growled at Koa, he nibbled on my arm.

"I know, I know!" Ailani's eyes opened wide in wonderment.

"There's stuff all over the human body that the analysts, I like that word, *analyst,* that they can look at under a microscope and figure out who the bad guy is."

"You don't have nightmares from stuff like this?"

"No. I have nightmares about Candy Land. You know that game?"

"I do."

"I have nightmares about the gumdrops. They chase me. I have nightmares about hopscotch, too."

"Hopscotch?"

"Yes, the squares turn into square aliens and try to eat me. That's why I like talking about criminals and crime more. It's more relaxing for me, and you know I'm sort of a nervous kid." She picked up a handful of my hair. "I'll brush your hair for you, Aunt Toni. You haven't brushed it in a long time, have you?" She scampered out of the room and danced back in a minute later with a brush and lipstick and started brushing my hair.

"Grandma says never leave the house without your lipstick and earrings on unless your house is on fire and, you silly, you forgot both. Okay, so. Aunt Toni. Also! Did you know that in crime labs they can . . ."

Ellie, Valerie, my mother, and I ate stoned monster birthday cake in the backyard together.

"The monster looks high," Ellie said.

"I know," Valerie said. "I tried. Koa wanted to make the cake with me and so I did. It was the best I could do."

"Well, with pot being legal in Oregon, at least we know the monster won't be arrested," I said.

"This cake delicious, Valeria," my mother announced. "Your papa, he eat two pieces."

"Thank you, Mama."

"You come and make dessert at restaurant, Valeria. Then you no have to be talking to bad mens. I no like your job, Valeria."

"I know, Mama. You tell me at least once a week."

"And you, Antonia!" She turned to give me some of her wrath.

"You too thin. What wrong with you? Poor Antonia, you not sick, are you?" She put a hand to my forehead. "No fever. Where your earrings?"

"Working too much, Mama, and I didn't have time to put on earrings." I had told Valerie and Ellie about Nick, but not my parents. I was not up to my mother's disappointed inquisition. I had told her Nick wasn't at the party because he had to work.

"I bring you food tomorrow night. You eat. I see your bones. See?" She tapped my collarbone. "I no like to see that. Too skinny. Nick not like a skinny lady, Antonia. They like the curvies. And you"—she turned to Ellie—"Elvira, where is that Gino? That Italian?"

Ellie seemed calm. She had no paper bag with her. "He came over a few nights ago. I told him I didn't want to marry him."

"What? No!" my mother exclaimed, hand to her bosom. "Alexei, my love!" she shouted to my father across the yard. "Come here. Elvira not marrying that Italian stallion anymore."

My father hurried over, sat down with us. "No more Gino?"

"No, Papa. We broke up."

"Ah. That fine news, Elvira. It not right marrying a man with bag on face. That was a sign. Sign from up there"—he pointed to the heavens—"that this not right."

"Not right," my mama said. "Thank you, God, helping my Elvira. But I not curse Gino."

"Gee. Thanks, Mama."

"What happened?" I asked.

"He came over and I told him I couldn't marry him and I gave him back the ring. I realized I just had to be brave and do what needed to be done. He cried. I felt so bad for hurting him."

"It hurt him more if he marry woman who can't breathe when he walk in front door every night," my mama said.

"It hurt him more if he marry woman who doesn't love him," my father said.

"We talked about all of our problems that I already told you about."

"What did he do?" Valerie asked.

"He told me he'd change everything. Told me his mom wouldn't live with us, ever. Told me we wouldn't have kids. Told me he supported my business. Told me he'd travel wherever I wanted to go in the world. Told me to go to any movie I wanted whenever I wanted. He said we'd have separate accounts."

"And?"

"I'd had time to think after we had that fight and he slammed out of my house. I felt so much better believing we'd broken up. Believing we were done. I could breathe again, be me again, plan my future and be happy. He wanted to get back together, and I said no."

"Must be the right decision, because you don't have a paper bag with you," I said.

"No paper bag. I haven't needed one since he left. The thing is that Gino will be a super husband. To someone else, not me. We are not right for each other. If he gave in on kids, he would come to resent me. We'd end up divorced anyhow. He wants a stay-at-home wife who doesn't work and who will have half a dozen kids. There are plenty of women who would love that, but not me."

"This right decision," my father said. "Gino nice man, but he doesn't make your heart do bumpity bump bump hump."

"Your papa right. He no make your heart go bump hump," my mother said.

My parents do not know what "hump" means in slang.

"Now," my mother said, pointing at my father so we could find him. "Your papa. He does that to me. He make my heart go bumpity bump hump humpy. I think we go home early tonight, what you say, Alexei?"

My father smiled, nodded. "I think nice idea, Svetlana."

What a love machine.

At Svetlana's the next night my mother made Russian Pizza and named it "Elvira Made Mama Proud."

I received many calls, all along the lines of "Why is your mama proud of Ellie? Did she and Gino break up? She's serving 'Elvira Made Mama Proud' pizza with a shot of vodka still, right?"

Our family's personal business—all played out on a restaurant's Specials board.

That night I climbed into my kayak, the single seater, and rowed it to the front of my tugboat. I tied it to the deck and stared up at the stars. In the distance I heard flapping against the water, and I knew it was one of the Sergeant Otts. Dixie was surely tucked in for the night. I didn't know where Mr. and Mrs. Quackenbusch were.

I sniffled. I wrapped my arms around my waist.

Sometimes I am haunted by what my and Marty's kids would have looked like. Would they have had black hair like me? Brown curls like Marty? A smile that took up their whole face, like Marty's? Tall and thin like a crane, for the boys? Shorter, with curves, for the girls?

I wish I had our child. Or six of our children. I ache for the children we did not have. Forever and beyond I will regret that we did not have children. No grandchildren for his kind, loving parents, little Marties for them.

In the midst of that shearing pain, I thought of Nick. What would our kids look like?

Blond-haired little Nicks. Or black-haired little Tonis with Nick's light blue eyes? Then I thought about Nick naked. Shoulders so broad I can't get my whole hand around them. Hard, packed chest. I liked the size of his hips. I liked his lips. I liked the way he moved when I was over him and when I was under him. I liked the way he held me close. I liked how warm he was.

I told myself when I started sleeping with him that it was only for sex. That was never true. I always liked Nick, in and out of bed. Nick always made me feel wanted. Needed. He was kind. Funny. So smart, quick, his conversation wide ranging, about everything.

He always wanted more, from day one. That was a threat to me. Paradoxically it also made me feel safe. This was not a man who was looking for sex and then would dump me. On the

other confused and mixed-up hand, I didn't want to love someone who had his type of job. Too dangerous. I couldn't go
through another loss. It would disintegrate me.

So I could live in fear and stay alone in my kayak, my tugboat, my life.

Or I could be brave.

I saw a shooting star light up the sky.

Daisy walked by, saw me, backed up, and sang "Amazing
Grace."

It was what I needed to hear. She is a generous and caring
lady.

21

The trial for Tyler Barton was wrapping up. I had gone several times, as had Ellie, and my parents once. My parents don't like going to the trials. "Upsetting," my father said. "Our Valeria up there. So proud, yes, she get rid of bad mens, but hard to watch and hear what the bad mens did. We had enough of that in Soviet Union."

The defense didn't have much of a defense. They implied someone else did the crimes. They implied it was one of Tyler's relatives, like Leroy or Dalton or Zeke, which meant that Bill Kortrand, the defense attorney, found two dead rats on his front porch the next day. His wife took the kids to her mother's house in North Dakota by nine that morning.

It would soon go to the jury. The ending of that trial made me more nervous than what was going on right now, because I knew Barton's family would pick up their meat cleavers and go to war when Tyler was found guilty.

"Any new threats?" I asked Valerie during Pillow Talk. None of us were sewing, we were too worried. Instead we were eating our mama's Russian tea cakes.

"Bobbi Jae's and Garrett's tires were slashed." Bobbi Jae and Garrett were attorneys assisting Valerie.

"They like slicing things, don't they?" I asked, feeling that frozen snake wrapping around my spine again. The problems were escalating.

"And there was a dead rat on Bobbi Jae's back doorstep."
Valerie started massaging the top of her widow's peak.

"They certainly like killing animals," Ellie said. She popped
another Russian tea cake in her mouth, the powder landing on
the tip of her nose.

"It's a specialty of theirs."

We sat in our silence, inhaling Russian tea cakes. Stress
eating.

"Security for them, too, now?" I asked.

"Yes."

We sat again in our silence.

"I'm trying to be brave," Valerie said. "Nothing else to do
but be brave."

I reached out my hand and held hers. *Be careful, Valerie.*

"I will," she said out loud.

What about the kids? What about Kai?

"We're moving the kids to Mama and Papa's tomorrow.
They're excited."

I squeezed her hand. I was scared to death. But Valerie was
Valerie, and she would do her job.

"I love you, Toni, love you, Ellie."

"I love you, too, Valerie."

"If anything happens to me—"

"Don't even say it, Valerie," I said. "We will help Kai take
care of the kids."

"Thank you."

"You're welcome," Ellie said. "Now don't talk about that
stuff anymore."

"Okay. But you need to wash your hair, Toni."

"I know."

"Can I wash it for you?" Ellie asked. "I'm worried about
you, too, Toni. Your hair. You're wearing the same jeans again
and again, and T-shirts. When did you ever wear T-shirts except
when you're exercising?"

"I like them." They knew I didn't want to talk about Nick.

"Let us wash your hair, Toni, please," Ellie said.

"If JJ saw you like this..." Valerie said. "It would be like Mt. Vesuvius."

"The screech of outrage," Ellie shuddered.

Valerie and Ellie washed my hair over the kitchen sink, then dried it and brushed it back from my widow's peak. My head felt a lot better when they were done. They filed my nails, plucked my eyebrows. We all polished our fingernails and toenails. When I noticed Valerie's hands shaking, I took over for her.

I love my sisters. We put our heads together.

"I'm scared," Valerie whispered.

"I am, too," Ellie and I said.

The snake's mouth was open, ready to strike.

We did not get any pillows sewn that night.

"Toni, the whole family is worried about you."

"I'm fine, Dmitry."

He let the silence hang.

"I am."

"You're not fine. I'm sorry about Nick. I heard you're not washing your hair."

"I wash my hair...."

"Be honest."

"Most of the time. When it needs it. I'll wash it more."

"Worse, I've heard you're not wearing your pretty clothes."

"I wear my pretty clothes."

I heard him crying.

"Dmitry, stop. Please. You're making me upset—"

"Toni, I don't like it when you're unhappy. When Marty was sick, after he died, watching you in so much pain, I thought I was going to have a heart attack. He was one of my best friends, the whole thing was awful, but watching you cry...and now you're unhappy again."

"I'll be fine. But I miss Nick." My voice was a pathetic whimper, which was irritating.

"You couldn't commit, could you?" I heard him sniffling and hiccupping. "I get it. We're both broken, aren't we? Like teacups or a vodka bottle or a rocking horse that rocks on its own...."

Broken. Yes. I could say that. "Broken but still standing, now that's something, right?"

"No," he wailed. "No, it isn't. I want you to be happy. Very, very happy."

"I'm working on it." No, I wasn't.

"I want to help you."

"You always help me, Dmitry, by being the best brother ever. . . ."

Dmitry is incredibly sensitive to other people's suffering, and when it comes to our family . . . he's a mess.

"I love you, Toni."

I had no interest in honing my skills in Keeping The Monsters At Bay: Shopping Defensive Strategies. None. I didn't want to shop. I didn't even want to get dressed in the morning.

Moscow, the Soviet Union

My father arrived half dead late on a Sunday night.

We heard a truck outside our apartment rumbling, five floors below us, the breaks screeching, doors slamming, laughter. The snow floated down onto the slushy roads. Minutes later we heard a thunk against our door, then silence.

My mother peered out through the peephole, her hands shaking. She was thin, too thin. She was often distracted, pained. She was nervous, weak, and still coughed from the pneumonia. She worked all hours into the night mending, sewing fancy dresses for the fancy wives of the men who had locked her own husband in jail.

My mother cried out, then yanked open the door. My sisters and I ran out of our bedroom and pulled our father into the house.

I hardly recognized him.

Elvira screamed. Valeria froze, as if she'd been hit. I stared, shocked, then ran and got the towels, soap, and bandages my mother yelled at me to get.

My father was bloodied, bruised, broken, unconscious.

Later, after my mother cleaned him up, bandaged his wounds, and we all hauled him into bed, I saw her leaning over the sink, rinsing my father's blood from her trembling hands, stooped, sobbing, shattered.

My father's recovery was slow.

His humor returned on the fifth day, when he woke up, no longer in another world, fighting a fever, fighting a demon. He peered out at my mother from the one eye that was not swollen shut.

He did not see his three daughters perched on the other side of the bed. He saw only my mother, kneeling, their heads close together.

"Ah, Svetlana," he said, his voice raspy. "I dreamed of you, during the day, during the night, every day. You were with me. Are you real?"

"Yes, my love, my Alexei. I am real. I am here. How are you?"

"Do not worry. I will be fine. I am here with you again. I will heal. And then we will leave. We have to get out of here, Svetlana. I am afraid they will come for you. I am surprised they did not."

"Your father. How is he?"

My father's eyes filled with tears. He shook his head. "He is gone."

"Oh, my God and Jesus, Mary, mother of God." My mother crossed herself, crying with my father. "I am so sorry, my love, so sorry."

"What?" I said. "Grandfather is gone?" I loved Grandfather Konstantin! His smile, his songs, the treats he brought us when he visited, the way he could cut animals out of paper. "What do you mean? Is he dead?"

Slowly, as if every inch pained him, which it probably did, as he was covered in bruises and lashes, my father turned his head.

"Hello, daughters. I love you. How I missed you."

We bent to kiss the one cheek that wasn't bashed.

"Grandfather's gone?" Elvira asked, her tiny hands clenched together.

"Yes, my angel, I am so sorry. He is dead. He is with Grandmother now, in heaven."

"But what happened?" Valeria said, her face crumbling. "I want Grandfather!"

"A bad man killed him."

"What?" Elvira wailed. "*What?*"

"Why did he kill Grandfather?" I asked.

"Because your grandfather spoke against the government. He spoke for God. He spoke for Jesus. He spoke for freedom. That is why."

It is surprising that the tears we shed did not drown the poor man when we kissed him again.

"Everything will be fine," our father croaked out later, holding my mother's trembling, weak hands. "You have kept up with your educations, your reading, mathematics, and science?"

We nodded that we had. We did not mention the pickpocketing or the trip to the police station for my mother and me or the bloody cloths.

"I knew you would. I love you all. So much." He turned back to our mother as his eyes started to close. "Svetlana, you are my gift."

"And you are mine, Alexei," she cried. "Always mine."

"We will leave. We will save our family, God help us."

He closed his eyes and went back to a comatose sleep.

Two nights later I saw my mother, with such tenderness, take off my father's shirt in their bedroom. My mother pressed a kiss against every whip line on my father's back, his head bent. My father was a muscled man, large, he had boxed for years. And yet, there he was, bent, beaten, and only showing his weakness in his bedroom, to his wife.

I would never forget my father's injuries. I would never forget the enduring love I saw between my parents that night.

The whispering started again immediately, a few friends who slipped in and out of our apartment at night, slinking through the shadows, hats and glasses disguising their faces as they took the stairs up to our apartment, the home of people who had been declared "enemies of the people," who would soon lose their apartment and might be arrested or forcibly moved to another part of the Soviet Union, my parents learned.

"You must leave," we heard them say again and again. "As soon as Alexei can walk, you must go, Svetlana. Go, go right away."

We were going, I knew it. I heard my parents talking. My father said he had to do something before we left, when he regained some strength, but then, immediately after that, "On to America, Svetlana, as we have dreamed about."

"When are we going?" Valeria asked.

"What is happening?" Elvira asked.

"Wait," I told them. "Don't tell anyone."

The silence began after that.

People did not come and tell us, "You have to leave."

I knew then. They did not tell us to leave because we were leaving.

"When are we leaving?" Valeria asked.

"What is happening?" Elvira said.

"Wait," I told them. "Don't tell anyone."

My grandfather Konstantin's body, my father's father, who had been imprisoned with my father, beaten and starved, was delivered to us in a can. Yes, a can. The prison cremated him. The official notice was that my grandfather had died, *unfortunately,* of a heart attack.

The letter enraged my father. I have never seen him so livid. He ran a hand over a shelf and knocked all of his books off, then another shelf, then another. My mother pointed at us to go to our room, so we did but, as always, we cracked the door so we could see. My father yelled, low and primal, his face a twisted mask of utter grief.

"A heart attack?" he screamed. "A heart attack?"

My mother, calm, tears slipping down her cheeks, let him rage until he could rage no more, then he fell to the floor, his body still battered and bruised, his mind still reeling from the trauma of his own imprisonment, of watching his father die, and my mother rocked him, as she rocked us when we cried.

"A heart attack? Rurik Nikonov killed him. He killed my father. I saw him do it. I was there, Svetlana. I will get revenge for my father."

"No, no, darling," my mother said, not bothering to hide her alarm. "We are leaving here. We will have a new life. We are getting out. Do not risk it."

"I will. I must, Svetlana."

"Alexei—"

"This is my final word."

And so it was.

My sisters and I crept away, crawled into bed, and hugged each other, crying silently until we went to sleep, our father's words, "I will get revenge for my father," echoing like the lash of the whip marks on his back through our minds.

My mother told each of us to pack one bag the next morning. "One, no more, girls. We must be ready to leave."

I packed my two pairs of pants, two skirts, and three sweaters, almost all I had. Mostly I packed my books and notebooks where I wrote stories.

Valeria packed a pair of old, high red heels that my aunt Polina gave her before she left and a blue ballerina skirt that Uncle Vladan had given her.

Elvira packed her two stuffed animals, fabric scraps, and her sewing kit. We would each wear coats, as it was winter, and two pairs of pants and our boots with three pairs of socks, as there were holes in the boots.

"When, Mama, are we leaving?" I asked.

"*Shhh.* I will tell you when. Do not say a word to anyone, Antonia. Do not forget." She tapped my lips. "We could die if someone knows who should not know."

Three nights later, I woke up to hear my mother begging my father not to leave the apartment. Crying, holding on to him, clutching at his coat, his hand on the doorknob.

My father was standing again, much stronger. He was eating. He had a look in his eye that scared me, but it was never directed at us. The cuts and new scars on his cheeks glowed, it seemed, in the darkness. I was scared of the scars, scared of how he got them, but not scared of my father.

"Go back to your room, Antonia," my mother snapped when she saw me. I started to cry, but instead of reacting with a hug, as always, she said, "Now, Antonia. *Do as you are told.*"

I pretended to shut the door, but I listened, Elvira and Valeria beside me, holding hands.

"Do not do this, Alexei. Please. For the family, for the girls, for us."

"Svetlana, I must. I cannot let go of what has happened. It is for my father, for our honor."

"Honor? What is honor if you are dead? We cannot, we will not, leave without you. We are ready, you know this. They will come for me soon, I'm sure of it."

"I will do this first. If I do not return by tomorrow night, you are to go without me."

"No. I refuse. I will not leave without you."

For the first time in my life, I saw my father get angry with my mother. He grabbed both of her arms and yanked her in close. It was at that moment that I realized that my loving father had another side. He was a Russian man born in a hard time, brought up with hard knocks, with a father who had suffered the same. "You will do as I say, Svetlana." I had never heard that tone. "You will leave with the children and begin a new life as we have planned."

"No."

My father cupped my mother's face with his hand, yanking her closer, his face flushed. "I will not listen to this, Svetlana. I am your husband. Do not disobey me."

My mother burst into tears, and my father's searing, surprising anger faded.

"Be strong, Svetlana. Be brave. I love you."

"You stupid, stupid man."

"I need your love, Svetlana."

"No."

"Please. I need to hear it, Svetlana."

"Stupid man."

"No, not that." He smiled.

"I am so mad at you, stupid man."

"Not that, either."

"I love you, Alexei."

"Yes, that. It is what I needed to hear. I will see you soon. Tomorrow night."

He kissed her. A long, passionate kiss. I closed the door before it ended.

When I woke up, the sun barely peeking over our frozen horizon, the streets of Moscow slushy and gray, I saw my mother in a chair by the window, sewing. She was leaning forward toward the front windows, bent over, stiff, her fingers shaking over the fabric.

"Good morning, Mama," I said.

"Good morning, Antonia."

I sat by her feet. She absentmindedly patted my shoulder with a trembling hand, a bird in flight, a frightened dove.

"Will he be home soon?"

"Pray, Antonia. You pray. Hard as you can." She turned back to the window. "Lord God, Jesus, Mary, mother of God, please protect my Alexei. Antonia, are you praying for your papa?"

"Yes, Mama."

"Do not stop."

"I won't."

"Valeria? Elvira? Are you praying for your papa?"

Valeria and Elvira sat beside me.

"Yes, Mama," Valeria said. "To Jesus and God and Mary, mother of God, who didn't get enough credit for her sacrifices, right, Mama?"

"I'm praying to Jesus," Elvira said. "He's nice."

My sisters and I went to school. The Bessonovs gave us food

to take home when we went to their house to play after school. Mr. Bessonov said to me, "All will be well, Antonia."

I hoped so.

We waited.

My father limped home late that night, the moon covered by rolling gray clouds. His face was bloodied again, bruised, swollen. There was blood covering his blue shirt underneath his jacket and on his hands. My mother cried out when she saw him. She hugged him close, not minding the blood, then quickly pulled away, a cry escaping her lips.

My father was holding something.

"Alexei, what?"

"Ours."

"No."

"Ours."

"But where—" My mother's eyes widened. "Oh no, Alexei."

"Yes. This is the way it will be."

My father held something in his arms. More blood.

My parents lied about where it came from.

I heard a bloodcurdling scream about eight o'clock on Tuesday night. I shot out the door and stood on the dock. Another scream, cut short. It was Lindy. I sprinted down the dock, then noticed that Daisy was running beside me. "Call the police, Daisy!" I yelled, and sped up.

I burst through Lindy's door. A hulk of a gargoyle man was leaning over her, where she lay on the couch like a crumpled doll in a pink negligee. "Get away from her."

He spun around, and all I saw was evil. Evil in his bulging, packed body, the weird shape of his rectangular face, his mouth a slash. "Get out. This ain't your business, bitch."

"It is my business." Lindy's face was swollen and bleeding. She was trying to roll off the couch.

"I'm warning you, tight ass, leave unless you want this to become a threesome." He charged toward me as Lindy opened a drawer next to the couch. I knew she had a gun in there.

"And I'm warning you!" Daisy flew past me and pointed a .45 at that gargoyle man, a foot from his chest. She was wearing a pink-flowered daisy robe. "Get out. Now." She cocked the gun, both hands on it, steady as could be.

He put his hands up as Lindy collapsed back on the sofa. I thought she might be dying. Daisy kept the gun pointed right at his chest.

"Hey, take it easy."

"Shut up, pig face."

Daisy stood her ground as he backed away, toward the door.

I stared at his crotch. He was peeing on himself, his face pale with fright.

"He's peeing himself," I said, almost amused.

"Get out!" Daisy yelled. "Lindy's home is clean and immaculate and clean. She doesn't want your urine in here!"

He backed out, his chest heaving in fear, and Daisy followed him. She pulled something out of her robe. I saw the glint of the blade. She thrust her arm back, and I knew she was going to throw the knife. So did he.

That hulking man turned and ran . . . right into the river. Daisy waited until his head appeared, his arms flapping about, obviously not a swimmer, then yelled, "I'm going to shoot your dick off." His face collapsed into horror. How would he know that Daisy's sons had removed all the bullets?

The gargoyle started dog-paddling the wrong way down the dock, toward the river. Daisy followed him, then threw the knife. It landed a foot from his face, and he sputtered and struggled. "Lady, stop it, please, she's just a hooker—"

"She's not just a hooker! She's my friend, Lindy! I'm going to shoot your butt off . . . I'm going to shoot your nose off . . . I'm going to shoot your flipper off . . ." He kept dog-paddling and gasping to the end of the dock and into the river. When he was beyond the dock, Daisy took out another knife and threw it. Landed a foot in front of him again. He screamed. Excellent aim, as I knew she wasn't trying to kill him.

When he was gone, the police sirens piercing the air, we hurried back to Lindy's.

"Don't you worry," Daisy told Lindy. "I'll tell my sons about this tinsel-toothed warthog and he won't bother you again. What was his name?"

Lindy told Daisy.

"He'll be in the river being eaten by my whale friend soon." She called Skippy. It was a short call. "All done. Skippy is angry."

I got an ice pack for Lindy's face and a dish towel for the blood and cradled her in my arms. I was trembling, and so was she. "I wish you'd quit."

"I think I might." She held my hand, her hand shaking hard. "Thank you, Toni. Thank you, Daisy."

"No problem. I'm glad I had my gun"—Daisy spread her robe open—"and my knife robe."

There were four different knife pockets. Each pocket was made of fabric with daisies on it.

"A knife robe comes in handy. I'll make you two girls one to protect yourselves."

"Thank you," we said.

Lindy nodded and then semi-passed out. I hugged her and her bleeding head close to me as the paramedics rushed in the door.

The police went out in their boats and found the man who beat Lindy climbing up a bank. They arrested him. He had a long record of assaults against women. It was also strike three for him. He was going to the slammer, so Daisy's boys wouldn't have to kill him after all. The police interviewed Daisy and me after the paramedics took Lindy to the hospital.

"You pointed a gun at him?" an officer asked Daisy.

"Yes. I had to. He was trying to eat my friend, Lindy."

"And you threw a knife at him?"

"Yes. Two."

"Two?"

"She has excellent aim," I said. "She missed on purpose."

And later, "Do you know what Lindy does for a living?"

"Yes," Daisy said.

"What?" the officer asked.

"What does that matter?" Daisy hit him on the knee. "A man shouldn't be able to beat up a woman no matter what she does."

"No, no, absolutely not," the policeman said, backing way off. "I didn't mean it like that."

"But I know what Lindy does for a living."

"What?" the policeman asked.

"She reads books," Daisy whispered. "She loves the smell of them."

I told the police officers that I didn't know what Lindy did for a living when they asked, but I also said it was irrelevant. I knew they didn't believe me, but one of the officers was Sammy Cho. He was a regular with his family at Svetlana's. I knew him from high school. On the way out he said, "Last week I had the rolled crepes with ahi. There was cabbage salad on the side. I didn't even think I liked cabbage until I had it. Your mama called it "Alexei Happy Husband." Do you know if it's on the specials for this week, too?"

I told him I'd let him know later.

I called my mother. "Tell Sammy I make it for him special. Tell him I say, bring your mother."

I told Sammy. He could not hide his delight. "Tell her I'm coming tonight. Bringing my parents with me. Thanks, Toni."

Lindy spent a night in the hospital with a concussion.

I stayed with her for hours and read her the first chapters of *Shōgun* by James Clavell, at her request. Jayla and Beth visited during their breaks. Charles and Vanessa brought her home. We took turns making her dinner.

She cancelled all her clients. Daisy went over every night and sang lullabies until Lindy went to sleep.

Or pretended she was asleep.

Daisy's sons, Georgie and Skippy, aka Slash and Slugger, sent Lindy an enormous bouquet of flowers and paid for an in-home nurse for a week. Lindy loved her. When she was better, the nurse and she reorganized her book collection. It took hours.

* * *

Daisy made Lindy and me soft, comfy knife robes. Mine was red with yellow daisy pockets inside. Lindy's was pink with white daisy pockets inside. Daisy made Lindy's first. "The hooker needs more protection than you do, widow. You're honky-tonking with Nick, the man with a pistol in his pants, I wish he would honky-tonk me, and he can protect a woman from Godzilla, but Lindy needs the knife robe now."

I didn't want to tell Daisy that I was no longer sleeping with the honky-tonk man. I was afraid it would upset her.

Nick and I left for work at the same time on a Thursday morning. There was a wind meandering in off the river, like an invisible ribbon, swaying, curling. Mr. and Mrs. Quackenbusch had settled in on my deck, and even Maxie, the golden eagle, had made a flighty appearance. It should have been a happy morning for me.

"Toni." Nick didn't smile. His hair was shorter, he had a goatee. He was positively eatable.

"Hi, Nick." Whew. We were back to his being intimidating.

I hadn't planned on seeing Nick, and I was dressed in my current sloppy style—jeans and a T-shirt and tennis shoes. Yes, this was what I was wearing to work. My coworkers hadn't said a thing, but I'd seen the quick glances. Certainly wasn't my usual style, but I had no energy for my usual style.

I also hadn't washed my hair. Again. Too much hair to wash, so it was stripped back into a ponytail. I paused. How long had it been since Valerie and Ellie had washed my hair? There was nothing I could do about the circles under my eyes.

"How are you, Toni?"

Dying. Lonely. Alone. Miss you. I smiled—bright and cheery. "I'm fine. How are you?" I fell into step beside him up the dock.

"Fine."

"How's work?" *Can I hug you? Can I kiss you?*

"It's busy. People want to sell drugs so they can make money off of other people's misery and addictions, and we don't want them to do that, so there's a clash. It's the usual."

He had a black jacket on. I could still see the gun. "Be careful."

"I am. How's your job? I saw the house out in eastern Oregon with that view of the mountains that you wrote about. I liked the article."

"Thanks. Writing about houses is more pleasant than writing about crime." *I think about you all the time. I can't get you out of my head. I want you, Nick.*

"What are you working on next?"

"I'm going down to the beach tomorrow to write about a house that was built by the owner's grandfather. The family has remodeled it." *What kind of house would I have with you, Nick, if we were together?*

"It's supposed to be sunny tomorrow. Perfect beach weather."

I wanted to say, "Want to come?" but I didn't. He would have said no, and then my heart would have felt as if it had been dropkicked. We had climbed the stairs from the dock and were at our cars.

"Okay. Well, nice to see you, Toni."

"Nice to see you, too, Nick." The formality crushed me. The lack of intimacy. The coldness, the distance in Nick's eyes. I smiled again, bright and cheery, so I wouldn't crack.

He pulled out of the parking lot first, in his black truck. I waited, pretended to follow, then when he was off, I parked, laid my forehead against the steering wheel, and let the waves of pain in my body rush on through.

When the destruction was done, I drove to work and shoved my emotions down hard and fast so they wouldn't come up and throttle me.

I drove to the beach the next day to interview the family that had gutted and remodeled their grandfather's beach house. The captain's wheel of his old boat—which had sustained irreparable damage in a storm—was in the family room by the window. They'd taken the deck of the boat and nailed it up as a hearth for the fireplace. The anchor was leaning against a corner, and a thick rope from the boat hung on a wall.

After the interview, I sat on the sand.

I needed the ocean. Needed the waves, the view, the sunset that I stayed to watch as the colors danced off the water. I missed Nick.

And yet. I couldn't get myself to walk down the dock, tell him I was sorry, tell him I could be in a relationship with him, that I would trust and love and be with him forever. There was a wall between him and me. The wall was made of Marty, a kayak, a wedding ring, a hospital bed, chemotherapy, a last kiss, and a coffin.

I was trying to be brave, but I was immobilized. I was frozen. I was in an emotional morgue where I'd buried one man and didn't want to betray that man and then bury another who had a dangerous job. I was stuck.

The waves rolled in. The seagulls dove. The burgundy, golden yellows, azure blues, and purples stretched across the sky until it was dark, the sun down, only the white foam of the waves visible.

How long are you going to live like this? I asked myself. *How long?*

22

It was Pavel's night.

Our whole family went to his school's musical, *Bennie and the Music*. I went from work straight to the theatre. I was in jeans, a T-shirt, and boots. No makeup. No earrings. I had forgotten about the play, or else I would have dressed up more. My mother would have a fit. I braced myself.

My father hugged me and said, "I no see you for a week. Start with Monday. What you do?"

Before I could answer, my mother, resplendent in a black dress and black heels, eyeballed me in the lobby of the high school, frowned, and dragged me off to the bathroom with JJ behind her, who saw me and rolled her eyes.

"I brush this rat in the nest," my mother said, digging in her purse for a brush after manhandling me in front of the mirror. "I say to you, many times, Antonia, always put on the lipstick and earrings before you leave the house unless the house on fire. Your boat on fire? No? Then why you look like that?"

"I'll do it, Mama."

"No. I do." She held the brush up and away from me. "You stand still, Antonia."

I had finally told her and my father about Nick because they were upset and confused about why I was upset. My mama cried with me, but that was no excuse to have a "rat in the nest," in her eyes.

"Here, Aunt Svetlana, it's my job." JJ took the brush.

"No, don't, JJ," I said. "My hair is fine. I'll do it."

"It is not fine." JJ kneed me—not gently—so I was up against the counter. "Stand still. What did you do, electrify yourself?"

Zoya and Tati burst through the door, laughing and chatting. I'm sure my father told them where we were. They were both in lacy bustiers, silky shirts, tight pants, heels, hair all floofed up.

"What happened?" Zoya said, hand to throat.

"What the heck?" Tati said, hands on hips.

"What is wrong with your hair, Toni?" they said together.

"Nothing is wrong with it." I fought for the brush. I grabbed it from JJ, she grabbed it back.

"Stop it, Toni!"

"You be still, Antonia!" my mother said, shaking her finger at me and swearing in French. "You let JJ fix the rat in the nest."

"I'm not seven, I'll brush my own hair." I grabbed the brush again.

JJ wrapped one arm around my waist and with the other hand struggled to get the brush. "You don't. You won't. I'll do it. I have a curling iron in my bag." JJ was panting. She lifted me up with a Tarzan/Jane yell.

"Put me down!"

"No. Not until you give me the brush and agree that I can brush your hair!"

I could not believe she was lifting me up like she did when we were kids. I put my foot against the counter of the sink and pushed. She slipped. She was wearing four-inch heels, and I fell right down on her.

We rolled on that bathroom floor. I grabbed the brush and held it high over my head as she lay on top of me. I was ticked. This was all stubborn, bossy, aggressive JJ's fault. "Get off of me, JJ!"

Ellie walked in. Her black hair was curled and clean, and she continued to breathe without a bag. "Ah. I see we're having a family fight."

Valerie was behind her. "Who's winning? Hard to tell."

"I think it's Toni," Zoya said. "Wow. She's really mad."

"No, JJ's winning," Tati said. "No, Toni. They're noisy!"

"What's the problem?" Valerie asked.

"I can brush my own hair!" I shrieked.

"No, she can't. She doesn't," JJ gasped. "It's a disgrace. It's been weeks, maybe years."

"She's right, Toni," Ellie said. "Your hair is a disgrace. When was the last time you washed it?"

"JJ, fix the hairs," my mother announced. "Antonia! You lie flat and let her give you a quickie. The brushing be all done soon." My mother peered down at me, on the floor of the bathroom. "You feel good when she done."

Anya walked in and gasped as if she had just come up for air after nearly drowning. She slapped her hands to her cheeks. "This isn't happening." She reached for both of us. "Get up, get up right now. There's bacteria and viruses and feces and urine on a bathroom floor. I'm going to be sick, sick, sick right here unless you two get up."

She put one high-heeled foot on either side of us and tried to yank us apart. JJ took a furious swipe at her with her foot, and Anya tumbled on top of us. "Oh no!" Anya howled, hands in the air so she wouldn't touch the floor "Germs! Germs!"

Because Anya would not push herself off the floor with her hands (bacteria, viruses), she lay on top of JJ and me, like a cross, my ears suffering from her high-pitched howls.

"If this is as entertaining as tonight gets, I'm going to be happy," Ellie said.

"I haven't seen JJ and Toni roll around on the ground for a long time," Valerie said. "Ouch! Toni, you should say you're sorry. I think you kicked JJ in her personal flower."

"This is making me think we should get into making outfits for the women's mud wrestling business," Tati said.

"Tati!" Zoya clapped her hands. "What an idea!"

"... also on a bathroom floor is old vomit," Anya said, anguished, still teetering on top of us, hands toward the ceiling. "Remnants of animal defecation brought in by people's shoes—"

"I had enough!" My mother swatted all three of us, then wrenched the brush out of my hand. JJ and I struggled up, panting, JJ's hair now a mess. Anya had to be helped up, complaining vociferously.

"Antonia!" my mother reprimanded me, smacking me on the butt with the brush. "You let JJ do it to you. She fix that." She circled her hand around my hair.

JJ and I were both sweating.

"Fine!" I shouted, wiping my brow. "Fine!"

"If you had given in from the start, we wouldn't have had to go rolling around on a bathroom floor." JJ pushed me toward the mirror, ripped out the rubber band holding my hair in a ponytail, and brushed it.

"Ouch! JJ, not so hard!"

"It smells, Toni. Wash it tonight." She dug in her voluminous bag, plugged a curling iron in, then sprayed my hair with something that smelled yummy. I sagged, defeated.

"Put a couple of those long, skinny braids in it, JJ," Valerie said. "I love that style on her."

"Stop squiggling, Toni," Ellie said. "Be still."

JJ brushed my hair, then added a couple of skinny braids on each side. "There, better."

It was better, up in some doopty-doo design. Not so rat's nesty. I would not admit it. "Done, JJ? Happy now, Mama?"

"You are hair talented, JJ," Zoya gushed.

"And you are beautiful, Toni," Tati said. "Sorry about Nick."

"Me too," Zoya said.

"I will have to immediately wash all the viruses and bacteria out of my clothes. . . ." Anya muttered, hot water blasting on her hands.

My mother took out her lipstick and pointed it at me. "Hold the lips still!"

"Mama, I can do it."

"No! I do." She swung the lipstick back like a spear. I gave in, furious, knowing if I moved, she'd wipe that lipstick all over my face, or JJ and my sisters would jump me and hold me down.

My mother dug in her purse and stuck earrings in my ears.

They were red feather earrings. Four inches long. "Your papa, he like those." She winked at me. "Turn the men on."

Tati whispered to me, "That'll teach you to remember to put earrings in your ears. Never leave your home without earrings and lipstick unless your home is on fire or you'll end up wearing red feathers."

I sighed in defeat.

We Kozlovskys stood in front of the mirror, straightened our clothes, patted our hair, checked our lipstick, and walked out as if nothing untoward or frighteningly odd had just happened.

JJ slung her arm around my shoulder. "Love you, Toni."

"Love you, too, JJ. Sorry about that."

"No problem. I understand. Sorry about Nick. I know I already said that a few weeks ago, but I'm saying it again: I'm sorry about Nick. You've had it rough, cousin, I get it."

"I'm fine."

"Whatever." She kissed my cheek. "But do wash that hair tonight."

In the lobby I hugged Hope, who said, "I feel like I've swallowed a bowling ball," and cried. Shockingly, against all odds, her boyfriend, Macky Talbot, and she were still together. He hugged her. She smiled through her tears.

Chelsea came up, black eye shadow ringing her eyes like a drunken raccoon, fist-bumped me, then said, "I joined a new band! I'm the singer. What do you think of that, Aunt Toni? My first song is going to be about moms who are too paranoid strict."

Kai hugged me off my feet. "Hello from a Hawaiian. Heard you had a wrestling match with JJ. Sorry I missed it."

Uncle Sasho wrapped me in a bear hug. "My Antonia. One of my favorite nieces in my life. Pavel, he ballerina. He wear tights. He like the boys. But what of that?" Uncle Sasho's bushy eyebrows shot up. "I don't know. He has the high grades, he do his chores, he help me with the trucking business on the weekends and the summer. Fine son. How you? Ah. Hair is nice. JJ do it to you. Look my daughters, Tati and Zoya. How they marry when they dress like that? How?" Eyebrows up again, weathered face creased in a sad frown. "How?"

Uncle Vladan and Aunt Holly gave me a hug and kiss.

"I had a kindergartener ask me today if I was a hundred years old." Aunt Holly groaned. "I have to retire, soon."

"Woe on my life," Uncle Vladan moaned. "Anya have crazy story about lying on bathroom floor with you. Now she think she may have the pneumonia or measles. At least her neck not disappearing. That what she thought last time. Bees in her knees, too."

Uncle Yuri and Aunt Polina wrapped me up in a three-way hug. "How are you, Toni? We hear you and JJ have fight on bathroom floor. That not true, right? Ah, your hair pretty. JJ did it."

Boris strode in with a new woman on his arm. "This is Rosa."

We shook hands. She looked like a Mexican model. She was getting a doctorate in physics, so she and my father chatted.

Boris slid me two tickets for *The Pirates of Penzance.* "Be ready for it, though, Toni. We'll both be crying by the end of it, you know what opera does to us. I have reservations at Henry's for our discussion afterward. JJ should do your hair like that again when we go."

We Kozlovskys sat in the center of the auditorium. It was packed.

Koa climbed across everyone and sat in my lap. He was wearing a blue monster outfit with huge rolling eyes on his head. "Hiya, Aunt Toni. I going to eat you up." He growled. I growled back.

Ailani scooted over and said to me, "I've decided to study the psychology of serial killers for my spring fifth-grade project. I like your feathered earrings and the braids JJ did."

The lights went down. The orchestra played. The curtains opened.

And there was our Pavel.

We clapped and cheered.

The show was incredible. The kids tap danced and sang. They had a modern dance number. A jazz piece. Two modern rock numbers. There was ballet. Pavel opened the show, he had a solo midway through, and he closed it.

Pavel was brilliant. He had obviously been working on ballet for years, diligently, with determination and passion. He spun, he twirled, he was on his toes, he lifted ballerinas up, he jumped, he twisted.

At one point I peered down the row, Koa on my lap, and saw Uncle Sasho blotting the tears on his cheeks. Uncle Vladan and Uncle Yuri did the same, as did my father. Rough men, raised in the Soviet Union, former boxers, noses all off to the side from punches, bawling their eyes out about "our boy ballerina."

When the curtains closed, Uncle Sasho was the first on his feet, clapping, shouting when Pavel came out. "That my boy! Right there! That my ballerina! Good job, Pavel! Good job!" We joined him in the ovation.

We yelled and cheered. We cried. We cry too much, we Kozlovskys.

Uncle Sasho treated everyone to banana splits, including Danny, Pavel's boyfriend. When we were served he said, "Cheers. To my boy, ballerina. I love you, my son."

We clinked our banana split dishes together. "Cheers to Pavel!"

"And cheers to family," my father said. "To the Kozlovskys."

"To the Kozlovskys!" We knocked our banana split dishes together again. Only two bananas slipped out.

Nick was home! I heard his footsteps on the dock, scrambled up the ladder to my wheelhouse, and snuck peeks through the windows with my sneaky binoculars. I wanted to hold him. I wanted to kiss that man. I did *not* want him to see me spying on him, because that would be pitiable.

Ah. There he was, coming on down. Blond. Strong. He seemed tired. He did not slow in front of my tugboat. Not a bit.

I waited until he was in his houseboat, then scrambled back down the ladder and slithered like a snake on the floor to my bedroom. I turned off the lights by my bed, then peered out into the blackness behind my curtains, again with the sneaky binoculars. Maybe he would go out on his deck. He loved being on his deck at night, as I did.

I scrunched down and . . . shoot! He turned toward me.

I dropped to the floor and curled up into a ball, as if that would make me disappear.

He couldn't have seen me.

No, it was dark.

He couldn't have seen me.

No, the lights were off.

He couldn't have seen me.

The sneaky binoculars were black.

I felt myself go hot.

He had seen me. I knew it. He had looked right at me. Maybe there was a glint on the binoculars. Maybe the curtains moved. He was a trained DEA agent. He would notice stuff like that.

I was pitiable.

I didn't even bother turning on the lights. I slithered like a snake into bed and pulled the covers straight over my head. I was an awkward goose. A poor excuse for a woman. A spying disgrace.

Three nights later Boris and I went to *The Pirates of Penzance.* During the opera we cried our eyes out. Opera does that to us. Then we went to Henry's. It's a fancy restaurant. Fancy tableware, fancy wine list, fancy food. Boris loves all that stuff.

"To have someone who understands opera, to her soul." Boris patted his chest. "It means everything to me."

"Me too, Boris."

We then discussed the next opera coming to town.

He steals cars (though I yell at him) and he loves opera.

"Antonia," my father said. "I cannot believe. Three waiters out sick. Flu. Please, can you come in and work? Eh? I'll make sure you have your favorite dinner when you are done. You tell me."

I was in the wheelhouse. I was not exactly trying to spy on Nick with the sneaky binoculars. I was trying to find Anony-

mous or Maxie the golden eagle, or the Sergeant Otts. If Nick
came out and I saw him, it was purely by coincidence.

"I'll come in, Papa. No problem."

"Ah, my daughter. You are loving to your mother and I."

Ellie was there, too. Valerie was swamped with the trial. We
waitressed, and afterward my parents brought us the special—
Russian stew, one of my favorites. The name of the special was
"Dmitry Come Home To Mama." We had hot bread and wine.

My mother said, "I know three things today." She held up
three fingers so we would not be confused by the number three.
"One, always have extra food. Maybe one day the government
go bad, like it was in the Soviet Union, and you want some hidden. Two, put money underneath the mattress sometimes, to keep
it safe. Three, a woman, she should kick a man out of house
with boot if he not right to her. And three again, I love you,
Alexei."

My father smiled, they kissed. Too much kissing.

Ellie poured me another glass of wine. We clinked our glasses
while our parents acted like teenagers in the back of a Chevy.

"It's not even embarrassing anymore," Ellie said.

"They're almost R rated though...."

Moscow, the Soviet Union

On that black night in Moscow, the moon covered by rolling
gray clouds, my father limped through our door, his face bruised
and bloody, blood on his shirt, blood on his hands. He was carrying something in a blanket. When he saw me, he said, "Go to
your room, Antonia, now."

"But, Papa, you have blood on you and who is—"

My mother stood in front of my father. "Now, Antonia. Obey
your papa."

"But who is that kid? He has blood on him! What happened?"

"We will tell you in the morning." My mother grabbed my

arm and put her face close to mine. "Do not tell anyone, ever, what you saw tonight, do you understand?"

"Mama—"

"Antonia, you must not tell."

"Go, Antonia," my father said, sinking into our sofa. "I will talk to you in the morning."

I went to bed and shook and cried, a vision of my beaten father, and the blood, charging through my mind. Valeria woke up and I pretended to be asleep, and then I fell asleep, a little girl who had had enough trauma in the last year to last a lifetime.

I was sure, when I woke up the next morning, that I'd had a bad dream. That my father had not had blood on him, that he had not carried a kid into our apartment with blood on him. But, in our cramped family room, that same kid with blond curls was sitting up on our couch, no blood on him now. He was staring straight ahead. Quiet. There, but not there.

My father took me aside when Elvira and Valeria tried to play with the little boy.

"Antonia," he said. "Your mother told you not to tell anyone what you saw last night, do you remember?"

"Yes."

"If anyone asks, ever, you are to say his name is Dmitry, and we adopted him from an orphanage."

"From an orphanage? At night? But why did he have blood on him?"

My father squeezed my arm, not hard. "Dmitry was adopted from an orphanage. Say it."

"But, what happened—"

"Do not argue with me, young lady." His face was so haggard, bandaged now in two places. "Dmitry was adopted from an orphanage. You and your sisters wanted a brother, so we adopted him."

"But why were you bleeding last night?" Tears burned behind my eyes.

"Antonia, forget what happened last night. We will not be talking about it again. Do not talk about it with anyone, including your sisters. What is important is that we are leaving for America later tonight for a better life."

"Papa—"

He put a finger to my lips. "This is a secret. Can you keep a secret?"

I nodded. Yes. I already had a ton of secrets.

"Say it: Dmitry was adopted from an orphanage."

"Dmitry was adopted from an orphanage." I thought of one more thing. "How old is he?"

"He's three or four, I'm not sure. He told me his name, and he held up three fingers when I asked how old he was, then four fingers. You will be his big sister now. Can you do that? Can you be a big sister to Dmitry?"

Yes, I could. This was something to be happy about. I smiled. "I've always wanted a brother."

He smiled back, hugged me. "And you have one now. I love you, Antonia."

"I love you, too."

My sisters and I went to school. When we came back, we tried to play with Dmitry, but he wouldn't say anything at all. He stared straight ahead. He didn't cry, smile, or laugh.

"Is he alive?" Elvira asked.

"Why doesn't he talk?" Valeria asked.

"What's wrong with him?" I asked.

"Give your new brother time," my father said.

"And hug him," my mother said. "He needs our hugs and love."

So we gave Dmitry time and we gave him hugs and love.

My parents woke us up in the middle of the night and we quietly left our apartment, snuck down the stairs, and headed to our small car. It used to be my grandfather's. It usually didn't work and we couldn't afford gas, but obviously my parents had had it fixed. As enemies of the people, my parents had to sneak out of the Soviet Union. We did not have permission to leave.

I held Dmitry on my lap, the black shadows whipping by, the petrified silence stifling.

At one point tears ran down Dmitry's face and he whimpered but didn't say a word.

The first night we fled Moscow, we stayed in the country, in a barn. Same with the second night. We met people, our parents talking quietly, furtively. Dmitry didn't speak.

The third night we stayed in a home outside of a village. The fourth night a garage in an industrial area. The fifth night behind a building. Dmitry still didn't speak.

My parents' fear zinged the air around us. For once in our lives, our parents kept telling us to be quiet. We were only allowed to whisper short prayers.

On the sixth night, out in the country, in a cottage with no electricity, our parents let us talk. My sisters and I played cards, whispering, our parents lying on the ground, on blankets, beside us. They were so tired, they looked dead.

"Where is Mama?" Dmitry said, his voice soft, like cotton. "Where is Mama?"

My parents sat straight up

"I want Mama. I want Mama." Dmitry's voice rose. "Mama by the trees." He pointed into the darkness. "He took her to the trees." He started crying, his sobs wretched and piercing, right from his young soul. My parents started to panic. Sounds carry in the night.

"Be quiet, son," my father hissed.

"Darling, please," my mother said.

"Stop crying, Dmitry," my sisters said.

He kept crying. My parents exchanged a look, resolute, hardened, saddened. I knew that one of them was going to do something drastic.

I pulled Dmitry onto my lap and rocked him, then I sang a song. He quieted, then went back into his semi-comatose state and finally fell asleep. My parents sighed with relief, then we all went back to being petrified.

After we left the Soviet Union, we went to Germany via Poland. We were crammed into one small room in Munich, the six of us, for a year. My mother went to work as a maid, paid under the table, cash. My father worked as a laborer, paid with cash. Two college professors with doctorates, but neither complained. Not a word.

My sisters and I were taunted and teased at school for being from the Soviet Union, for our clothes and braided hair piled on top of our heads and for not speaking German, for about two weeks. Kids can smell weakness, they smelled ours, and they attacked. We Kozlovskaya girls decided to fight back. One punch, two punches, down they went. Our father had taught his girls to box. The teasing stopped enough for us to learn German and make a few friends.

We didn't pickpocket again, though. My mother had talked to us about it, realizing the extent of the stealing that we had done in Moscow. I knew she did not tell our father, not wanting to hurt him, but she told us what would happen if we were arrested in Germany. "We could be deported back to the Soviet Union, do you want that? For us? For your father?"

The threat of returning to the Soviet Union, where our grandfather had been murdered, our father near murdered, our uncle Leonid "disappeared," was enough to make us keep our hands in our own pockets, as was the searing memory of what happened to my mother when she came to get me in jail. Plus, though we were very poor in Germany, we weren't starving. We had food. We had electricity, heat, hot water, a refrigerator that worked all the time. Our parents were with us and healthy. There was no need for survival stealing.

Uncle Vladan and Aunt Holly were officially sponsoring us from America. When our interviews were over, the endless paperwork filled out, and with help from three professors in the United States whom my parents had been friends with for years, we finally left Munich.

Dmitry still hardly spoke. He cuddled up to me most of the time. To my mother, to Elvira and Valeria, but mostly to me. He did not warm to my father. He often cringed when my father said hello. He pulled away from his hugs. He was scared of him. It hurt my father, I could tell, but he didn't force Dmitry to hug him, to talk to him. He gave him his space.

The same questions kept coming. "Mama? You know where Mama is, Antonia? By the trees?"

"I'm sorry, Dmitry. I don't know where she is. I'm your sister. We're your family now." I was almost eleven. I said this over and over, as my father and mother had told me to do. "I don't know what happened. I don't know where she is."

"I thought Dmitry was from an orphanage," Valeria said.

"I thought he didn't have a mother," Elvira said.

"The past is in the past," my father said. "Let it lie. Dmitry is from an orphanage. I am his papa, your mother is his mama. That is my final word."

And so it was.

Dmitry cried, but silently, tears streaming down his small face. He would stare vacantly for hours, sometimes hardly moving, as if he was staring at something, or someone, we couldn't see. Other times, he would rock back and forth, the tears flowing, and he would repeatedly say, "Mama, Mama."

The paperwork came through. The interviews were over. We dropped our meager belongings into beaten-up bags and climbed on the plane, my parents terrified, waiting to be stopped, to be denied, to be deported back to the Soviet Union. Instead, smiling flight attendants greeted us, this ragtag bunch.

The flights to JFK, and then to Portland, Oregon, felt luxurious to us. My parents both slept, conked out, for the entire trip to JFK. Once the plane took off they not only knew we were safe, they also knew that the four of us weren't going anywhere.

Dmitry, Elvira, Valeria, and I were spoiled by the flight attendants. I will never forget that. They brought us meals and snacks. We were starving and when we ate everything they brought more food. And pop. We loved the pop. Our parents slept, we ate.

We had to be "processed" when we landed at the airport. Customs, paperwork, stamps, much that I did not understand as a child, except that we had to wait and it made my parents nervous all over again.

We officially became the Kozlovskys then, in that airport, not Kozlovsky and Kozlovskaya. The paperwork that we filled out had only Kozlovsky on it. There would be no more feminine and masculine separation. We would do what my uncles' families had done before us. One last name per family, like the Americans did.

When we were finally done, and told we could go, my father turned to my mother and said, "Welcome to America, Svetlana. We are here, finally."

We cheered.

My parents, who had endured the impossible, their journeys tragic, held each other and cried and cried.

Then they kissed. The kiss took too long.

"Mama! Papa!" we all cried. "Stop!"

The customs officials smiled.

"Welcome to America," they told us.

My parents turned and hugged, and kissed, on both cheeks, the customs officials.

We Kozlovskys have never forgotten the gift and safety of American citizenship.

Not for one day.

Uncle Vladan and Aunt Holly and Anya and Boris met us at the airport, along with Uncle Yuri, Aunt Polina, and JJ; Uncle Sasho and Aunt Yelena, who had not yet run off with the plumber; and Zoya and Tati. The brothers sobbed in each other's arms. Uncle Vladan looked at the scars on my father's face, drawing his fingers over them, and cried again.

"Now, finally, we are together," my father said. "All the Kozlovskys."

Uncle Vladan's successful landscaping business, plus Aunt Holly's job as a kindergarten teacher, had allowed them to buy a nice home on the west side of Portland. Not fancy, thirty years old. It had three stories, with a full daylight basement with one bedroom, and a bathroom, where we lived. Two sets of bunk beds were put in the bedroom, and my parents had a couch that unfolded into a bed in the family room.

Uncle Vladan and Aunt Holly, a woman who could sew or paint anything and make it new and modern, had painted the basement all white. Aunt Holly put red-and-white slipcovers on two couches, found a blue rug to go over the wood floors, and painted two dressers yellow. She added red-and-white checked curtains to the sliding glass doors and the three large windows. Each of us had two blankets and our own comforters and pillows.

Uncle Yuri put his electrical skills to work and added canned lights in the ceiling, a pretty chandelier over a table, and standing lamps. In our room he installed a pink light shaped like a tulip. We loved it.

Uncle Sasho, with income from his new trucking business, bought my parents a used truck.

The basement was far brighter, larger, and more cheerful than our apartment in Moscow.

When Aunt Holly walked my mother down to the basement, my mother put her hands to her mouth and gasped. I gaped. My sisters couldn't speak. Dmitry clung to me.

"I cannot thank you all enough," my father said. "Ever."

"Brother," Uncle Vladan said, "you never need to thank me. When I left the Soviet Union, you and Svetlana gave me money to survive. Now, a small token of my appreciation, I give to you."

Uncle Yuri and Uncle Sasho said the same.

Uncle Vladan and Aunt Holly also had a sprawling backyard with towering maple and fir trees, a tire swing, a play structure, and a tree house. We were in awe of all that space to run in, trees to climb, flowers blooming and vegetables growing in Aunt Holly's garden. She allowed us to take apples and pears straight off her trees.

Once we dropped off our bags in the basement, we all ate together, after a long, long prayer of thanks from my father, with everyone chirping in with, "Thank you, God."

"To the Kozlovskys," my uncle Yuri shouted, his glass in the air when the long, long prayer was over. "To family."

When we were done, I went outside to play in the sunshine with my sisters and my cousins. Dmitry sat and stared at us, in that backyard, his little back ramrod straight, that dead expression in his eyes. He wouldn't play no matter how many times we asked.

"The orphanage," Uncle Vladan said, his shoulders slumping. "That's what did it. It brought the sadness to his eyes and soul."

"Those orphanages are housing from hell," Aunt Polina said. Uncle Yuri nodded.

"A disgrace to the Soviet Union," Uncle Sasho said. "A danger to the children."

"They are jails for children," my aunt Yelena said. She blinked rapidly. I later learned that she had spent years in and out of those orphanages, her mother too poor to feed her.

My father stared off into the distance, as if he could see the threat from Moscow on the horizon.

My mother held his hand, a loving couple who had a secret.

The secret keeper went back to climbing a tree with her cousins.

We grew to love living in Oregon.

No men in uniform ever came in the middle of the night and dragged my father out and beat him half to death, then dumped him in front of our apartment.

No one ever attacked my mother. There were no bloody cloths to deal with. There was no pneumonia that could not be treated immediately.

There was always food. The first time we went to a grocery store, none of us could speak. "Where are the lines?" my mother asked. No lines.

"All this food," my father marveled.

"Milk," my mother breathed. "Alexei, look. Rows of milk."

People did not disappear.

The police were not people to run from, to hide from.

The schools were safe and bright. Our teachers were kind, not rigid and intimidating, lecturing us about being well behaved so we could become Pioneers, little Communists, wearing red scarves, in the future.

The streets were clean, the sun shone, the rain poured, the flowers grew.

There was a library where we could get free books, anytime, stacks of them.

We could read anything we wanted. We did not need to hide that we were Christians. In fact, most of our classmates were Christian, and a bunch of us went to the same church.

Our life became, as my mother said, "filled with color, not with the hands of death, praise God, Jesus, and Mary, mother of Jesus, who never got the credit she deserved, and may God strike down his mighty fist on the men of the KGB, and the men of the jails, who have hurt the Kozlovskys, good people. May they be turned to dust."

There were things we missed about Moscow. Our friends. Bogdan and Gavriil. Our home country. Our traditions. Being new, not knowing the language, not fitting in, starting over for my parents, not being professors anymore, it was all hard, exhausting, sometimes demoralizing.

But the safety and freedom here in America, not having a death threat over my parents' heads, all worth it.

We never pickpocketed again.

There was no need. Stealing is acceptable only when you are starving to death.

There was no chance of starving to death in America.

The Kozlovsky family was happy.

Except for Dmitry.

A week later, at one o'clock in the morning, my insomnia clutching me, visions of Nick and his warm body and smile dancing through my banging head, I heard someone knock on my tugboat.

I actually gasped. Was it Nick? Joy and lust sizzled on through me, and I flipped off my covers.

Maybe he couldn't stay away from me! My heart pittered and pattered. I got caught in my covers and crashed to my floor but, undeterred, I pounded down the stairs, spun around the corner, and just in case, my history in the Soviet Union taking over, I peered through the keyhole to make sure it was my lust muffin.

Whew! *Not Nick.*

Shorter. Not my six foot five Nick.

Smaller. No mountain-sized shoulders.

A hoodie on.

I put my hand to my throat.

The man raised his hand to knock again, strong, loud. It echoed.

I panted, fear ripping through me. Was it one of the Bartons? Had they looked up Valerie's relatives? Oh, my God, save me. Were my parents safe? Were Valerie and Ellie safe? Oh, my God, save *us*. Would he break down the door and attack me for revenge? Would he smash his way in like the KGB had with my father?

Was it someone else?

I whipped around and grabbed my cell phone out of my purse, my knees all gooey.

I did what I had to do. I called Nick. I told him who I thought it could be, my voice wobbling and shaking.

"Do not open the door, Toni," Nick ordered. "Go upstairs. Lock your bedroom door. I'm coming now."

I held on to the phone even when he disconnected. I tucked myself into the kitchen. Within seconds I heard Nick's voice outside my tugboat.

"Hello. Can I help you?"

I heard the man answer. I knew that voice. The cadence. The tone.

I ran to the door and ripped it open. "Dmitry!" I cried, and jumped straight into his arms. He laughed and twirled me around the dock, as if we were in some cheesy movie.

Dmitry and I lay in my bed together that night holding hands.

"I'm so glad you're here."

"Me too, Toni."

"You're staying for a while?"

"Yes. I thought I'd come for the wedding, but that date didn't materialize, so here I am anyhow."

I didn't even bother to hide the tears that swam down my face.

"Aw, Toni."

"What? I missed you."

After Dmitry put me down, I had introduced him to Nick.

"We've met," Dmitry said, smiling. Nick smiled back.

"He told me he was your brother, but I didn't believe him until you came flying out of the tugboat."

Being that close to Nick set my body on slow sizzle. I smiled at him, smiled more. Gave him one more smile. . . .

"Well, I'll let you two go inside," Nick said. "It's late."

"Do you want to come in and talk, Nick?" I couldn't believe I said that. I couldn't believe I was that brave. Or desperate. Probably the latter.

For one second, his expression opened, like a tiny door, and I could see his emotions, raw anguish and hurt, and then it slammed shut. "No, but thank you. I have to get up early."

"Nick, I'm sorry I woke you up—"

"I wasn't asleep."

"Are you sure, man?" Dmitry asked. "Love to have you over. We'll call it a one o'clock in the morning nightcap."

"No, not this time. Next time."

"I owe you, man. Thanks for not beating me up."

"No problem."

We said good-bye, I smiled, smiled, smiled, Nick turned. I lusted after his body, his mind, his laughter, and the way he made burritos and margaritas.

"Come on in, Dmitry."

We had chocolate chip cookies, then headed to bed.

"Toni," Dmitry said, soft, caring. "You need to get past Marty so you can get to Nick."

"I'll never get past Marty."

"Marty will always be a part of your life, who you are, but you have to get past the pain so you can live."

"I'm living."

"You're living in a numb way."

"Numb insulates me from crying all the time."

"Does it work?"

"No. Not at all. My crying doesn't appear to like to limit itself to a time schedule."

"I've been thinking about this a lot, thinking about you, and I have a solution. I think you should go on a kayaking trip."

"No."

"Entertain the idea for a sec, sister. Embrace the music of the idea."

"Too painful. Kayak alone?"

"No. I'll come."

"You would go with me on a kayaking trip?"

"Yes." He handed me an envelope. "But let me rephrase this. I *am* going with you on a kayaking trip. Already paid. Valerie and Ellie are coming, too. We're all going to embrace the music together."

"What?" I opened the envelope. A brochure fell out. A confirmation sheet. Pictures of kayaks in an ocean, green islands, orcas, birds, a tiny town next to a dock.

"It's all arranged. We're going as soon as Valerie's trial is over. The four Kozlovsky kids."

"I don't understand. You planned a kayaking trip and all four of us are going to the San Juan Islands?"

"Yes. We're going to kayak our way to you smiling again. We'll kayak, eat, sing songs, write poetry, drink wine, the works. Peace and paddling."

I sniffled. "I love the islands, but I don't know if I can do this."

"I'll help you."

"I don't know if I can pick up the paddles."

"I'll put them in your hands."

"I don't know if I can sit in a kayak in the ocean."

"I will help you. I'll be in the ocean with you."

"I'll think of Marty and get upset and depressed."

"I know you'll think of Marty. That's why we're doing this. We're reaching into the grief and dealing with it. It'll be cathartic. I think you'll cry. And I think, sister"—he patted my hand—"it's what you have to do to heal and see where things can go with Nick."

"I'm scared."

"I'm scared a lot."

"You are?"

"Sure. I have problems. You know my problems. But what I am most scared about now is that you are still grieving so deeply, that you're not moving into your future. Especially with Mr. I'm Going To Bash Your Face In, who was so protective of you. I want to see you happy again. I want to know you're happy. It hurts me when you're not. So"—he grinned—"it's selfish. I want my old sister happy so I can be happy, too. What do you say?"

My eyes filled. "You're the best brother."

"That's because I have the best sisters."

"I love you, Dmitry. I loved you from the first second I saw you."

"I love you, too. And same with me. So what's your answer? Yes or no to the kayak music?"

"Yes. For sure, yes."

Dmitry told me the next morning over coffee on my deck, the river blue and gray and cool, that he had rented a small house.

"You're kidding. Where?"

"Here. In Portland. About four blocks from Mama and Papa."

"Whooee! I can't believe it. You're finally going to settle down for a bit?"

"Until I want to wander again. I don't know when that will be. Could be in a few weeks, could be months."

"I am thrilled, Dmitry, to have you around again. You're going to tell Mama and Papa today?"

"Yep. I know you have to leave for work in a few minutes, so I'll walk out with you and surprise them at their house for breakfast before they go to the restaurant for the lunch rush. Then I'll surprise Valerie at the trial, give her a hug, then Ellie, while she's sewing up her pillows."

"I'm so glad you're home. I can't believe you've rented a house."

"I can't either, Toni, but it feels . . . right. That's the word for it. I want to plant a garden."

I thought of what my parents had said about Dmitry and a garden. "You're kidding. Mama and Papa said that you would like that."

"They know me."

"I'll help you. I'll get a floppy hat."

He smiled, high-fived me. "Thanks, Toni. We'll plant carrots together." His face shut down, but only for a sec. "No potatoes, no beets."

"Absolutely not." No to his nightmare vegetables.

"It's so odd that a couple of vegetables could cause me such anxiety. . . ."

"Potato and beet anxiety." Sounded funny; it wasn't.

"I think I'll write a poem for my blog today about anxiety. It'll be called 'The Debilitator.' Everyone hates anxiety, that's what I've learned. And so many people are chased down by The Debilitator, including me sometimes."

"I've been chased, too."

He gave my hand a sympathetic squeeze, then Maxie flew overhead.

"Look at that!" Dmitry pointed. "A golden eagle. It's a sign I should stay in Portland."

"I'll take it." I hugged him.

As Dmitry and I left my tugboat, I snuck a peek back at Nick's houseboat. No Nick.

23

On Saturday, the Kozlovsky gang was invited to Dmitry's new home for a barbeque. It was a yellow bungalow with a sprawling backyard, fir and willow trees, and a huge deck. He made ribs.

I walked to the end of the backyard with my father in my sloppy jeans and T-shirt. I did give myself credit for being clean. He put his arm around my shoulders and pointed to the sunny spot of Dmitry's yard. "See? Dmitry needed a garden. I knew it."

"He needs a garden, and he needs the truth, Papa." My father's scars on his face had faded over the years, but they were still a reminder of the hell he'd been through.

"The garden will be better for him." He answered in Russian. I knew it was because my question brought him back to Moscow. "The garden will bring him peace, his truth will not. It will hurt him and I do not want to hurt my son." He rubbed his face. "But I will tell him, Antonia, you are right, he needs to know. We will wait until after the kayaking trip, okay? Let him have that. Let the four of you have that time together."

"He may hate me when he knows what I didn't tell him," I said, also in Russian.

"He will not hate you. He will understand. But I am sorry, Antonia, for putting you in the position that we have all these years, with that secret, I truly am. You have always been a beautiful daughter to me and to your mama. I want nothing more than for you, and your brother and sisters, to all be happy. You four are our lives." He thumped his chest, and two tears slipped down his cheeks. "Our whole lives."

My father makes me emotional sometimes.

Everyone had a plateful of ribs, coleslaw, hot bread, and salad. My father said a long, long prayer of thanks for bringing his son home to him, then Dmitry raised his glass. "To family," he said. "To the Kozlovskys."

"To the Kozlovskys!" we shouted.

Then we all sat down and ate. We Kozlovskys are talented at eating.

And secret keeping.

Never tell, Antonia, never, ever tell.

We would be telling. Soon.

Valerie won.

Tyler Barton was convicted for all four murders, and there were other unsolved murders that would surely be pinned on him in the future.

I was there when the jury came back and announced the verdict. The victims' relatives and friends stood and cheered and clapped. Victory! Justice, finally.

The Barton family stood, too, but not to cheer. They hollered, they swore like the mean, half-cocked people they are.

The security was already tight in that room, and the police and security officers swarmed.

The people who were cheering stopped cheering and told the Barton family to "Shut up" and swore back at them as they struggled against the officers. Two fathers of the victims lost it but were outdone by two mothers, who took the opportunity in the middle of the mayhem to try to get to Tyler. Complete, utter yelling, hitting, chaos.

More security officers ran down the aisle and hauled the Bartons out, pushing the victims' loved ones who tried to attack Tyler out of the way.

I was scared to death for Valerie. They were hungry jackals with sickening, vengeful expressions.

I heard her in my head, clear as day.

They're coming for me.

She turned toward me amidst the upheaval, the cacophony. She had two fingers on her widow's peak, rubbing it.

They want me dead.

My whole body felt as if it had been dipped in ice. *I'll be with you.*

Valerie was hustled out one door, Tyler the other.

I did not miss Tyler's hateful expression when he smirked at Valerie or what he shouted at her. "You're dead."

Valerie didn't miss it, either.

The snake and his family were gunning for her.

Kai took the kids to Hawaii to visit his family when Valerie went kayaking with Ellie, Dmitry, and me.

The kayaking trip in the San Juans was not arduous. Valerie and Ellie hadn't kayaked before, but the ocean sparkled, the orca jumped, the eagles soared, the seals peeked at us, and otters played nearby. We saw forests, sandy beaches, cliffs, and rocky shores.

We went with a guided tour, as they made it easy for us. They assembled our tents, provided the food.

"We're not exactly roughing it," Valerie said, glancing at the outdoor shower the crew was setting up.

"We can't say we're out in the wilds," Ellie said, eyeing the steak sandwiches

"We are not going to be able to go home and talk about the joys of eating off the land," Dmitry said, as the chef handed out glasses of wine.

"But we can pretend that we're adventurers," I said. "Cheers."

We fell over in our kayaks, coming up drenched. We crashed into each other. We camped, sang, wrote funny poetry, and watched shooting stars. I cried about Marty, and Nick, Valerie cried because of the trial, Ellie cried because she was so happy she didn't get married, and Dmitry cried because of a locket, a rocking horse, and a woman with bloody golden hair.

I worried about Nick's job, the danger, how he could die, too, but then I reminded myself that Marty had a safe job, so safe, and he died, and I could not hinge love on an occupation.

We drank too much one night and had hangovers the next day. The guides jokingly threatened to have us arrested for drunken kayak driving.

I sank into my kayak, into that ocean, as if I'd never been gone. Hello, ocean. Hello, nature. Hello, beauty that will be here forever, millions of years after I'm gone. Endless and eternal. Stunning and surprising.

Maybe it was the simple beauty of the exquisite emerald islands. Maybe it was being outside again, finding myself, the self that I'd lost after Marty had died. Maybe it was time. Time to know that I would always love Marty, but he was gone, and I had grieved so deeply I wanted to die and I didn't want to want to die anymore.

I wanted to live. I wanted to be happy. I was not who I had been before. But I was still me, and I decided that I would live again.

I would be brave and honest and I would tell Nick I loved him, and I would hope it wasn't too late.

I love him with everything that I am. I would love him forever, I knew that. That love did not take away from the love I had with Marty.

My kayak flipped over, again. This time I came up laughing. I heard Marty laughing, too, then his laugh faded and I heard Nick.

Nick.

At the end of our trip, on the white ferry taking us back to civilization, the islands fading in the distance, the four of us stood at the rail, our arms wrapped around each other.

We watched the rays of the sun tunnel through white, puffy clouds, to the blue waves, creating that golden staircase up to heaven.

The staircase reminded me of Marty, the loss still there, but this time, for the first time, I also felt gratefulness and acceptance. Gratefulness for the time that I had with Marty and acceptance that he was gone. It was not my time for the golden staircase. It would be, in the future, but for now I needed to move forward and begin again.

With Nick.

"Thank you," I said to them. My sisters and I put our widow's peaks together with Dmitry's blond curls. "I love you."

"We love you, too, Toni."

"I am never kayaking with a hangover again," Ellie said. "That hurt."

"Hi, Nick."

"Hi, Toni."

Nick was guarded. He seemed to take up most of the doorway of his houseboat. He was wearing a black tank top and jeans, and he was so sexy I could feel myself tingling. It was about nine o'clock, Friday night. I'd been home from the island for two hours. The dock was quiet, the river flowed, and the stars had their dimmers on but were becoming brighter.

"How are you?" I took a deep, deep breath and told myself to be brave.

"Fine."

"Can I come in? Please?" Please, Nick.

He hesitated, and my stomach pitched and headed toward my feet.

"Sure." He stepped aside. "Have a seat." He indicated his couch, and I sat down before my pudding knees gave out from fright. He sat down about three feet away from me.

I had taken a shower, washed my hair, and put on my clothing armor. Thigh-length black skirt, black tights, knee-high boots, low-cut purplish silk blouse, a push-up bra, earrings, and lipstick.

"Haven't seen you around."

"Dmitry and my sisters and I went kayaking."

"Ah." His eyes flickered. I could tell he understood the significance of my little journey. "How'd it go?"

"It was what I needed to do." I sat on my hands to hide the shaking. "It went well. Valerie rolled herself twice, which was hilarious. Ellie tripped straight into the ocean one night holding a beer. Dmitry somehow ended up going backward, often, and I ran into a rock, a log, and a downed tree, but we made it."

"I'm glad you went." Nick seemed tired. He had lost weight. He was wary, evaluating why I was there.

"Do you—" I stopped, words stuck. Too much was weighing on this one question. "Do you want to meet my family?"

He didn't respond at first, his elbows on his knees, those warm and magically perfect hands linked together.

"I would like that very much."

"You would?" Yay!

"Yes." He smiled. "Yes, I would."

"They're uh . . . different."

"I like different."

"But none of them deals drugs."

"That's a plus, or I would have to arrest them."

"No arrests necessary." I smiled. I felt much better! "I was also wondering if you would like to spend the night on my tugboat."

Nick's smile grew. Something flashed in those light blue eyes. Perhaps a spark of light blue hope.

"I would like that, babe. But I have to ask, so we're clear, would it be for only one night?"

"I was hoping it would be for . . . for many nights." I scooted over and grabbed his warm hand in both of mine, I couldn't help it.

"Ah." His smile was now full, happy.

"Yes. Hundreds of nights. Thousands. Tens of thousands."

He picked me up, dropped me on his lap, wrapped those strong arms around me, and kissed me, long and macho manly like. "I would like to stay over for tens of thousands of nights. It's what I want more than anything."

"Then you're invited." I kissed him, then pulled away. "I love you, Nick."

"I love you, too, baby."

"And I'm sorry. I'm sorry I couldn't commit, couldn't be with you. I am truly sorry that I hurt you."

"Don't be. I understand."

"I'll make it up to you." I kissed him again, then started kissing lower.

"I'm going to hold you to that." Macho man wiped a hand across his face, and I grabbed it and kissed the tears away on his palm and on his cheeks. I hugged him. I hugged my Nick, a strong, courageous man who looked like a hardened criminal but who had a warm and patient heart.

We made love on his couch, clothes flying everywhere, then we went to my houseboat for the sleepover.

Making love with Nick is my favorite thing to do.

The next morning I had no trouble finding an outfit to wear to work. What color? That was easy: red.

Living on a Tugboat, Talking About Homes

BY TONI KOZLOVSKY

My father brought home a present on my parents' fourteenth wedding anniversary. He had a huge smile on his face. It was a long box, and it was heavy.

"What's in the box, Papa?" I asked, but he wouldn't tell my sisters, my brother, and me. He told us to sit on the couch with him and wait for my mother to come out of their bedroom.

My sisters, my brother, my mother, and I had made a five-layer peppermint cake together that day to celebrate their anniversary. We had also made our parents cards, pictures with the two of them on the front, drawn from a photo we had of their wedding day.

I had accidentally drawn my mother far taller than my father; my sister Valerie had trouble drawing their faces, so there was some resemblance to pigs; Ellie, my youngest sister, had drawn them each holding oversized dogs, as she wanted my parents to buy her two dogs; and my brother, Dmitry, drew a picture of my father upside-down, we don't know why.

"Alexei!" my mother said. "You are home early. What is that?"

"Happy anniversary, Svetlana."

"What is this?" My mother carefully removed the wrapping paper so she could save it.

Inside the box were cast-iron pans. Heavy. Strong. Top of the line. The type a cook craves. My mother burst into tears. So did, surprisingly, my father. Together they held hands across that box, their tears streaming down their faces. My sisters and brother and I were baffled. They were only pans!

I asked my mother, when she was done kissing my father, why they were crying over pans, and she told us a story, in Russian, as if we were back in our cramped, tiny apartment on the snowy streets of Moscow.

During a hard time, after my father was arrested and jailed for his political views and for his fervent, outspoken belief that we, as Christians, should be able to worship openly, we were dead poor. My mother sold the pans that had been her mother's so that she and my sisters and I could eat. I remember watching her walk out the door with those pans.

She didn't have a choice. We didn't have enough money for food at the shops. We had no extra money for the black market. I knew selling the pans broke my mother's heart. They weren't just pans, they were her mother's pans. They were part of her history, part of her family.

"When your papa returned from prison," she told us, "he asked where the pans were, and I told him. He told me that he would buy me the best pans in the world as soon as he could to make up for the loss.

"This is about losing everything, then coming here

to America and starting over. It's about having nothing, not even a dollar, and building something together. It's about love. It's about you children and the sacrifices we all made. It's about your papa and me and our marriage. Mostly, it is about how your papa kept his word to me."

She leaned over and kissed my father over the box of pans again. We said, "Ew!"

They laughed and put their cheeks together so their tears blended into one. "Thank you, Alexei," she said.

"You are welcome, Svetlana."

My mother still uses the pans my father bought her, every day.

"Because what I make in those pans," my mother told me, "is filled with love."

We ran the column with a picture of my parents and their pans, in their kitchen. They had both dressed up—my father in a blue suit, my mother in a burgundy dress and heels, regal and elegant. We also printed their wedding photo.

"I famous now," my mother told me over the phone. "I wear my wine color dress. I think I still have the, what you call it? The va va voom? Your papa, he thinks I do. Last night he—"

"Mama!"

"Ack. You prune, Antonia. I know what I call special tonight at restaurant. I call it 'I Am Va Va Voom.' "

I tried not to groan, thinking of the calls I would get tomorrow.

My father got on the phone, too. "Antonia! I like the article. Your mama and me. She look pretty in that wine dress, no? Yes. I think so. I not talk to you since Monday. Start with Tuesday. What you do? Who you talk to. . . ."

Daisy sang that night on the dock, every note dipping and soaring, catching the natural serenity of the river, then flowing toward the tips of the trees, the twinkling lights of Portland.

"You Don't Bring Me Flowers" by Neil Diamond. "America the Beautiful." "Here You Come Again" by Dolly Parton. "I Say a Little Prayer" by Dionne Warwick.

It was like listening to an angel with a daisy hat.

It was tremendously sad.

What to do as Daisy's mind slipped, as if it were tumbling down a cranium chute? Skippy and Georgie continued to check on their mother daily. Georgie called me the other day and told me his mother had shown him and his brother the whale hat she was working on.

"She always wears daisies on her hats, not whales. What the f-word is going on? The other day, Skippy and I had to write a huge check to a charity that studies whales. She insisted. Don't tell anyone, Toni, it's embarrassin' because of our...uh... business."

What was the solution? Trap her in a nursing home, or let her live her life out here until there was absolutely no room for any wriggling and for her own safety she had to be moved. She was clean, safe, eating.

I voted for the latter.

It's what I would want for myself.

I drove by the white house with the red door on Thursday afternoon. The garage doors were up, but the family was sitting on the porch, one kid each in a parent's lap.

I could see the kayak. It had been repainted red. Well done. Looked new now. There were four people in the family, though. They needed two kayaks, not one. I wondered if they were planning on buying a second one.

Nick and I went out on *Sanchez One*. He bought a pizza. I made a salad. We anchored down in a quiet area of the river, the city lights way off in the distance.

"Do you want to tell me more about your childhood in Russia?"

I tried to make it a short story. "I lived with my mother and father, Valerie and Ellie. They were called Valeria and Elvira then. I was Antonia. There were uncles, aunts, cousins, grand-parents. We wanted to live in America, so we immigrated."

"Nice short version. Let's hear the rest."

"It's grim."

"I can take it, and I'd like to know. Your childhood affects your life now. I know there were problems in Russia, because you won't talk about it."

I told him about the deprivations in Moscow.

I told him about Uncle Leonid.

I told him what they did to my father and grandfather and why.

I told him about the pickpocketing.

I told him the story about my mother, her secret.

I told him about my parents and that last night at home, the blood.

I told him about Dmitry.

I told him what I hadn't told Dmitry, and how the secret—*Never tell, Antonia, never, ever tell*—had followed me, like a Russian scythe wrapped in guilt.

I told him how I didn't feel that I fit in for so many years in America, why I dress the way I do, and how lonely I had been here as a kid, speaking no English.

He listened. He didn't interrupt. He held my hand. He asked questions. I knew my secrets were safe with him. It was like talking to a vault. He was sympathetic, compassionate.

"Babe, I'm so sorry for what you went through. I have never met a woman like you, Toni, or any people like your family. You lost everything, came here, worked hard, stayed sane, and here you are. All great people."

"I don't know about the sane part."

"You're the most sane person I know." He kissed me, and I kissed him back.

The sun was down when we parked his boat at his house and cleaned it up.

Making love that night with Nick was more mind blasting than usual.

*   *   *

We had a family dinner at Svetlana's the next night to celebrate my parents' anniversary. The Kozlovsky gang was out in
full force, as were longtime friends and neighbors, the staff,
Ralph, and Charlie. My father said a long, long prayer thanking
God for my mother, how wonderful she was, until my mother
interrupted and said, "Amen, Alexei."

Our family then officially welcomed Nick, my father introducing him. "Welcome to the family, Nick Sanchez. We are . . ."
He swept his hand out. "We are American Russians. We say
American first, then Russian. Some of us more crazy than others. It's a large family. We fight. We love. We laugh. We drink
vodka. I think you fit in to us good."

My mother stood next, and smiled, so sweet, black hair in a
ball, the white streak from her widow's peak striking. She wore
a sleek white lace dress. "Nick. Our daughter, Antonia, is very
special. I love her. Her father loves her. We all love her." Her
face turned stern. "You take care of her, or I kill you, okay?"

"I'll do that," he said, in all seriousness, as everyone laughed.
"I promise."

We raised our glasses to Nick. He was gallant and respectful
and thanked everyone for including him and then made a toast
to my parents and congratulated them on their anniversary and
thanked them for creating me, "the love of my life."

My uncle Vladan stood next and made a toast to my parents.
"My brother, Alexei, my longtime friend, Svetlana, we grow old
together, right, and it my honor and privilege. But Alexei . . ."
He paused. "Your wife looks much better than you. Looks like
your daughter, old man. Yes, she does. Woe on your life. You
got to do something about your face."

Ah, Uncle Vladan. So funny. . . .

Not to be outdone, my uncle Yuri stood and said, "Alexei,
you have been married to Svetlana for many years and I must be
honest. You got the better part of the deal, brother. I still cannot
understand why she say yes. Maybe she drunk? Were you drunk
the day of your wedding, Svetlana? Come on, you can tell all of

us now. Must have been drunk! No? Well, to my brother and to my sister by marriage, I raise my glass to you. To the beauty and what is my brother called? The beast."

My uncle Sasho said, those bushy eyebrows up, "Svetlana, you are bright woman. What you still doing with Alexei? Come. I not married. I need wife. I take you, Svetlana."

Oh, they were funny.

Zoya and Tati gave my mother a red box. She unwrapped it and pulled out a purple, lacy negligee. It was exquisite, I have to say. We clapped and cheered.

My mother held it up over her white lace dress and turned to my father. "Alexei, I think we leave this party early."

My father stood up. "No, Svetlana. We not leaving early. We leave now." He grabbed her and danced her toward the door. "Good-bye everyone. I have better things to do."

We ate our favorite Russian food. We drank vodka shots, and my father got out the key to the wine cellar.

We again toasted my parents. We shouted, "To family! To the Kozlovskys!" and clinked our glasses together.

The only one not happy was Valerie. She looked ill. She tried to fake it.

I heard her voice in my head.

They'll come for me, I know it.

Ellie dropped her fork and stared at Valerie.

I put my wineglass down.

Listen for me, she told us. *Listen.*

Nick hooked an arm around me as we walked back to his truck that night. "Nothing is ever dull in your family, is it?"

"No."

He laughed.

"Are you sure you want to be around these people?"

"Yes, baby. Positive."

I kissed him.

I do love my white bedroom in my yellow tugboat. It is even better with Nick in bed with me. I fell asleep hugging Nick, the river no longer lonely.

* * *

My mother was very pleased with Nick. She named a new special after him at the restaurant. It was called "Welcome To The Family, Nick." It was a beef and lamb dish with sauerkraut on the side. She and my father stood in church and asked everyone to pray for the happiness of their daughter, Antonia, and her new man, Nick. My mother would let them know when the wedding was! I received many, many calls and e-mails of congratulations. What to do with a mother like that?

Keeping The Monsters At Bay: Shopping Defensive Strategies meant that I should buy Nick a cool coat I saw . . . and I should buy a pile of lingerie.

24

⌇

"Mama, Papa, first off, I love you." Dmitry leaned forward on our parents' kitchen table.

"We love you, too, Dmitry," my parents said, together.

"I need to talk to you. I need to ask you some questions, and I need the truth."

It was time. My parents knew it, we all knew it.

Valerie, Ellie, Dmitry, and I were at my parents' home for Sunday dinner. Knowing the topic, Valerie had not invited her family, and I had not invited Nick. On the kayaking trip Dmitry had told us, "I can't stand it anymore. If I don't find out the truth, I'm going to lose it."

The table was set with a white tablecloth, peonies, and candles. My mother had made chicken Kiev, my brother's favorite. When we were done, we got down to the secrets that have followed our family like a continuing train wreck from Moscow to Oregon.

"I know you're hiding something. I've asked about my past many times, but you both shut me down. Papa, you tell me that I am your son and that I came from an orphanage. Mama, you tell me to forget my life in the Soviet Union. I can't forget it. It's still in me, these snatches of another life. The rocking horse, a blue box with a woman on it with a parasol, a red and purple butterfly, wooden ducks, a blue door, a vegetable garden. And that white dog, I think he's dead. A locket, for God's sakes. I keep seeing a blond woman, who I think may be my mother, and I have seen woods, scary and dark, my whole life. I have no memory of an orphanage. I do, however, have memories of blood."

My father slumped back in his chair at the head of the table. He put a hand to the scars on his face, a parting shot from the Soviet Union. I knew he did not realize he was doing it. My mother, at the other end, slumped at the same time.

"I remember blood, too," I said.

"What?" Dmitry said, whipping his head around to me.

"You had blood on you, Dmitry, when Papa brought you home late that night. Your first night with us."

"You never told me this, Toni. Never."

I heard the accusation. The hurt betrayal. My chest tightened, as if my guilt and regret were lodged there. "I was ten. They told me not to tell. They told me I was to tell you that Papa got you at the orphanage, but even as a kid I knew that an orphanage would not have released a child in the middle of the night, Papa wouldn't have been beat up, and there would not have been blood on both of you."

My father went gray. My mother closed her eyes, hands together, praying.

"Oh, my God. Why was there blood on me? On Papa?" Dmitry shouted. "Why? What happened? Whose blood was it?"

"Dmitry, I am sorry," I said, my tone begging for forgiveness. "I kept a secret when I shouldn't have. I kept something from you that you had a right to know."

Dmitry stared at me in shock. "How could you not tell me this, Toni? I have told you so many times that I kept remembering blood. You could have told me that I came in with blood, that I wasn't imagining it. That it was part of my history, not a nightmare that kept repeating itself. At least I would know I wasn't losing my mind."

"I knew, too," Valerie said.

It was as if a silent bomb exploded in that room.

"Me too," Ellie said.

Second bomb.

"You two knew about the blood, too?" Dmitry said, incredulous.

They had known? My sisters, who I could sometimes hear in my head, they knew, too?

"That night when Dmitry arrived, you crawled back in bed and started to cry, Toni," Valerie said. "I got up and looked out the bedroom door, and I saw Papa carrying Dmitry to the bathroom. I saw the blood on both of them. Mama saw me and told me to shut the door and later she told me, *Never tell, Valeria, never, ever tell.* Papa told me the same thing the next morning, and I promised I wouldn't. And I haven't. I wish I had. I am so sorry, Dmitry. I should have told you."

"I got up after Valerie came back to bed," Ellie said, "I went to the bathroom. The water . . ." Ellie closed her eyes. "It was red. The curtain was drawn. Papa was in there but I could still see. Dmitry had blood on his hands and his clothes. Mama turned and told me to go to bed. The next morning she said, *Never tell, Elvira, never, ever tell.* Papa said the same thing to me."

"Oh God," Dmitry said. "Really? All three of you?"

"I didn't know they knew," I said, which my sisters echoed. All these years, we hadn't known the other sisters knew.

"The truth. Now. Tell me." Dmitry pushed a hand through his blond curls. "Did you kill my mother, Papa? Did you? Did you kill my father? Why? Why would you do that?"

My parents seemed to crumble, my mother visibly shaking. I felt ill.

"No, son," my father said in Russian. "No, I did not kill your mother."

"Your papa would never have killed your mother, Dmitry," my mother said, also in Russian, so I started thinking in Russian. "He would not lay a hand on a woman in violence." My mother wiped her eyes. "We must tell him, Alexei. He cannot rest."

"Tell me," Dmitry said, in Russian, slamming his fists on the table. "Tell me now."

My father closed his eyes then said, "You are right, son. There is more. Much more. It begins before you were born. In

Moscow. In a university, with me, your mother, your uncles, our ideas, our faith, our beliefs. We wanted a free, democratic society. Freedom of press, of protest, of religion. I was jailed for my beliefs. Your mother, I was sure of it, would soon be jailed, too.

"The man who tortured me in prison was named Rurik. He never thought I would be released. He thought I would die there, that he would kill me or that I would die later, working in hard labor. He talked to me, often, sometimes as if I was a friend. I would have a wrist chained to a wall and he would tell me about his wife. I would be starving and he would eat dinner in front of me while he told me about his childhood. I would be bleeding, or beaten, by him, and he would tell me about the women he'd slept with."

I shuddered, sickened for my father.

"Rurik said his own father had beat him, that he had been a drunk. He was out on his own at thirteen. Became a beggar, then a criminal, never caught, then came to the prison as a guard. He showed no mercy. He was relentless. He laughed at our pain, mine, my father's, the other prisoners'.

"He would say to me, 'You think you are smarter than me, a farmer's son, because you are a professor? No, you are not. Who is on the ground in his waste and who is standing, Professor Kozlovsky? You think you are better than me? Who has a job and who is dying?' "

My mother put her hand over her mouth as a sob escaped. I reached for her other hand.

"Rurik talked about his wife all the time. He was obsessed with her, said she was the most beautiful woman in all of the Soviet Union. Said she was his. That he would never let her go. That he owned her." The candles flickered, my father studied them. "Rurik killed his wife."

My sisters gasped. Dmitry's temple beat. My mother, however, was not surprised. She had always known.

"For weeks before he killed her, he thought she was having an affair with one of the men in town, so he beat her to get her to tell him the truth. One day he came back to the prison and whispered to me that he had killed her and dragged her outside into the woods and buried her by a large rock. He was enflamed at her betrayal. He said he put a piece of cement over her grave. 'So she can't get out and go to heaven.' He laughed at that, too. He did not believe in God. His wife did, and he told me he heard her praying when he beat her. He mocked her prayers as he mocked the prayers of my father and me. He told me that she got what she deserved. He went from rage to tears. He would cry for hours over his wife—her betrayal and her death.

"Within days it was clear he was having a breakdown. He started fighting with the other guards, so he was told to take a vacation. I was released, ironically, the day after he left. The Bessonovs bribed me out of prison. Your uncles tried but had not been able to do so from the States. They had no influence, but Stas Bessonov did.

"Anyhow, I am sure, if Rurik was there, he would have fought against my release, maybe to the death. My death. He never thought I would get out. The timing was God-given."

"Was Rurik arrested for killing his wife?" Ellie asked, so pale.

"He was not. Rurik and his wife lived outside of a small village, in the country. No car for her. He said that he didn't let her leave the house. How he thought she could have an affair, I don't know. He was insane. Anyhow, he was planning on going to the pub soon and telling everyone that his wife had run off. Left him. That she had a boyfriend. Then he could avoid suspicion."

"How do you know, though, Papa," Valerie said, ever the prosecutor, "that he was not arrested? Didn't we leave Moscow about two weeks after you were released?"

"Yes, we did. When I was better. When your mother, when you all"—he nodded at my sisters and me—"nursed me back to health."

"He could have been arrested then. Later." Valerie always wanted justice. "After we left. Did you tell the police?"

"No. They would not have believed me, an enemy of the people, accusing his jailer of being a murderer. And Rurik would have known that. He was never arrested."

There was more. So much more. I felt it coming like a tank. We all did.

"How, though?" Dmitry asked. "How are you sure?"

My father's back was ramrod straight. "Because I killed Rurik."

Because I killed Rurik.

What? It was like being hit by a sledgehammer. We struggled to get our minds around it. Our father killed a man: his jailer.

"I went to his home, two days before we left for America. It took me awhile to find it, but the next day I killed him. We fought. I killed him with your grandfather's knife, a knife he had from the war. It was my way of allowing my father the chance to be a part of killing the man who killed him."

Sometimes it is hard to understand everything, all at once. It's too brain scrambling. It's too graphic. You can't get your mind to react, because it's overwhelmed. It's like trying to swallow verbal thunder.

We sat in that verbal thunder, stricken into silence.

"What?" Ellie whispered.

"You killed the man who—" Dmitry started.

". . . who killed grandfather . . ." Valerie said.

". . . the man who tortured you—" Ellie said.

". . . the man who told you he had recently killed his wife?" I said.

"Your papa," my mother said, and I dare say she was proud. "He is an expert fighter. He was a boxer. I am proud of his skills."

"Thank you," he murmured.

"I was scared that night," my mother said. "So scared. I waited up for you all night. Praying. I begged you not to go, but you did."

"I know you prayed, Svetlana. I felt your prayers."

I remembered, as if it happened last week. My mother begging my father not to go, his telling her it was for his honor, his father's honor, insisting we leave without him if he did not immediately return. The next morning, my mother praying, asking us to pray, sitting by our window in that tiny, freezing apartment in Moscow.

"And here, my son," my father said to Dmitry, "is where this story takes another turn, one I did not expect amidst the revenge I knew I had to take against Rurik. You are not from an orphanage, Dmitry. I lied to you."

"Yes, we lied," my mother said. "Do not be angry only at your papa. Be angry at me, too, my love."

"Where then?" Dmitry said, hands flat down on the table, as if to steady himself, face flushed. "Where did you get me?" But understanding dawned on his face, inch by inch.

"Oh, my mother of God and holy crap," Valerie said.

"Oh," Ellie said. "Oh."

"Oh, Lord," I said.

"Dmitry," my father said, so gently, "you are Rurik's son."

Dmitry's face froze, stunned, for long seconds, then he lowered his head to the table, his hands over his blond curls. I patted his back, reeling.

"I didn't know he had a son, Dmitry. He never talked about you, only his wife. I killed your father, Dmitry, with my father's knife, for what he did to me and my father. When he was dead, I dragged him to the woods, when it was dark, as far in as I could, and buried him. I cleaned up the blood, then burned the rags. I hoped that no one would come looking for Rurik, at least for a while.

"I planned it so that we could immediately escape to America before the police had any chance to figure out who had killed him when they discovered he was gone." He grabbed Dmitry's hand, his beloved son whom he never quite bonded with, Dmitry's memories dancing like demons in the back of his head. Dmitry pulled his hand away.

"I heard you cry, son, in a back room, down a hallway. I didn't know you were there. I swear I didn't, and there you were, standing up in a cardboard box, no crib. You had blood all over you. At first I thought you were hurt, then I realized what had happened. While I was burying your father in the woods, you came into the room and you must have slipped on the blood from our fight."

"I slipped on my father's blood." Dmitry's eyes were dazed.

"You slipped on your father's blood," my father corrected, "mine, and you slipped on Rurik's blood."

I leaned back against the chair, weak. Ellie put a hand to her mouth. Valerie looked drained.

"I couldn't leave you," my father said, "which is what I think Rurik did after he killed your mother and then came to work. He left you. Alone. It was winter, it was freezing. I could not leave you. You would have died in that house. I couldn't take you to the village and drop you off, try to find other family members. I would have been caught. Jailed. Killed. What then, for your mother, your sisters? Your mother had been investigated for our meetings, for our faith, too. We knew she would go to jail soon. We were shocked she had not already gone.

"Who would take care of your sisters without us? Your uncle Vladan had been gone for years. Your uncle Yuri and uncle Sasho were gone, too, in the last year. I would have had to sacrifice my wife, your mother, your sisters, and I couldn't do that. It was a small village anyhow, no orphanage. I picked you up and you stopped crying. I comforted you. I needed to move quickly, and that's what I did. I didn't have time to clean you up, to clean us up. I put you in the car wrapped in a blanket.

"On the way home you fell asleep against me, your head in my lap. It was a long trip home. When you woke up I sang to you, fed you a sandwich your mother had made me. I could not take you to an orphanage in Moscow. Those are no place for children. No love or kindness. Abuse. Not enough food. I could not do that to you. There were no viable choices. I could not sacrifice my family by trying to find yours, and I could not sacrifice you by putting you in an orphanage. The decision was made. You had to come with us, to America."

Dmitry was white. "But let's get this straight. I am the son of your torturer."

My father closed his eyes. "You are *my* son. *Our* son. You are not my biological son, but the son of my heart. I loved you from that first day."

"You are our love son," my mother said. "The son of our souls."

"*I am the son of your torturer,*" Dmitry said again, his face twisting. "The son of the man who tortured, starved, beat, and killed your father and who almost killed you."

"You are a Kozlovsky. A *Kozlovsky,*" my father said, his face insisting that Dmitry understand. "We are a proud family, and we are proud of you."

"When I held you in my arms, Dmitry, I felt the same as your papa," my mother said. "It was as if you were always supposed to be with us, always, a son who came to us later, a gift."

"No. I don't believe this," Dmitry said, his face flushed, the tears falling. "How can you love the son of the man who did what he did to you, to your father?"

"Because you are not his true son," my father said. "You are mine. Mine. *Our son.* Rurik did not deserve you. He did not treat you as a father should. He did not treat your mother with love and kindness."

"Why didn't you tell me any of this sooner? You knew. You both knew my struggle. I knew I had a mother. And I remembered someone else, someone who scared me. That would have been my father. I remembered blood."

"I didn't tell you the truth, son, because this is a story that rakes your soul over coals and back again. Your poor mother, killed by her husband. I didn't want this blackness, this well of hate and violence, to have any place in your mind. You were so young when you came to us. I wanted you to forget. I thought it would be better if you thought you were from an orphanage. As a boy, you used to ask me where your mother was, and I said that she loved you and gave you up because she couldn't care for you. That is a hard story, but it is a better story than this one. This one is much more difficult to live with."

"We wanted you to put everything in the past, to shut the door," my mother said. "To never think of it again. You were young. We thought you would forget, that you would block it all out, but you didn't. Parts of your life have followed you."

"Dmitry," Ellie said. "You've always talked about a woman with golden hair. Papa, did Rurik say what color her hair was?"

My father's face sagged. "Rurik said his wife had hair like gold."

"I have seen that gold hair my whole life," Dmitry whispered. "I remember bloody golden hair."

"That must have been the night he killed her, son."

It was a nightmare. Dmitry's past was a nightmare.

"What is my last name?" Dmitry asked. "What is it?"

"It is Nikonov," my father said. "Nikonov."

"And what . . ." He choked on his loss, his eternal loss. "What was my mother's name?"

"Nelly." My father's eyes were so sad. "Your beautiful mother's name was Nelly."

Our parents heaved out long, tearful sighs, then my father got up and removed a picture from the living room wall.

"Papa?" I said.

Behind the picture was a safe. I had no idea there was a safe there. Neither did my sisters or brother.

My mother did, though.

My father started turning the lock. He pulled out a piece of paper. There was a Russian address on it. He also pulled out a tiny white box and handed it to Dmitry. Dmitry lifted the lid. We all gasped as he held up a golden, heart-shaped locket and opened it up.

Dmitry tilted his head back, a mixture of grief, relief, and devastation on his face. On one side was a picture of a baby, on the other side a picture of a blond, smiling woman.

"On the way out, I saw that necklace, on a table. I grabbed it," my father said. "I knew it was your mother's, and I took it, for you, and later I realized that I shouldn't give it to you, because I wanted you to leave your life in the Soviet Union behind you, those memories behind."

Dmitry stared at the picture of his mother, then he wiped his eyes. He stood up, walked unsteadily to the door, and put on his shoes.

"Please stay, Dmitry." I grabbed his arm.

"Don't take off again," Valerie said. "We'll miss you. We always miss you."

"Be with us. Let's talk," Ellie begged.

"Son—" my mother said, then cried, ragged sobs.

He hugged my mother, he hugged my father, who had a hard time letting him go, then us. He left, closing the door behind him quietly, the golden locket with photos of his mother and himself in his hand.

He would wander, he would travel, as if the pain would not go away without it, as if he walked long enough, searched long enough, wrote enough poems and songs, he could bury it down, further than a grave next to a rock and covered in cement.

"He is gone again, my son," my father wailed, his voice defeated. "I only just got him back, Svetlana, and now, gone. Is he gone forever this time? Will I see him again? He hates me, I know he does. I cannot blame him. I killed his father."

"You killed the man who killed your father," my mother said, wrapping him in a hug, still sobbing. "You did not know, my love, that he was a father, too."

My father had aged years in an hour. I had never seen him like that before, as if life had finally pushed him down so hard, he couldn't get up.

"See what revenge does," he said. "Revenge is toxic. It spreads. It never ends. Rurik killed my father. I killed him. I took Dmitry and Dmitry leaves me. Rurik has had his revenge on me."

"Dmitry will come back," my mother said, her voice a raspy whisper, her tears running into his. "He will come back."

My father cried until I thought he would run out of tears.

I told Nick that night what happened. He listened, holding me close, and we went to bed. I couldn't sleep. In the morning, he took me out on his boat and we watched the sunrise. He brought coffee and bagels and jelly.

We hardly said anything. He knew I needed the sunrise, the color, that vibrant sign of life, to even begin thinking about starting my day.

Dmitry was the son of my father's torturer, my grandfather's murderer.

He would hate himself for it, though he had no connection at all.

"I love you, Dmitry," I whispered. Somewhere out there, I hoped, with all that I had, that he felt that love.

"That's it, Toni, I'm done." Boris's cheerful voice came over the phone as I sat at my cubicle at work, editing an article on a home that had been built with all recycled materials.

"Done with what?"

"Stealing, uh ..." He coughed. "Borrowing a car now and then from the wealthy and spoiled. I have three full-time mechanics working with me and I'm running an honest shop."

"Perfect. I didn't like seeing you in jail. The orange jumpsuit didn't go well with your coloring."

"Orange doesn't go well with anyone's coloring. I cannot wait to see what's upcoming in the next opera season, can you?"

No, I couldn't.

I chatted with Boris.

I missed Dmitry. Having him gone again felt like a slash against my heart.

"I'm leaving my business, Toni. Shutting it down. Doors closed."

"You are?" Lindy and I were making two apple pie crusts in my kitchen, rolling out the dough.

"Yes. I'm tired of it. I don't want to have so much sex anymore. I don't want middle-aged and old men touching me. It's disgusting now."

"Glad to hear it." Wow. Boris, now Lindy. Lucky week. "What are you going to do?"

"I'm going to become a librarian."

I stopped rolling out the dough. I envisioned that. Lindy, a librarian. Yep. It would work.

"I loved your idea," Lindy said. "I love books. I read all the time, as you know, and I love libraries. I love the smell of books. I love the feel of books."

"You're a book addict."

"Yes. A book addict. I can help anyone find a book. Even my clients ask me for book suggestions sometimes. I loan my books out to them. They always bring them back. Plus, I love research, love studying. So I'm going to college to become a librarian. I want to work at a university."

"I think that's a dandy idea, Lindy. I do."

"A dandy idea. I like the way you say it."

"You're supersmart and you know a whole bunch about everything."

"Not about everything, but I do have this need to learn something new each day. Being an expensive call girl, that profession, I didn't learn anything. Same old, same old. The men want to talk, they want you to listen, they want to think that their sticks are bigger than other men's sticks, so you lie and tell them yes, they are, praise them, make some noises, and they think they're Superman in bed. Like I said, I never learned anything new."

"It's important. Learning, I think."

"Me too, and thanks, Toni."

"For what?"

"For saying that I'm supersmart."

"You are supersmart. You're a brain."

"I think I'll use my brain instead of my secret passageway from now on."

"I think it's your dream job."

"Me too."

We used our hands to scoop up chopped apples, cinnamon, brown sugar, and nutmeg.

"I really like you, Toni."

"I like you, too, Lindy. And I'll definitely come and check out books at your library."

"I'll waive your late fines for you."

"You're a true pal."

On a Monday night, at eight o'clock, reading a book in bed, hoping it would distract me from a prison in the Soviet Union, a sadistic jailer, and a house out in the country with a little boy slipping in blood, I heard Valerie in my head.

Help me, Toni. Help me.

I closed my eyes as my whole body tightened, my breath coming to a halt. I blocked everything out, even warm and cuddly Nick snuggled up with me. *Where are you?*

I'm in a cellar. House across the street is 12756.

Valerie? Valerie?

"What is it, Toni?" Nick sat straight up. "Are you all right?"

My lungs lost air. I felt dizzy.

"Can you breathe, Toni?" Nick leaned over me. "Baby, can you breathe?"

I hit my chest with my hand and dragged in air, sagging. "Valerie needs help. She's going to get hurt."

"What? How do you know?"

"There's one thing I haven't told you, Nick." I flew out of bed and started to dress.

"What is it?"

"I can hear Valerie and Ellie in my head. Now and then. Rarely. I just heard Valerie."

I told him what I knew. He looked as if I'd hit him with a two-by-four.

"Please, Nick. We'll talk about it later. You have to believe me."

"Okay." He made a call, then another, getting dressed.

I called Kai. He said that Valerie had said she was going by the restaurant. "She said she'd be home by nine-thirty." His voice was sharp, worried.

"Where are the kids?"

"They're here." I told him what I heard.

"I'm calling Chief Crighton."

Ellie called me. "12756. We have to go now to the police station. Now!"

Nick and I raced down the dock to his black truck and met Ellie and Kai at the police station. Chief Crighton was there. There were police officers and detectives buzzing around, working the computers, on the phone, trying to find Valerie. Valerie's security officer had been found knocked out and bleeding in the back corner of Svetlana's Kitchen parking lot.

"Look for 12756," I told them. "It's the address of a home across the street from where Valerie is being held."

"She called you?" Chief Crighton asked. Crighton was a tall, strong, tough, honest man. I knew him from my work at the newspaper. I liked him.

"No." I saw his confusion. "It's . . . it's weird. It's down our family line. From the Sabonises. We have it. We have a language, only in the worst circumstances, we can . . ."

"You can . . . ?" the chief prodded.

"We can hear each other in our heads."

Everyone in the room froze. I could feel their disbelief, ridicule from a few of them.

The chief stared at me. He evaluated.

"Believe her," Nick said.

And that was it. Nick knew the chief, too. Chief Crighton said to everyone, "We're working this from all angles. We've got people at Svetlana's, we've got addresses and cell phones for the Barton family, we've got officers going to their homes now. And we're going to investigate this number, 12756. Joe, Ismael, Sierra, you're on it. Move."

In minutes there were a number of addresses up on computer screens. The chief looked at them, yelled them out to officers. There were houses with the number 12756 all over the Portland metro area. "Go. Remember it's across the street," the chief said. Officers ran out of the room with their addresses, along with Kai.

"One more," one of the officers called out. "This one."

"12756 SW Moreland Lane," the chief said. "Looks like it's in Schollton, out in the country."

Another two officers took off.

Valerie! Are you in the country?

It was weak, dim, hopeful. *Yes.*

"She's in the country," Ellie said.

We sprinted out of that police station.

Nick drove Ellie and me in his truck, following the police car as it rushed through the city, lights and siren on, down a freeway, out onto winding rural roads, the countryside black except for occasional lights from homes.

"Almost there," Nick said, looking at his GPS.

The police officers turned off the lights and siren, then slowed in front of a house with the number 12756, its porch light on. It was well manicured, painted light blue, flowerpots hanging from the porch.

The lights in the dilapidated house across the street, and down a short dirt road, were all off except for one dim light in the back. The curtains were closed. The front porch tilted. There were broken-down cars in the front yard, a lopsided trailer in the back, stacks of wood, and piles of trash and junk.

The police officers hid the cruiser down the road, behind a grove of trees. Nick parked in back of their car.

I didn't wait. I clambered out of the truck and slid through the shadows to the house. Nick and the police officers ordered me to stop, to get back in the truck. I didn't listen, because I had to get to Valerie. It was primal sister pull. That faint *yes* made me think she was dying or believed she was going to die. That the Bartons or one of their sewer-dwelling friends had her made that a distinct possibility.

I scrambled down low, hiding behind hollowed-out cars, a refrigerator, and a metal shed as I moved toward the house. Darting through the shadows came second nature to me, as if I were back in Moscow, after pickpocketing someone, and I needed to escape, quick as could be.

Nick, the officers, and Ellie were behind me. I searched for a cellar window, a slit near the ground that would have allowed

Valerie to peek out and see the address of the house across the street.

I'm here, I told Valerie. *Where are you? Valerie?* Was she hurt? Was she dead now? "Valerie!" I whispered, as loud as I dared.

"Toni!" A faint voice. "Toni!"

Relief swept through me as I hugged the edge of the house, Nick, the police officers, and Ellie right behind me. Several bricks had been pushed out around a six-inch opening next to the ground. I knelt and peered into the darkness.

"Valerie," I whispered. "Are you okay?"

"Yes. No. Toni," she whimpered. "They're coming back."

"Oh, my Lord, you're bleeding." She had blood on her face and one eye was swollen shut.

"Bashed me up. It's the Barton gang."

"We're getting you out of here, Valerie," an officer said. She was very calming. "Hang on."

I put my hand through the opening and held her hand. Ellie did, too. "I love you. Everything will be fine."

The police officer behind me called for backup. The other one had her gun out and was crouched protectively in front of me. Nick was beside me.

"Car," Nick said. "Everyone down."

The headlights zoomed down the highway, too fast, swerving. Drunk, I thought. Nick pushed me down lower. Ellie flattened out on the ground. We did not let go of Valerie's hand.

One of the officers slid behind a tree, her gun gripped in both hands. The car turned, screeching, sliding, and then ground to a halt in the driveway, hard rock music blaring. Two men stumbled out of the car. They were swearing and smashed. I recognized them from the trial. Wasted away. Matted, long hair.

"Backup on the way," the police officer whispered. "Unless something happens, then we'll be going in immediately."

"Valerie," Nick said, getting his gun out and lying in front of the opening. "If the men come downstairs, I'm going to shoot them. You will need to move out of the way, i.e., onto the floor, and cover your head. Do you understand?"

"Yes." She looked at Ellie and me, tears spilling out. "Promise me."

"We will," we assured her. We knew what she was talking about: her kids.

The minutes while we waited for backup were some of the scariest of my life. We did not let go of Valerie's hand. We knew we would have to let go if those hellions came through the door, as Nick would shoot.

"I'm scared," she whispered, her voice wobbling. The men in the house turned music on. Suicide music, that's what I called that banging, clanging crap. They yelled and swore, a bottle broke, then another. I heard one of them say, "I want a crack at that bitch." Another said, "Yeah, you first then me, brother."

I saw a look of cold fury in Nick's eyes.

"Everything will be fine," I said to Valerie.

"You'll be safe, Valerie," Nick said. "I don't miss."

I heard police cars speeding down the street, but they were quiet. No sirens, no lights. They crept in. Soon the house was surrounded by police officers, Chief Crighton, and SWAT.

They burst into the home, exactly like on TV, back and front, yelling, swearing for everyone to get down, hands up, guns out. Nick stayed with us, flat on the ground, his gun pointed at the door to the cellar.

Quickly, so quickly, the police stormed into the cellar, to Valerie, held underground, no walls, no floor, only mud, beaten up. "It felt like a tomb," she told me later. "Like a tomb."

Five men were arrested. Two were passed out from drugs upstairs. They were all from the Barton family. They would spend years in jail. Kidnapping and assaulting a prosecutor does not go over well. Maybe their cellmate would be their kin, Tyler Barton. It could be a family thing.

Valerie, "shaken but not stirred," as she told me later, was fine.

As fine as one can be after being hit and kidnapped in the parking lot of her own parents' restaurant, driven in the trunk of a car to the country, and shoved into a wet, dirty cellar in preparation for being attacked later.

"They were waiting for two other members of the gang to arrive and then my fate was signed, sealed, and delivered," she said to us later that night at my parents' home. She had been to the hospital, had six stitches on her forehead. She did not want the kids to see her, so a neighbor was at her house, Kai by her side. The rest of the family was coming over. Her ordeal was already on the news.

My parents were ashen, holding hands. I held Nick's hand.

"It is the language of sisters then," my father said.

"Again," my mother said. "It is from the Sabonis family line, through our genes, through our widow's peaks."

Then my poor mother burst into tears. My father followed her lead.

I had called Dmitry from the hospital to tell him what had happened to Valerie.

"I'm coming," he asked.

"Where are you?"

"I'm home."

"What do you mean, you're home?"

"I'm at my house."

I was flummoxed. "What house?"

"The one I'm renting."

"Wait. You mean . . . you didn't leave? You're not traveling?"

"No."

"Oh. My."

"I'm home now, Toni. I'm staying with you all for a while. You're my home."

I couldn't even speak.

"You're crying aren't you, Toni?"

I still couldn't speak.

"You're making that hiccupping sound you do when you cry. I'll be there in five minutes. See you, sister."

* * *

The Kozlovsky family is deafening. Valerie, kidnapped, beaten? Oh, woe on *all* our lives. It was an emotional Kozlovsky night. My father said a long, long prayer of thanks for saving Valerie, then we all had a small glass of wine to calm our fried nerves.

Okay. We all had two small glasses.

And maybe a shot of Russian vodka.

It had been a bad night!

"To family. To the Kozlovskys." We clinked glasses.

"And may the Barton family be locked away in jail for years," my mother said, in Russian. "And may the Kozlovskys live with love forever. We are good people."

"I'll drink to that," Dmitry said.

We clinked the ol' shot glasses again. Bottoms up.

Dmitry and I sat on my deck in my chaise lounges for a long time the next day. I apologized repeatedly. He quickly told me, "Stop, Toni. It's okay. I forgive you."

"You do?"

"Yes, I do. You're my sister. You kept a secret you were told to keep." He ran a hand through his curls. "I wish you had told me, but I understand. I can't be angry at you, I love you too much, and in every single other area of my life, you have been my best friend. I don't want to lose my best friend."

Forgiveness is healing. Down to the deepest part of who I am I was relieved to have it from Dmitry. It was humbling, but I wouldn't forgive myself for a long time. I should have told him. It would have helped him to unravel his past, a thread pulling out. I had done Dmitry wrong, and I'd known it for years.

It had been ingrained: *Never tell, Antonia, never tell.*

"I understand now why Mama and Papa kept my real identity from me," Dmitry said. "They're right. It's been..." He paused. "It's taken a lot not to bust out of my own head and leave for Antarctica, knowing my own reality. I have the genetics of a psychopath. My biological father murdered my mother. Our papa killed him, killed Rurik, for killing his father and torturing him in jail. That's my past. No wonder Mama and Papa wanted to keep it from me. I get it."

"You have the truth now."

"And it would probably be easier to swallow a mountain than grasp this truth." We sat in our silence for a while. Dixie, the great blue heron I loved, took off, so strong and graceful. Mr. and Mrs. Quackenbusch climbed up on the deck and quacked at me. I finally saw Anonymous flapping overhead. It had been weeks. I was glad he was still alive.

Dmitry lay back on my chaise longue. "If you make me some of your brownies with extra chocolate chips it will help things between us, though."

I made him the brownies with extra chocolate chips. It was the least I could do.

That night I disentangled myself from Nick's arms, wrapped a blanket around myself, and sat on the top deck of my tugboat. I thought about the guilt that had traipsed through life with me, like rocks that were tied to a rope that was tied to my waist.

I couldn't live like this anymore. I had pickpocketed to help feed my destitute family in Moscow when I was a child and my father was in jail. I was caught and jailed. My mother was attacked. That was the fault of a broken system that did not provide enough food for their people and a Communist state that did not protect its people. In fact, it endangered them.

I had kept a secret that my parents told me to keep. Dmitry's true past, with his lunatic father and the murder of his mother, was heinous. My parents had a rational reason to keep it from him.

And Marty? I had been a devoted, loving wife. Even when I started sleeping with Nick, it had been twenty-one emotionally ruined months since he died. There was nothing wrong with what I did. There is nothing wrong with what I'm doing now, and how I am in love with Nick.

I told myself to say good-bye to all the rocks filled with guilt that were drowning me.

I was done with the rocks.

25

Moscow, Russia

When Ellie, Dmitry, Valerie, and I arrived in Moscow, we flew in.

We were not being throttled by fear as we were when we escaped the last night we were here, our father beaten, Dmitry not speaking.

We walked out of the airport and hailed a cab.

We did not have to pick anyone's pockets for money for food.

We went to our hotel, elegant and safe, off a side street. There was heat, hot water.

We did not have to stand in long lines for bread.

We were all healthy. Our mother was not stricken with pneumonia, her lungs crowded with disease, our father upside-down in a prison.

We walked the streets in warm clothes. We did not have holes in our coats or in our shoes. Moscow was not as bleak as I remembered it from my childhood. The streets were cleaner, brighter. There were more shops and stores, more color, more life, skyscrapers and well-tended parks, Old-World traditional and incredible modern architecture.

We walked with our heads up, not down, trying to be invisible, always ready to hide around concrete buildings, grasping a stolen wallet. We were Americans. We were visitors. Valerie is a prosecuting attorney. I'm a reporter. Ellie owns a pillow business and Dmitry is a well-loved writer and blogger.

It was here, in Red Square, near St. Basil's Cathedral, that I found out I was talented at pickpocketing.

I knew how to slip my fingers in, soft and smooth, like moving silk. I was lightning quick, a sleight of hand, a twist of the wrist. I was adept at disappearing, at hiding, at waiting, until it was safe to run, to escape.

I was a whisper, drifting smoke, a breeze.

I was a little girl, in the frigid cold of Moscow, under the looming shadow of the Soviet Union, my coat too small, my shoes too tight, my stomach an empty shell.

I was desperate. We were desperate.

Survival stealing, my sisters and I called it.

Had we not stolen, we might not have survived.

But we did. We survived.

We left as Kozlovskys and Kozlovskayas and returned as Kozlovskys, but there was a world of difference between the two sets of people.

My sisters and I and Dmitry held hands in the middle of Red Square. Sometimes it is hard to believe you have come so far.

We had one more place to visit before we headed out of Moscow.

"I can't believe we're here," Ellie said, staring up at our apartment building. It looked the same—drab, dull, old.

"Doesn't feel like home, does it?" I asked.

My mouth dropped as three little girls opened the door and headed down the stairs.

"Would you look at that," Valerie whispered.

The girls were poor. We could see ourselves in them. The sleeves of their coats were too short. One girl's boots were obviously too big, and she tripped over them, her sister pulling her back up. The other girl had tape over the front of her tennis shoe.

They held hands as they headed down the street. Their mother leaned out the window, five floors up, from our apartment, the fourth window over from the left, and watched them, her hair up in a red kerchief. She could not have been more than thirty, but she looked fifty, her face worn, her dress faded.

"This is the strangest thing I've ever seen," I said. "I . . . I . . ." I didn't know what else to say.

The mother's body sagged.

We entered the building when another person came out and held the door for us. We went up five floors. We didn't trust the elevator. It still seemed ragged, but there were improvements. There were lights on the ceiling now. The ancient floor had been changed out to tile. But it was still depressing inside.

I took out my wallet when we were in front of our old apartment. Ellie, Dmitry, and Valerie took out theirs. We put the rubles under the mat, half sticking out. I nodded at my siblings and they walked away and turned the corner. I rang the doorbell, scooted off. My skills at disappearing quickly were still sharp.

I watched from around the corner, with my siblings, as the mother opened the door, looked around, her brow creasing in confusion, then down.

We will never, ever forget the expression on her face when she saw that money, or the way she sank to her knees, grabbed it, shoved it into the top of her shirt. The relief, the gratefulness.

That could have been our mother, right there. Exhausted. Poor. Watching her girls disappear around the corner and worried each second until they came home.

The next day, we took a drive out of the city, hours into the country, a prison lurking like an avenging gargoyle up in the hills.

We stopped and got out of the car, holding our coats close to us, the wind chilly.

"That's it," Dmitry said.

We stared up at the place where our father and grandfather had been imprisoned and tortured for a long time, and where our grandfather had died.

"May all the men who hurt innocent men die slow and suffocating deaths," Valerie said. "May their wives and children leave them, may they be alone at the end, may they be paralyzed as they watch maggots invade their bodies."

"Wow," I said. "Impressive."

"Nice one," Dmitry said.

"Vindictive," Ellie said. "I like it."

We drove through to the next village. We knew we were close to Dmitry's house, based on the directions our father had given us.

"Dmitry," he said, in Russian, "this is where you spent the first few years of your life, three or four, we were never exactly sure how old you are. You will find your mother's grave east of the house, next to a large rock. Rurik told me he walked into the rising sun. There is a cement slab there. You will find your father's grave in the forest, about thirty yards in. Walk directly toward the woods from the kitchen window. On top of his grave I piled stones to keep the animals out. Perhaps I should not have added the rocks. Let the jackals get him. It may be there still, it may not."

The village was small, one of those places where everyone knew everyone, so we stuck out, four Americans who all spoke fluent Russian.

The owner of one of only three local restaurants, about sixty-five years old and stocky, saw Dmitry, smiled, spread his arms out to give him a hug, then stopped. He seemed confused, stared hard, then said, "You look like a young man who lives here, Ruslan Fyodorova. The resemblance..." He shook his head, "Come, sit down, sit down. Welcome."

We ordered chicken Kiev—to test it against our mother's—cold kvass soup, and cake soaked in liquors, frosted with chocolate icing. We chatted with the owner, Kirill, his wife, Lubov, and three neighbors who were there for a beer, while our meal was prepared. We all sat at the same table.

"Ah, you look like the Fyodorova brothers," one of the neighbors said to Dmitry.

"When you walked in, I almost said, 'Hello, Ruslan,'" Lubov said. "So unusual. You look exactly like him. You are from America, then? Now, why have you returned to Russia? When people go, they usually do not return."

Dmitry told them he had lived in a house outside the village as a little boy until his adoptive father came and took him with us to America. He left out many details.

The sudden quiet in that restaurant could only be comparable to a roar.

Lubov was the first to recover. "You lived here as a little boy until your adoptive father came and took you to America?"

"What," Kirill said, still appearing stunned, "was your mother's name?"

"Her name was Nelly. My father's name was Rurik Nikonov."

The silence was so electrified, I could almost hear the sizzle. No one moved. One person dropped his glass, and it shattered on the stone floor. Still no one moved.

"You are Dmitry Nikonov," Lubov said.

"Yes. But my name is Dmitry Kozlovsky now."

"I cannot believe this," Kirill whispered. "I cannot. Quick, quick, Stepan, go and get Lucya and Nestor and the boys." Stepan, a man about thirty, eyes wide, sprinted out of the restaurant.

"All these years," Kirill said, his eyes overflowing with tears. "Lucya, Nestor, they will be so happy."

"What?" Dmitry said. "Who is Lucya? Who is Nestor?"

Lubov was aghast. "You do not know?"

"I know nothing," Dmitry said. "Nothing."

We would soon know everything.

"Your mother was my younger sister," Lucya Fyodorova said, hugging Dmitry one more time. "I loved Nelly with my whole heart."

Lucya—gold hair with a few white streaks, high cheekbones, classically beautiful—had taken one look at Dmitry in the restaurant and almost fainted. Nestor, her husband, held her up, his face shocked, her four sons fretting over her and shooting confused glances Dmitry's way.

Dmitry was an exact replica of Lucya and Nestor's sons—Ruslan, Rodian, Andon, Artur. If you were to line him up with those four, you would not be able to tell which one was not a full sibling. All blond curls. Green eyes. Tall. Lanky. Same high cheekbones, same friendly smile.

When everyone recovered, and we were all introduced to one another, Nestor invited us over to their home across the street and down the road, small but comfy, a fire soon burning, candles lit, a huge wood table that Nestor had made in the center of the room.

Lucya did exactly what my mother did. She fed us, though we had just eaten, ordering her husband and sons around, who obediently did as told until a meal was on the table.

"Did I used to call you Aunt Lu Lu?" Dmitry asked.

"Yes!" she cried. "You did. You couldn't say Lucya."

"And did I have a little white dog?"

"Yes. You did. We called her Snow."

"What happened to her?"

Lucya hesitated. "Your father killed her. Your mother told me. He was trying to scare her. Threw Snow against the wall."

"I remember that. I remember Snow not moving."

"I wanted to kill Rurik when I found out," Nestor said.

We all sat in that bleak, horrifying moment.

"And did you . . ."—he turned to his uncle Nestor—"did you carve me wooden ducks?"

"Yes, my boy." Nestor, burly, weathered face, gentled. "Yes, I did. I loved you. You played with those ducks all the time."

"I remember," Dmitry said, his face lighting up. "Were there were red trucks, too—"

"Ours!" his cousins Rodian and Ruslan said. "We played with them together."

"My nephew, my sister's son," Lucya said, still trembling, tearful. "So long gone. Oh, today is one of the best days of my life. I have never stopped believing that you would return. I felt you." She pointed to her heart. "Here. I felt you. What happened, what do you remember? Where is Rurik, do you know?"

Ah, now that took a lot of time to explain.

* * *

"Rurik was a criminal," Nestor spat out.

"The devil," Lucya said. "He wanted my sister from the second he saw her. He pursued her, flirted with her. She had no idea the type of man he was. She was young and innocent, only nineteen when she married him, pressured by our parents and, Dmitry, pregnant with you. She had nowhere to turn when he started to beat her."

I could not help but wonder if Rurik had raped her. I'll bet he did. Trapped her into marriage through rape and pregnancy.

"Our parents never would have supported a divorce. They thought it was a sin. Our father drank heavily, and sometimes he took a hand to our mother. I suppose he didn't think that was a sin." Her mouth twisted, bitter. "They were unhelpful, unkind. Nestor and I begged Nelly to come live with us, we told her we would protect her, and you, but she didn't come. She was afraid of Rurik, afraid of what he would do to her, or to you, Dmitry. He had threatened to take you from her. Rurik thought Nelly was having an affair. He told her he would kill her if she did.

"There were weeks when we did not see her that winter. We were buried in snow. They lived about forty-five minutes from here. I was busy with the children, Nestor with work, but we drove out to check on her one day when we thought Rurik would be at work. We had heard that he had gone to a bar and told everyone that my sister had had an affair and left town. He told everyone he was glad she was gone because he wouldn't want to be with a slut. My sister would not have cheated on him. I knew he was lying. I was so scared for her, scared for what I would find.

"Oh, the blood," she moaned, hand over her mouth. "I will never forget. The home had been cleaned, but not well, and we saw it. Blood in the wood. Blood in their bedroom. Blood on the hearth. We called the police, and they came, but no one could find you, Dmitry, no one could find Rurik. We believed that he'd killed Nelly, kidnapped you, and left."

"I would have been there when he killed her," Dmitry said. "I have always remembered blood in blond hair. I remember blood on the floor. I remember this dark shadow. I remember scream-ing, it must have been her. I remember saying when I was a child that my mother was in the woods. Now I know it's where he buried her. My father told me that Rurik told him."

"Rurik should have been locked up in the jail, not working as a guard." Nestor's face was murderous. "He was more of a criminal than most of the men there. How did your father kill Rurik?"

"He used his own father's knife. From the war," Dmitry said. "It was personal, for revenge, a way for his own father to be a part of killing the man who tortured and killed him."

There was no need to hide the truth when we started talking. Dmitry's family would not go to the authorities. They were glad that my father had killed Rurik. There was nothing to be gained except peace in knowing that Rurik had died years ago.

"Bless that man," Lucya said, her husband and sons nodding. "But why did he take you? It broke me, not having my sister, not having my nephew. I missed you, Dmitry. We all grieved for you both."

"My father told me that he knew I would freeze out there alone in the house, that I would die, but that he couldn't bring me to the village, as then it would raise suspicion. We were leav-ing the Soviet Union immediately and he couldn't risk it, couldn't risk his daughters, his wife, not getting out. He had been warned by the KGB not to try to leave Moscow. My mother, they be-lieved, was soon to be arrested for her outspokenness against the government, about her Christian faith, so my father took me with him. He said he thought about dropping me off at an or-phanage in Moscow but couldn't because he knew my life would have been ruined."

"Ruined without question," Nestor said. "The orphanages are abusive. Desolate."

"My father said he has felt guilty his whole life, that he knew I probably had other family who would miss me. Please." Dmitry put up his hands. "I know it will be impossible to forgive my fa-ther for taking me, but he didn't know what else to do. He was panicked. He had been jailed, he had been tortured by Rurik, he was trying to get his family out alive. He had a window to escape through, and he took it. He saved his family, knowing he was causing grief to another. If he had more time, would he have done the same? No. I speak on behalf of my father, please try to forgive him."

"I forgive your father," Lucya said. "If you had lived with Rurik, he might well have killed you, too. If not, you would have been motherless and a victim of his abuse. My grief on losing you, and my sister, has never ended, but you had a better life in America than here, and now you are home. Tell me, darling Dmitry, tell us about your parents, your life in America . . . you are so fortunate to have these three lovely sisters . . ."

And he did. Dmitry's family loved his blog, and they treated Valerie, Ellie, and me like well-loved family.

Later, we all went to Dmitry's childhood home, two cars. We drove down a winding street, then onto gravel, then dirt, to get to the home, small, tucked away, in the woods, isolated. For a young mother beaten by her husband, a sadist, it would have been her prison.

The home slouched on the land, rustic, ugly. I felt sorry for Dmitry's young mother. Only twenty-two or twenty-three when she died and she had to live here. The roof was now caving in on one side, the paint was chipping, the shutters hanging haphazardly.

"Dmitry, the door is blue," I said.

"Yes, it is." He told his family how a blue door kept coming to him in his dreams.

The door unlocked with a key that Nestor had, but he and Dmitry and Ruslan had to lean a shoulder into it to get it open. Dust fell down from the rafters. The floors squeaked. The mice scurried away. A larger animal skittered on out. I hoped it was only a cat. We all entered the cramped, bleak house. It was like entering a tomb.

Inside, everything was covered in dust. It was eerie, unearthly quiet. If there had been anything, ever, of value, which was unlikely, it was long gone.

Dmitry stood in the center of the living area, turning to see it all. His eyes landed on something. He crossed the room, dusted it off. It was the blue box he'd told us about. There was a woman in a dress from the 1890s or so, a parasol, a carriage.

"There she is," Ellie said. "It wasn't your imagination, Dmitry."

"It's the box you have seen so many times," Valerie said.

He opened it, and inside was a brooch. It was the red and purple butterfly that he remembered. He sniffled. "I remember playing with this butterfly, holding it."

"I gave your mother the box and the butterfly for her birthday," Lucya said.

Next to the blue ceramic box were the carved wooden ducks. Dmitry held them in his hands. "Thank you, Nestor."

Nestor nodded. "It was my pleasure, Dmitry, to make those for you."

Dmitry didn't even bother wiping his tears, and Rodian handed him a handkerchief.

"Thank you, Rodian."

"You are welcome, friend."

Dmitry held the ducks, reverently, one by one, a tear dropping on each.

Andon and Artur each put a hand on his shoulders.

"Take them," Lucya said. "Take the ducks, the box, the butterfly."

"Really? Are you sure?"

"Yes," Lucya said. "They are yours, Dmitry. Everything in here is yours. Not ours."

"We couldn't take anything," Nestor said. "It was too painful. It belongs to you, Dmitry. These are your mother's things."

In the corner of a back bedroom was the rocking horse. "I've seen this rocking horse in my mind so many times." He turned to Nestor. "Did you?"

Nestor nodded. "I made it for you. I made one for all my boys. You loved it. You were a loving boy. Our fifth son."

"Thank you, Nestor, Lucya." He hugged them both, hugged his cousins, everyone emotional and sniffling. "Was there a garden?"

"Oh yes," Lucya said, running her hands over her wet cheeks. "Your mother had one every year. The soil here, the temperature, it's tough to grow in. But she planted potatoes, cabbage, tomatoes, kale."

"Were there beets?"

"Yes, but you wouldn't eat them. Your father"—she spat on the floor—"when you were a baby, my sister told me that he forced you to eat them, one after another, until you threw up. She had a bruise on her face the next day. She was crying." Lucya stopped, unable to go on.

"And potatoes. I hate potatoes," Dmitry said. "It's the strangest thing. I don't know why."

"I do," Nestor said. "Rurik threw them at you when you wouldn't stop crying as a baby. He knocked you off your feet."

"I wish that my father had come to kill Rurik before Rurik killed my mother."

"Us too," Lucya said, taking Dmitry's face in her hands. "Us too."

We followed our father's directions to the graves. We walked east into the woods. We had to walk a long way. No wonder the grave had never been found. We found a large rock. At first we found nothing more than that. No cement slab. But the earth shifts, weather changes the landscape, and there it was, overgrown, buried under inches of dirt, further than expected from the rock. Lucya found it.

We stood around the slab and held hands, all of us. Dmitry, me, Ellie, Valerie, Dmitry's aunt and uncle, his four cousins. Lucya said a prayer, then said, sobbing, "Nelly, Nelly . . . sister, see who has returned. Your beloved son, Dmitry. He is back."

Nestor cried, too. Then we all cried, hugged each other, for Nelly, for Dmitry, for his Russian family.

Dmitry said, "I'm home, Mama. I am home." We let Dmitry have his time alone with her, the gold locket in his hands. When he rejoined us, he was sadder, pale, eyes puffy, and his cousins surrounded him, arms along his shoulders.

We found Rurik's grave. We had to return to the house and then walk back into the woods, a straight line from the kitchen window. We found the rocks, still piled up.

Nestor swore, furious. Lucya picked up a rock and threw it at the grave and swore, too.

Dmitry said, "I hate you, Rurik, for killing my mother. You are not my father, you never have been."

Nestor indicated that Lucya, my sisters, and I were to leave. We didn't understand why, but then a quick peek back told us.

All the men were peeing on Rurik's grave.

That night we stayed with Dmitry's family. We had dinner. We talked and heard all about Nelly. They gave Dmitry photos of her to take. We sang songs. At five in the morning, we finally went to sleep under blankets on the floor of their home. We insisted on buying the groceries and making lunch for Dmitry's family the next day. My mother would have been proud of the feast we made.

We hugged Dmitry's family good-bye, tears blending face to face. There were promises of a return visit, soon, and we left. Dmitry's treasures from his home—the box with the woman with the parasol, the butterfly, the wooden ducks, a red truck, the rocking horse, which we would have to ship out—in the car, where they would soon find a new home, with Dmitry, where they always should have been.

We had dinner with Gavriil and Bogdan and their parents, Stas and Irina Bessonov, in Moscow. It was as if we had never been away from each other, except Gavriil and Bogdan were wealthy, which was unsurprising. There had been accusations of their being in the Russian Mafia, but it also appeared they had normal businesses in gas, oil, and minerals. Each had four children. The children were charming. We ate at Bogdan's house. Formal. White linens. Crystal. Expensive wine.

We told Gavriil and Bogdan's children about our exploits as children—although not the pickpocketing. We told them about

Gavriil and Bogdan saving Valerie, how their grandparents gave us food and cash. Stas and Irina said, "It was nothing."

We laughed and laughed.

We thanked Stas and Irina for bribing and buying our father out of prison.

"You saved his life," I said

Irina waved her hand. "We loved your parents."

Stas said, "I am glad that you all left and built a new life, although we have missed you. From our family to yours, it has been a long friendship."

"A friendship that calls for more wine," Bogdan said.

"To the Bessonovs and the Kozlovskys," Gavriil said. "To our friendship. May we all have long and happy lives."

We cheered to that.

We had one more thing to do in Russia. Gavriil and Bogdan helped us. There may have been a bribe or a threat involved. Some things you don't need to know.

Two days later we were on a plane leaving Moscow.

Peace, finally, for Dmitry.

And for our mother.

We met at my parents' house, in the kitchen, on a rainy afternoon, the rainbow tiles a welcome reprieve from the weather. They always reminded my mother that she was no longer in the Soviet Union. She had made her chocolate fudge cookies and coffee strong enough to give me a hairy chest. The cookies were on the train station table.

My mother held in her trembling hands the paper that we brought to her, stamped by a Russian prison.

It told her officially what she had always wanted to know.

Leonid Sabonis. Entered February 18, 1984. Death of natural causes May 3, 1984.

The date of Leonid's death was the day he came to her and told her he was not going to last the night.

"Natural causes," my mother snapped, a look of such thundering rage coming over her face, I thought she'd scream. "I hate them. I curse them. They murdered my brother."

My father hugged her. "Svetlana, I have spent years of my life, like you, missing your brother, missing our parents. The grief and anger has been a constant for both of us. But we must let it go. We cannot let the grief win, we cannot let bitterness win, we cannot let the KGB or the Communists win for one more minute. They win every time they bring us to our knees."

She nodded. "You are right, Alexei. I have cried a million tears for Leonid already. I have raged enough already."

All of the Kozlovskys came for dinner that night. We lit candles for Leonid. We turned down the lights, and my mother talked about Leonid, then Uncle Yuri and Aunt Polina spoke, followed by Uncle Sasho, Uncle Vladan, and my father. We turned on his favorite piece, Rachmaninoff's Concerto No. 2 in C Minor, and listened to it, as if Uncle Leonid were there with us. We took a moment to raise our glasses to Leonid. My father said, "To you, Leonid, my brother-in-law who became my brother, my friend, we bless you, we will see you again one day."

We clinked glasses.

Then we did what Kozlovskys do best.

We ate, we laughed, we had a couple of shots of vodka. Leonid would have approved.

26

〜

"The other day Ailani called me from school," Valerie said, as she sewed a pillow at Ellie's house. Her pillow was for a young boy. It would have a green dinosaur on a blue background.

"And?" I said. I was making a furry pillow in the shape of a blue teddy bear. It would have a huge, pink plaid bow around its neck and paws made from leather.

"Did she get in trouble again for detailing a crime scene?" Ellie asked. Her pillow was a patchwork quilt in blues, greens, and browns.

"No. She heard Koa. Koa had crawled up on the bookshelf when he was at home with Kai, and the bookshelf tumbled down. He cut his head open."

"And Ailani heard that?"

"She said he told her, in her head, 'Blood on my face.'"

Wow.

"It's the Sabonis line," I said.

"Through our widow's peaks," Ellie said.

"And it's on to the next generation," Valerie said.

"Are we ready to cart this load of pillows to the children's hospital soon?" Ellie asked, later that night. "I got a call from the director today...."

You Are Toast Day started with a bang.

I could feel the buzz at the newspaper when I walked to the

third floor. People were laughing, chuckling, staring at computers, and pointing.

"What is it?" I asked Ricki. She was in a red wraparound dress and black heels.

"This is the reason I get up in the morning." She put her hands out, palms up, her rings glittering under the lights. "For glorious moments such as this. Ball-banging moments. Rip-your-spleen-open-laughing moments. Momentous moments on a grand, gossipy scale that resonate with you forever."

"What's going on?"

Shantay was laughing so hard, she was bent over. Zoe was leaning over her, cackling like a witch.

"Look here, my friend, feast your eyes. I believe you know these fine feathered people." Ricki sat down at her computer. "Behold YouTube."

I pulled up a chair. "What in heck . . . is that? . . . Yes, it is, isn't it? . . . Oh, this is ripe. . . . There's another video? Such a surprise . . . a *hilarious* surprise. . . . Who knew the truth about those two?"

So that was it. You Are Toast Day.

I started to laugh. Ricki laughed, too, then laughing Zoe hobbled over, her legs crossed, followed by laughing Shantay, who handed me a Kleenex for my laugh-tears. I crossed my legs and had to run to the bathroom. Ricki was right behind me.

"I'll need a diaper to get through today," she yelled, still laughing. "A diaper!"

Lindy had told us "not to worry," repeatedly, that she had Tweedle Dum Dee and Tweedle Dee Dum "handled" and the dock would not close.

She certainly did have things . . . *handled.*

Tweedle Dee Dum and Tweedle Dum Dee, otherwise known as Shane and Jerald Shrock, were "new" clients of Lindy's. She had propositioned them both at a bar they frequented. They came to her houseboat and told her what they wanted. She told us that they came in disguise, as we would have recognized the two Tweedles.

Tweedle Dee Dum, for some reason, wanted to act out his fantasy of being a woman with long blond hair, a velvety red dress, and sparkly red heels. He was heavy, paunchy, balding.

He wanted to be spanked and ordered around. Lindy dressed up as a dominatrix with brown hair and tons of makeup. She was unrecognizable as they acted out his fantasy. She filmed him dancing, kicking up his heels, and twirling. He didn't know the camera was up and rollin'.

Tweedle Dum Dee had a fantasy of wanting to dress up like a medieval knight. Lindy was supposed to be a young male knight. She dressed up in the outfit he brought, hair tucked beneath a hat—as a young man. They jousted with their swords, they rode their "horses," they fought in battle.

The videos landed on YouTube with an untraceable URL, or something like that. Lindy used another client who was a computer whiz to set it up. She also had him add entertaining music and songs.

When the brothers called her, out of their minds with humiliation, she told them that if they didn't back off the dock project that she would post the other videos she had made of them in different costumes, including the Scottish warrior and the pirate.

The brothers made threats of impending lawsuits. She referred them to the contracts she had them sign, and of which they had copies. She had had her attorney slip in a clause about how Tweedle Dee Dum and Tweedle Dum Dee gave her permission to film them and to "use the film and their names in advertisements, marketing, or in any public domain, including Facebook, Instagram, and YouTube." Lindy stripped while they were "studying the contract," and they signed it.

Tweedle Dee Dum had a poor kick and was an unattractive woman.

Tweedle Dum Dee could not joust. No princess would ever want him now.

The brothers were toast, hence, You Are Toast Day.

*   *   *

"You Are Toast Day was today. Did you see it?"

"I did," Nick said.

I rarely called him at work. I couldn't say anything more. We both laughed until I was making hyena-like sounds, which made us laugh harder.

I saw Ricki laughing again, hobbling back to the bathroom. "I'm going to have to run home for fresh panties!" she yelled.

Nick heard it and cracked up. I made the hyena sound again.

I called Lindy next. All I could do was laugh. She said, "I waited until you came back from Russia. I didn't want you to miss out on You Are Toast Day."

"You're a true friend," I gasped out.

"So are you, Toni. My best friend."

My hyena laugh and I hung up.

That night I went to Lindy's place to celebrate You Are Toast Day. I was still laughing thinking of the slumlord man-woman in a red dress and a knight who could not joust.

I was not the first one there. Vanessa and Charles had already arrived. Jayla and Beth were there, both in scrubs. Daisy was there in a blue hat with daisies around the rim. Take-out dinners from a local seafood restaurant arrived, from Georgie and Skippy, aka Slash and Slugger.

Nick walked in, strong and lovable, and I hugged him. Lindy was smiling. She was wearing a pink blouse and brown skirt and a new pair of glasses.

"I don't think we have to worry about the dock shutting down," Charles said.

We cheered to that, glasses clinking.

"Splendid work, Lindy," Vanessa said. "Although"—she tipped her head down and glared—"I don't want you to do this anymore." She waved her hand.

"There are other jobs that you would enjoy," Charles said, "and are better suited to your intellect and your ambitions."

"Safer," Jayla said.

"More interesting," Beth said.

"This job needs to stop," Nick said, his tone brooking no argument from her, "before you're killed."

"I quit. I'm going to school to become a librarian. Being around books makes me happy. I like the smell of them."

We cheered.

"Being around whales makes me happy," Daisy said, her daisy hat bopping. "Being with my river family makes me happy, too. I love you."

"We love you, too, Daisy," we said.

"Being around shrimp and steak makes me happy," Charles said. "Shall we eat while it's hot? And thanks to Slugger and Slash." Charles cleared his throat. "I mean, uh, thanks to Georgie and Skippy."

"Thanks to my sons, naughty boys!" Daisy said. "They took my bullets out of my condom box."

Those naughty boys. We ate shrimp and steak on Lindy's houseboat, the sun went down, and we celebrated. Jayla did a spot-on imitation of Tweedle Dee Dum in his red dress dancing like an electrified pig, and Beth was clearly talented in her saber skills. "My name is Tweedle Dum Dee, and I'm a knight," she declared. "See me fence." She put the "sword," a small stick, between her legs, up by her crotch.

We about died laughing.

Daisy sang at the edge of the dock that night, the moon in front of her, high and white, like a ball dropped from the clouds, an invisible string holding it in place. She wore her whale hat. I had never seen it before. It was blue. She'd sewn a blue tail and flippers. Googly eyes. A yellow daisy was sewn onto its head.

Nick and I sat together in my chaise lounge. I leaned against his chest, his arms wrapped around me as Daisy sang "You Are My Sunshine"; "Yesterday," by the Beatles; and "Crocodile Rock," by Elton John. She finished off with "Hallelujah" and "Jesus Loves Me."

Every note soared into the sky, waltzing or crashing or busting along, depending on the tune, a story in itself.

I could see why Skippy and Georgie couldn't sleep at night until their mother had sung them a lullaby.

At the end of a song about a mother's love for her son, she shouted, "Whale, whale, where are you? Laughing with the fish, dancing with the dolphins, into the deep blue, I'll come and visit you."

We heard her footsteps down the dock, then she opened the door to her houseboat and stepped inside.

The Tweedles agreed not to close the dock if Lindy took down the videos. They agreed to all repairs. They agreed not to build any slumlord apartments near us, or anywhere else, and to make repairs in the existing slumlord apartments. "Or else."

The videos came down.

The next day, by coincidence, a court date was set for all of their slumlord crimes. The Tweedles' callous recklessness had finally caught up with them.

The Tweedles' wives filed for divorce.

Rumor had it that both men were moving to Idaho.

Skippy pounded on my door at seven-thirty in the morning on Saturday.

Nick flew up and was at the door, his jeans yanked on, before I even made it to the stairs.

"Momma's gone," Skippy panted.

I skidded up behind Nick in my socks. "What?"

"Momma's gone." Skippy had his hands in his hair. He was pulling it. "I came by to check on her this mornin'. Last night Georgie was here, and he said Momma was makin' up rhymes about whales, talkin' to her whale hat. He got her into bed about ten, stayed to make sure she was asleep until midnight, then went home."

"Maybe she's on a walk," I said.

"She likes to walk," Nick said. "I see her often."

"I know, I know, but the problem is"—Skippy said, almost hyperventilating—"that she left all of her daisy hats on her dresser stand. She has twenty-one. I counted. All there today, but her whale hat with the daisy on it isn't there."

I felt cold. Sick. "That's not right."

"I know, I know!" Skippy, in his expensive clothes, shined shoes, a face that had been hit more than once, started to cry. "It's not right."

"We'll help you," Nick said, a hand on his shoulder.

"I'm coming, Skippy." I ran up the stairs, Nick behind me, and we threw on clothes, then ran back out. Skippy was on the phone, crying harder, talking to Georgie. Then he said something that I'm sure neither Episcopo son has ever said. "Call the cops, Georgie! Call the cops!"

Everyone in the marina was soon searching for Daisy. We covered the dock, people's boats and homes, the streets above, the neighborhoods and shops beyond that. People drove downtown, following the route that Daisy always took.

Charles and Vanessa took their boat out, as did others, including Lindy, who had the most expensive boat. She'd named it *Hookin' It*. The police were there, on the dock and out on boats in the water. Nick and I went out on *Sanchez One*, knowing the futility of it all, but trying anyhow.

Daisy was eighty-five years old. If she was in the water, she was long gone.

And that's what it ended up being. Daisy was long gone.

We searched all day long, into the night. She was on the news. She was on our online newspaper immediately. I wrote the article. She was listed as missing. We hoped that she had taken a walk and simply gotten lost, but I knew that wasn't true.

Nick and I stood at the end of the dock at two that morning holding hands. It had been a long, long day. Jayla and Beth were there beside us, as were Vanessa and Charles, and Lindy. Georgie sat on the dock, his feet in the water, and cried. Skippy had his arm slung over Georgie's shoulders.

Daisy Episcopo was a ball breaker, a bar owner, a tough single mother who had kicked a man out of her house because he beat her, and raised her boys on her own. She was smart, hilarious, generous, and loyal. She was an outstanding businesswoman. She sang like a nightingale, like a Madonna, like a beer-brawling, rough-talking son of a gun.

I knew without a doubt that she had gone to talk to the whales, to take her last ride on their backs. My guess is that her mind slipped that last millimeter and she took a step off the edge of the dock, drowned quickly, her mind and body shutting down, and the river took her out to the whales in the ocean.

She had been headed for a nursing home, probably within weeks. She would have hated it. She would have felt as claustrophobic and trapped as she had when her own hard-drinking father locked her in a closet. This death was more merciful than any nursing home could ever be.

I would miss her. We would miss her.

Nick pulled me in and hugged me.

It was Skippy who started singing.

We joined him in "Amazing Grace."

Daisy would have like that.

Then we sang Elvis Presley's "Hound Dog" and followed it up with a couple of raucous drinking songs.

She would have liked that, too.

I had Nick help me. We waited until it was nighttime, stars sprinkled across the sky, a few clouds, grayish blue across the black.

"Are you sure you want to do this, Toni?"

"Yes, I'm positive."

We carried it up the dock and into his truck. We drove to the white house with the red door. We quietly grabbed the two-seater red kayak and put it to the side of the house.

I left a note. "I hope you enjoy many happy days kayaking with your family."

I knew that I could not be in that two-seater kayak again, nor did it belong with me anymore. It belonged to a new family who would make new memories.

Nick and I climbed back into the truck and drove off.

We held hands all the way home, then he spent the night on my tugboat and we made love on the red bench in the captain's wheelhouse.

"I like being the captain," Nick murmured.

"Aye, aye, handsome."

We watched for shooting stars together.

"There's one." He pointed. I hugged him close.

The next afternoon, coming home from work, I saw a huge cardboard sign in front of the white house with the red door. Clearly, the kids had painted it. There was a picture of the red kayak and four people in it, with the words, in purple, THANK YOU! WE LOVE IT!

I smiled.

27
◞

Nick took me out on his boat. We headed downriver, to the quiet part, then stopped, dropped anchor, and watched the sunset, our lounge chairs side by side. Nick was wearing a sweater and jeans, as was I. I had borrowed one of his coats.

I felt it then . . . peace. Utter peace, the sky glowing, a mammoth, moving painting.

He took my hand and held it. We didn't talk. Nature was enough. Geese flew overhead. We watched a river otter swim by. A fish jumped, then another.

When the sky was still purple, lush and soft on top, orange and yellow swirled together below, he sat up, turned toward me, and said, his voice skimming on the edges of ragged, "Toni, we need to talk."

"Okay." I tensed.

"I love you." He held my hand, and I sat up and faced him.

"I love you, too, Nick."

He leaned over, and we had a soul-touching kiss, warm and yummy. The wind drifted around us, and I relaxed into his kiss, into him. He pulled away, kissed my forehead, then leaned our heads together for a few seconds before pulling back.

"I started falling in love with you the day we met, babe. You know why I love you, I've told you a hundred times."

I smiled, kissed him again. Yes, he had.

"I remember being in my houseboat, the first time we made love, after months of trying to get you to go out with me, to be friends, and I thought to myself, 'This woman is now my life.' I meant it then, I mean it now, I'll always mean it. You are my life. I'm happy with you. I'm truly happy. I know we can be happy together, forever. I know we can grow to be a hundred together, and we'll still have things to say to each other, we'll still laugh, and we'll still be in love."

I was so happy, I almost embarrassed myself by giggling.

"I want to marry you, Toni. I would have asked you before we even made love the first time, but I knew you weren't ready and you'd bolt. But please, honey, marry me."

"Marry you." I whispered it, trying those words out for size. I waited to feel guilty, but I didn't. I felt Marty, but only for a second. I saw him smiling at me, then he was gone, into the sunset, and Nick filled my vision, and hope filled me, hope of a future with Nick, with a bunch of kids, with love.

I laughed. "I love you, Nick Sanchez."

"Is that a yes?"

"Yes. That's a yes." He smiled. I loved that face. Loved that smile. Loved that man.

"Now you have made my whole life happy. We'll get married and we'll have kids and eat bananas dipped in melted chocolate chips in the bathtub as you like to do."

"Kids, plural?"

"Yes. You've said you want kids, and so do I."

I knew that truth to my bones. "I do. Many children."

"We can have as many as you want. Pick a number. Try to keep it out of the double digits. And I hope they all look like you. If they look like me, they'll look like criminals."

We laughed. "You don't look like a criminal, Nick." I kissed him, linked my arms around his shoulders. "Okay. Maybe you do. A sexy criminal."

He pulled me up into those mongo-sized arms, and we made love on his boat, on his bed.

We really rocked that boat.

The next night, at sunset, waiting for Nick to come by so we could go to dinner at Pepper's Grill, I saw Dixie, my blue heron.

She was on the bank, blue and elegant. She turned and stared right at me for long seconds, then spread her wings out, majestic and proud. The sun was tunneling through the puffy clouds, creating that golden staircase, from here to heaven.

I watched as Dixie soared this way and that, following the wind, before climbing higher, soaring near the trees, closer and closer to the staircase. When she disappeared, I knew I would not see her again.

"Ready to go, babe?" Nick called, stepping onto my tugboat.

He was smiling, strong and gentle, protective and smart. I loved that man with all my heart. "Yes, I'm ready."

Our wedding was beautiful. I wore a red, lacy dress. We had it overlooking the river on a sunny day, then my parents closed down Svetlana's for the reception. There were about 250 people there. My family, Nick's family, his parents loving and welcoming, his uncles, aunts, cousins, our friends from high school and college, everyone from the dock, Ricki and my friends at the paper, Nick's friends from the DEA, friends from the church, the staff at Svetlana's, Ralph and Charlie, who played the piano, and Marty's parents, of course.

At my parents' invitation, Nick's mother brought her favorite Italian recipes and Nick's father brought his favorite Mexican recipes. The staff cooked the food, along with our Russian favorites. Yes, at Svetlana's Kitchen on our wedding we served something other than Russian food. Miracles do happen.

We danced. We drank wine. We had a couple shots of vodka. There were funny toasts.

Nick and I were married, and everyone had a fabulous time.

But Nick and I had the most fabulous time of all.

28

I told Ellie and Valerie, in my head.

Ellie called me immediately, joyful. "I heard that!"

She was teary, I was teary. We talked for an hour. "Congratulations, Toni."

Valerie called me. "I've been trying to get through. You were talking to Ellie, I'm sure. Anyhow, I am thrilled."

We laughed, she was teary, I was teary.

"Congratulations, big sister."

"Thank you."

Ellie, Valerie, and I met at Ellie's house later that week. We were each making two pillows.

I am having twins.

When Nick found out, he was so happy he said, "Nice work, Toni," then wiped a napkin across his eyes.

My parents were, for once, speechless.

They are not shy about crying. "We love you, Antonia. We love you, Nick. And that," my father said, "is my final word."

And so it was.

The language of sisters is a gift from our mother. It came down the Sabonis line, like genes, through our widow's peaks. From the Romanovs, to Lenin, Stalin, Germany's invasion, the siege of Leningrad, the Cold War, we have heard each other.

Passed from mother to daughter.

Father to son.
Sisters and brothers, we hear each other.
It's a gift. It's a curse.
It is us.

Living on a Tugboat, Talking About Homes

BY TONI KOZLOVSKY

I am moving. As I have told you all before, I live on a yellow tugboat in the Willamette River.

I am pregnant with twins, and morning sickness is not pleasant when waves are rolling underneath you. In fact, it feels like my stomach is being constantly shifted by an invisible, watery hand. The slight movement never bothered me before, but the storm we had last weekend was enough for this pregnant woman.

I will miss my ducks, Mr. and Mrs. Quackenbusch; the Sergeant Otts, the otters; Anonymous, the bald eagle who makes rare appearances; Maxie, the golden eagle; and Big Teeth and Big Tooth, the beavers who built a new home. I will take the memories of my blue heron, Dixie, with me. I will miss the river, the weather, the views.

I will miss my tugboat. I will miss my friends here. I will miss Jayla and Beth, Charles and Vanessa. I will miss Lindy, a true friend, and a soon-to-be librarian. I will miss Daisy, gone now, but the songs she sang on the dock will forever be with me. I will not miss Nick, my neighbor on the dock, because as I mentioned in a previous column, I married him, and we are leaving together.

It's hard to leave my tugboat. I arrived eighteen months after my husband died of cancer. I am leaving with a new husband, a strong man, a wonderful man, but a tugboat is not the place to raise babies, toddlers, or young kids.

The new owner has promised me she will let the ducks up on the deck. She will be friends with my friends here, I know it.

I have lived in Moscow, Germany, the suburbs of Portland, a tugboat, and now I'm moving to a home in the country where we will have land and space, peace and quiet.

We have bought a light blue house with a wraparound deck, a white porch swing, a view of the coast mountains and, I'm told, daisies that grow profusely in summer, all over the property.

It will be our new home, for a new life, a new family.

Wishing you well, wishing you love, wishing you a happy home.

THE LANGUAGE
OF SISTERS

Cathy Lamb

ABOUT THIS GUIDE

The suggested questions are included
to enhance your group's reading of
Cathy Lamb's *The Language of Sisters*.

DISCUSSION QUESTIONS

1. What was your overall impression of *The Language of Sisters?*

2. Toni Kozlovsky says:

   I was talented at pickpocketing.

   I knew how to slip my fingers in, soft and smooth, like moving silk. I was lightning quick, a sleight of hand, a twist of the wrist. I was adept at disappearing, at hiding, at waiting, until it was safe to run, to escape.

   I was a whisper, drifting smoke, a breeze.

   I was a little girl, in the frigid cold of Moscow, under the looming shadow of the Soviet Union, my coat too small, my shoes too tight, my stomach an empty shell.

   I was desperate. We were desperate.

   Survival stealing, my sisters and I called it.

   Had we not stolen, we might not have survived.

   But we did. We survived.

   How would you describe Toni? How did she change from the beginning of the book to the end? Would you be friends with her? Why or why not?

3. Of the three sisters, whom do you relate to most—Toni, Ellie, or Valerie? Did they go through anything in their lives that you have gone through, or are going through now? If you had to be a prosecutor, a pillow business owner, or a newspaper reporter, which would you choose?

4. Ellie Kozlovsky was engaged to Gino. The engagement and Gino were giving her panic attacks. Were the panic

attacks because of Gino or because Ellie didn't want to get married, or both? Could you relate to the reasons— losing her independence, not wanting children, problems with her future in-laws, financial issues, and so on—Ellie didn't want to get married?

5. The Kozlovsky family is huge. Who were your favorite members? Were there any members whom you didn't like? Can you relate to the family dynamics?

6. The Kozlovsky family endured much hardship in Moscow. They didn't want to talk about it when they came to America. As Alexei Kozlovsky said, "Forget it happened. It another life, no? This here, this our true life. We Americans now. Americans!" Was covering up the past the right thing to do? What would you have done?

7. Toni, Ellie, and Valerie all lied by omission to Dmitry about the night he came into their lives in Moscow, which would have shed some truth on his past. Alexei and Svetlana lied about who Dmitry's parents were and his life in the Soviet Union. They wanted him to forget his history, forget the trauma. Were the lies justified? Why or why not?

8. Dmitry wandered. If you wandered, where would you go? What would you want to learn about yourself?

9. Toni said, "The language of sisters is a gift from our mother. It came down the Sabonis line, like genes, through our widow's peaks. From the Romanovs, to Lenin, Stalin, Germany's invasion, the siege of Leningrad, the Cold War, we have heard each other. Passed from mother to daughter. Father to son. Sisters and brothers, we hear each other." What did you think of this magical element? Did it enhance or take away from the story?

10. Toni writes a column titled "Living on a Tugboat, Talking About Homes." If you wrote a column, what would it be titled? What would you write about?

Please e-mail Cathy Lamb at CathyLamb@frontier.com if you would like her to visit (in the Portland, Oregon, area) or Skype with your book group.

Connect with Us

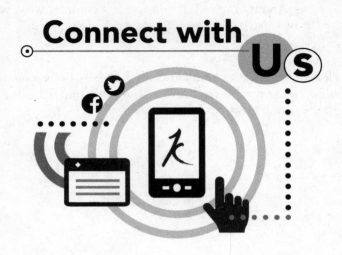

Visit us online at
KensingtonBooks.com
to read more from your favorite authors, see books
by series, view reading group guides, and more.

for sneak peeks, chances to win books and prize packs,
and to share your thoughts with other readers.

facebook.com/kensingtonpublishing
twitter.com/kensingtonbooks

Tell us what you think!

To share your thoughts, submit a review,
or sign up for our eNewsletters, please visit:
KensingtonBooks.com/TellUs.